Ignatius Jeiler, Clementine Deymann

Life of the Ven. Mary Crescentia Höss

Ignatius Jeiler, Clementine Deymann

Life of the Ven. Mary Crescentia Höss

ISBN/EAN: 9783337333300

Printed in Europe, USA, Canada, Australia, Japan

Cover: Foto ©Raphael Reischuk / pixelio.de

More available books at **www.hansebooks.com**

OF THE

Ven. Mary Crescentia Höss,

OF THE THIRD ORDER OF ST. FRANCIS.

Drawn from the Acts of her Beatification, and other reliable Sources,

BY

FATHER IGNATIUS JEILER, O. S. F.

TRANSLATED BY

REV. CLEMENTINUS DEYMANN, O. S. F.

NEW YORK, CINCINNATI, AND ST. LOUIS:

BENZIGER BROTHERS,

PRINTERS TO THE HOLY APOSTOLIC SEE.

R. WASHBOURNE,
18 PATERNOSTER ROW, LONDON.

M. H. GILL & SON,
50 UPPER O'CONNELL STREET, DUBLIN.

1886.

AUTHOR'S PREFACE.

The Venerable Sister Mary Crescentia Höss, of the Third
Order Regular of St. Francis of Assisi, whose biography we
now propose to set forth in a faithful and complete manner before our readers, lived in an age when the higher
classes of society had already begun to fall away from Christian principles and morals, and had thus prepared the way
for the minds of the masses to adopt those destructive ideas
which finally culminated in a revolution that shook the
whole world. The Ven. Sister herself saw, in a prophetic
light, the dark clouds gathering on the spiritual horizon,
and announced in plain terms the storm about to break
forth at no distant period against convent-life, and religious
institutions. This, in point of fact, began about thirty years
after her death, and in a comparatively short time brought
its destructive work to completion.

Yet, before the ancient tree of religious life in Germany
was finally to be hewn down, it was, by a decree of Divine
Providence, to produce a glorious blossom, by means of
which the whole beauty and exalted character of the cloistral life were to be exhibited. This great praise, this sublime encomium, we venture to confer on Sister Mary Crescentia of Kaufbeuren, without fearing to be accused of exaggeration ; nay, in our own humble opinion, we may venture to call her one of the greatest ornaments of our own
Church (Germany), and challenge comparison for her with
the canonized Saints of other nations.

To promote veneration for the Ven. M. Crescentia in wi-
der circles than those in which she has hitherto been known
is the first object of this book, which is written with the

special view of increasing the interest necessary for the resumption of the process of her beatification. To this end, also, the materials have been selected and arranged. Yet it must be obvious to all that the main object aimed at in a biography of this description, is to increase religious instruction and devotion. The sources whence we derive our materials are ample. The life of this servant of God presents, indeed, on the one side, a series of extraordinary phenomena, since from childhood upwards, nay, from her very infancy, she was called to modes of prayer and of interior life, which are vouchsafed by God but to the few, and to which none unbidden may dare to intrude ; yet this expansion of soul, which is not suitable for all, remained, in her case, before her death, as also after it, on the whole, a hidden fact, a secret to the world.

Her superiors had indeed taken measures to commit to writing the account of her extraordinary states, her visions and revelations for the benefit of posterity, but their efforts to produce the effects they desired were frustrated, as will be seen in the subsequent history. The Lord, however, has so ordered it that we possess exact and appropriate information of the virtues and exercises by the practice of which, as a child, as a young maiden, and as a religious, she became a mirror of perfection and a complete model for imitation.

Following these indications of Divine Providence, we have carefully selected the characteristics of her life, and those expressions to which she gave utterance which bear upon the pious practices of her genuine life, whether interiorly or exteriorly. We even venture to say that that which she taught by word and deed is a sufficient and safe guide to the interior life. Only the smallest portion of this refers exclusively to religious Orders ; consequently, good Christians living in the world may find instruction and edification in the words and example of this consecrated virgin. Every one, who by baptism is incorporated with Christ, should live an interior, supernatural life, proceeding from the grace of Jesus Christ, the Head, and not resulting from the exercise of our natural faculties.

In order to comply with the well-known decree of Pope Urban VIII., we state that the Church has conferred on Crescentia the title of "Venerable" (Venerabilis), declaring that she practised all virtues in an heroic degree. Should we, in the course of this narrative, attribute to her any other appellation, we hereby declare such other titles and appellations shall have no other meaning or certainty than such as appertains to mere human assertions.

May this narrative conduce to the honor of the Most Holy Trinity, the Father, the Son, and the Holy Ghost, from whom proceedeth "every good and perfect gift;" may it increase the veneration felt for the amiable and venerable spouse of Christ and contribute to the edification of the reader.

THE AUTHOR.

PADERBORN, Feb. 14, 1874.

TRANSLATOR'S PREFACE.

The translator fully endorses the sentiments of the learned and Reverend author; and wishes that Ven. Sister Mary Crescentia Höss may be accepted as a model to all religious, but especially to the Regular Tertiaries of St. Francis; also, that she may become a model of every virtue to all Christians:

The translator considers himself happy in having an opportunity to acknowledge his indebtedness to Mrs. M. A. Stace, a well-known authoress in American literature, who has, most willingly, undertaken to revise and prepare the manuscript for the press.

May God in His goodness fully reward this zealous convert for all she has done for the good of religion and the Order of St. Francis, of which she has been a fervent Tertiary for many years.

THE TRANSLATOR.

Feast of St. John Baptist.
    CHILLICOTHE, Mo., 1885.

CONTENTS.

PAGE

Author's Preface, ... 3

Translator's Preface, ... 6

FIRST BOOK.—*The Life of Ven. Mary Crescentia.*

CHAPTER

I. The Family Record.—Birth of Crescentia, . . 9

II. The Child of Grace, ... 14

III. Crescentia a Model for Young Women, . . 23

IV. The Convent of Mayrhoff, ... 29

V. The Year of Probation, ... 40

VI. The Lion's Den, ... 53

VII. The Redemption, ... 64

VIII. Her Religious Life, ... 71

SECOND BOOK.—*Picture of Her Virtues.*

I. Faith, the Root of her Life, ... 86

II. Hope, her Strength, ... 104

III. Love without Reservation, ... 116

IV. The Blessed Sacrament her Heaven on Earth, . 135

V. The Life and Passion of Christ the Subject of her Constant Meditation, ... 150

VI. The Holy Ghost the Sweet Guest of her Soul, . 160

VII. Her Fervor in Honoring the Mother of God, the Angels, and the Saints, ... 168

VIII. The Great Gift of Prayer and Contemplation which God Bestowed on Ven. M. Crescentia, . . 183

IX. How Crescentia Loved Christ in Every One, . 196

X. On the Love and Assistance Conferred by Crescentia, on the Suffering Souls in Purgatory, . . 211

XI. Her Fortitude and Love of the Cross, . . 219

CHAPTER
                                                                                PAGE

XII. Crescentia Crucified with Christ by Severe Penances and Mortifications, ... [illegible]

XIII. How the Humble Servant of God takes the Last Place. [illegible]

XIV. How perfectly Crescentia Practised the Obedience of Faith, ... [illegible]

XV. Crescentia an Angel in the Flesh, . . [illegible]

XVI. How truly Crescentia Loved Poverty, . [illegible]

THIRD BOOK.—*Crescentia's Work for Others.—Her Death and the Veneration Paid Her.*

I. Crescentia as Mistress of Novices, . . . [illegible]

II. Crescentia as Mother Superior, . . . 2[illegible]

III. How much and how successfully Crescentia Labored in and outside of the Community, . . [illegible]

IV. How Crescentia was Endowed with the Spirit of Prophecy and the Gift of Curing the Sick, . 29[illegible]

V. Last Sickness and Happy Death of Ven. Crescentia, 31[illegible]

VI. Remarkable Occurrences after the Death of Ven. Crescentia.—Her Death, ... 32[illegible]

VII. Surprising Spread of the Veneration Paid to her.—Pilgrimages to her Grave.—Conversion of many Sinners, ... 329

VIII. Selection of Miracles, ... 33[illegible]

IX. Process of her Beatification.—Opening of the Grave, 351

APPENDIX.

Decretum Augustanae in matters referring to the Beatification and Canonization of the Venerable Servant of God, Sister M. Crescentia Höss, ... 355

customed to carry very bitter pills about him, to chew before and at his meals, to subdue any sensual pleasure which
he might feel and which he dreaded might arise, even from
his scanty fare.[1]

Poor as he was himself, he never refused an alms to a
needy person who begged of him ; or if he had no means of
affording substantial relief, he never failed to say some consoling and sympathizing words, adding a promise to help as
soon as he should be able. The words of the Wise Man [2]
seem to have been fulfilled in regard to this truly devout
man: "A good wife is a good portion; she shall be given in
the portion of them that fear God, to a man for his good
deeds." His wife was, in very fact, truly ennobled by her
Christian virtues. Her name was Lucy Hörmann; she was
the daughter of a barber and surgeon of Füssen, a neighboring town on the borders of the Tyrol. She was specially
remarkable for the love she manifested towards the sick
poor, whom she was ever ready to tend gratuitously day and
night, with the zeal, tenderness, and skill worthy of a Sister
of Mercy. As she had acquired some knowledge of surgery
from her father, the poor people from the whole town had
recourse to this most charitable neighbor, when they wanted to have their sores dressed, their wounds healed, or even
their broken limbs set.

God blessed their union with eight children, three of
whom were boys.[3] Two boys and two girls died while yet
very young; the third son, who was named Joseph, lost his
life by an untoward accident when nearly grown up : a
heedless boy gave him a push by which he fell into a cellar,
and was so seriously injured that he died shortly after. The
good, pious boy sincerely pardoned the youth who had
caused his death, and departed this life entirely resigned
to the will of God.

Thus three daughters only remained to survive their
parents: of these one was older than our Crescentia, the

---

[1] Aȼt. B. Summ. Object. no. 15, § 2 et 3.
[2] Ecclesiasticus xxvi, 3.   [3] Otto, Book I., ch. 1.

other younger. Mary, the eldest sister (born April 19, 1679), experienced an early vocation to the religious life, and having surmounted all obstacles, which were such as arose chiefly from poverty, she was received by the Sisters of St. Francis at St. Joseph's convent at Hagenau, Alsace, far away from her native town. Here, under the name in religion of Mary Angelina, she led a very edifying life and died at the advanced age of eighty-three.

Regina, the youngest of the sisters (born in 1697), also proved faithful to the good education she had received from her pious parents. She married a poor but honest citizen of Kaufbeuren, named Joseph Heinritz, who carried on the same trade as her father. Sixteen children sprang from this marriage, five of whom entered different orders in religion. One of them, who became a member of the Congregation of the Knights of the Cross at Memmingen, so distinguished himself that he attained to the dignity of a prelate. But the mother of so many children had necessarily many and severe hardships to endure. She became a widow while her children were as yet unprovided for ; to which may be added that constant sickness and severe pain hindered her from continuing her husband's trade ; she consequently fell into the greatest distress. The sanctity of her sister then came to her assistance. Several persons of high rank, both gentlemen and ladies who had a special veneration for the revered Crescentia, and among these the Duchess of Savoy, *née* Princess of Lichtenstein, came to the succor of the distressed widow and provided for the education of her children. She herself edified every one by the heroic patience with which she bore all these trials : and thus purified in the furnace of suffering, she slept in the Lord in 1758, aged seventy-one years.

These two sisters have both left to posterity written reminiscences of the Ven. Sister M. Crescentia, reminiscences which they had retained from childhood of her life and virtues ; these valuable documents are still preserved among the archives of the convent of Kaufbeuren. The one written by the eldest sister is dated May 26, 1748; the other is of July 11, of the same year.

Both of these sisters were far surpassed in grace and virtue by her whose life we are now writing. Crescentia was born Oct. 20, 1682; she was baptized on the day following in the parish church of St. Martin, and named Anna. The parish priest, Philip Gäch, doctor of divinity and dean of the chapter at Kaufbeuren, performed the holy rite. Two pious Catholics, Matthias Propst and Mary Vögel, stood sponsors.

The fructifying germ of the higher life, implanted at baptism by the Holy Ghost in this child's soul, was fostered by Him with special love, until it grew into a flower of grace of wondrous beauty, which delighted the eye of the heavenly Gardener and filled the world, far and wide, with the fragrance of the most glorious virtues. And if it be true that Christian parents can receive from God no higher gift than that of having good and pious children, then these poor weavers of Kaufbeuren were rewarded for their godliness in a manner for which emperors and kings might envy them.

Though poor in worldly goods, they were rich in grace and blessed with good children. Throughout this biography two sayings of the Wise Man are continually verified: "The house of the just is very much strength: and in the fruits of the wicked is trouble."[1]

"One is, as it were, rich, when he hath nothing: and another is, as it were, poor, when he hath great riches."[2]

---

[1] Prov. xv. 6.   [2] Ibid. xiii. 7.

CHAPTER II.

The Child of Grace.

IN the lives of many Saints it has been observed that the fulness of grace which the Lord was to confer upon them in the course of their lives, was already announced by certain extraordinary signs accompanying their birth or occurring in the first years of their childhood. Thus a beautiful morning dawn of an evidently supernatural character heralded the brilliant sun of grace, which at a later period was destined to transfigure the entire life of Crescentia into a blaze of light and love.

Her elder sister, Sister M. Angelina, says, in her memoir, that she had frequently heard her mother affirm that she had brought forth this child of the elect without pain ; and the germ of Divine Life planted within her soul by the Holy Ghost at her baptism, already manifested itself while little Anna was yet in the cradle. This, indeed, would be scarcely credible, were not similar facts recorded in the history of many other Saints, in which the manifestations of grace preceded the physical development of nature. To mention only facts concerning well-known Saints of the last century, similar manifestations occur in the lives of St. Rose of Lima, of St. Juliana Falconieri, of St. Veronica Juliani, of St. M. Frances of the Five Wounds, and of the pious Anna Catherine Emmerich, who lived in our very midst.

While little Anna was yet a babe in her mother's arms, that mother often remarked, as she frequently told her daughters, that the sweet, quiet child appeared to have a wondrous sense of the Divine. The pious mother was a zealous frequenter of the daily Mass, and as she had no one with whom she dared to trust her darling child, she took it along with her to the church, where it made no disturbance, as other children are wont to do, but kept still and quiet, even appearing to be contented and happy, raising its hands devoutly and fixing its eyes immovably on the altar. And when the priest, after the consecration, elevated the Host for the adoration of the faithful, this little child appeared to be filled with joy and devotion, and its lovely countenance beamed with the glow of roseate brilliancy.[1] The first words which the tongue of the infant learned to lisp, were "Our Father." She was scarcely three years old, when of her own accord, she, with great fervor and earnestness, would recite the "Our Father" and "Hail Mary" many times a day. At the same age she never wearied of hearing others speak of God and of things divine, and would even ask for instruction. In a very short time she knew the articles of faith by heart, and astonished every one by her ready and lucid answers to the questions of the catechism.

From her fourth year upwards she manifested a great and continuous fervor in prayer. She was often seen on her knees for a long time in a corner of the house, immovable as a statue. But her favorite place for devotion was the Church. Other children at her age love to play, but little Anna seemed to be driven by an irresistible impulse to the House of God. She hardly asked her parents for anything else, save for permission to go to Church. There she tarried, kneeling, often for hours together, with a devotion truly angelic. Her delight was to be near the altar, because there the magnet of her heart, the Sacred Heart of her Saviour, was present. She was not content with hearing one holy Mass, she would remain at all that were said, unless her parents called her away. Even at other times, when there was no Mass, she would, if permitted, hasten to the Church, which was for her the gate of heaven. Her parents knew very well, whenever she was absent from home, that they should find her there, kneeling before the altar, absorbed in prayer.

Thus did this infant soul, at that early age, already look

---

[1] Act B. Summ. N. 5.

for the " things above " with a fervor and perseverance that
may well put many, if not most, Christians, to the blush.
From this childish heart a prayer like to the fragrance of
sweet incense ascended to the throne of the heavenly Father, surpassing in simplicity, purity, and fervor most of
the prayers so often mechanically offered up by grown-up
Christians.

All who knew the child were witnesses of her astonishing piety ; yet, its deeper source was hidden from their
view. It was not till after years that, being compelled
thereto by holy obedience, she disclosed to her confessors
the mysteries of her childhood. The Act of her Beatification states in general terms that from her third or fourth
year she had wonderful visions of the Infant Jesus and of
her guardian angel.[1] Father Ott relates some particulars
concerning these visions ; he writes :[2] When she was three
years old the Infant Jesus appeared to her in a form of
wondrous beauty : He was dressed in a coat of violet-color
embroidered with flowers, with a red mantle ; His head and
feet were bare. She was all alone, but had some milk, an
apple, and a pear, which her mother had just given her.
The little girl spoke to the Boy Jesus, and invited Him to
eat with her. The Boy replied: " My Father has much
better food and much sweeter fruit than these in His garden." "Who is your Father, and where do you live?
What is your name, and your Mother's name?" inquired
the little one. "My Father is the heavenly Father, and
My dwelling place is in the heavenly Jerusalem. My
name is Jesus, and the name of My beloved Mother is
Mary." When Anna heard this she was exceedingly glad
and begged the child to take her to His Father in the garden, and immediately she was rapt in ecstasy and carried
off to Paradise to the heavenly Father, who said to her :
" If you wish to be My child, you must love Me and this
My Son alone: you must have no communication with
other children, you must love retirement and obey your

---

[1] Act B. Summ. Obj. N. 11. § 4.   [2] Ott. B. III. Ch. 4.

parents in everything." Then the Divine Child, smiling at her most lovingly, said: "There is but one God in whom you must believe ; but there are three Divine Persons : the heavenly Father, I Myself, the Son of God, and the Holy Ghost, and we three are but one God. This is the first thing you must believe and know." On this she received, as a special grace, the use of reason, and when she came to herself, she was lying on her bed. Her mother had brought her in and laid her there, as she mistook this ecstasy for a profound sleep. The effect produced by this vision was extraordinary : a powerful desire to possess and eternally to retain this Sublime Good was enkindled in her heart, and from that time forth prayer and meditation formed her only delight.

This extraordinary intercourse with the supernatural world was repeated from time to time. We will here relate another vision which she had of the Infant Jesus, following the same author : [1] The Divine Child appeared to her and said : " My delight is to be with the children of men. "[2] " My child, give Me thy heart, and everything that I possess is thine." Lovingly embracing her, the Infant then placed a ring on her finger, saying : " Now, I have espoused thee to Myself ; thou art Mine, and I am thine : thy heart and My heart shall be but one heart."

Like so many other mystical Saints, she also carried on a most remarkable intercourse with her holy angel guardian ; he often appeared to her in a visible form ; he accompanied her to Church and school, and stationed himself by her side ; he instructed her in the articles of faith, especially teaching her how to perform all her actions with a good intention.[3] Her elder sister, M. Angelina, even asserts that Crescentia once received from him a cilice (hair shirt), with the injunction to wear it for love of Jesus. It is certain that from her fourth year upwards she was accustomed to chastise her guileless body in many ways, even with fastings and scourgings.

---

[1] Ott, B. I. p. 58.　　[2] Prov. viii. 31.　　[3] Ott, B. III. Ch. 4.

God Himself so ordained matters that this privileged child received the Sacraments of Confirmation and Holy Eucharist earlier than is customary in the Roman Catholic Church. She was confirmed in her third or fourth year, together with her sister Mary, who was some six years older, by the Coadjutor-bishop of Augsburg, May 23, 1685, or according to other records, 1686. She received Holy Communion at the age of seven years, which is in itself a striking proof of her piety, otherwise the parish priest would not have permitted it. Her desire for this heavenly food had for a long time previously been extraordinarily great; so much so that for years before she would make frequent spiritual communions, with so much devotion that she sometimes spent a whole hour in doing so. [1]

While yet very young she was sent to school and to the catechetical instruction given in the Church. According to the testimony of many trustworthy witnesses, she attracted the attention of everybody by her conduct and by her answers to the questions proposed. John Baptist Neth, a councilman of the city, says that when the other children failed to answer, the priest used to ask Anna, who never missed giving so clear and defined a reply that all present were astonished at her words. Father Ignatius Wagner, of the Society of Jesus, was at that time giving the instructions; and many times he could not repress his feeling of admiration, and publicly exclaimed: " My child, you must have had a higher Teacher ! " Sometimes he even made the little child stand on a bench, and speak from it, that all present might see, hear, and admire her. In very fact, she had had that higher Teacher, who enlightened the prophets and Apostles and who communicates understanding and life, not by letters and words, but by interior inspirations of light and love.

At school she likewise manifested the early maturity of her mind. Her teacher acknowledged that she had

---

[1] Ott, B. II. Ch. 5.

never seen a child like her, and that she must have received instructions from above. In a very short time she learned to read and write well, and that was all the schooling she ever received, except that at a later date she took lessons for one year in music, in which she continued to delight up to her old age. Mr. Biber, the director of the choir, who was her music teacher, often expressed his astonishment at the facility with which this child surmounted all difficulties. [1] She had a pleasing voice and a good enunciation, so that her singing was universally applauded.

Speaking in general terms, she had received from Almighty God an extraordinary number of natural gifts: she had a very keen and penetrating intellect, an exuberant imagination, an extremely kind and tractable disposition, pure and clear as the crystal spring from the rock, a heart so tender, so full of love, and withal so magnanimous and vigorous, that it was ready for any heroic act, whether of work or of suffering. Although her body was extremely frail and delicate, she was competent for any task, being equally at home with the works of busy Martha, as with the contemplations of the quiet, thoughtful Mary.

These precious germs of good were constantly fostered, fructified, and developed by the excellent education which she received at home, in the bosom of a Christian family. A rare flower never flourishes along the public roadside; it needs to be well tended in an enclosed garden; so, also, the child of God flourishes well only in the garden appointed by nature and by God Himself, and this garden is the Christian family. On this account the heavenly Gardener chose the poor and plain, but holy, family of the obscure citizen of Kaufbeuren, that His dear child might, at ease and unmolested, lay the foundation of her spiritual life within these homely walls, as in a peaceful, well-protected garden.

The child saw and heard at home nothing but the prac-

---

[1] Ott, B. 1. Ch. 1.

tical exemplification of Christian virtue. This personified Christianity replaces, and in reality infinitely surpasses, all theoretical rules of training. Above all, the deep religious feeling of her noble-minded father could not fail to make an impression on the susceptible heart of little Anna, and bring forth fruit a hundred-fold. His tender devotion to the bitter passion of our Lord, his mortifications, his fervor in prayer, urged her onward to do the like.

And when this pious father, as he often did, spoke of the sufferings of Christ, Anna, when scarcely four years old, would shed abundant tears. Nay, soon she herself began to open her mouth and from the fulness of her agitated heart to utter marvellous words concerning the passion of our Lord, so that her father, excited and astonished at her expressions, exclaimed : "Child, where did you learn that?" She herself could not tell this ; silence and tears were her only reply.

The rare combination of such great interior and exterior graces could not fail very early to produce the happiest effects. The heart of the little Anna was, by the special influence of the Holy Ghost, opened prematurely to the light of reason and faith, and she followed the invigorating movement of divine grace, which led her on to the last aim and end, and directed all her longing and desires, her affections, nay, her life itself to the Sun of all justice. This early tendency of the soul to God is assuredly of rare occurrence; but even more rare, and still more precious, is the fidelity with which this chosen soul advanced to sanctity, without interruption, without relaxation or repose, constantly increasing in perfection and constantly hurrying forward with rapid and still more rapid step to complete sanctity. We find in the lives of almost all the Saints, even of those who are held up as models of innocence from having never committed a mortal sin, a period of lukewarmness, and a time when the spirit of the world seemed to obtain entrance. A time which, at a later date, offers matter to humility, gives occasion to unceasing interior contrition and thanksgiving to God, in that He has, as they term it, given them the grace of conversion.

Of such a crisis as this the most searching inquiry into the life of Crescentia discovers not the least symptom. Like a true flower of Heaven, planted by God Himself on earth, she, even as a child, opened her fragrant blossoms, and developed them more and more in the fulness of that grace which so harmoniously pervaded her being, until the time came that Christ alone appeared to live in her. This may appear of less practical interest to our eyes, which love the contrast of light and shadow; but, in reality, what can be more wonderfully beautiful than to see this lily beneath the thorns of earth, in whom the love and beauty of Christ are so victoriously revealed that it almost seems as if she had never sinned in Adam.

At the age of six, before her first communion, she took the vow of perpetual chastity in honor of the Immaculate Virgin Mary.[1] This she did of her own accord, or rather, impelled thereto by the inspiration of the Holy Ghost. Pure as an angel was she then, and pure as an angel did she ever remain, as according to the testimony of her confession, she was never tempted to violate purity in any way. Even in her exterior conduct, the power of grace manifested itself in so striking a manner that she was known all over the neighborhood by the name of the little angel.

Even good children occasionally give their parents cause for sadness or uneasiness, from the levity and inconsiderateness of their age. But both the parents of this child in after times assured the Superioress of the convent at Kaufbeuren that she had never given them reason to complain of her. And that this docility of her's and this purity were not the consequence of her natural disposition is proved by the fact that from her earliest years she cherished such a hatred of sin, even of the smallest description, as is seldom found even among pious grown-up peo-

---

[1] Summ. N. 5. A document signed by ten Sisters, Aug. 28, 1753, testifies that she herself revealed it to her Superioress Johanna, in obedience.

ple in an equal degree. It was the work of grace. She would frequently say to her father: "Oh, father! may God grant that I may not commit a sin during my whole life. Oh, father! no sin; I would rather die a thousand times than commit one sin." When asked why she feared sin so much, she replied: "Because it offends God."

Children generally love games and the company of other children, but little Anna would never stir from the house, except to go to Church and to school. She spoke but little, and then only of God with deep emotion. To remain alone and pray in a little oratory erected under the roof, or remain for hours on her knees before the Blessed Sacrament; these were her games and recreations. Even at that time she had the grace to use all creatures as a mirror in which she could perceive the Divinity. A glance at a flower, at the stars, nay, even at a blade of grass, sufficed to raise her thoughts to Heaven and to God in holy gratitude. Her soul resembled the sun-flower, which, awakened by the first bright ray of light, still turns its golden chalice to the day-star as it revolves, accompanies it in its course, and imbibes from it light and life. Fortunate child! What the greatest number of men scarcely understand in their old age, and after a bitter experience, you have practised from the very cradle. You have given your heart to God for life and death. By the grace of God you are what you are: but you have not to lament, as we too often have, that the grace of God has remained void for you. And since we, in the time of our youth, opened our hearts too early and too widely to the world, may God grant that at least in our old age we may fulfil the words of Holy Writ: "Give, therefore, your hearts and your souls to seek the Lord your God." [1]

---

[1] I. Paral. xxii. 19.

CHAPTER III.

Crescentia a Model for Young Women.[1]

WHEN Crescentia grew up to young womanhood, the blessed child, as she increased in age, increased also in wisdom and grace before God and man. All who knew her, both Protestants and Catholics, are unanimous in their assertions "that the pious Annerl was more like an angel than a mortal." Long after her death parents and teachers used to refer to this holy virgin as an example and mirror of all virtues, especially of that of prompt and cheerful obedience.[2]

She never was seen at public gatherings; never with persons of the other sex ; in a word, she was never found outside of the house, except when visiting the Church or when business compelled her so to do ; and in every case her whole demeanor, her dress, gait, manner of talking, with her angelic modesty, bore public testimony to the purity and interior collectedness of her soul.

At home she was the help and consolation of her parents. She assisted her mother with diligence and skill in her domestic duties and household work, as well as in the education and instruction of the other children. She helped her father by winding the yarn on the spools and in other matters connected with his trade. She herself even learnt to weave, and afterwards, when she was at the convent, she not only wove the cloth for the habits of the Order, but taught other Sisters how to do it.

The promptitude and alacrity with which she obeyed every hint or word given by her parents was not unlike that of the angels, who always do the will of the Most High. Her piety, flowing from the pure and deep fountain of faith, betrayed no mark of hypocritical devotion, or of sadness, nor yet of self-seeking ; her beaming countenance

---

[1] Summ. N. 5. passim. [2] Summ. N. 15. § 162.

mirrored the heart's peace and joy in the Holy Ghost. She spoke but seldom and never of herself, not even to excuse herself when accused of faults committed by others.

Her practical charity towards the sick and needy manifested itself more and more; so that, in truth, the words of the pious Job might be applied to her: "For from my infancy mercy grew up with me : and it came out with me from my mother's womb."[1]   The example of her good mother must certainly have been a great encouragement to her, while her own lively faith, which saw Jesus Christ Himself in the persons of the poor and suffering, imparted to her love not only a sublime Christian character, but raised it to a height on which she appeared absolutely to forget herself.   Her sister Regina bears witness that Crescentia had the tenderest compassion for every afflicted person ; even animals were not excluded from her sympathy, and whenever she heard that one of them was to be butchered, her heart was pierced with grief.   When a beggar knocked at the door she hastened as cheerfully to greet him as if the King of Heaven Himself had been there, and received him in the kindest manner.   If she happened to be at table she would beg permission of her parents to be allowed to give her own share to the poor person.   As often as this request was granted, it was easily seen in her countenance that she considered it a great gain.   And indeed, it is much sweeter to give than to receive : and whoever gives for God's sake, gains more than a hundred-fold.

Knowing that the victory over one's self and one's natural inclinations is the first lesson in the school of Christ, she mortified herself in all her natural inclinations and tried to impress the cross of Christ on her body, her heart, and her soul.   In eating, drinking, and sleeping she was more than moderate, as also in all her bodily needs; she always used to take the worst for herself and even of that only a little.   To subject the body more completely to the spirit, she tortured it by the use of hair-cloth (ciliciums),

---

[1] Job xxxi. 18.

scourges, bitter herbs, and long vigils. Even then she had opportunity given her to exercise patience, the true test of virtue, for, as her sister Angelina relates, she had to suffer from extraordinary attacks of Satan. In short, the sufferings of Christ, on which she so frequently meditated interiorly, were outwardly imprinted on her body. The spirit of devotion and of prayer were constantly developing themselves in her to still greater degrees of perfection. She practised an almost unbroken prayer at her work and most assuredly devoted to it every moment of leisure. She had selected a corner in a secluded part of the house, where she could give herself up to prayer and mortification. For hours together she knelt there, her body as immovable as a statue ; and there she listened with all the powers of her soul to the mysterious voice of her only Beloved. She shortened her sleep, and very often, even in the severest winter time, would kneel for hours beside her bed. From her earliest childhood she assisted at the first Mass in the early morning, and remained there on her knees, immovable, until obedience to her parents called her hence. This recollection of spirit and perseverance in prayer inflamed her heart with the glow of that supernatural love which alone is able to elevate the soul above all distractions from without, and all affections from within, and thus strengthen its union with God. It was this very love which communicated to her body that immovability which astonished all who beheld her, and caused them, as councilman Neth, an eye-witness, assures us, to call her, " the statue."

Father Heiland, of the Society of Jesus, was at that time her confessor.[1] He acknowledges that he never knew a soul which united such purity to such humility and such a spirit of mortification, and that he was frequently at a loss to find matter on which to base an absolution. With his permission she received the Blessed Sacrament on all Sundays and feast-days. Nothing could be more edifying than to see her approach the table of the Lord. In conse-

---

[1] Ott. B. I. ch. 1.

quence of the long preparation she made, she had become
a living picture of devotion, and many persons bore witness
that they were excited to piety and recollection by the mere
sight of the angelical fervor of this virgin. When at Holy
Communion she seemed rapt almost to ecstasy, and her
countenance glowed with the beauty of a rose. Having
completed a long thanksgiving in the Church, she yet continued it through the day, being more silent than usual,
and more occupied with God. We know, however, but
little of the interior action of the Holy Ghost on her soul,
and of the extraordinary light and grace which were communicated to her at Holy Communion, because she concealed, with the utmost care, the interior state of her mind.
Only once, when she was Mistress of Novices, the remark
escaped her in the presence of her pupils, the novices, that
her communion days had been by far the happiest days
of her youth.

For the rest, we know that on the day before she so prepared herself for Holy Communion by fervent prayer, and
virtuous exercises, that her desire to be united with her
Redeemer in the Blessed Sacrament increased to that degree that she could scarcely sleep the previous night.[1]
Before the morning dawned this desire called her to the
Church to seek her Saviour. She was very often kneeling
before the Church door at two o'clock in the morning,
seeking her Bridegroom in the Tabernacle with the eyes of
her heart, while patiently awaiting the opening of the
Church-door.

Hence we can scarcely be surprised that the same spirit
of God, that worked such miracles of devotion in the heart
of this virgin, should at times change the exterior order of
things in order to reward the fidelity of His servant, as also
to confirm her in her devotion. Her confessor, Father
Pamer, heard from herself that the Church-doors, which
had been closed with heavy bolts, often opened of themselves when she knelt before them, and were shut in the

---

[1] Ott, p. 32.

same way when she had entered the Church.' The pious
maiden then tarried in a corner of the Church, rapt in
thanksgiving, love, and prayer, and was unobserved by
the sacristan when he came to open the Church.

The devotion to the passion of Christ which she inherited
from her father gradually developed itself, until it took possession of her whole soul. Almost every exterior object reminded her of the sufferings of Christ, and stirred up
within her a burning desire to be crucified with the
Saviour, and to know of nothing, hear of nothing, and love
nothing but Jesus Christ and Him crucified.

Such sublime virtues, in this modest, amiable, and affa-
ble maiden, could scarcely fail to call forth the greatest
love on the part of her parents, or to secure the respect and
admiration of all who knew her. Every one said that not
even the smallest fault could be found in her, but that, on
the contrary, she showed a perfection more like that of angels than that of human beings. There were many who
could not refrain from praising her greatly to her face,
which might have proved very dangerous had not the
Spirit of God watched over her and early taught her that
no danger is to be more carefully fled from and avoided
than that of vanity and the desire of pleasing ; consequently, the sweet poison of praise, too sweet, alas, to poor fallen
humanity, found no admittance into her soul. She rejected every emotion of self-complacency with the utmost
care, and when, as happened quite often, she heard others
express admiration for her bodily or spiritual superiority,
she would shrink back as from a venomous serpent, and
blushing with shame, while interiorly suffering, ² would
quit the company in all haste ! As she was applauded on
account of her beautiful singing she would frequently make
mistakes on purpose to avoid this, rightly considering that
the discord of one vain thought is a greater injury to
Eternal Truth than a false tone in a piece of music swiftly
passing away. From the same spirit of love and of humil-

---

¹ Summ. N. 5. § 16, § 126, § 195.　　² Ott, p. 9.

ity arose her practice of taking for her own share the
most menial and laborious part of the house-work, and
thus sparing her sisters the trouble.

The youth of this soul, thus called to angelical perfection,
was in this way passed in innocence, in simplicity, and in
undisturbed peace, even as a clear brook glides through a
quiet valley. She was a lovely child, in the fullest sense of
the word, admired by every one and set up for an example
to young women. The darkening storm-clouds, which at a
later date broke over her, had not yet appeared. The clear
sky of her outward life was not as yet darkened by the
faintest speck of mist. Loving everybody and beloved by
everybody, she might, in the very love that filled her heart,
have found a temptation to seek to satisfy that love by
bestowing it on a creature, had not faith long since taught
her soul the true direction, by pointing out the path in
which alone rest can be attained by a human being endowed
with reason.

We do not by this intend to affirm that she had nothing
to suffer. In that case she would not have been led by God,
who chastises all whom He loves. We know that from her
very childhood she wandered at times through the great
wilderness of interior desolation ; and that she was exposed
to satanic temptations and vexations, the particulars concerning which have not come down to us. Besides this,
there was always a desire, nestling in her soul from her very
earliest years, which prevented her from feeling wholly at
rest, even in the bosom of her family ; it was the longing
to consecrate herself entirely to her Redeemer in the religious state. "Go forth out of thy country, and from thy
kindred, and out of thy father's house, and come into the
land which I shall show thee."[1] Thus spoke the Lord to
her as He had done to Abraham. Great obstacles seemed
to render the fulfilment of this wish of her heart impossible.
Nevertheless, nothing could weaken her hope of becoming
a spouse of the Lord ; God Himself had awakened this

---

[1] Genesis xii. 1.

hope within her and had confirmed it in an extraordinary manner.

According to Father Ott's testimony,[1] her guardian angel appeared to her when she was fourteen years old, carrying in one hand a red cross, in the other the habit of St. Francis. He addressed her in these words : " See, my child, a dress like this has been prepared for thee." In this way her future lot was plainly indicated. A life of the Cross, a cross of love in the garment of St. Francis,—such was to be her path to Heaven when youth had passed away. Another vocation than this could scarcely be expected for a virgin to whom the words of the Holy Ghost could so appropriately be applied: " O how beautiful is the chaste generation with glory: for the memory thereof is immortal: because it is known both with God and with men."[2]

CHAPTER IV.

The Convent of Mayrhoff.—Extraordinary Vocation.

HERE was a convent of the Third Order of St. Francis at Kaufbeuren in which the Sisters lived in great poverty. According to the statements found in the records of said convent, it must have been built in 1023 by a noble lady who took the veil therein. To what Order the Sisters belonged who inhabited the convent in those first centuries is unknown. In the year 1470 the city was almost destroyed by a tremendous fire, by which the convent was also reduced to a heap of ashes. The Mother Superior, Anna Scherich, however, by the help of kind benefactors, rebuilt the convent, which still stands. It appears that it was at that time that the Sisters adopted the Rule of the Third Order of St. Francis. This Rule, as is well known, was originally written for penitents, married or single, living in the world. In the fifteenth century it was first

---

[1] Ott, B. III. Ch. 4.   [2] Wisdom iv. 1.

adapted by blessed Angelina, Countess Marschiani (✠ 1435) to community life, and in that form was approved by Popes Urban VI., Boniface IX., Martin V., and, in a special manner, by Leo X. Cloisters following this Rule were soon to be found in every land, although with constitutions differing from each other. In this convent, called Mayrhoff, the Mother Superior was elected for life. From the year 1470 to 1874 the names of twenty-four are registered in the annuals of the convent, with the number of years they were in office.

In the fearful storm of the sixteenth century the convent suffered great distress, as a considerable number of the inhabitants of Kaufbeuren, particularly from the year 1544, embraced the new doctrine. The Mother Superior of that period, Regina Kirchmayr, however, with the Sisters under her rule, courageously withstood all temptations. The Sisters remained firm in their faith, and true to their vocation, but for nearly a century had to suffer so many persecutions and losses that they fell into a degree of poverty which was really oppressive.

When our servant of God felt herself called to the religious state, she first applied to this community, with which she had been acquainted from youth upwards. Whoever would have considered this step in the light of worldly wisdom would have found but little attraction to induce any one to enter this particular convent, for its poverty was well known and was very great. How great this poverty was may be learned from the fact that Mother Johanna Altweger, who ruled the community in a most praiseworthy manner from 1707 to 1741, found on her installation a multitude of pressing wants, and only half-a-florin in the treasury. The income of the convent was so small that the Sisters, with their utmost efforts at their hard work, could scarcely manage to live, even in the sparing fashion to which they were accustomed. This circumstance could not fail to be detrimental to cloistral discipline, and yet, on the whole, it was not a poor religious spirit that reigned therein. Some Sisters served the Lord in true piety and simplicity, while some others seem not to have possessed a high degree of the spirit of devotion and love. But God had, from all eternity, chosen the poor weaver's daughter, who, in her humility, considered herself unworthy to hold even the last place in the house, to make this religious community a model of perfection in a temporal as well as spiritual point of view, although from circumstances it had yielded a little to lukewarmness in religious discipline. Indisputably is the Ven. Sister M. Crescentia to be considered as the second foundress of this community, for she impressed it with the stamp of her own spirit and, so to speak, remodelled it. The Coadjutor-bishop of Augsburg, assuredly a competent judge, testifies to the excellent standing of the community in 1782, almost forty years after her death ; he states: "That it is perfectly entitled to be called the most prosperous institution of religious piety and perfection, wherein the least thing that offends truth and conscience can find no admission." [1]

After this short digression we will turn back to consider the state of the convent, previous to the entering therein of this pious virgin. The convent had not only to suffer from poverty, but also from arbitrary and exceptional laws made by an over-wise magistrate in a mean and exclusive spirit, put forth ostensibly for the common good. One of these ordinances strictly forbade "that any real estate be made over to the convent, whether by sale, donation, or otherwise." [2]

Now, the Sisters had scarcely the necessaries of life, and certainly had not the means to purchase superfluities, to say nothing of buying real estate ; nevertheless, this prohibition fell heavily upon them, because it prevented them from putting a stop to an evil that had become almost unbearable.

There was situated near the convent chapel a saloon of a low character, which, with its infernal carousings, disturbed

---

[1] Positis addit, super causæ introductione, p. 24. [2] Ott, B. I. Ch. 2.

the Sisters when at divine service, both day and night. There was no other way of getting rid of this nuisance than that of buying the house; but this had hitherto been impossible, partly because the Sisters in their poverty could not compass the price, partly because the wise (?) aldermen of the city council had inexorably rejected their petition, as an encroachment on the welfare of the State. We shall, however, soon see how the Lord made use of this vexatious embarrassment to open the convent doors to our pious Anna.

The Sisters did not then, as they do now, attend to the education of youth, neither did they, unless in exceptional cases, minister to the wants of the sick. Prayer and manual labor formed their only occupations. Added to this they did not observe strict enclosure, and were not under the immediate jurisdiction of the bishop, but like so many other convents of those times, they were under obedience to the Franciscan Order, and more immediately under that of the Provincial of the province of Upper Germany (Provincia Argentina). He had annually to perform the canonical visitation, to preside at the election to office, particularly at that of the Rev. Mother, and to decide in all weighty matters, as when important business had to be transacted or abuses abolished. [1]

Yet their ordinary confessors were not from the Franciscan Order, but, up to the year 1719, from the secular clergy; after that time, when the Society of Jesus had established a high institute of learning in Kaufbeuren, Fathers of that society became their confessors. [2]

---

[1] During Crescentia's time the following Provincials are mentioned : P. Odoricus Schnable (1703) : P. Thomas Baudrexel (1707) ; P. Marcellinus Wedl ; P. Luchesis ; P. Sebastianus Höss (1721) ; P. Quintilianus Weez (1726) ; P. Kilianus Katzenberger ; P. Benjamin Elbel (1737), the well-known moralist ; and P. Bonifacius Schmidt,—at the time of her death.

[2] The following confessors to the convent are mentioned in Crescentia's time : Dr. Damian Küllestadt (1704—1715) ; Rev. Philip James Meichelbeck, parish priest of Kemnath for two years ; Rev. John Picheln, parish priest of Oberbeuren. From the Society of Jesus : P. Ignatius Lieb (5 years); P. Ortulph Lachner (6 years); P. Ferdinand Schitzinger (1 year); P. Peter Schneller (1 year); P. Athanasius Baier (1 year); P. Bartholomew Binner (2 years); P. Joseph Burger (2 years); P. Thomas Faber (2 years); P. Michael Bauer (1 year); P. Januarius Mayer (2 years): P. John Baptist Pamer,—at the time of her death.—Act B. Summ. Obj. N. 15. § 19.

The reader will certainly be well pleased to ascertain what became of the convent after the death of Ven. Crescentia. It continued to flourish remarkably well throughout the last century, that is, the eighteenth century. Two of her faithful daughters in religion, Mother Joachim Kōgl (1744–1769) and Mother Rafael Miller up to 1799, presided over the Sisters in the spirit of their venerable mistress. They were succeeded by Mother Elizabeth Ibel up to 1822. She had the sorrow of witnessing the suppression of the convent. In the universal storm which broke forth against convents this lovely place of prayer and virtue was not spared.

In the year 1802 the Sisters were forbidden to receive novices, all their possessions were confiscated, innumerable votive tablets, many of which were set in gold and silver, were placed on wagons and carried off, and the Sisters themselves would have been expelled the convent, had not repeated examinations proved that the accommodations therein were too poor and too limited in extent to be available for State purposes.

As not one of the Sisters yielded to the request that they should return to the world, the authorities, who seemed to be less timid or more tolerant than those of modern times, finally yielded to the urgent entreaties of the Sisters and allowed them to live together in the same house. On this, the good Sisters continued their wonted exercises as if nothing had happened, relying on the prophecy of Ven. Crescentia that the convent would be suppressed, the number of Sisters be reduced to a very few, yet not entirely die out, but on the contrary, that after a while the number of Sisters should be greater than in her own time. The result fully verified the truth of this prophecy. This convent, doomed to die out, retained life till the year 1831, through the courageous perseverance of the Sisters and a special dispensation of Providence. Then the noble King Ludwig (1831) granted them permission to receive novices on condition that they devoted themselves to the education of the youth of the female sex. At that time there were six Sisters living, out of the twenty who had witnessed the suppression of the convent in 1802, under the direction of Rev. Mother M. Francisca Wiedeman ; she was the last of the old school of our Ven. Crescentia. Sister M. Ignatia Bögin did not die till Feb. 15, 1864. Of late the number of Sisters has wonderfully increased. In earlier times there were never more than twenty Sisters ; at the present time there are between thirty and forty, who conduct parochial schools, a school in a manufacturing district, and a Normal School for ladies preparing to become teachers. The constant increase in the number of novices rendered it necessary to build additions to the convent. The old buildings and the Church, with their interior arrangement, have, however, been preserved in their simple and poor condition, with praiseworthy reverence which forbade the altering anything from the state in which it was when the servant of God dwelt therein. Thus the whole house is filled with the fragrance of the reminiscences, and with relics of this blessed spouse of Christ. The Church itself, notwithstanding its lofty steeple, is of low pitch and of small dimensions, and should rather be called a chapel ; nevertheless, it contains three altars. The choir for the Sisters is built over the whole nave of the Church, and with two side extensions embraces the little sanctuary with a small main altar. This choir is richly adorned with pious pictures, which stimulate devotion. This was the very sanctuary in which the Ven. Crescentia spent the greater part of her earthly life ; this was where she received most of the marvellous blessings from above. The somewhat strange and peculiar kneeling-desks enclosed by curtains date from olden times. The one occupied by Crescentia, when Superioress, is still adorned with her pictures and other objects of devotion.

Having thus described the field of our future narrative, we turn back to the pious virgin herself. The conviction that she was called by God to the most perfect interior and exterior separation from the world and to the state of giv-

ing her entire being to Christ remained unshaken, and at
length the desire to attain this end gave her no rest, and
compelled her to disclose her wish to her beloved father,
that he might help her, or at least give her good advice as
to how she might obtain admission into the cloister of the
city.

She had, however, scarcely uttered her petition, than she
met with a firm resistance, which she had not expected
from a man of her father's extraordinary. piety. He opposed her most resolutely and sought every means to make
her give up her notion, alleging that it was altogether impossible to get the dower necessary to procure her reception
into the convent; that the convent itself was so very poor and
life there so hard, that she would not be able to stand it.
It would be much better and easier for her to remain at
.home with him, leading a single life and earning her bread
by the work of her hands.

Her good father proved by such discourses as these,
which were certainly well-meant excuses, the truth of the
old saying, that parents are rarely good counsellors, when
the question concerns the vocation of a child to the religious state. It was so difficult for him to reconcile himself to the thought of being separated from his beloved
daughter, that it dimmed the light of faith which had ever
shone so brightly, so that he took a purely human view of
the matter and consequently went astray in his judgment.
God's thoughts and ways were quite different, and consequently, this virgin, who was guided by the Spirit of God,
for the first time in her life could not acquiesce in her father's decision. Her resolution held firm and the hope she
cherished that God would assist her was not to be shaken.
When her repeated petitions had no effect in inducing her
father to permit her to make the trial of her vocation to
the religious life, she went herself to the Superioress of
the convent, Rev. Mother M. Teresa Schmid, and with
humble gestures and a beating heart prayed for admission. It turned out as her father had foretold; she

was refused, on the ground that the convent was too poor and dared not receive a young woman without a dower. She repeated her request many times, but without any other result. "For one or two years," says her confessor, John Baptist Pamer,[1] "her entreaties were in vain; even tears that might have melted a stone were unheeded by men."

Nevertheless, the resolute virgin, hoping against hope, relied on the all-powerful arm of God, to whom that is possible which is impossible to man. She redoubled her ardent prayers for the help of God, and brought into exercise that faith which, according to the words of Holy Writ, can remove mountains of difficulties. This heroic hope could not, therefore, be confounded; and meanwhile it pleased the heavenly Father to console His child even in a miraculous manner. In the dormitory of the Sisters, near the entrance to the oratory, was a crucifix, which is still to be seen there. When passing this the pious Anna knelt down before it and prayed with a heavy heart that the Lord would grant her the favor she desired. She distinctly heard from the lips of the image these words: "Here shall be your dwelling-place."[2] Another circumstance is added by many witnesses,[3] which is, perhaps, the only one of its kind, and which the thoroughly trustworthy witness, Sister M. Gabriel Merz,[4] relates in the following words: "This image of the Crucified One previously had its mouth closed, as all the other Sisters saw with their own eyes, and told me and my fellow-Sisters of it; but from the moment it spoke these words to Crescentia it remained open, as any one may see at the present day, where it hangs in the same place as it did then." Even now that crucifix may be seen, having that remarkable peculiarity, as if, with wide-open mouth, it would tell something to the beholder.

This change in the crucifix naturally gave rise to much wonder and gossip among the Sisters; but no one suspected

---

[1] Act B. Summ. Add. p. 6. [2] Summ. N. 6 passim.
[3] Ibid. § 5, § 53 passim. [4] Ibid. § 4.

how it had come to pass. It was not till many years later, when the virtue of the servant of God had been put to the test, that it occurred to the afore-named distinguished Mother M. Johanna Altweger to ask Crescentia about it. Crescentia blushed, and compelled by obedience, related the whole occurrence, which the Superioress communicated to many other witnesses.

Crescentia, meanwhile, though consoled in so miraculous a manner, did not even reveal it to her father ; she simply said to him :[1] "Father, I really believe and hope for certain that I shall enter the convent here." But her father rebuked her with these words : "Child, what are you talking about ? What are you fancying ? You know how poor we are ; don't cherish such a thought as that, while you live. I can give you nothing, and without temporal means they will not take you." Crescentia, however, continued quietly yet confidently to await the hour when God would open for her the convent doors.

Meanwhile, the news that the "pious Annerl" had been rejected by the Superioress spread through the city. The veneration and love with which the maiden was regarded were such that all blamed the Superioress in the severest manner : "Such an angel would be an ornament to the convent," was the universal conviction ; even Protestants joined in blaming the Mother who had refused her. Divine Providence had, however, already paved the way for her reception, and for this purpose made use of a Protestant, namely, of Matthias Wörle, of Wöhrburg, mayor of the city of Kaufbeuren. He was the instrument by which God willed to deliver the convent from a long-felt and much deplored nuisance, and at the same time confer a rich, though as yet unprized, treasure. The good man did not suffer difference of religious creed to hinder him from seeing the great injustice suffered by the convent, in the city not permitting the removal of the saloon which caused such disturbance during the religious exercises. He argued

---

[1] Gabriel, p. 10.

the matter in favor of the convent, before the city council, in so forcible a manner, that the council unanimously agreed to buy the said saloon at the moderate price asked for it and give it to the Sisters.   By this great service he earned a title to their gratitude, and insured a respectful attention to his wishes.

Now, he had known and admired the pious but poor Anna from childhood upwards, and had heard with regret that she had been refused admittance.   He at once resolved to use all his influence in her favor.   Without the knowledge either of the young woman or of her parents, he went to the Superioress and represented to her and to the community that they should not reject the incomparable Anna Höss, who, as he had heard, had applied for admission and been refused, "For though poor in earthly possessions, she was rich in virtue; and," he added, "it were a pity for so innocent an angel to remain in the world."

All objections naturally vanished before so influential a patron, especially when this same gentleman applied to the Father Provincial, Odoricus Schnabel, who happened to be present, and reiterated his recommendation.   Father Odoricus immediately sent for Anna, who suspected nothing of what had passed, and he conceived so high an opinion of her virtue that he insisted with decision that she should be received immediately and without dower.

The prescribed voting of the community then took place, and on the 5th of June, 1703, it was unanimously resolved that the pious Anna should be permitted to enter on her novitiate.   Her long-cherished desires were thus fulfilled, her persevering prayers were thus answered in a manner and at a time when no one could have imagined or expected it.   This was truly the work of Divine Providence; it is the prerogative of the Supreme Ruler, the highest King, to come to the rescue when human wisdom is at a loss what to do, and to open a door where the mortal eye sees but an impenetrable, insurmountable wall.

The joy of the good maiden surpasses expression; all

who knew her shared her satisfaction, especially the good mayor. Her happiness was the greater because her actual admission was to take place in eleven days. On the 16th of June, when she was twenty years and nine months old, she left her father's house, that home which, under the loving eyes of pious parents, had always been to her a place of peace, of innocence, and of tranquil happiness.

She followed the call of the Crucified One, who deeply in her heart had impressed the words : "Every one of you that doth not renounce all that he possesseth, cannot be my disciple." [1]

It is probable that some regret might have mingled with her joy as she left her beloved home and its cherished inmates, and perhaps her heart was beating when she passed through the convent portals, and was anticipating what weal or woe, what struggle and victory, she might meet in this new arena of her life. By a special privilege never before or since granted to any other Sister, the customary days of preparation were remitted ; she received the habit on the very next day. At the direction of the Father Provincial this ceremony was performed by Father Francis Imhoff, O. S. F., guardian of the Friars Minor at Augsburg.

A new period was now opened in her life ; she had commenced to walk on that road of the Cross which was to lead her to the summit of the purest and holiest love, the love in which human affection is transfigured in the divine. The Spirit of the Lord, which had guided her from youth upwards, which " reacheth from end to end mightily, and ordereth all things sweetly," [2] continued to conduct her with marvellous firmness from step to step, and transformed all obstacles into rounds of the golden ladder that leads up to Christ Himself.

O Christian soul, learn from Ven. Crescentia always to follow the indications of Providence ; accomplish what the Psalmist says : " Commit thy way to the Lord and trust in Him : and He will do it." [3]

---

[1] Luke xiv. 33.   [2] Wisdom viii. 1.   [3] Psalms xxxvi. 5.

CHAPTER V.

The Year of Probation.[1]

AS soon as the servant of Christ had been clothed with the penitential habit of St. Francis, she forgot what lay behind her and for the future strove only for the sublimest perfection of pure love of the Cross, to acquire which she considered her only mission on earth, a possession compared to which she considered everything pleasing to the mere human sense as dross or refuse. She was so utterly a stranger to self-complacency that she viewed her past life as a simple aberration, or even as a resistance to the divine will, and resolved to atone for it by the practise of severe penance.

For the Lord had sent a ray of light into her soul, which disclosed to her the truth of the nothingness of all earthly things, and the misery and sinfulness of the human soul fallen in Adam. At the same time He excited within her an insatiable hunger after justice, so that she thirsted after the living God, as the "hart panteth for the fountains of water." The following fragment of her resolutions will show the spirit with which she entered on her task; these resolutions were written down some years later, but they will, nevertheless, be a true expression of her aim at the time she commenced her religious life.

"O Jesus, most loving Ruler of all things, I know that all my happiness comes from Thee alone, and I fully understand that I must not, even for a moment, depart from Thee. Therefore, may it please Thee, O my God, that I make this covenant with Thee : even as I draw breath every moment, so do I desire that not one instant should pass, in which I do not love, praise, and adore Thee. I desire every moment to be inflamed with ardor for Thy divine honor, and for the salvation of souls ; I desire to honor Thee, to subject myself to Thee, to atone for my

---

[1] Summ. N. 6.

sins, to love my neighbor, and to imitate Thy humility, poverty, chastity, and obedience, and by constant prayer for these graces, to keep myself ever near to Thee. In attestation of this, I acknowledge, with the most humble subjection, in the presence of Thy divine Majesty, of the Blessed Virgin, and of the whole court of Heaven, that this is my will, purpose, and earnest resolution, which do Thou, O Lord, my God, deign to accept, now and forever, and confirm with the seal of Thy divine grace for all eternity."

Even as a novice she put into practice what she wrote down in the year 1721 : [1]   " In following my King, I will courageously take in hand the sword of the love of God, and in full trust in that love, hoping for His all-powerful aid in the assaults and temptations of the evil one and in all the adverse circumstances of life, I will in His name, under which I have enlisted, fight for my King, suffer, struggle, and contend, and by His grace, conquer ; and all this with no other purpose in view, save that my Omnipotent King be honored and loved."

These resolutions did not remain mere wishes and unfruitful attempts; they were immediately put into practice with so great fidelity and to such a degree, that the most fervent of the Sisters were far behind our novice in zeal. Her resolutions show that she was principally intent on building up the interior life according to the principles of a genuine asceticism. These resolutions principally refer to the purification of the soul by the extirpation of the slightest evil inclination ; to the entire subjection of one's own will to that of God ; to putting all lukewarmness to flight; to attaining peace of mind, love of one's enemy, love of the Cross, obedience to superiors and confessors, and especially to interior recollection. All these virtues, but especially those of humility, obedience, of unshaken peace and serenity amid the severest sufferings, manifested themselves in so exalted a form from the very commencement

---

[1] Kolb, p. 11.

of her religious life, that the eyes of all who were connected with her were attracted towards her, whether for or against her.   But she, herself, was occupied only with the "sweet guest of her heart" and her only struggle was to subdue any emotion that might disturb her inward peace and to accept with love every cross as a messenger from Heaven. Two resolutions, from the year 1718, may serve to illustrate the sentiments of her heart: [1]

"I will cherish interior peace, that I may hear and understand what the Holy Ghost speaks to me ; and when my passions and cares make themselves heard within me, as soon as I perceive their voice, I will tell them to 'keep silent,' while with Samuel I say :   'Speak, Lord, for Thy servant heareth.'"

Under the title of "love of the Cross" she says :   "O my dearly loved Father, if Thou, in Thine infinite goodness, wilt give me a little cross, I would rejoice out of pure love for Thee, that Thou deignest to be mindful of Thy unworthy child."

Yes, indeed, her beloved Father in Heaven was mindful of her ; He who had enkindled within her these pious desires, also made provision that exterior circumstances should correspond with the interior longing and strong impulse of her soul.   He cast His beloved child into the crucible of painful trials and of unjust persecutions, that the pure gold of grace might be separated from the dross of nature, which the eye of God alone could perceive ; that the purified gold might daily increase through heroic acts of humility, of obedience, of love of enemies ; that the work might be brought by endurance to perfection, and that the golden ladder to Heaven might be erected on the foundation-stone of patience, as St. Paul describes in these words :   "We glory also in tribulations : knowing that tribulation worketh patience, and patience trial, and trial hope, and hope confoundeth not, because the charity of God is poured forth in our hearts by the Holy Ghost, who

---

[1] Kolb, p. 2.

is given to us." [1] There is nothing that could give us a clearer proof of the height of virtue which she had already attained, than the measure of the sufferings which God permitted to be meted out to her in the very beginning of her religious life ; it far surpasses ordinary occurrences. And she had to bear this heavy cross upwards of four years, without human aid, alone, forsaken, and forgotten. And she did bear it, not only without a murmur, complaint, or wavering, but with joy and gratitude. Hard, nay, fearfully unjust treatment from her companions, terrible, hardly credible temptations and assaults from the devil, were means in the hand of God to cleanse her more and more from the dust of human misery. We begin in this chapter to narrate the process of this purification, by relating how hardly she was treated by her fellow-beings. And that nobody may be scandalized by what we have to tell, we premise a few remarks, to afford the reader a right point of view, when he has to consider these and similar occurrences in the lives of the Saints.

It is the unanimous teaching of all the masters of spiritual life, who have written on the Mystical State, [2] that all souls who are called to the higher degrees of prayer, and to the mystical union with God Himself, must pass several stages of the so-called passive purification by suffering. Among these stages the passive purification of the sensitive part of the soul, termed by that great master of mystics, St. John of the Cross, " the dark night of the senses," is especially to be considered. During the time that this purification is going on, contradiction, contempt, calumny, and unjust persecution are regularly poured over the soul in a thousand different forms, with the violence of roaring mountain streams; added to which, God Himself often so orders it that this persecution arises from one's near neighbors, well-intentioned persons, sometimes even from moderately saintly persons, which latter circumstance adds a

---

[1] Rom. v. 3-5.

[2] Comp. Thomas a Jesu. De Oratione Divinæ.—L. ii. c. xi. 15 : Schram, Institutiones. Theolog. Mysticæ.—P. 1. 198 seq.

deep, cutting pang to the soul. Let us listen to an experienced man of the olden time, who belonged to the Order of St. Francis;[1] he says on this subject: " I say in truth that before God would leave a soul which He has selected and set apart in special love, without such a preparation, He would take occasion to permit a hundred thousand men to do some injury to this soul, or close the interior eyes of a thousand Saints, so that by their severe, yet false, judgments, they might purify and polish this vessel of the elect."

The lives of the Saints bear ample testimony to the truth of this assertion. Just think of St. Elizabeth of Thuringia, against whom her nearest friends, and some of them far from ignoble, permitted themselves to use expressions which seem almost incredible from their harshness; of St. Francis of Assisi, who was ill treated by his own father in the presence of the bishop; of St. Catherine of Sienna, who had to do the work of a hired girl in the house of her parents; of St. Peter Damian who, as Baronius relates (1049), had to suffer injustice from the holy but deceived Pope Leo IX. ; of St. Alphonsus Liguori, and many others who verify the words of St. Paul : " All that will live godly in Christ Jesus, shall suffer persecution."[2]

These observations should make every one careful in regard to judging others, particularly holy persons, and at the same time lenient in reference to those who, for want of this precaution, have maltreated saintly souls. The words of our Lord, " They know not what they do," are sometimes very applicable to them. This was very probably the case with the most of those who persecuted our novice. They afterwards acknowledged their mistake; it was as if a veil had been withdrawn from their eyes; so much so that they, declaring that their blindness had been incomprehensible, made public reparation.[3]

<hr>

[1] Heuricus Harphius, Theologia Mystica.—L. ii. c. 11.
[2] II. Tim. iii. 12.   [3] Act B. Defensio, N. 72.

The Father of mercies, however, prepared His child for these sufferings by a vision.[1] She saw her Redeemer coming out of the room of the Mother Superior, Sister Theresa Schmid, carrying a heavy cross on His shoulders. She knew at once that this cross was to be her portion and that her Superioress would be the instrument by which God would send suffering to her. So, in fact, it came to pass : the character of the Superioress made this cross heavier than might be expected. She was born in Munich, 1670, the daughter of the physician to the Elector. She had been elected to office as Mother Superior in 1698 ; but it seems as if at her election more attention had been paid to her exterior qualifications and to her connections, than to her virtues ; for it soon became manifest that she was utterly unfitted for the office, and disorder soon assumed such a shape, that the Superiors found themselves obliged, in the year 1707, to proceed to a formal deposition, as she had been elected for life, according to the ancient custom of the convent. And we may here mention that this deposition, or removal from office, is the only one in the records of that convent, though they embrace several centuries ; also, that the name of Theresa Schmid is not found in the catalogue of Mother Superiors preserved in their archives. This Superioress could not fail to have some Sisters on her side to join in this persecution ; among these one old Sister Anthony is particularly mentioned, with four or five others.

The proximate exterior cause for the harshness of the Mother Superior, lay probably in the fact that she had been urged to receive this poor young woman, without a dowry, and in opposition to her own previous decisions. It might be that she considered this reception a wrong inflicted on the community. Hence the antipathy of the Superioress, which vented itself in upbraiding the poor child with the injustice which she (Crescentia) had committed by entering the convent. This blindness very soon increased to

---

[1] Act B. Summ. Obj. N. 11. § 20.

that degree, that she held herself justified in treating the poor novice so badly that it might induce her to leave of her own accord. Perhaps she believed she was thus doing a service to God and the cloister, when she treated the innocent girl, not like a fellow-Sister, but like a slave.

To this may be added the very singular conduct of the Ven. Crescentia, whose ideas on spiritual life were far in advance of the somewhat circumscribed notions of her persecutors and to those already prejudiced against her, might possibly give occasion for false interpretation and rash judgment. This could less easily be avoided because of those strange influences and assaults of the devil which very soon took place, and of which we will speak in the next chapter. In the kitchen, in which she had to help, strange disturbances and accidents frequently occurred: the yeast was upset, the fire would go out, dishes were broken, and all this under such circumstances that the servant of God was sometimes accused of awkwardness, sometimes of wickedness, and sometimes of being possessed ; so that the Sisters believed that she must, in one way or another, be compelled to leave the convent.

Envy and jealousy, vices which so easily enter the human heart, particularly that of the female sex, may have concurred in producing this effect ; and the custom in vogue among half-pious people of measuring everybody by their own standard and of sitting in judgment to con-demn those who do more than themselves, may have con-firmed them in their perverseness.

Sources as foul as these gave rise to the vilest judgments, to the most uncharitable accusations, and finally, occa-sioned Crescentia to be very harshly, even cruelly, treated. Even the most innocent of her actions were distorted and a wrong interpretation set upon them, while her vir-tues were converted into faults. Her kindness and will-ingness to help appeared to the blinded eyes of her enemies as hypocrisy and a desire of pleasing ; her patient silence at unjust accusations was ascribed to stubbornness, or want of feeling ; her piety was assumed; she never could do anything right ; the Superioress treated her only to wry faces and harsh words; reprimands, false accusations, and severe penances were her daily portion. She was accused before her confessor, nay, before the Father Provincial, of faults of which she was entirely free ; as, for instance, of not observing the prescribed silence ; she who was the most silent of the whole cloister; she who never spoke, save in reply.

The hardest and most menial works, such as were usually performed by hired servants, were assigned to her, without regard to her weakness, and indeed, so much was required of her that she could scarcely perform it all, no matter how hard she tried. She was seldom admitted to table with the community, but had to be contented with the remnants of food left on the dishes ; often with musty black bread, stale beer, or with water. Even this poor diet was given in such a small quantity that she was fearfully tormented by hunger while at her hard work. The Mistress of Novices often wept for her in compassion, and at times helped her by stealthily giving her a piece of bread.[1]

Her greatest trial, however, was that the obdurate Superioress often commanded the obedient child to do silly and ridiculous things, which were extremely painful to her tender modesty. Even before strangers the novice, in a comical dress, had to perform all kinds of nonsensical fooleries and tricks. Blind obedience heroically conquered the natural repugnance she felt to such performances ; and immediately afterwards she was summoned before the whole community, sharply rebuked, and punished for what she had done from simple obedience. The humble maiden confessed her fault on her knees, and uttered no word save that of thanks for the maternal correction. Such unworthy treatment as this was many times repeated, and the

---

[1] Summ. N. 15. § 36.

heroic novice never wavered or hesitated a moment, first to expose herself with a kind countenance to the laughter and derision of strangers and then to submit to the most severe reproaches and corrections. This conduct at length became too outrageous to be endured by the other Sisters; they advised the novice who was so miserably used to resist any command to perform such fooleries, assuring her that obedience did not require such things as that of her.[1] She answered in a cheerful tone: "Oh, my beloved Sisters, holy obedience alone suffices me. Contempt, disgrace, and ridicule are all welcome to me, if only I can be obedient. In this I find God, and in God all; what else can I wish or desire, when I possess God?"[2]

The heart of this pious virgin, accustomed, up to that time, to the kindest and most considerate treatment, could hardly help feeling deeply the pressure of her present position; but she was already confirmed in a life of faith, so mortified in her feelings, so filled with the desire to participate in the sufferings and disgrace of Christ, that she never wavered an instant, never was sad or confused. Her soul stood as firmly as granite amid the rush of the waves, for her hope was placed on her heavenly Father, and all her love was enclosed in the heart of Jesus. Many witnesses assert that never a word of complaint passed her lips, never did she defend herself, never did she resist. Neither did she ever doubt her vocation, and what is still more remarkable, her countenance never lost its expression of peace or of interior serenity. The greater that the pressure from without became, the more her soul was directed to the interior life, and blossomed like a lily among thorns, constantly increasing in beauty, and shedding around her, far and wide, the fragrance of humility, patience, and love of her enemies. If others complained of the unjust treatment she received, which they could not see without compassion, she excused everything, said that she was leniently dealt with, and that everything was done with a

---

[1] Summ. N. 15. § 22, § 50, § 99.   [2] Gabriel, p. 186.

good intention. She gave thanks for the meagre nourishment she received as for an unmerited alms ;. she requited
evil with good, especially by praying day and night for the
chief instrument of her persecution, and these prayers she
continued unceasingly for many years after another Superioress had been elected. Thus she, as St. Paul recom-
mends, overcame evil by good. God rewarded her fidelity
by granting her great graces, and by assisting her in other
more dangerous temptations, in which the devil, under
the mask of an angel of light, sought to withdraw her
from her vocation.

She had a very great love for her father, and from
this affection the devil sought to spin a web, by means of
which he could withdraw her from the convent. He
brought vividly before her mind how unhappy her father
had been rendered by her absence; he made her reflect on
the great happiness which she had enjoyed at home, and
what a hard life, full of disgrace, she was leading at the
convent. She answered all the evil suggestions in words of
her wonted faith : "Who is like unto God ? I am prepared, nay, I wish to suffer harder things."

It was thus, with the shield of faith, that she repelled the
fiery darts of the enemy. Thereupon the old serpent es-
sayed to deceive her by delusive representations, which, by
permission of God, he produced before her. Twice he appeared before her in the figure of her younger sister,
Regina, telling her, in most moving words, that their
parents were constantly weeping and lamenting in the
home she had abandoned ; that they could not get along
without her, and insisted on her returning to them ; it was
the urgent duty of a child to assist her parents and she
could certainly live more piously and more peacefully at
home than at the convent, where she found nothing but
work, want, and persecution. Her father could not endure
her absence any longer; he had sent her on and he was
waiting at the convent-gate to conduct her home. Then
the supposed sister at one time showed her the key of the

convent portal, and at another secular dresses she had brought for her use. In this dangerous struggle the oppressed maiden raised her heart to God, made the sign of the cross and invoked the holy names of Jesus and Mary ; then, being immediately enlightened by the Holy Ghost, she said : "I did not come to the convent for thy sake, and for thy sake I will not leave it." At these words the delusive apparition disappeared.

Sister Gabriel [1] recounts yet another story similar in character, wherein the devil appeared to her in the shape of a hunter, bringing her worldly clothing, and with specious words advised her to escape by crossing the brook flowing by the church-yard, and making her way to the distant country.

In all these struggles the maiden was utterly devoid of temporal aid ; even her father confessors for many years afforded her little assistance. For even they were, by the repeated complaints of the Superioress, if not prejudiced against her, yet rendered cautious and wavering ; or, it may be, they thought fit to try her by severe probations and humiliations.

In this way she continued to be, during her novitiate and even longer, a stumbling block to the greater number of the Sisters, a puzzle to others, yet to the more enlightened an object of high admiration. Among the last, three Sisters were found, who were distinguished for their solid virtues and who could not be persuaded by any gossip to take part against the good novice ; these were Sister M. Constantia Leder, Sister M. Benedicta Pez, and above all, Sister M. Johanna Altweger, who succeeded Mother Theresa in her office of Superioress.

The influence of these distinguished ladies was great enough to hinder any obstacle being laid in the way of Crescentia's profession, when the year of probation had expired. She was looking forward with ardent desire to this decisive day, on which she was irrevocably to consecrate

---

[1] Gabriel, p. 14.

herself to God by the three vows and thus place herself in the happy necessity of always following Christ and of carrying the Cross after Him. With the greatest care she prepared herself for this solemn act, which took place on June 18th, 1704. The ceremony was conducted by the Rev. Father Provincial, Odoricus Schnabel, who delivered a most touching address on the occasion. But those present were even more edified by the sight of the devout virgin than by the preacher's words. The astonishing piety with which she offered herself as a victim to the Most High with Christ and in Christ, attracted the admiration of all. As she approached the altar, first to take the vows, and afterwards to receive Holy Communion, the eyes of every one were fastened on her and fascinated, as at a spectacle never seen before. A holy awe impressed the souls of the whole audience and many shed tears abundantly. The virgin seemed rapt above the world of sense, so as no longer to belong to earth, and the presence of heavenly powers was perceptible ; an atmosphere of angelic purity seemed to breathe its fragrance even into such souls as had hitherto tasted only the ordinary piety of common life. Even these felt the rays of a mysterious fire and perceived that the heart of this extraordinary virgin must be the hearth and starting point of this glow of warmth. But beyond this sensation all was unknown. It was many years after this that, in holy obedience to her spiritual director, she communicated to him what had then passed between God and herself.[1]

She said that she had been wrapt in ecstasy immediately before making her vows ; that it had seemed to her as if she were no longer on earth, among men ; Christ, her heavenly Bridegroom, and His holy Mother had visibly appeared to her ; her guardian angel was standing at her side and conducted her to the place where the divine espousals were to take place ; there her Redeemer bowed most graciously to her, placed a most beautiful ring on her finger,

---

[1] Ott. B. I. Ch. 2.

and said : "Now I have taken thee to be My spouse ; go, suffer and fight ; I will always assist thee with My grace, and My Mother will take thee under her maternal protection."

Immediately on this, she made the vows of poverty, chastity, and obedience, in the presence of the Father Provincial, and, according to the custom of that convent, received the name in religion she was to bear, that of the holy Virgin and Martyr, Crescentia, with the surname Mary. A fit name, indeed ; a pure virgin, free even from a breath of carnal temptation, she continued throughout her life a martyr of love, bearing the hardest sufferings with unheard-of patience, while the fact of increasing in perfection without intermission is the distinguishing characteristic of her life.

This vision at her profession sheds its light over her state of mind at that time sufficiently to prove that she had already attained the higher degrees of the passive prayer of suffering and had at least reached the first degree of sublime union, the so-called mystical espousals which is ever attended with a similar vision.[1] This degree, already attained, was in itself a pledge that in future she should be called to yet higher graces of the mystic life. These, however, can only be acquired by fearful interior and exterior trials, which terminate in the transformation of the whole being into Christ ; so that such a soul can truly exclaim with St. Paul : "I live, now not I, but Christ liveth in me."[2] Both of these, heavy crosses and bitter suffering with unswerving fidelity, form from this time forth the substance of the life of this soul, so precious to God ; for it is absolutely the unalterable law of God, that none can receive a great reward save by undergoing great labors and crosses.

Oh, that every Christian, led by easier paths than these

---

[1] See St. Theresa, Seelenburg. 7 Dwelling, ch. 1, 2. Thomas a Jesu. De Oratione Divina. L. I. IV. ch. 14, 15. Schram, Inst. Theol. Myst. T. 1 § 322. Schol.—Scaramelli, Myst. Vol. 1. ninth degree.

[2] Gal. ii. 20.

of the Saints, would at least, with equal fidelity, follow the conducting hand of God! For: "Blessed is the man that endureth temptation : for when he has been proved, he shall receive the crown of life, which God hath promised to them that love Him." [1]

CHAPTER VI.

The Lion's Den. [2]

E read in the life of St. Mary Magdalen di Pazzi of a vision wherein the Lord told her that she would be thrown into a lion's den, namely, that she would have to suffer horribly from the attacks of the devil. This frightful state lasted five years, and left her thoroughly purified and prepared for the highest degrees of the interior life. In like manner our heroine had to descend into the lion's den and for four years to endure the assaults of the old serpent, and these seem to have been so extraordinary and to have assumed such a glaring aspect, that perhaps some of our readers may not feel inclined to believe the most important statements of eye-witnesses. If the facts which we are about to relate were the only ones of their kind spoken of in history, hesitation and doubt concerning them might appear to be somewhat justified ; but the history of the Saints in all ages, even up to the present time, presents us with many similar cases, perhaps even more extraordinary ones, and these occur at certain periods and degrees of the mystical life in regular gradation. Therefore the masters of the spiritual life teach, that for such souls as are led to the highest degree of prayer by means of the passive purification, these extraordinary and palpable temptations and

---

[1] James i. 12.   [2] Summ. N. 6.—Act B. Summ. Obj. N. 13, and Resp. p. 50.

torments of the devil are not exceptional cases, but occur according to a fixed rule.[1]

We take occasion to remark, however, that this state is by no means the same as that which is called possession (possessio). Rather is it a kind of circum-possessio called obsession (obsessio), and consists, according to Scaramelli[2] in this :—that evil spirits, by God's special permission, surround persons, excruciating them by some extraordinary assaults for their purification and sanctification. To speak figuratively, the evil spirits have not taken possession of the fort, but besiege and attack it.

With the Ven. Crescentia these vexatious proceedings commenced immediately on her entering the convent; nay, some say they had even occurred before that time. At first no one noticed them, because she never spoke to any one about them. Many disturbances which happened to her when at work, such as snatching the dishes from her hands and breaking them by throwing them on the ground, extinguishing the fire and the like, were attributed to her awkwardness or perversity, but these diabolical persecutions soon assumed so visible and tangible a character, that they threw the whole house into commotion.

One evening Sister Mary Beatrice Leder noticed in the corridor of the dormitory a frightful form, dressed like a hunter, but without a head, enter the cell of Sister M. Crescentia. Crescentia soon came up and was about to enter her cell, because the Rule of the house required that every Sister should withdraw to her cell at eight

---

[1] See Scaramelli, Myst. T. II. p. 292-364. Thomas a Jesu, De Orat. Divina, L. II. c. 14, 15.—Schram, Instit. Theol. Myst. T. 1. 6. 217-225.—Especially Görres, Myst. Vol. III. p. 430-470, who enumerates many examples, which may, however, easily be increased. Not to mention the tortures undergone by Christina Mirabilis, which are beyond measure, we find the same trials in the life of St. Rosa of Lima, of St. Frances of Rome, of St. Peter of Alcantara, of St. Paschal, of the Ven. Dominicus Jesu Maria, and in our times of the late Venerated Curé D'Ars, M. de Vianney, of the pious Anne Catherine Emmerich and of Maria Mörl. Görres, in his Mystik, relates (L. C.) at length the assaults undergone by our Crescentia, and cites the reports of Sister Gabriel Merz verbatim. He agrees, in the main, with those cited in the Act of Beatification; but we have preferred strictly to adhere to those acts.

[2] Loco cit. p. 302.

o'clock in the evening. Sister Beatrice ran up to her, held her back by her clothes, and warned her not to go into her cell, as there was a frightful spectre there. Undismayed, however, she replied that obedience required her to go into her cell, and this she did without delay. This incident, in itself scarcely worth noticing, was, notwithstanding the earnest entreaties of Crescentia, related on the following day to the Superioress by the other Sister; in the explanation demanded of her, the young woman was compelled to confess that she had often been tormented by the devil in her cell, sometimes even whipped.

From that time forth, even in clear daylight and before the whole community, strange vexations beset Crescentia. When she knelt down to kiss the floor, according to a custom in the community, or when in the chapter-room she bowed her head, it was frequently struck to the ground so forcibly by an invisible power, that the worst result might be expected and, in fact, blood streamed from her nose and mouth.

At table she sat near the wall and her head was frequently hammered against it, in such a way that all the Sisters were terrified and believed that her skull must certainly be smashed to pieces. The Superioress was consequently compelled to assign her another place. But now she was at two different times seized upon by an unseen power, as she was sitting at table with the Sisters, and carried off with the quickness of lightning from the refectory without her feet touching the ground. The Sisters hastened after her, but she was soon out of sight; they found her after a long search in a remote corner of the house. Once she was under a pile of turnips that had been heaped over her; at another time she was in the cellar, jammed in between beams of timber on which hogsheads had been laden. The Sisters rescued her from this perilous position with much difficulty.

But it was at night, in her room, that she was most cruelly tormented. At first she heard a fearful noise before her

door, soon it came into the cell itself ; then she saw herself surrounded by all kinds of frightfully fantastic figures,
such as we read of in the lives of other Saints.   Poisonous
or disgusting animals, such as snakes, toads, spiders, craw-
fishes, in great numbers, appeared to fill her room and even
to come near her bed.   She, however, conquered her natural repugnance, raised her soul to God in faith and with
more than masculine courage stuck to her post, saying :
"Obedience appointed this room to me, not to you; it is I
that must stay here, not you ; begone with you."   Thereupon the illusions disappeared.

Frequently she was roughly torn from the bed and merci-
lessly beaten.   One night a hellish noise of fifes, rattling
of chains, and cracking of whips, was heard coming from
her room.   After that the poor creature was snatched away
from her cell by invisible agency and in the twinkling of
an eye dragged down the stairs, through two doors, out of
the house to the creek, which was then running swiftly
through a corner of the convent property.   There she was
first dipped into the water, then packed away under a pile
of wood.   Some of the Sisters, awakened by the noise,
hastened to her assistance, and when they heard the opening and closing of the door and of the stone covering of the
creek, they searched for their Sister in religion, both in the
creek and in the court-yard.   After a long time they noticed
that one of their many wood-piles had been thrown down
and torn apart ; there they at length found Crescentia,
stretched on the snow-covered ground, with her face down-
wards, covered with several logs of wood, stiff with the
frost and half-dead. [1]   The same tormenting occurrence
was repeated several times, at least in substance.   She was
dragged over the ground by night, in the severest cold
weather, thrown into the mill-stream, and held so long
under water that it is incomprehensible how she escaped
being drowned or frozen to death, for her clothes stuck together with the ice which covered them. [2]

---

[1] Act B. Summ. Obj. N. 13. § 12 et 21.   [2] Ott. N. 20. Summ. N. 6.

Frequently she was thrown with force to the ground, or down the stair-case, was pressed against the wall and at the same time ruthlessly beaten. Many times she received such a blow in her face that she bled at her nose and mouth and her cheek swelled up. Once, when she was busy in the loft, the noise of a heavy fall was heard. The Superioress immediately sent up some Sisters to see what was the matter; they found Crescentia had fainted and was lying bleeding between two beams of wood. She had been thrown down from the height of the roof, so that she lost two teeth, and the bone of her nose was fractured so badly that it formed a little hump, which remained visible all her life.

Once in the yard she was thrust under a box filled with old iron, and it was a long while before the Sisters found her and released her from this painful position. Another time, as Father Ott relates, she was discovered under a heavy chest in the garret.

The vexations in the kitchen were even increased. The following cases are related by many witnesses :[1] She was holding a vessel containing boiling milk and dumplings, when Sister M. Johanna Altweger, who was near, saw that the vessel was snatched from Crescentia's hand by an invisible power and its contents poured over her head, so that she received several severe wounds from the scalding, all over her body. Another instance that is related is this: Crescentia was just ready to serve up a wine soup prepared for the community, when a dark figure appeared and began to carry off the vessel. The courageous virgin called on her Redeemer for help, and soup-ladle in hand, pursued the strange robber, beat him lustily and forced him to give up the vessel, on doing which he at once disappeared. The Sisters who tasted of this soup, the price of this heroic combat, affirmed, all of them, even her greatest enemies, that they had never eaten so delicious a dish.

These acts of ill-usage, so many of which happened be-

---

[1] Summ. N. 6 et 16. § 204.

fore eye or ear-witnesses, in so striking a form that the
idea of attributing them to the effect of the imagination
falls of itself, lasted during the first three years after
her profession. They are so terrible in themselves, that
only one possessing an heroic fortitude could have preserved her soul in peace while enduring them, but in this
case their pressure was rendered greater, both in sharpness
and extent, by the persecution Crescentia also underwent at
the hands of her fellow-beings.

It can hardly excite our surprise to learn that such un-
usual occurrences created a great stir among all the Sisterhood of the convent ; those who had been already against
Crescentia, now suffered themselves to utter such severe
criticisms, that even those who had not hitherto been un-
favorable to her began to entertain doubts in her regard,
and to avoid meeting her, as if they really suspected that
she was possessed by the devil.

The evil-minded among them scrupled not to say that she
was a " witch" and had entered into a compact with the
devil to acquire the halo of sanctity. These opinions were
favored by the prejudices of the age, which, as we know, was
very credulous in such matters, and thus it came to pass
that this grievous calumny was promulgated even outside
the convent, and that many persons believed it.

It is easy to imagine that such accusations became a fertile germ of bitterness to our much-tried heroine. The reproaches of sham-holiness, possession, devilish delusion,
were frequently cast at her. Most of her Sisters in religion
systematically avoided her, blessed themselves when she
passed by, and spell-bound by superstitious fears, were careful not even to touch the dress of the supposed witch. The
Mother Superior now laid altogether aside justice and
toleration in Crescentia's regard. One single occurrence will show how far she carried out her harshness towards her.

By the direction of their actual father confessor, the Rev.
Thomas Damian Kuilestadt, parish priest of Kaufbeuren,

his niece, Miss Catherine Kempter, was received into the community, although the number of sisters (20) for whom cells were provided was complete. To prepare a cell for the new novice, who in religion was to be called Sister M. Felicitas, the Superioress commanded Crescentia to vacate her own room in favor of the new-comer, although, as a professed nun, Crescentia had the first right to the cell. The Superioress enforced her command with the stinging remark that she had brought nothing to the convent and was but a burden upon them, while Miss Kempter had a good dower. To this speech she added, with revolting asperity, that Crescentia might look out a place to sleep in for herself.

She was now literally like the Saviour, in this respect, that in the convent she had not where to lay her head. She had to go round among her Sisters and beg of them permission to spread her mattress in a corner of their cell, for a night's repose. This she did for two years, in all humility and gentle quietness, until the Mistress of the Novices, M. Dorothea Osterrieder, took sick and had to exchange her cell for the infirmary, where she afterwards died.

We are reminded of St. Elizabeth, Landgravine of Thuringia, expelled by her brother-in-law from her husband's castle at Wartburg and wandering from door to door in Eisenach, seeking a night's lodging for herself and her little ones and seeking it in vain, until finally she found shelter in a stable used for pigs, whence the swine had to be driven out to make room for her. And they who admire the greatness of soul shown by this daughter of princes, in requesting the Friars Minor to chant the Te Deum at the midnight office in order to give thanks to the Almighty for likening her in this way to the poor yet great King, will not refuse a tribute of honor and admiration to the poor weaver's daughter, when they learn how sublimely she conducted herself in these most severe trials. No word of complaint, no defence of herself, not a prayer to be spared this injustice escaped her lips, and no dark or gloomy looks betrayed any irritability. On the contrary, contemplating the matter from the high observatory of faith, she believed and said that this treatment was the just one for her; that she, a poor weaver's daughter, who had been taken in for love of God, deserved no better. Nay, her spirit triumphed over all purely human considerations and she discovered honor and wealth where the carnal eye sees extreme neglect and poverty. To be compelled to taste of the contempt and poverty of Eternal Love made Flesh appeared to her a priceless gain of riches and of honor. And she expressed her gratitude not only in words but with her whole heart, for what she called unmerited alms, when the worst, worn-out clothes were given to her, or when the hardly eatable remnants of food were left for her, or when a corner of a cell was assigned her for a night's rest. It was never noticed that she in any way avoided her persecutors; in fact, she requited evil with good to such an extent that very soon the general cry among the Sisters was: "If you wish to be a favorite of Crescentia's, you must offend her."

But even more painful than the treatment she received from the Superioress, harsh as it was, must have been that which the forsaken young woman experienced at the hands of her father confessor, of the Father Provincial, and of the other influential persons before whom she had been falsely accused. Although these persons were not so far led away as absolutely to condemn the accused, they nevertheless began to hesitate. and doubt if she was guided by the right spirit, and did not scruple to communicate their suspicions to her, and to subject her to strict examinations, in order to ascertain the truth. One of the father confessors even proposed to resign his office, because he doubted his own ability to decide correctly on so singular, remarkable, and critical an occurrence and to maintain peace amid the diversity of opinions and party-strifes.

Two young priests of the Order of St. Francis, probably instigated thereto or requested so to do by the Mother Superior, undertook to institute a kind of investigation respecting the spirit that animated Crescentia; that is to say, whether she was possessed of the devil, and guilty of sorcery and hypocrisy. Governed by prejudice, their proceedings were carried on without love or discretion. The less that Crescentia said in her own defence, the more humbly that she demeaned herself at all the reproaches they cast at her, simply replying that she did not know what a witch was, so much the more rashly and harshly did these uncalled-for judges pass sentence. They asserted that Crescentia was in league with the devil, and was thereby rendered as stupid, as devoid of feeling, and as perverse as possible.[1]

Such a judgment could but confirm the Superioress in her harsh behavior; she went so far as to shut up the Sister in a dark, lonely room and leave her there for a long time, with scarcely any food. Here the Father of all consolation came to her assistance with such heavenly illuminations and spiritual delights, that she declared her stay in that dark place had given her the sweetest and greatest happiness, and that it was a grace altogether unmerited.

Some years later, when Mother Johanna was Superioress, Crescentia was again subjected to a severe trial instituted by Rev. Weindach, a spiritual counsellor from Augsburg, and was repeatedly examined and condemned. He publicly declared in a threatening tone that she must be sent to another convent and there kept in strict custody; he would himself see the spiritual authorities and have this measure carried out.

Nothing came of these threats, however, but for a long time they hovered over the head of the virgin, who appeared to be thoroughly resigned to a fate apparently unavoidable, and which at least brought on new sufferings by sharp speeches uttered against her outside the convent, which some tattling tongues repeated to her. To all this storm of accusation, the heroic servant of the Crucified opposed only her wonted text: *" Jesus autem tacebat,"* " But Jesus held His peace." This divine silence at the severest accusations was her model.

---

[1] Summ. N. R. § 153.—N. 16. § 13.

In fact, there is no defence more effective, and more meritorious than humbly to remain silent before the unjust, and to commit one's self and one's affairs, without reservation, to the hands of the Judge of the living and the dead. It could scarcely fail but that the Lord would eventually take the matter into His all-powerful hands, and in the end exalt her as highly before men, as she, of her own free-will, had humbled herself before them.

How painful must have been this evil-speaking of her, coming to her from all sides, even from persons whom she held in great reverence, we may easily imagine. Her profound humility made her look on her lightest defects as grievous sins, and on herself as a creature of reprobation ; thus she was naturally inclined to think the worst of herself, and to assent to every accusation made against her, especially when advanced by Superior or priest. Her soul must, therefore, have been frequently harassed and restless, and her heart have been overwhelmed by bitter feelings ; nay, she must have despaired of herself, if the hand of God had not upheld her by inspiring her soul with an heroic confidence in the Redeemer. To be persecuted by good people, or by those holding God's place to us, is, of all the bitter sufferings of exterior life, the bitterest. So, at least, St. Theresa judged from her own experience.[1] She says : " What happened to me, namely, the evil opinions of, and doubts entertained by, her superiors and confessors, respecting the spirit that inspired her, would have been sufficient to drive me crazy ; sometimes I was in such a state that I could do nothing but simply raise my eyes unto my Lord. Although I have during my life suffered very great pains, this opposition of excellent persons was the worst of all."

And yet, even all this would have been endurable, if, during this time, her soul had experienced sensible devotion and interior consolation. For the suffering of the outward person is scarcely felt when the spirit is in Heaven, penetrated by the rays of light and love. But this conso-

---

[1] Autobiography, p. 28.

lation, which in earlier times she had so abundantly enjoyed, was now, for the most part, withdrawn. She was assailed by painful scruples, tormented with aridity, abandonment, and darkness of spirit, and what usually happens in such cases, violent temptations against faith, and hope were constantly knocking at her heart ; the terrible thought that she did not belong to the elect pursued her incessantly.

Thus, no protection was left her, nothing but a naked, dim faith, which faith, however, was "the shield" wherewith she was able "to extinguish all the fiery darts of the most wicked one."[1] Sustained by this faith, she clung firmly to the feet of the Redeemer, and gave herself up to Him for life or death. From this faith sprung the incredible firmness with which, without wavering, without losing peace in the higher part of her soul, she felt the bitter waves of sorrow rush over her. She was like unto the wise man who hears the word of the Lord and keeps it, namely, who believes and lives according to his belief, and whose house is built upon a solid rock.[2] However much the storms of temptation came and the waters of suffering rushed against this soul confirmed in God, she fell not, but rather was she purified to the depths of her being from all thoughts of self-complacency, self-confidence, and self-will, and marvellously advanced in every virtue, especially in faith, hope, and charity.

Dear reader, be you also careful not to build upon the sand of human feelings or human opinions, but upon the rock of faith, and marvel not that God permits violent tempests, both by man and devil, to be excited against you. Direct the eyes of your soul to the Cross, and ponder over the words of the Wise Man : "Take all that shall be brought upon thee : and in thy sorrow endure, and in thy humiliation keep patience : for gold and silver are tried in the fire, but acceptable men in the furnace of humiliation."[3]

---

[1] Ephes. vi. 16.   [2] Matth. vii. 24, 25.   [3] Ecclus. ii. 4, 5.

CHAPTER VII.

The Redemption.[1]

OR two years and a half had the dark night, just described, lasted, when a ray of hope came to announce her deliverance to the severely-tried virgin. She had perseveringly had recourse to Mary, the Queen of Heaven, and to her alone had complained of the oppressions she received. Now, "her beloved Mother," as she called Mary, appeared to her, consoled and encouraged her to persevere, promising that very soon she should be freed from this tyranny of Satan. At the same time she was commanded, with the permission of the Mother Superior, to make a pilgrimage to the picture of the Mother of God in the Church of the Friars Minor at Lechsfeld; that would be the place where she should be forever delivered from satanical persecutions. With a heart full of consolation and gratitude, Sister Mary Crescentia went to the Mother Superior and in all simplicity requested permission to perform that pious pilgrimage; but she met with a denial, and when she got others to intercede for her and make the same request for her, she had to put up with harsh reproaches, instead of the favor being granted. There seemed then no prospect of changing the mind of the Superioress and obtaining the promised redemption, notwithstanding that the rules, being exempt from canonical enclosure, were in no way opposed to such a pilgrimage ; the will of the Superior, influenced by a blind antipathy, was the only obstacle in the way.

Meantime, the Lord made use of this perverse will to obtain His end, and that for the best interests of His beloved child, to wit : the opportunity of exercising patience and holy obedience for a length of time, a far more precious favor than the one requested. Not a murmur, not a com-

---

[1] Summ. N. 6.

plaint escaped her lips ; she submitted to the harsh rule of her Superioress, and in all humility and patience adored the all-wise and merciful will of God. In this way she was sure to attain, with ever greater certainty, the terminus appointed by God, and if apparently her redemption was delayed, she was in reality approaching it in a more glorious and more speedy way. The moment soon arrived when the measure of certain sufferings and trials was filled up. The Lord then cast aside the human tool of which, for His own high purposes, He had made use of, and changed the whole state of affairs.

The mis-government of Mother M. Theresa Schmid had become so flagrant that the Father Provincial had to interfere, and, in the year 1707, she was removed from office. This, as we have noted before, is the only case of the kind in the history of that convent. Sister M. Johanna Altweger was elected in her stead. This Sister was one distinguished in every way, one to whom the reports of her fellow-religious, as well as those of outsiders, bear favorable testimony. It may suffice to quote what Father Ott [1] says of her: "She was a very prudent, pious, and able religious, who presided over the convent for thirty-four years, governing it with eminent virtue and prudence, not only in spiritual but also in temporal affairs, so that from her inferiors she merited honor, love, and gratitude, as well as the greatest veneration from those outside, and with these sentiments they carried her to the grave. Sister M. Johanna seems to have been specially elected by Almighty God, that she might direct Sister M. Crescentia according to the rules of prudence, might scrutinize her virtues, and afford her occasion and opportunity for those greatest and most difficult exercises practised by the most renowned Saints." Thus far Father Ott.

Mother M. Johanna had scarcely entered on the duties of her office, ere she thought of liberating the over-burdened Crescentia, for whose sufferings she had always felt com-

---

[1] Ott, B. I. Ch. 3.

passion, and whose virtues she had admired, from the diabolical influences which distressed her. She sent the pious virgin, accompanied by Sister M. Anna Neth, to Lechsfeld, that at length the proposed pilgrimage might take place. Many extraordinary things occurred in this pilgrimage which we cannot omit to notice, since they are affirmed, not only by Sister M. Anna Neth, whose testimony might be esteemed dubious, but by the repeated[1] assertions of the Superioress, who immediately investigated the matter and questioned Crescentia herself about it. [1]

When the Sisters were preparing for their journey (which was at least six hours' walk) to the miraculous picture, the Superioress felt at a loss, because she had no reliable person to accompany the Sisters, neither of whom knew the road. Suddenly a messenger was announced at the convent-gate, who asked if any of the Sisterhood wished to go to Lechsfeld, in which case he was ready to accompany them, and show them the way. The portress informed the Mother Superior of this offer, adding that she had never seen such a modest and well-behaved young man before. The Mother accepted the kind offer without hesitation. The stranger refused to take refreshment and added that he would wait outside the city for the Sisters and conduct them safely. And so it happened. On the road they repeatedly said the beads together, and the unknown guide spoke of spiritual things, especially of the prerogatives of the Queen of Heaven, with so much unction and in so pleasing a manner, that the pilgrims forgot the tedium of the way ; they did not even notice the length of the journey until they came into the neighborhood of the sanctuary, when all at once their companion vanished and on the far-extending plain no human form save their own was visible. A shudder passed through Sister Mary Anna. "What is that ? Who was he ?" she inquired of Crescentia ; but she who knew that it was good to "hide the secret of the King," [2] answered evasively that they were

---

now in sight of the convent and of the Church, that the man had guided them far enough ; they should offer up a thanksgiving to their heavenly Father for the protection His Providence had granted them.

In silence, but much moved in spirit, both of them then entered the Church. Sister M. Crescentia remained during the rest of the day, until late in the night, kneeling before the miraculous picture, motionless as a statue. Before the break of day, on the following morning, they were waiting at the Church door, and very carefully prepared themselves for Holy Communion. After which, Ven. Crescentia was rapt in ecstasy. She remained in that state for an hour, as stiff as a statue, now pale, now glowing with red, entirely absorbed, so that her companion did not know what to make of it, and became embarrassed and frightened. [1] Meantime, the Mother of Mercy had appeared to the servant of God and had accosted her with great kindness, telling her she should _in_ future be free from any outward persecution by Satan, while for her spiritual benefit she would often have to bear interior sufferings. " Though," she added, " do not fear; I myself will be thy protection."

Filled with indescribable consolation, returning thanks and giving honor to the heavenly Father and her beloved Mother Mary, she returned to her dear convent the very same day. She herself said nothing of these extraordinary occurrences, but her companion could not keep from telling Mother Johanna all that she remarked that was marvellous in Crescentia and in their companion ; concerning the latter she stated, that at the conversation of this unknown friend she had felt like the disciples at Emmaus ; her heart burned within her, and the thought that they were accompanied by an angel became certainty when he vanished in an inexplicable manner.

The prudent Superioress laid no great stress on this narrative of Sister M. Anna. She reflected carefully on

---

[1] Ott, p. 30.

the circumstances detailed, and held her tongue. After the lapse of a considerable time, she came upon Crescentia unawares with the question, whether she knew who the pilgrim was that had borne them company. The young woman shrank from answering. She dared not lie, and to reveal an extraordinary grace was very painful to her. Blushing painfully, she most humbly made known the truth that it was her special patron, St. Anthony of Padua. When questioned more closely, she communicated to the Superioress the vision she had had, and the promise that had been made to her after Holy Communion.

This being accompanied by St. Anthony, remarkable as it may appear, is not incredible, since similar and even more wonderful occurrences are related in the lives of other Saints, as in those of St. Rose of Lima, and of St. Mary Frances of the Five Wounds. The communion of Saints often discloses itself in a manner exceeding the power of comprehension of the wise people of the world.

The promise of the Blessed Virgin to Crescentia was completely fulfilled : the dark night was followed by the dawn of day in the soul of the servant of Christ, nay, even by the bright day of a peaceful evolution of a close and still closer union with Christ. The power of Satan to produce exterior disturbance was altogether broken ; and the deposition of the former Superioress also improved her exterior condition in the convent. Persecution lost its harshness, although it still revived at times, through the talk of credulous or evil people ; a rooted prejudice, or aversion, does not disappear all at once, and many considered themselves justified in asserting that she had at least been deceived by Satan, from some singular occurrences that took place. This occasioned many painful examinations and evil reports against her, which Mother Johanna—however much she loved Crescentia, and was for her own part convinced of her virtue—did not repress, for important reasons. She herself treated her with a strict and wholesome severity. In this she was confirmed and assisted by the Rev.

Father Provincial,[1] who had commanded her, when she
assumed the office, to mortify Crescentia, wherever and
whenever she could, to exercise her in obedience by laying
on her harsh and, according to the natural reason, irrational commands; she should even, when she judged her innocent, impose strict and humiliating penances on her and
never speak a friendly word to her. This ordinance of the
Father Provincial was not only appropriate, it was necessary: souls walking in such extraordinary paths must be
strictly and severely tried, that a safe judgment may be
arrived at, as to whether their spirit really is from God.
And when this has been ascertained, they must, for the
sake of their own selves, be exercised in heroic virtues,
namely, in humility and privation of all the natural affections of the heart and mind, as a protection against
the dangers of self-aggrandizement and self-esteem, and to
afford them occasions and inducements to prove their
fidelity towards the Giver of all grace, by thus conquering
themselves. Humility and obedience are alike the only
sure touchstone of spirits, and the best means of advance-
ment. The carrying out of these orders was a greater
conquest to the heart of the Mother Superioress, than the
trials were to Crescentia, who had to undergo them.
To use a Sister she so dearly loved harshly, nay, apparently unjustly, was very grievous to her. But obedience and the conviction that this was the best treatment for
her, did not permit her to doubt that this was God's will.

After many years she used to say[1] to the other Sisters,
with tears in her eyes, that she believed no one had been
so severely tried in every way as Crescentia, and that she
had often been afraid she had gone beyond the due limits
with her; had been apprehensive that Crescentia might
lose courage, but that she, on the contrary, had endured the
hardest trials and had always been tranquil, cheerful, and
ready for every new one. In short, she sooner became
weary of issuing such commands than Crescentia of obey-

---

[1] Summ. N. 15. § 42.   [4] Summ. N. 15. § 186.

ing them. At a later period we shall hear more of this, and at the same time see how God rewarded such marvellous virtue with equally marvellous success, which He made known to the public.

We may, as St. Augustine remarks, conceal truth for a time, but never conquer it ; it will at length burst forth only the more gloriously through the clouds with which wickedness and ignorance have darkened it. This was verified in Crescentia. All the doubts which her Superiors had entertained, especially concerning her ecstasies and revelations, vanished by degrees, for God Himself bore testimony to her worth in an unmistakable manner. Rev. Father Provincial Sebastian Höss became aware of this in the following manner : [1]

As he, in November, 1716, was holding the visitation of the convent, and could not come to a definite decision concerning the spirit of the servant of God, he thought he might ask of God Himself a proof of her supernatural graces. He was alone in the reception-room and wished to seal a letter, when the thought came into his mind : "If Sister M. Crescentia should come in at this moment without being summoned, with a lighted candle, I will consider this as a sign that she is led by the Spirit of God." Thereupon he actually commanded her, though only in thought, to bring him a light. A few moments later, there was a tap on the door, and Crescentia came into the room with a lighted taper. He suppressed his surprise and said simply : "What is that for, Crescentia ? It is broad day-light and you bring me a light." She replied : "And does not your reverence want a lighted taper to seal your letter with ? I felt an impulse to bring it to you." Without saying a word to her, the Provincial, now fully convinced of her virtue, related the circumstance to the Superioress and the other Sisters, and concluded by saying : "Crescentia is truly and genuinely pious ; God is with her and leads her."

---

[1] Summ. N. 21, § 34, 104, 167.

Had we in our light trials only a little firmness of faith and patience, then after our short sufferings we should be able to repeat with a joyful heart the words of Holy Writ : "For Thou (O God) art not delighted in our being lost ; because after a storm Thou makest a calm, and after tears and weeping Thou pourest in joyfulness. Be Thy name, O God of Israel, blessed forever."[1]

CHAPTER VIII.

Her Religious Life.

TO pray, to work, and to suffer, these comprehend the whole circuit of the forty-one years which Crescentia passed in religion. These occupations, indeed, fall to the lot of every religious, and thus it would appear as if there were nothing peculiar in respect to these related of Ven. Crescentia. And yet it is precisely the manner in which she performed this treble duty that calls forth the highest degree of our admiration. Her bodily frame was weak and tender, but her iron will, her diligence, and skill enabled her to execute the work and business of the community of every description to the general satisfaction. During the first years she spent in the convent, she worked in the kitchen and at other toilsome labor ; she also wove the Sisters' clothing, and taught the art of weaving to others of the Sisterhood.

Thus she was almost the whole day engaged in labor of some sort, but her heart was still more occupied with God than was her hand with work. For from her very youth she had—they say instructed by her guardian angel—acquired the sublime art, until it became a habit, of honoring the divine mysteries by interior intentions, while occupied in exterior matters. All her confessors have expressed their surprise at her manner, which was unique in

---

[1] Tob. III. 22, 23.

its kind, of forming at every kind of work, and on every occasion, with inexhaustible fertility and a playful facility, the sublimest reflections and intentions. Her soul lived so entirely in the supernatural order, faith illumined her interior life so brightly, and the life and sufferings of Christ were so deeply impressed on her heart, that all she said, thought, or did, was stamped with the word of the Apostle : " Christ is all and in all." [1] In everything she saw or heard, in everything she did herself, or saw others do, there was mirrored, to her spiritual eye, some mystery of the supernatural world ; she discovered similitudes to the divine in objects the most remote, where an ordinary person would see a mere nothing, and therefore would consider conclusions, which were natural and spontaneous in her, as far-fetched and almost forced analogies. For instance, when she was weaving and throwing the shuttle to and fro, she would remember the stripes Christ had received at the pillar of scourging, and would offer them up to the heavenly Father with the petition to be permitted to receive the same strokes. If she were scrubbing the kitchen-floor, she would, in spirit, gather up the blood of the Redeemer running to the ground from the scourging ; when winding up the clock she would wish that the movements of the wheel-work might become a sweet music before the throne of God ; when, according to her custom and great love for poverty, she gathered the splinters of wood which were scattered in the yard and carried them to the fire, that they might serve the end for which they were created, her intention was, either to kindle a fire of love to her Redeemer, or to present Him with a golden sceptre and do homage to Him as the King of kings.

These few examples,[2] taken from the papers written by her disciples, will give to the reader an idea of the manner in which, throughout the day, while her hands were at work, her heart was ever with God. These sublime intentions, practised with an ease and variety which seem incredi-

---

[1] Col. iii. 11.   [2] Good Intentions of Ven. Mother Crescentia.

blo to us of the lower grade, will go far to explain why she was so often rapt in ecstasy, was in actual conference with heavenly persons, and actually received divine visions.

With regard to temporal necessities and everything else around her, she seemed to forget them or to remember them only as the duty of charity or of obedience required. Prayer, contemplation, spiritual reading, pious conversations, formed her sole recreation and spiritual nourishment. Spiritual hymns and music she loved very much, not for the sake of the pleasure they give the senses, but because they impart to the spirit a new impetus to soar on high.[1] Her heart was then on fire with the longing for the eternal harmonies and with love for Him who comprises within Himself all sweetness and all harmony. A tune played by an instrument, or sung by a human voice, was sufficient to set the chords of her heart in motion, and cause them to vibrate to the praise and love of God.

"My God," she would say, "Thou Creator and Beginning of all things ! this little creature praises Thee after its own fashion, by sending forth this tune to Thee. Praise be to Thy infinite power by which Thou didst create it ; praise be to Thy wisdom, by which Thou dost regulate it ; praise be to Thy eternal goodness, by which Thou dost sustain it every moment. And since this creature is unable to offer itself to Thee, therefore do I present and offer it to Thee as Thy creature and the work of Thy hands."

Some years after the persecution had stopped, and when her virtues were acknowledged, she was made portress of the convent. For sixteen years she filled this office,[2] discharging it with so much fidelity and virtue that every one wondered how she could unite the greatest propriety and love, with the strict reserve becoming a portress, in such a manner that she did not offend any one, but rather edified all.

---

[1] Gabriel, p. 245.

[2] It is thus stated in a document subscribed with the names of many Sisters, Aug. 24, 1752 while others affirm that she served seventeen years in that office.

Every unnecessary conversation she knew how to avoid ; even when her beloved old parents came to the convent-gate, which seldom happened, she would not converse with them till she had obtained an express permission to do so. The poor, who were to her the representatives of Crucified Love, she treated with the same veneration and charity as if Christ Himself had been personally present to accept the tribute of her love. She preferred converse with the poor and needy, rather than that with the rich. She found means to obtain many extra gifts for the poor besides the usual alms, and shared these among them with so friendly a countenance and such loving words that her foster-children, as these beggars were, gave her the beautiful name of " Mother of the Poor." They were inconsolable when she was removed from the office of portress.[1]

Other more important offices were now intrusted to her. She became Mistress of Novices for many years, and for the three last years of her life was Mother Superior. How she fulfilled the duties of these two offices we will relate in separate chapters. She was infirmarian from five to six years, and for a time was guest-mistress, receiving such strangers as were admitted to enjoy the hospitality of the convent. She was indefatigable in her fulfilment of all these offices ; and yet her frail body became constantly weaker, and she was often tormented with almost unendurable pains. She suffered severely from head-ache and tooth-ache from the first years of her religious life to the time of her death ; her face and head were for the most part greatly swollen from this cause ; violent fever often rendered her unable to stand on her feet. To this was added that she often heard evil-disposed persons assert that her sicknesses were but idleness or assumed, or at least that she was but a burden to the community and a stumbling-block to the other Sisters.

The fortitude of her soul, which never lost its peace or

---

even its cheerfulness for a moment, is really admirable. To a priest of the Order who found this incomprehensible, she replied in deep humility :[1] "I can do all things in Him who strengtheneth me. He is the Lord who works in nothingness. Who can injure me, when God is my Helper? To Him I give myself utterly, for time and for eternity."

Her bodily sufferings increased year by year, disclosing symptoms often inexplicable to the physicians. A burning heat consumed her veins, creating a continual thirst which she increased by refraining from drink. Violent pains in the side frequently beset her so that she could not stir a step. Medical aid was ineffective in her behalf, while on the contrary, she at times recovered suddenly, unexpectedly to every one. Let us listen to some reports on these matters, and first to one drawn up by the confessor of the convent at that time. "In the month of February, 1718,[2] Sister M. Crescentia was seized with a very dangerous fever, that was occasioned by inflammation of the interior parts, in which, but especially in the heart, she felt extreme heat, accompanied by intense thirst and sleeplessness, while the extremities of the body were cold and freezing. I supposed, from the weak and sanguine temperament of this Sister, this sickness would result in death, especially as no medicine took any effect on her, and finally all human aid had to be laid aside. Seeing there was such small hope of her recovery, we directed our attention to endeavor to prepare her for eternity by administering the holy Viaticum and Extreme Unction. But when, humanly speaking, there was no hope left, Divine Goodness restored her almost instantaneously to health. On the 4th of February she told me that her Divine Spouse had said to her, that on the following day she should suddenly be restored to health, and at the time appointed for hearing Mass, she should rise from her bed free from all pain.

"I hereby certify that this prediction was fulfilled to the

---

letter, that the aforenamed Sister was suddenly cured in my presence and before my eyes, and so thoroughly healed that it was as if she had never been sick ; that she rose from her bed and heard Mass. We could not sufficiently express our wonder and admiration that God should have granted so great a favor, and healed this, His creature, in so marvellous a manner.

"In witness whereof, 1 affix my own signature and seal to this attestation, this 24th day of February, 1718. (Signed) Philip James Meichelbeck, Doctor of Theology, parish priest of Kemnath, and at the time Confessor in Ordinary of the convent of Mayrhoff, of the Order of St. Francis."

In an equally wonderful manner, she was cured of a very dangerous sickness in 1742, which will be related in Chapter II., Book III.

Once she was suddenly healed of a very painful malady in her foot.[1] Her right foot had become stiff and was so much contracted with the great pain it had suffered, that she could not put it to the floor. When she went to receive Holy Communion, Sister Felicitas Kempter and Sister Elizabeth Krunner, one on each side, supported or rather carried her to the Oratory and back again to the kneeling-bench. But immediately after that the whole malady disappeared in a moment, so that she could, without inconvenience, leave the Church without help and attend to her own affairs. According to a statement of Mother Superior Sister M. Johanna, who asked for particulars of this occurrence, Christ had appeared to Crescentia immediately after Holy Communion, and touching her foot with His divine hands, had healed it. Her numerous attacks of sickness at length unfitted her for laborious employments, although they in no wise affected the elasticity of her mind, or hindered her uninterrupted prayer, which was never disturbed, either by exterior works or by bodily pains, which but increased their merit. The principle which was often on her lips, that "all

---

[1] According to a document kept in the archives of the Convent, and subscribed by the two Sisters named in the text, April 9, 1743.

time not spent in prayer is lost," spurred her onwards to dedicate every available moment to this holy exercise.

The usual routine of her daily life while in the convent was as follows: At two o'clock in the morning, and often earlier, nay, at midnight, when the Superioress permitted it, she arose, and either in her cell or in the Church, prayed and meditated till four o'clock, when the Sisters were called. She was always the first in the choir. The severest winter cold could not hinder her from rising thus early and remaining in the unwarmed rooms; she never missed attendance in the choir, unless chained to her bed by mortal sickness. Even when she was so sick that she could not go alone to Church, which was often the case in later years, she accepted the assistance of a Sister, to drag herself along to the beloved spot. There, before the Blessed Sacrament, all weakness and pain seemed to disappear and a supernatural strength enabled her to accomplish what healthy and robust persons would find difficulty in doing. Motionless and without leaning against anything, she would kneel for hours as if she had no body. She recited the Office with angelic devotion, and prepared herself most fervently for Holy Communion, which, from the year 1723 to her happy death, she received every day. After that she tarried as long as obedience permitted in her prie-dieu, which was curtained off from the gaze of the public, and she was then generally in an ecstatic state. In later years, the Sisters used to leave her to her devotions, which generally continued till noon. They avoided disturbing her, partly that they might not lose the fruit of such prayers, partly because she, suffering so much bodily sickness that she was not able to do much work, would not feel her suffering so acutely while at prayer.

The rest of her time she employed in common work and exercises, and during the last years of her life, in advising and consoling persons of every state and condition of life, who came flocking to her for help and counsel. All her free time she spent before the Blessed Sacrament, where this enlightened soul had built her tabernacle, and there, in a manner far surpassing our understanding, she found the fulfilment of St. Peter's words: "Lord, it is good for us to be here." [1]

Obedience and love alone could induce her to be with others, for she cautiously avoided every diversion, every idle word, every loss of time, and when she deemed that she had committed the least fault in these respects, she wept bitterly for it. As long as she had no office imposing on her the duty of watching over others, she literally fulfilled the wise counsel of St. John of the Cross: "Think that God and thou are the only ones in the convent." She seemed to see nothing save her own sins, as she expressed it, and to hear nothing but the voice of her Beloved in her heart.

Once only she made an exception. [2] The great poverty of the community compelled the Sisters to gain their living by manual labor. This had given rise to the abuse which had been confirmed by the custom of many years' standing, that a part of the office, namely Vespers and Compline, was not recited in the Chapel but in the room, while they were at work. Scarcely had Mother M. Johanna assumed her official duties, than Sister M. Crescentia, usually so bashful and reticent, and at that time one of the youngest, besides always considering herself the last, went to her, stating very emphatically, though very respectfully, that it was the will of God that this abuse should be done away with, and that the office should be recited in the Church. God, she affirmed, would reward the act with His choicest blessing.

This decisive step surprised the Mother Superior not a little; at once she put a stop to the irregularity, and the promised blessing followed at once, abundantly and visibly, so that Mother Johanna, in her old age, speaking of this turning point, when they had been by frequent alms gradually relieved from their financial embarrassments, certifies that the abundant blessing of God, both in temporal and spiritual affairs, which was received by the community

---

[1] Matth. xvii. 4.   [2] Summ. N. 16, § 27.   N. 20, § 23.

from the beginning of her holding office as Superioress, was to be ascribed to the holy life and the prayers of Sister M. Crescentia. "I best know," she said, "what poverty and want of everything there was in the convent before she entered, and I—when I accepted my office—found only half-a-florin[1] in the treasury. If I had not had Crescentia here, I would not have known what to do to find a way out of our poverty and want." For this reason this worthy Mother Superior used to have recourse to the prayers of her spiritual daughter in every pressing emergency; she always found help from above and very often in a manner that bordered on the miraculous.

When in want of funds, there came just at the right time, from unknown persons living at a distance, considerable pecuniary alms. Disastrous storms of hail and overwhelming floods of rain spared the convent gardens and fields, while they spread devastation all around; and not only the Superioress, but all the Sisters acknowledged, taught by a long experience, that the food, such as flour, butter, lard, bread, and the like, when committed to the charge of Crescentia, the servant of God, multiplied, by the blessing of God, in her hands, so as to go farther than they would naturally have done. This was particularly noticeable when as portress she distributed bread and other food among the poor. The provision was often out of all proportion small when compared to the number of the mendicants; she raised her heart to the heavenly Father of the poor and it came to pass that not only was there enough to satisfy all the poor, but there was yet much remaining. Father Ott[2] relates one case in particular:

One day there came unexpectedly such a rush of people from the city and the neighboring villages, that the provision, which had already been cut into portions, was very far from being enough to go round. Crescentia, full of faith, called on Him who with five loaves and two fishes had satisfied five thousand persons; she then broke what she

---

[1] About twenty-five cents.　　　[2] Ott, p. 54.

had with her, and not only not a single poor person went empty away, but there was a remarkable quantity left, a fact utterly inexplicable to those present. Confidence in the efficacy of her prayers, after a while, became general, and it was especially her fellow-religious who had recourse to her in every need and perplexity, even in matters of no apparent consequence. A few instances will suffice to prove this.

One Friday on the feast of the Portiuncula (August 2d), a day on which many visitors were accustomed to call at the convent, and, according to an ancient custom, received hospitality, the Sisters, notwithstanding their endeavors, had not been able to procure any fish for the guest-table. In this exigency Sister M. Crescentia was again called upon to help. She exhorted them to trust in God, who was well aware of their needs, and added: "St. Peter will certainly catch abundance of fish." These words, uttered on August 1st, referred to the feast of that day, which was that of St. Peter in Chains. Very early the next morning a great abundance of fine fish, which had not been ordered, was delivered at the convent gate. A similar thing occurred when Sister M. Joachim was superintendent of the kitchen; she was a disciple of Crescentia's and subsequently succeeded her in office. One day she was in trouble because she could get no fish; she came to Crescentia, who replied: "My dear Sister, you worry yourself too much about temporal affairs; pray, and hope, and leave it to God to provide; we shall have fish enough." And so it turned out and that in a manner quite unexpected by them.

Another time the altar wine that had been ordered was not forthcoming; and their stock of it was reduced so low that there was not enough for the holy Mass on the following day. When the Sisters who had charge of the cellar, Sister M. Anna Neth and Sister M. Rosa Weber, came to tell this to Crescentia, who was then Superioress, she admonished them to trust in God and sent them back to the cellar. Father Ott says that they begged her rosary of her, and hung it through the bung-hole. How surprised they were to find the cask, which they had found empty, pour forth a rich pure wine, which continued to flow for them at need, for three weeks; it dried up, however, when the wine which had been ordered arrived.

Some of the Sisters were once trying to lift a large statue upon the high altar, from which it had been taken down. Its weight was so great, however, that all their efforts to do so were unavailing; they could not raise it. The servant of God now came, and just laid her hand on the image, when immediately it raised itself, before the eyes of the astonished Sisters, and settled itself in the right place. A little picture of the Blessed Virgin had fallen into the fire and had become as black as coal. Crescentia breathed on it, wiped it with a little cloth, and it became at once brilliant and beautiful. It was placed in the choir, where every one marvelled at it, and when Crescentia was praying before it, several Sisters, among whom was Joachima Kögl, afterwards Superioress, remarked that tears flowed from the eyes of the picture.[1] We will add one more remarkable case:

A countess of Vienna had made her a present of a very beautiful Infant Jesus, formed of wax. As she had a special devotion to the Infant Jesus, she wished to set up the image in the Church and to adorn it with a beautiful dress. But she had nothing wherewith to pay for the dress; nevertheless, with the permission of the Superioress, she bought it, saying : "The Divine Child will certainly pay for it Himself." When the wax figure was clothed she brought it to the community room to show it to the Sisters. Whilst they were considering it with pleasure and admiration, the little bell of the convent-gate rang. The portress returned with a letter to Crescentia, which had been given her by an unknown person, and one who never was seen by them again. The letter was opened in the presence of the Sisters ; it contained nothing but money; and, in fact, neither more nor less than the price of the dress; with one

---

[1] These two last cases are taken from a document of Mother Joachima, kept in the archives, and bearing the date of September 1st, 1753.

voice, all the Sisters broke out with the exclamation: "See ! the Infant Himself has sent the money." The reader who is possessed of the true faith, will willingly assent to this exclamation, and rejoice that he has so good a Father in Heaven, who reveals to His children, even in small matters, the greatness of His love, provided the eye is simple and the heart loving.

Thus, like to a quiet brook in a lovely meadow, her days flowed on in peace, in their monotonous course, all unobserved by the outward world. Yet, without noticing it, she gradually became the central-point and the soul of the religious community, in which God Himself had placed her. No heart could, for any length of time, resist her heart, which was overflowing with love. She ruled by humility and charity. Would that true love held the sceptre in every Christian community, then the kingdom of love, to establish which Christ came on earth, would quickly take possession of the whole world.

Great as was her severity against herself, she was full of tenderness and sweetness, boundlessly considerate and accommodating to the Sisterhood. She herself loved and practised, to a high degree, solitude and silence, yet she was anything but sad and gloomy, for she was ever ready to sympathize with others, whether in joy or sorrow. Her countenance, even when enduring the greatest suffering, presented a cheerful mirror of peace and happiness, which the Holy Ghost communicated to her heart. In all the exercises of the convent, and especially at the most menial and hardest labors, she was ever the first and the last, and the most active; and without sufficient reason and permission she was never absent from the customary recreations which, like salt in the food, can never be dispensed with in convent life without spiritual loss. At recreation she was ever pleasant and amiable, and understood how to combine cheerfulness with edification. She was rich in original thoughts and imagery, and did not hesitate to indulge in jokes and witticisms for the amusement of her Sisters. As soon as she had engaged her Sisters in cheerful conversation, she would withdraw from it herself, leaving it to others to carry it on, yet so directing it as to conduce to edification. Like a true daughter of St. Francis, she was much pleased to see the Sisters enjoying themselves, but doing so in the Lord.

She even acquired the difficult art of rendering glad the whole circle surrounding her, by raising what was merely a natural hilarity to God, and by intermingling ordinary conversation with heavenly harmonies. At the close of a recreation the Sisters would often say :[1] "Now we are entirely refreshed in mind and body." Nay, they even acknowledged that they left the recreations, which she had conducted, more recollected and with greater elevation of spirit, than when they rose from their ordinary prayers.

We have no reliable account of the development of her interior life, no chronological particulars of time or of the gradations she passed through. Isolated traits are abundantly related, but without indicating the time when they occurred. We are, therefore, compelled to abandon the chronological order, and in the following Book, simply seek to unite her characteristics so as to form a picture of her several virtues. In Book Third we will again take up the narrative. A short description of her person may appropriately close this Book and introduce the second.

The most complete and most reliable description of Crescentia's appearance is given in Father Ott's book;[2] he says:

Crescentia was of medium height and well formed. The expression of her countenance was spiritual, cheerful, and frank, while full of earnestness and dignity ; her complexion was delicate, so that the smallest arteries were visible. The color of her face was white, yet streaked with a tender red. Her voice was very melodious, her words easily touched the heart. Her whole demeanor was stamped with a maidenly modesty and with natural grace, joined

---

to a higher religious dignity, so that a single glance of hers inspired the love of purity, together with that of reverence and attraction to herself. It was palpable that in such a body, only a noble and holy soul could dwell."

And concerning this noble soul, it is beyond all doubt that it was endowed with extraordinary natural qualities; that she possessed a clear understanding, quickness of comprehension, a faithful memory, and a very fruitful imagination; she could with great ease present her thoughts in new imagery and find similitudes for the spiritual and corporal world. She united a firm will to a very tender heart. These natural endowments, however, scarcely deserve mention, in comparison with the wealth of grace and virtue which the Holy Ghost had lavished upon her. The following testimony of a father confessor who knew her well and wrote his statement during her life-time, namely, in 1736, may give the reader a view of her virtues and thereby introduce and render credible the more copious details given in Book Second. The literal translation from the Latin runs as follows: [1]

"I, the undersigned, after mature deliberation, with full knowledge, by reason of two years' close observation, having been for that length of time confessor to the Sisters of the Third Order of St. Francis, at Kaufbeuren, hereby make the statement and bear witness before God, as if I were really before His tribunal, that concerning Sister M. Crescentia Höss, as far as I can judge after a careful examination, made before God and my own conscience, that not the least deception or imposition exists. On the contrary, her extraordinary and profound humility, her ever ready obedience in all things, her complete resignation in numberless sufferings and pains, both interior and exterior, her insatiable fervor in prayer, both vocal and mental, with the view of union with God, her extreme abhorrence of anything that could sully angelic purity, her interior uninter-

---

[1] Act B. Summ. Add. p. 12.

rupted recollections, her fervent love for God and her neighbor, moreover, her most astonishing readiness to and practice of exalting the most trivial acts and ordinary works to the sublimity of religiously offering up her intention to God while performing them, in a word, HER TRULY SERAPHIC LIFE IS, IN ITSELF, AN EPITOME OF ALL WHICH THE WORLD ADMIRES AND PRIZES IN ITS GREATEST SAINTS.

"Heaven itself bears witness to this, since God has imparted many and most remarkable graces, in a wonderful manner, to those persons who recommended themselves to the prayers of Sister Crescentia, or prayed for divine help through her merits. Of which events, I, myself, although unworthy, could recount some of my own experience. To all this I bear witness according to my knowledge and my conscience, on my priestly honor before God, in my own handwriting and sealed with my ordinary seal: Kaufbeuren, 15th of September, 1736. Bartholomew Binner, of the Society of Jesus, confessor of the convent of Mayrhoff."

Similar testimonies are given by other confessors. Among these is one dictated to his superior by Father Januarius Mayer, S. J., on his death-bed; this we omit and add only the beautiful words of her last confessor, Father Pamer, who concludes a copious report as follows : [1] "I say freely and openly, that as in a chain one ring is linked in another ring, so in Crescentia one virtue is linked to another virtue, and one sublime act of heroism follows another, till the highest degree of intensity of inward force and fervor is attained, thus forming an uninterrupted chain of a holy life."

How poverty-stricken, how full of defects and contradictions, how full of resolves not put into practice, of beginnings which are not persevered in, are the lives of most of those who are even called pious Christians ! The golden thread of grace is continually being broken. "BUT THE PATH OF THE JUST, AS A SHINING LIGHT, GOETH FORWARDS AND INCREASETH EVEN TO PERFECT DAY." [2]

---

[1] Act B. Summ. Add. p. 12.   [2] Prov. iv. 18.

Second Book.

Picture of Her Virtues.

CHAPTER I.

Faith, the Root of Her Life.[1]

The vital power of a tree in its extension and duration depends on the strength, depth, and soundness of its roots: in like manner the entire development of the supernatural life in Christ depends on faith which, according to the Council of Trent[2] is "the beginning of man's salvation, the foundation and root of all justification." The purer, firmer, and more lively this faith is, the more brilliantly will the heavenly flower of Christian perfection spring forth from this root of life.

The Ven. Crescentia expresses this doctrine in these words: "Faith is the only safe road that leads unerringly to God, and that gives us the power to enjoy Him as far as it is permitted us to do, on earth." Convinced of this truth, she esteemed the grace of faith above all other gifts. Her mouth overflowed with inexhaustible praises of the glories of faith and with constant gratitude towards God for having granted to her the grace of being born of and brought up by Catholic parents, and that in a city in which one-half of the inhabitants were Protestants. She frequently repeated, as Sister Gabriel heard from her own mouth:[3] "I should not have rejoiced had I been created

---

[1] Summ. N. 7. § 1–305 and Act B. Inform. N. 31–58.
[2] Sess. vi. ch. 5.   [3] Gabriel, p. 19.

without faith ; I mean, if God had not conferred on me. the great grace of making me a member of the true Catholic Church, for which grace I can never thank Him enough, not even throughout eternity. Faith is a supernatural gift of God, a gift far greater than that of creation, for unbelievers are also created by God, yet, without faith, they cannot be saved."

From this great value which she set on faith, combined with that interior love which she felt for all men, particularly for her fellow-citizens, came those abundant tears with which, to the hour of her death, she bewailed the unhappy separation, in matters of faith, which kept so many of her fellow-citizens aloof from the true Church founded by Jesus Christ. Incessantly she offered up to the Father of mercies, prayers, fastings, and severe mortifications, for the souls who had strayed from the one fold of Christ, and with glowing words she admonished her fellow-Sisters, particularly the novices, to do the like. When she spoke on this subject, her countenance, before pale, glowed like a rose, large tears flowed from her eyes, and she was frequently checked in her speech by inward excitement, or, at best, could only stammer out : "Oh, would that every one believed in God, would that every one knew God well !"

This zeal for the propagation of the true Faith knew no limitation of country. It embraced the unbeliever and the heretic without exception : no sacrifice appeared too great if she could but procure the grace of the true Faith to a single one : it was her daily practice to offer herself for suffering, nay, even for a cruel death, to obtain this end ; and this offering was not a mere formula, it was a strong, ardent desire, springing from the utmost depths of her heart, piercing her soul with a poignant sorrow that seemed to overmaster every other feeling, even her love for solitude. If God's will had not opposed it, she would not have been able to withstand the longing of her heart, to go into foreign countries to gain souls to the Faith, by shedding her blood. She often exclaimed with sobs : "If I were not a woman, I would go by the next vessel to the Indies, either to bring Christ to the heathen, or to offer to God the sacrifice of my own blood."

What she could not accomplish in act, she supplied for by offering up burning desires, by continual prayers, and by severe penances. When she spoke with priests, especially missionaries, she could not refrain from giving vent to the ardor of her soul, beseeching them to perform the duties of their high calling with zeal and fervor, and to endeavor to propagate the Faith. With daily prayers she accompanied preachers and missionaries, and exhorted her Sisters in religion to perform this same duty of love with fervor. The extension of the kingdom of God was the only thing that interested her here below. To other occurrences and events she turned a deaf ear, but no sooner was faith spoken of, or the affairs of the Church became the subject of discourse, than she was all attention. If on these occasions she heard of conversions and of progress in religion, she rejoiced in the Lord, and words full of fire, many times repeated, expressed her gratitude to the Father of light, to the great edification of all present. This was especially the case on two occasions: the one when a whole family in her native city was converted to the Church; the other when she heard that a Protestant child had died in his baptismal innocence, and thus, as a member of the mystical body of Christ, had received the heavenly crown; at this, all the sympathies of her believing heart were enlisted and rejoiced.

On the other hand, when she heard of apostasies, and of scandals in the Church, every heart must have been moved with the indescribable sorrow which pierced her heart, venting itself in bitter sobs and moans as she bewailed the triumph won by the enemies of Christ over His Church. At such times she could only regain her peace by prayer and by entire submission to God's holy will.

The extraordinary veneration she entertained for the holy martyrs also had its origin in her sublime faith. To sacrifice one's life, to shed one's blood for Christ, she held to be the most enviable lot for a Christian ; she lamented bitterly that so desirable and so noble a lot could not be her's, on account of her unworthiness. The mere mention of martyrs excited within her feelings of joy, of admiration, of longing after so great a happiness, to so great a degree that she could not master the exterior expression of them. Afterwards, she would relieve herself a little of this burning fervor by bloody scourgings and other penitential works, so as to sacrifice, in some way, her blood, by the martyrdom of love through the martyrdom of faith. Neither sickness, weakness, nor age could restrain her from this voluntary martyrdom ; recent traces of it were even noticed on her corpse. On the feast-days of the holy martyrs she was, as it were, almost beside herself, and reserved as she usually was in the expression of her feelings, the power of the spirit then overleaped all bounds, and she often lavished the most ardent praises upon the witness of blood afforded by the martyrs, and would then exhort the Sisters to aim at their happiness and partake of it by a life of penance.

What has been said is sufficient to show that her faith far surpassed the ordinary degree; this will appear still more clearly if we contemplate how pure and firm, how enlightened, and how lively this virtue was in her. Her faith was—holding for truth, that which rested on one foundation alone, to wit : The authenticity of God, the first Truth—revealing Himself to us. Every other conclusion which the spirit may derive from its own reflections, vanished before the full light of the Divine Truth casting its rays into her soul by faith.

Her soul was, by this faith, raised far above the natural feelings and imaginings, above purely human notions and ideas, above the consideration due to natural wisdom and knowledge. In child-like simplicity she raised her spiritual eye to the Word of her Father in Heaven, clinging fast to the Divine Truth, which can neither err nor deceive. She in all humility sacrificed her intellect to this first and highest truth with so much resolution, in the obedience of faith, and clung with such firmness to this first source of all light, that the certainty of faith surpassed, beyond comparison, every other certainty, whether coming from a perception obtained through the senses, or from spiritual knowledge.

She found a special consolation in repeating the Act of Faith many times a day in these or similar words : " Thou, O God, who art the all-knowing, the Eternal Truth, hast said this ; I believe it without hesitation, I believe it absolutely." Or : "O great mysteries of the Lord, how holy and wonderful ye are ! I will always truly and steadfastly believe in them and with heart and mouth confess them." By this pure faith, free from every mixture of her own thoughts and affections, she overcame the dangers on the way of the interior life which lie so near to souls who pass the limits of ordinary virtue and who on that account are frequently subject to a reaction, alternating their feelings as night succeeds to day. Whether her soul was rapt in marvellous visions of light and beauty, with her feelings entranced in ecstasy, or whether she was groping through the fearful death-like shadows of spiritual night, her spirit was ever elevated above all these transitory occurrences which are infinitely below Divine Truth, following the admonition of the Apostle: " To attend (to faith) as to a light that shineth in a dark place, until the day dawn and the day-star arise in your hearts." [1]

Let us hear what she herself says, respecting these extraordinary inspirations : "I prize one article of faith higher than all revelations to myself ; in these I could easily be deceived, but not so in the articles of faith, in which I rely on the infinite, infallible Truth." Sister M. Gabriel [2] gives a more detailed account of her principles : "It is, " she used to say, "a great privilege, indeed, if Christ appeared to any one ; but I do not envy such a person, because faith is sufficient for me. It is much more meritorious, if we believe without seeing, for we cannot

---

[1] II. Peter I. 19.   [2] Gabriel, p. 24.

believe in the visible any more, because we see it. Let us, therefore, believe in the invisible, and seek by faith ; for the Gospel calls those blessed who having not seen, yet believe." She acted on these principles with regard to the many supernatural visions and colloquies with which she was favored, however full of light they might be. She never permitted herself to be drawn down by them, from the height of faith which, however dark it may appear to the groping intellect, is in itself far more sublime than anything that man can comprehend in a natural way, and is at the same time the only means which leads to an intimate union with God. On the contrary, all these illuminations assisted her in passing beyond them, to dive more deeply into matters of faith, and to adhere more firmly to the Word of the Lord.

The purity and firmness of faith is best tested, at such times when God withdraws every other light from the soul and places it in what St. John of the Cross calls, "the dark night." Those painful trials, in which the soul, deprived of all sensible devotion, has nothing to rest upon save faith alone, plainly show how firmly this virtue must have been rooted in this chosen soul. With the compass of faith for her guidance, she pursued her course through the darkness, ever directing her way towards God, and seeking Him alone with ever-increasing fervor. This apparent darkening of the interior light served but to bring out her faith "from glory to glory"[1] until it arrived at that perfection which is like the morning-dawn of that perfect day wherein the soul sees God face to face.

Saint Bonaventure, a Doctor of the Church, distinguishes three degrees of faith.[2] The first degree is that of ordinary Christians who, being without high learning or sanctity, accept the teachings of the Church as the Word of God. In the second degree, the things believed are, as it were, penetrated by a higher supernatural power communicating the gift of understanding. The third degree con-

---

[1] II. Cor. III. 18.   [2] De gradibus virtutum.

sists in believing as if the things believed were seen by one's own eyes. To this last degree the Ven. M. Crescentia had, beyond all doubt, arrived. The Holy Ghost had given her such a fulness of His gifts, that she seemed not so much to believe as to see these mysteries, like Moses, of whom St. Paul says : "For he endured as seeing Him that is invisible."[1] The veil which keeps the Holy of Holies from our view, here on earth, was not, indeed withdrawn for her, but it had become so transparent that no bodily eye could have given her so great and so perceptible a certainty as faith did. A few sayings of hers will confirm this :

"O God," she once exclaimed, "were all men to fall away from the Faith, yet I trust, by Thy grace, not to wander a hair's-breadth from the truth which Thou hast revealed, even were all men to rise up against me and inflict all sorts of torture upon me ; for I know and believe that Thou, O my God, art infallible in all that Thou hast revealed, and by Thy Church hast proposed to our belief." She once assured the Sisters that if Jesus Christ were to appear visibly in a Sacred Host, she would not, if she could do so easily, even look at it, but would shut her eyes, as by faith she had an infinitely greater certainty of the Lord's presence than all the senses of the body could afford her. Faith of such purity and firmness was naturally united with the peace and consolation which St. Paul, the Apostle, wishes to the Romans : "Now the God of hope fill you with all joy and peace in believing, that you may abound in hope and in the power of the Holy Ghost."[2]

The inward light governing her mind inflamed it so thoroughly, that she could not repress the deep emotion she experienced when a mystery of faith was mentioned. This was frequently noticed by all at the spiritual readings or conversations. Were the words, Trinity, Incarnation, Sacrament of the altar mentioned, even casually, before

---

[1] Heb. xi. 27.   [2] Rom. xv. 13.

her, she would change color, sometimes turning pale as death, at other times becoming crimson ; frequently tears flowed from her eyes, nay, often her nose bled profusely, and at times she became completely wrapt in ecstasy. The word "Bethlehem" produced the same effect upon her. Once, on the Vigil of Christmas, when it was her turn to read at table the announcement of the Nativity of Christ, from the martyrology, notwithstanding all her efforts to master her emotion, she could only utter the first words : "To-morrow Jesus Christ is"—when her voice was choked by a flood of tears. She was carried out of herself, to the great edification of her fellow-Sisters in religion. Another Sister had to continue the reading ; as soon as Crescentia recovered consciousness, she knelt down to acknowledge her fault and asked for a penance.

No one, without being edified, could observe how devoutly, when at the Divine Office, she pronounced the words: " Glory be to the Father, etc.," lowly bowing her head, while her countenance became brilliant. She then felt the most ardent desire to be beheaded for God's sake. Once she exclaimed : "O God ! the beauty of Thy faith darts its rays so brightly into the eyes of my mind, that it would be no wonder if, for love of it, I should entirely melt away."

The illuminations she received concerning matters of faith conferred on her such a knowledge of Holy Scripture and of the most difficult theological questions, that all her confessors and many other highly educated and learned men were exceedingly surprised at this "infused knowledge," as it is called by theologians. She had received but a scanty education in the elementary schools, and had only read the New Testament and those ascetical books as are suitable to religious, yet she could speak on the most profound mysteries of religion with such intuitive clearness and correctness and in such fitting terms, that the most learned of the theologians were those who wondered at her the most.

She once had a conversation about the "Magnificat" with Father Pamer, and from its words, taken singly, she evolved such sublime and profound mysteries, and did it with so much clearness, grace, and unction, that he was obliged to confess that he had never heard or read the like. [1] The Father Provincial, Benjamin Elbel, O.S.F., bears similar testimony to this prodigious knowledge; he was certainly a competent judge. His works on moral theology are well known to Catholic moralists, and are in use up to the present time. [2]

Holy Writ was to her an inexhaustible ocean of light and consolation. The Spirit under whose influence this wonderful book was written, dwelt in her heart by holy love, and unlocked and unsealed for her its mystic meanings, in a way which puts to shame many learned men, who with profane criticism tear to pieces the letter of the Holy Scripture, as the Jews did the Body of the Lord, without comprehending any of its spirit, and, having no spiritual life in themselves, are killed by the letter. She had a special love for the Holy Gospels, from which she usually took the points of her meditations. She almost knew them by heart, knew where to find any text therein and from each separate word to take abundant material for pious reflection and instruction. She likewise exhorted her Sisters in religion not to let the precious treasure of Heaven given us in the Gospels lie unused, but to read them diligently and devoutly, by the light of the Catholic Faith, to ponder over every word and, as it were, to chew and eat it, converting it into food for the life of the soul. She maintained [3] that the Gospels were of themselves sufficient, without any other book, to instruct and urge a faithful soul to sanctity. The power of this Divine Word penetrates to the inmost depths of the heart, works into bone and marrow; it teaches us how to love, suffer, and act, how to struggle and endure, and how in patience to remain faithful to the Saviour unto the end.

---

[1] Ott. B. 11. Ch. 5.   [2] He died June 4, 1756.   [3] Summ. N. 21, § 54.

It was very evident, from the spiritual conversations which she held with her religious Sisters, and especially with the novices, that she herself had been accustomed to draw heavenly nourishment from this Holy Book. She could take any short text from Holy Scripture, explain it elaborately in all its bearings, and for hours together discourse on it in so edifying, devout, fascinating, and sublime a manner, that her hearers were never weary of listening to her. The young woman, otherwise so reserved, became, under these influences, entirely changed : select passages from Holy Writ, clothed in eloquent words, with appropriate examples and quotations from the Saints, flowed as a flood from her mouth. These thoughts she presented to the circle of her listeners dressed in forcible language and in imagery taken usually from the labors and occupations of the common life, as known to the Sisterhood.

The substance of some of these spiritual discourses has been written down by her pupils, and is still extant in manuscript. But these scanty notices can afford but a very imperfect picture of their delivery by herself, so full of life and unction; nevertheless, we wish to give some fragments of them to the reader. Though the far-fetched allegories and similes are far more in accordance with the spirit of that age, than they are with that of our own, yet they will serve to illustrate, in a high degree, her manner of teaching and of impressing her lessons on the memory.

Once, in Advent, when her novices had asked her how best to prepare for Christmas, she said that it had occurred to her that instead of a dirty stable and miserable crib they should build a grand palace for Jesus, in a spiritual manner, and that they could construct it thus :

Five things are wanted to build a house : First, a good foundation in this projected spiritual edifice must, with the help of God, be laid by the exercise of a profound humility ; secondly, by the plumb-line of perfect obedience must the regular work go forward ; thirdly, unity among the workers and a mutual good understanding, which require, before all, sisterly love and union, are absolutely necessary; fourthly, suitable materials for building must be sought for, such as wood, stone, lime, sand, and water: these can be attained by pious meditations. The wood is to be hewn down and cut to pieces in the Garden of Olives, by contemplating the sufferings of Jesus and Mary. The beams must be made from the holy Cross and the staff of office broken before Pilate. The stones must be broken on Mount Calvary. Clay for the brick may be taken from the depths of their own nothingness and sinfulness, and burnt in the hot kiln of the Sacred Heart of Jesus: their own daily exercises might serve them for sand, and the brook Cedron furnish them with water. Fifthly, they needed tools, and these should be the tools used at the death of Christ, as the hammer, tongs, nails, ladders, ropes, and staves; they could every day select one of these for pious contemplation, and throughout the day, when at work, endeavor to keep it before their minds.

After this she gives some practical rules as to how to erect this spiritual edifice during the four weeks of Advent. They should choose the heavenly Father as Architect, and the Holy Ghost as Contractor, to prepare a palace worthy of the Divine Son. St. Joseph should be the carpenter, the holy angels should be the workmen. On awaking in the morning they should immediately make an act of faith, thinking: "That is the voice of the heavenly Master calling thee to work." They should rise without delay, in obedience, and make an act of hope in God, thereby intrusting the work to Him who balances the whole world in the hands of His omnipotence. Then they should proceed to the chapel, "the armory of love," and from the tabernacle draw forth all the tools for their work, putting up prayers to the Saviour that everything they should do that day might be done according to His sovereign will and pleasure. The prayers, good intentions, and acts of virtue, which they should make in reciting their office, are then specified: namely, the meditations on the incarnation during Mass and at work. For that work they should especially endeavor to compare the tools used thereat, with the instruments of the passion of Christ ; added to which, they should often say in their hearts, and by word of mouth, when they met one another : " Praised be the blessed Fruit of Mary," and the answer : " May He be praised forever and ever :"—or this salutation : " Praised and blessed be the. noble Treasure thou didst receive of the Holy Ghost, O Mary," with the response : Praise be to Him, forever and ever.

When the bell rings for meals, they should ponder on the generous love of the Lord and Father for whom they work, and receive the good food as if He served them with His own hand, although they had done their work so badly as not to deserve a bit of bread or a drop of water : here they should make an act of true contrition, with a firm purpose of amendment. At the examination of conscience, they were to present themselves before the Divine Architect, to entreat for light to inspect the building, especially in regard to the first stories or points. Before retiring to sleep, they should earnestly crave forgiveness for every failure by fault or neglect ; they should then put back their tools into the tabernacle, request the holy angels to watch over and guard the property of the future Messias, and then they should lie down to rest—to rest in safety in the bosom of Mary.

That Ven. Mother Crescentia not only read the Sacred Scriptures with an enlightened mind, but also the book of nature, is proved by the following conversation, which she held with Sister M. Raphael, at that time a novice— afterwards (from 1769–1799) Superioress of the convent. With some slight change in the language the naïve report is here verbally reproduced from a manuscript of this same Sister.

" One day Mother Crescentia called me, Sister Raphael Miller, into her cell, saying : " I am going to make you a little present." When I came at once, she gave me a leaf from a tree and said : 'There you have a particle from the almighty power of God.' I thought to myself : What can she mean by that ? but I dared not trust myself to inquire. Thereupon she took the leaflet into her own hand and said: 'Look here, in this apparently worthless creature lie concealed the divine omnipotence, wisdom, and goodness. Omnipotence is shown in the fact that it is what it is. God's almighty power created it and upholds it in its existence, else in one moment it would become nothing. Wisdom so ordered it that all its veins and points conduce to the highest end and aim, so that, in a manner, the whole tree is figured in this leaf. Goodness is manifested, by its being created for our eternal and temporal benefit : for our eternal benefit, in that we may know, love, praise, and worship God through it, for our temporal benefit, because, as the trunk puts forth its green foliage and increases for our enjoyment and pleasure, it also is in the end useful as fuel to warm us, or to cook our food.

" 'We can also,' she continued, 'contemplate the ocean in this leaflet. All the rivers and brooks have their origin from the ocean, and run through hill and dale, over gravel-pits and rocks, till they reach the goal appointed by God. These are signified by the little arteries of the leaf, which point out, as it were, the roads to Heaven which traverse this earthly kingdom. The tiny points of the leaf represent the boundaries which the Lord has set to the ocean, lest it should overflow the earth and do harm. For God Himself is the unfathomable Ocean of all grace and perfection. The little ribs of the leaf represent, not only rivers and brooks, but also all natural and supernatural gifts of God, more especially His holy inspirations, that penetrate the hills and dales, the rocks and stones, which are also found in the human soul : and when the soul, on her part, opposes no obstacle to divine grace, but co-operates with it, then will all virtues be built up within her.' "

What we have said about this individual case, namely, that in the smallest creatures she recognized, praised, and loved the glory of the great King, as if in a mirror, was constantly true of her, for this holy recognition was everywhere and at all times her conspicuous habit. She said sometimes before the Sisters: "O God, Thou marvellous Builder, how great is Thy power, how incomprehensible Thy skill! Be Thou praised in the work of Thy hands."[1] Then she called the attention of the Sisters to the fact that the infinite power, wisdom, and goodness of God are to be seen and admired in the smallest creatures; such as flies, ants, bees, etc., because, notwithstanding the smallness of their size, nothing is wanting to them : their eyes, ears, mouth, feet, wings, and all other members and parts are so perfect in their construction as to surpass all human understanding.

Her enlightened faith was not alone exuberant in beautiful thoughts and expressions which might possibly be likened to leaves without fruit ; it manifested itself, on the contrary, in what St. Paul terms "the fruit of the light,"[2] in a holy interior and exterior life, flowing clear, pure, and full from the fountain of faith. But "my just man liveth by faith."[3] This saying of the Lord best expresses the peculiar character of her life. From the depths of that light of faith, which radiates from the vision of God and fully eclipses all the enlightenment which proceeds from any finite spirit, she drew forth the rule and the impulse to whatever she thought, wished, said, and did. She laid the highest value on this life of faith; she prayed most earnestly to God to lead her soul by the infallible road of mystic faith, and in her spiritual conversations impressed this main point on the other Sisters, bitterly lamenting that God is so little loved, and is so often offended, because man does not live by faith. "If," said she, "men but knew it, and truly believed in the infinite greatness of God, and in His desire and readiness to make us happy, both in time and in eternity, no one would be found who did not truly love Him."

---

[1] Gabriel, p. 26.   [2] Eph. v. 9.   [3] Heb. x. 38.

The melancholy experience that many pious persons make no progress in spiritual life, but retrograde, in spite of performing many spiritual exercises, she ascribed to their keeping the talent of faith buried, that is, to their neglecting to apply and exercise this divine power. "O happy is the soul," she exclaimed, "who utterly mistrusts its own feelings and judgment and blindly follows the leadership of so clear a light as faith is ! What gratitude do I not owe to God, for having led me by this road!"

She applied the maxims of faith to everything concerning the soul, and to all interior and exterior actions, with a facility, perseverance, and energy that seemed to measure all things with eye and heart from the stand-point of eternity. Being completely immersed in divine light, she held the world and all temporal things as nothing, God as everything. That which the natural man loves and seeks, she looked upon as the refuse of the streets ; trampling it under foot, and stretching forward with all the powers of her soul for the attainment of that one Good which lasts forever. Yes, verily, she stood in this light of faith, like unto the angels, always before the face of our Blessed Lord, and scarcely for a moment ever lost sight of His presence. She herself confessed that it seemed to her as if there was nothing in the world except God and herself alone. She said to the Sisters on this subject : "What an infinite blessing it is that the Sovereign Good is constantly with us! Wherefore I beg of you in all your actions to practise a living faith."

All the following chapters of this Second Book will sufficiently prove in what a high degree "the fruit of the light"[1] in all goodness, and justice, and truth, revealed itself in her whole exterior and interior life. The astonishing purity of her conscience, the child-like simplicity of her heart, which saw beyond the exterior of things and their temporal use and convenience, and traced them and all things to their roots in the holy will of God,

---

[1] Eph. v. 9.

the immovable peace of her heart, the harmony in the quiet, progressive development of her interior life, her devotion in prayer and her continuous recollection—all these were the fruits of her firm, pure, living faith. Her strength in temptations also was the result of her "taking in all things the shield of faith, wherewith you may be able to extinguish all the fiery darts of the most wicked one."[1] From that same source sprang that peace that not the severest sufferings or unexpected rush of accidents could disturb. It was then she fled immediately to the region of faith, or rather she was always there, and raised herself, by its power, above the often destructive pressure of feelings which pain makes upon the feeble will of a soul not based on God.

In this place we would also mention that her vivid faith inspired her with an incredible love, veneration, and subjection to the visible Church of God here on earth. It could not be otherwise; the true spirit of Jesus Christ embraces with one and the same love the Head and the members, Christ and the Church, the Father and the Mother. As St. Augustine says, "Let us love God as our Father, let us love the Church as our Mother," she usually called the Church her beloved Mother, and really practised, in regard to it, love, obedience and respect; fulfilling towards this good Mother the precept of the fourth commandment with such ready obedience and perfection that the best child could hardly rival her in fulfilling its duties towards its own mother.

She received the Word of God from the mouth of Holy Church with the docility of an innocent child; and not only the expressed articles of faith, but every doctrine, decision, custom, and ceremony of the Catholic Church was highly revered by her. This was especially the case with regard to the Holy See. In the Pope she acknowledged not alone her Father, but Christ Himself. To be united to him by fidelity, obedience, and love, should it

---

[1] Eph. vi. 16.

even cost one's blood and life, she declared to be the duty of every Christian. She exhorted all with whom she came into communication, especially her religious Sisters, to persevere in these sentiments : " Remain ever faithful to the Church," she said : [1] " faithful even unto death ; if necessary, you must count it joy to shed your blood and give your life for her. The Eternal Truth itself testifies that the Church cannot err, and that must be sufficient for us. Should you have no opportunity to show your love in great things, show it in little things. Keep her rules, ordinances, and precepts perfectly ; cultivate a high esteem for her ceremonial, celebrate her feasts with great devotion, in a word, be always and in everything obedient children of the holy Catholic Church."

She valued every pious devotion precisely in the degree in which it had been recommended by the Church. When asked for a rule of life, she replied : " Follow the teachings, rules, and customs of the Church, which knows and teaches what is best to do." Hence, she held in utter abhorrence, not only every error, but the all too liberal and novel opinions in religious matters. A report had been spread abroad, and was believed by many, that the rosaries which she distributed, and which, before distribution, she always caused to be blessed and indulgenced by a priest possessing the proper faculties, had been blessed by Christ Himself, and by Him were enriched with indulgences. When this report, the offspring of an easy credulity, came to her ears, she was so stricken with pain and fear, that she was almost beside herself, and with tears protested against it. She used every means in her power to remove this error, which was disseminated even more widely after her death, and gave occasion to many objections being raised to her beatification. A thorough investigation was therefore made, by which the falsity of her having spread this rumor was incontrovertibly proved. [2]

---

[1] Ott, p. 42, and Act. passim.   [2] Act. B. Respons. N. 101 et seq.

From the same living faith arose her great respect for every priest. She frequently repeated the saying of St. Francis of Assisi, that if she met a priest and an angel at the same time, she would first salute, in all honor and respect, the priest ; because in the angel she beheld only an angel, but in the priest she beheld Christ Himself. Secular authority was also venerable in her believing eyes as representing that of God. She never permitted hard and derogatory language to be used in this regard: "Although this is often occasioned by the conduct of the bearers of authority themselves, we owe them respect," she used to say, "because our Redeemer and Law-giver has commanded it."

In this living faith she passed her life, and by continuing thus to the end, won the victory over death. What she had said so often during life : "O mysteries of the Lord, O mysteries of the Lord ! I will always firmly believe in them, and confess them with my last breath," she did, in fact, when she was dying.

When death was near, she turned to her confessor, Father Pamer, S. J., and said : "I testify before Heaven and earth, that I will die in the holy Roman Church." To her Sisters who were compassionating her for her terrible sufferings, she sweetly said these beautiful words, which came from the depths of her liveliest faith : "Oh! how little, how insignificant are my sufferings to be considered, when compared to the horrible torments which the holy martyrs so heroically endured for the faith ! Would to God I might suffer the same, after their example !" Thus had she, like the prudent man in the Gospel,[1] built the house of her temporal life upon the rock of faith, and when the rains poured in, and the rivers of suffering overflowed, when the winds blew and diabolical temptations stormed against this house, it fell not, for it was founded, not on the sand of human feelings and opinions, but on the rock of faith; it defied the power of death and stood firm in eternity.

[1] Matt. vii. 24, 25.

O Christian, if you do not desire that your house, built on sand, should one day fall down and bury you beneath its ruins, follow the example of this wise virgin and fulfil the admonition of the Apostle : "Let us draw near (to Christ), with a true heart in fulness of faith."[1]

CHAPTER II.

Hope, Her Strength.[2]

THE first-born daughter of faith is the theological virtue of hope. She directs the heart of the earthly pilgrim upwards, that it may dilate with desire for God as for its highest happiness, and she places its firm trust on the almighty arm of Him, who "continueth faithful and cannot deny Himself."[3] Thus, as St. Thomas Aquinas says :[4] "Hope takes hold of God, relying on His help, in order to obtain the desired good." In this virtue principally lies the vital force or motive power which moves the soul to its supernatural end, and from it also springs the fortitude to resist the pressure of the endless difficulties of this mortal life. We have hope, says St. Paul, "as an anchor of the soul, sure and firm, and which entereth in, even within the veil."[5] St. Thomas gives a beautiful explanation of this text, in these words:[6] "Hope is likened to an anchor, because, as the anchor renders the ship immovable in the ocean, so hope confirms the soul in God, in this world, which resembles an ocean. Yet, there is this difference between an anchor, in that the anchor does the fastening below, in the depths, while hope's work is above, in the Most High, in God. And, in fact, there is, in this life, nothing solid on which the soul could take its stand, support itself, and find rest."

---

[1] Heb. x. 22.   [2] Summ. N. 8. § 1, 317.   [3] II. Tim. ii. 13.
[4] Summa 2 : 2, q. 17 A. 1.   [5] Heb. vi. 19.   [6] In Epist. ad Hebr. l. c.

The Holy Ghost, the Teacher of Crescentia, had from her very infancy taught her to cast the anchor of her hope on high, above all visible and created things. No storms, how terribly soever they dashed against the ship of her heart, were able to wrest the anchor of her hope from its hold on the divine Father-heart, or even to shake its firmness; on the contrary, her hope in God and her strength in Him grew by that very suffering. She was herself quite conscious that her strength was grounded in hope, and she expressed this conviction in the maxim she often repeated: "We ought to part with life itself, rather than lose our hope in God."

It was the light of faith that first enkindled within her heart an ardent desire for God; everything beneath this Supreme Good she "counted as dung in order to gain Christ."[1] She practised what she often said : "We must turn the eyes of our hearts entirely aside from the visible and fix them upon the invisible, directing all our hope to God alone."

In that heart, purified from the deceptive love which binds us to temporal things, the ardent desire for the Supreme Good increased till it became a consuming fire. The Sisters often watched, unnoticed, when she raised her eyes, streaming with tears towards Heaven, sighing forth: "*Adveniat regnum tuum*," "Thy kingdom come," or uttering the burning words : "Who will give me wings, that I may fly away and rest in the wounds of my Beloved ?" In the evening she loved to contemplate the starry heavens ; then from her heart, wounded by love and desire, these words poured forth : "Ye stars, beautiful are ye, indeed, but oh! how far more beautiful is He who created you ! Ye, who adorn the head of my Beloved, as with a crown, tell Him, I beseech you, that I am pining away for love of Him ; that I am fainting with desire to see Him after this little while."[2]

The same faith produced in her heart the most child-

---

[1] Phil. iii. 8. [2] Summ. N. 8, § 149.

like and firm confidence in the most merciful and most faithful Father in Heaven.   In her greatest dereliction she did as St. Paul bids us do, " to hold fast the confession of our hope without wavering, (for He is faithful that hath promised)." [1]   By which she proved that she had attained the highest degree of hope, which, according to St. Bonaventure, consists in utterly abandoning all created help, and in relying confidently on the mercy and faithfulness of the Lord. [2]

She sometimes exclaimed, with a radiant face: "O faith, O holy faith, thou teachest me that God is my Father! O sweetest words, O remembrance full of hope, God, my Father! God, my Father!" It was from this thought that the beginning of the Lord's Prayer made a special impression on her, carrying her beyond herself; and causing her to repeat, over and over again, with indescribable emotion : " Our Father, who art in Heaven! O what is that ? God, my Father! God, my Father!" The usual formula in which she expressed her confidence in God was this one: " O almighty and ever-faithful God, I rely upon Thy infinite mercy and most faithful promises, and I will always trust that with the help of Thy grace, with which I will co-operate to the best of my power, and through the merits of Jesus, I may attain to Thee, my only blessed end and aim. Who has ever trusted in Thee, O Lord, and been confounded ?"

The reader will be edified if we add, in this place, the following words, which she wrote down in her exercises, during a retreat in 1741 : [2] " My crucified, loving God! Thou hast healed all my wounds, and I am the cause of all Thy sufferings ! Ah ! have mercy ! I will prostrate myself before Thy most holy feet, at the cross, I will trust in Thee with an invincible confidence, that I may not be led into any distractions, on account of my sinful life. Annihilate in me everything that could excite a vain confidence in creatures or in myself.   All creatures are but as

---

[1] Heb. x. 23.   [2] De gradibus virtutum, c. 27.   [3] Kolb. p. 50.

reeds of the marsh ; I can place no hope in them or in myself. I hope against hope when I find myself in great dejection, and weep because I have lost Heaven. If Thou shouldst kill me, yet will I hope in Thee.' The more I appear to be abandoned by Thee, the greater shall be my trust in Thee. If I enjoy but little light, yet I have much hope. My God, Thou art my strength !"

This confidence of hers was by no means the result of a natural disposition ; on the contrary, she had to struggle with anxiety, all her life, and for many years was beset with grievous temptations concerning the grace of the elect. She confessed to her novices[2] that the devil had continually troubled her with the thought : "Thou wilt be condemned, do what thou wilt ; everything is for nothing ; thou art an abomination in the sight of God ; thou dost but offend God the more with thy prayers and other good works." At these painful attacks and doubts her soul rose in faith, plunged all the deeper into the depths of the Divine Heart, and as she expressed it, she cast herself into the arms of so good, so merciful, and so amiable a Father, who is full of love and sweetness towards His children, asking of them nothing in return but love and trustful confidence. "O Thou, my God," she exclaimed ; "how often, nay, always do I find Thee faithful ! Thou knowest my needs and art ready to help me, for I am Thy creature and the work of Thy hands!"

Once she said in a spiritual discourse : "Whenever the devil assails me with gloomy thoughts concerning my eternal predestination, I flee to my crucified Redeemer, conceal myself in His wounds and say to Him with filial confidence : 'My Beloved, if for no fault of mine Thou shouldst condemn me to hell, I should yet be consoled, should still trust in Thy infinite kindness and fidelity that Thou wouldst never desert me, and if Thou wert with me, hell itself would be a paradise to me.' God is infinitely good ; He is never the first to depart. It is His peculiar property

---

[1] Job xiii. 15. [2] Gabriel, p. 15.

to be over merciful and to spare. Yes, He is my hope and my salvation."

As it was against this virtue that she was most tempted, and as she was fully aware of its decided importance on the bearing of the whole spiritual life, she kept constantly on hand some texts from Holy Writ, or sayings from the Lives of the Saints, and therewith rebuked the tempter, as with the sword of the Spirit, after the example of the Saviour. Such were : "It is not the will of my Father that one of these little ones should perish."—"God is my Redeemer, I will fear nothing."—"My help is in the name of the Lord."—"God is the Lord ; who can injure me, when God is my helper ?"—"Lord, who that has hoped in Thee, has ever been confounded ?"—"Thy grace, O Lord, is sufficient for me." She especially loved these two sayings :[1] "If armies in camp should stand together against me, my heart shall not fear."—"His heart is ready to hope in the Lord ; his heart is strengthened : he shall not be moved until he look over his enemies."[2] With such sentences she also consoled others.

Genuine hope is combined with a holy filial fear, lest, on our part, obstacles should arise to hinder the action of the mercy and grace of God. This fear surrounded her heart like the wall of a fortress, protecting her from presumption and sloth. "No sin, only no sin," she frequently exclaimed. "May God send whatever He pleases, so that no sin be committed ! I hope His infinite mercy will guard me." Her prayer for this fear was :[3] "O, my God, give me a child-like fear, that I may fear everything that displeases Thee ; give me a reverential fear that I may always stand in Thy presence and endeavor to obtain the fear inspired by love. Since Thou, O Man-God, hast, as man, trembled before Thy heavenly Father, what must not I do as a worm of the earth ?"

She ever imagined she could see faults in herself, when the strictest eye of her confessor could not detect a trace or

---

[1] Ps. xxvi. 3.　　　[2] Ps. cxl. 7, 8.　　　[3] Kolb, p. 43.

shadow of sin ; and even when she herself could not discover any sin in a thing, she did not on that account justify
herself, but said : "If, through the infinite grace of God, I
do not find myself guilty, I am not on that account justified, and know not whether I am worthy of love or hatred."[1] And again : "Let him that thinketh he standeth
take heed lest he fall."[2] Thus fear and hope were balanced
in her soul, as it is the will of God they should be in this
mortal life. This she expressed in these words : "I am
a great sinner, but God's mercy is greater than all my sins.
I am but a feeble reed, a mere nothing ; my whole skill
consists in sinning ; but it is on that account that I hope
and pray that God will not withdraw His merciful hand
from me."

When it happened that she really thought that she had
committed a sin, although her sorrow for it was indescrib-
ably great, yet her hope for pardon was not thereby diminished. Many pusillanimous souls would do well to take
to heart the following instruction of this servant of God :
"I rest entirely safe in the goodness and blood of my Beloved. I acknowledge that I have often offended my God,
but I will not offend Him by not hoping in Him ; and
therefore I do not entertain the least distrust in His inexhaustible goodness and in His fidelity to His promises.
Nay, even if I alone had committed all the sins of all mankind, I would still rely on the infinite value of the blood of
Christ. I would then immerse my sins in the wounds of
my Redeemer, believing that I could not do Him a greater
honor than by putting the greatest trust in Him, notwithstanding my being the greatest sinner. I know, indeed,
that God deserves to be loved for His justice as well as for
His love ; yet, I gather all my sins together, in the abyss
of my nothingness, and cast them into the abyss of the divine mercy."

These glorious sentiments manifested themselves more
gloriously yet, in the heroic firmness she exhibited in all

---

[1] Eccles. ix. 1.   [2] I. Cor. x. 12.

the exterior and interior sufferings that befell her; or rather, it may be said that her fortitude in suffering is nothing else than her firmness in hope. Concerning this she once expressed herself thus:[1]   "God is specially well pleased with those who firmly hope in Him, when they are abandoned by every one.   Such, too, He usually helps; they do Him violence, as it were, by their firm and courageous hope." In the cases wherein the ordinary man seemed to have failed and everything appeared lost, she used to be quite comforted and to say :   "Oh ! now is the right time to hope in God, and the more every hope is frustrated, the more will I trust in Him who is the author and fulfiller of hope."

Once some of the Sisters were compassionating the suffering state of this servant of God and marvelled that she was so tranquil while enduring so much pain.   Whereupon she revealed her interior life to them in these admirable words: "I am resting in security, in the bosom of my Beloved, my heavenly Father ; and I hope that I should there rest peaceably, were the whole world, nay, were all hell to rise up against me.   More than this, were Heaven and earth to fall to pieces, I should rest securely ; for, who can hurt me, if God is my helper and the anchor of my hope ?   Beloved Sisters, always trust in the good and powerful God, who imposes on no one a burden heavier than he can bear, and who bids the sun rise again when the fearful storm is past.   There would be no excellence, but rather a sign of meanness, in loving God only when He caresses us ; to love Him when He strikes us is the proof of true love.   We must part with life, rather than lose hope."

When she was decried as a hypocrite and a witch, and many of her fellow-Sisters avoided her from uneasiness, the peace of her soul was in no way disturbed.   "God is my Father," she said ;   "He will not desert me ; He will make all things work together for His honor and my salvation."   At the second investigation made by the ecclesias-

---

[1] Gabriel, p. 42,

tical authority of Augsburg concerning her, it was currently reported and believed that she would be sent away, imprisoned, and most severely punished as a witch. Sister Johanna, then Mother Superior, and the other Sisters, became extremely excited and terrified. She alone, though the very person threatened, remained completely at peace and only said : "God is the Lord ; in Him alone do I trust. If He takes care of me, no one can hurt me."

At this opposition by men, wherein many openly proclaimed her a hypocrite, and when even her confessors expressed their doubts and suspicions, her heroic courage once found vent in these words : "This is indeed the happiest position in the world ; it sets everybody at liberty to mock at me and tread me under foot. Nothing now remains to me but to place my hope in the Almighty God alone, trusting that He will turn all things to His glory and my salvation." The fortitude with which she endured the horribly vexatious tortures inflicted by the devil is yet more remarkable. When the Sisters were beside themselves from fright, she only smiled and said : "You may be able to kill me, but conquer me you cannot, for my hope is firmly placed in God."

Thus, finally she came to know no fear but the fear of God ; the sufferings and losses of this life which the natural man dreads, she looked on as passing shadows, which can indeed touch and inflict pain on the outward man, but cannot stand before the sun when it brilliantly lights up his interior life. Such shadows she did not fear. She once acknowledged this to Sister Joachim, with whom she was intimate, and who was tending her in a sickness. "Although I am the most feeble reed, yet I should not be afraid, were all hell and all men permitted to exercise their utmost fury and cruelty against me ; for I would then place my hope so firmly in God, that by the assistance of His grace, I should assuredly conquer. His grace is sufficient for me."

O happy soul ! looking neither forward nor backward,

neither to the right nor the left, but ever glancing upward; who, with her body, walked the earth, but with her heart was "in Heaven, from whence also we look for the Saviour, our Lord Jesus Christ, who will reform the body of our lowness, made like to the body of His glory." [1]   In this disposition, she frequently prayed :   "O God, send me only crosses, sicknesses, contempt and disgrace, and a whole ocean of persecutions!   Then so much the more will I hope in Thee, O powerful God !   And shouldst Thou even kill me, I will still hope in Thee, and cling to Thee immovably, O almighty and at the same time most merciful Father !"

Such heroic hope deserved, and in all real necessities actually obtained, extraordinary graces and miraculous assistance from God.   That "hope confoundeth not," [2] is most strikingly proved by her whole life : she obtained, by virtue of hope, more than mere deliverance from the pressure of distress, she received such consolation and strength in her needs that their pressure did not bend her soul to earth, but raised it up higher towards Heaven.   Neither did the Lord fail to grant her extraordinary consolations in the painful situations in which she was placed.   Most of these she concealed in silence, according to her wont, yet we know from the communications of her confessor, that when the persecutions were at their height, the Lord appeared to her and said these consoling words : [3]   "My child, trust in Me : I am thy Father who takes care of thee in every way.   Fear nothing, but to offend Me.   Remain faithful to Me ; love Me ever, and above all things ; My grace will be great."   Also in the later persecution, when it was proposed to remove her from the convent, according to the same witness, our Saviour appeared to her, saying: "Fear not ; I will defend thee against thine enemies ; thou shalt not be confounded in thy hope."

As she expected and obtained such great things from God, we must naturally conclude that in temporal matters

---

[1] Phil. iii. 20, 21.   [2] Rom. v. 5.   [3] Ott, B. II. C. 2.

she also placed her trust in God alone. She did this in so sublime a manner that the Lord often interfered with the usual order of things in her favor. Her principle that : "God and all the inhabitants of Heaven usually grant the most efficacious and powerful assistance to those who are without human assistance," has always proved true. She also admonished most earnestly her spiritual Sisters to cast all their cares upon the Father in Heaven. "Be not solicitous for the morrow. *Our* true business is to love God : it is *His* to provide for our needs." Was there anything wanting in the supply for temporal needs, or were great losses threatening, she immediately directed the attention of all to God, with the words : "Provision of these things can never be exhausted with God ;" [1] or, "I trust in God ; He is a loving Father, providing everything we need; He never forsakes His children ; if we trust Him with a child-like trust, and keep our vows and rules, we shall certainly never be in want of our daily bread. He so lovingly feeds even the irrational creatures; how much more will He feed us, if we love Him from our hearts. Seek ye first the kingdom of God, and bread will be given to you without fail. Our part is to serve God, God's part is to preserve us."

We have already related some striking instances of the help accorded by God in temporal affairs, but we shall here add some other cases. She had a set of Stations of the Cross painted for the convent, but had no money to defray the cost. She had recourse, as ever, to prayer, and a benefactor who knew nothing of the Stations or the price asked for them, brought, as an offering, without being requested to do so, the exact sum needed to pay for them. Certain justifiable reasons induced her to wish to present a beautiful crucifix to an honorable gentleman. She had none; her confidence in God, however, came to her aid at once : a most beautiful crucifix was most unexpectedly donated to her. Once she was in need of 200 florins.

[1] Ott, B. II. C. 2.

She opened an old chest, which she herself had shortly before emptied, and found that amount therein. Nobody knew or could imagine whence this money came.

A grace to be valued more highly yet and which it would seem was granted her by God as a reward for the heroism of her hope, was the gift conferred upon her of being able to console despairing souls, and of re-awakening hope within them. Her Sisters in religion had many times experienced this influence, and in later times, when the renown of her sanctity drew persons of every class to her from far and near, all those who went to her for consolation bore witness to this experience. God frequently led great sinners to her, who had long since given themselves up to despair, and had lost courage to open their minds to their confessors. Her mere presence and a word from her mouth dispelled the gloomy spirit of despair. The heart of the poor sinners overflowed, they revealed to her of their own free-will and consent what previously they could not resolve to tell the representative of Christ under the seal of confession. After this her consoling words infused into these depressed souls the firm hope in Christ which was living in her own heart. She told them that no sinner, so long as he sojourns in time, has any well-founded cause for mistrust, much less for despair; after sinning, there is indeed cause for sorrow, but the very thing that leads us to contrition, namely, that we have offended such a good God, is also an effectual reason for hoping in Him. God is good to all who hope in Him; and a soul seeking Him with a true confidence will find Him. Then she exhorted those she had consoled to make a good confession, recommended them to a father-confessor, and so far as is known, every one departed from her with an altered soul, full of trust.

This virtue she had so much at heart, that she was never tired of speaking, hearing, pondering over or reading of the fidelity and infinite mercy of God towards us. She eagerly cautioned them against the snares of Satan, who inspires pusillanimity under the guise of humility, well knowing that he labors in vain so long as the soul cherishes the true hope. She exhorted every one, especially in the hour of suffering and trial, to protect themselves with the shield of a firm trust in God. Sufferings were sent by God not for our destruction, but to purify us from our faults, and to exercise us in virtue. To live in pains and temptations is the greatest gain. Accompanied and supported by this brilliant virtue, she trod the narrow path of life courageously, perseveringly, progressing from virtue to virtue and as she increased in age increasing also in peace, in love, in interior recollection, and in longing to possess the Beloved One. She sighed like a turtle dove, with the Psalmist: "When shall I come and appear before the face of God?"[1] "I await death," she said with pleasure, "because it opens for me the door of the banqueting-room of Heaven." And when on her death-bed this desire for God shone brilliantly in her soul, and in the firmest confidence in God poured itself forth in ardent aspirations. "I wish to be dissolved," she frequently repeated, "as soon as possible, yet not a moment sooner than it pleases God. For the present, my Heaven consists in suffering, and in fulfilling God's holy will by suffering." Whoever so lives and dies in such hope may courageously say: "In Thee, O Lord, have I hoped; let me never be confounded."[2]

O Christian! In all the storms of life and death, never lose hold of the saving anchor which God has given you, and the more it seems to you that everything is lost, so much the firmer must your hold be of the word of the Apostle: "Let us hold fast the confession of our hope without wavering (for He is faithful, that hath promised)."[3]

---

[1] Ps. xli. 8.　　[2] Ps. xxx. 1.　　[3] Heb. x. 23.

CHAPTER III.

Love without Reservation.[1]

HE words of St. Gregory may be appropriately applied to this seraphic virgin:[2] "There are some who, inflamed by the torches of the higher contemplation, languish with desire and pant after their Creator. These never rest : they are consumed by the glow of love which burns in themselves and they kindle the flame of the love of God in others, as soon as they touch them, though with but a single word. What could I call these souls, but Seraphim, since their hearts, transformed into fire, illumine and burn?"

From the time that Crescentia, as a child, had been favored with the vision of the Infant Jesus which we have already mentioned, this spark of heavenly love, not seeking its own, was enkindled in her heart, and with an ever-increasing glow became so intense as finally to consume, not only her natural failings, but at length her bodily life also. What she understood by love she expresses in the following beautiful words:[3] "It is and shall be the only business of my heart to love and know God and to work for love of Him, even as He loves and knows Himself and works for His own honor; to live for love of God, even as God Himself lives for love; to speak of divine things with such a love as God speaks of Himself and of His eternal truths; to rivet the powers of the soul so completely to the Divine Power, that nothing be loved save God only and what belongs to God; to be grateful with a divine love, to the highest love of God. For God is Love, and Power, and Strength." This flame she could not keep entirely inclosed within her heart, no matter how hard she tried to conceal her virtues: she revealed herself in everything she said, thought, and did ; nay, her very appearance reflected clearly and warmly the

---

[1] Summ. N. 9, § 1, C30.   [2] Hom. in Ev. l. II. N. 34.   [3] Kolb, p. 33.

interior fire, namely, "the charity of God, poured forth in our hearts by the Holy Ghost, who is given to us."[1]

Her conversations on love could only proceed from a heart entirely filled with that sentiment. Words cannot depict the fire wherewith she exhorted her Sisters in religion and every one who lent an attentive ear to her, to love God and to retain nothing for themselves which they would not be willing to sacrifice to this love. Those who listened to her when speaking on this subject, acknowledged that they had never heard anything that could be compared in lucidness and intensity of fervor to the words of this simple and uneducated soul, glowing with ardent love. "No one ever left her presence," says a witness, "without taking some sparks of the divine love caught from her." One had to see and hear her, in order to obtain an idea of the efficacy of her words, whenever she spoke of divine love. "Dearly beloved Sisters," she said, "love God, love God alone; let no moment pass without the love of God. Gild all your tasks, even the smallest, with the fire of love ; and this when you work as well as when you suffer. By day and night say hundreds and thousands of times : O my God, I love Thee ! I love Thee purely for Thine own sake, because Thou art the Supreme Good. O my God ! I rejoice with my whole heart that Thou art this Supreme Good ; that Thou art all, and I am nothing. O God, most deserving of our entire love, would that I could love Thee, as Thy Divine Mother, as the holy angels, the Saints of God, and all godly souls, including the souls in purgatory, love Thee ! "[2]

It was her wish that the Sisters should every day ask three favors of God, viz.: The greatest hatred of every sin, even the tiniest ; the most perfect love of God ; a pure and holy love of their neighbor. "O dear Lord !" she would then exclaim ; "Love, Love itself ! O how sad it is, that Love is not loved ; taste and see how sweet the Lord is." These words flashed from her mouth like flames

---

[1] Rom. v. 5.   [2] Summ. N. 9, § 92.

of fire, so that even obdurate hearts were moved thereby.

If any one was present who understood how to speak of the love of God, her soul would rejoice and she listened in silence like an humble pupil, apparently quite refreshed, both in soul and body, by this water of life. Often, however, her own fervor broke forth in flaming words. The following passages, written down by herself in 1723, will give the reader a faint idea of the way in which she spoke of love.[1]

"Love gives me wings with which I may soar up to the throne of the Most Holy Trinity, there to present the needs of the Catholic Church and of Christianity, the state of infidels, together with that of sinners, and of the souls in purgatory. Love gives me wings that, like a dove, I may fly to near and distant lands, there, by the power of God, to preach the true doctrine and announce the Gospel to unbelievers. Love gives me wings that, like a bee, I may approach every creature and extract from it the honey of love. Love, too, is the best teacher; it instructs me how to conquer myself, how to obey, how to suffer, and how to keep silence. For this reason I surrender myself entirely to love. If I love Thee, O my God, I am, by that very love, as strong as death. By love, I can draw down from Heaven, into my heart, Thee, the Supreme Good, and with Thee I can pass through every wall. By love, I can soften the obdurate hearts of sinners; I can break the chains made through sin. By love, I can redeem the captives of purgatory. By love, I can conquer my evil wishes, my vicious nature, my wicked self-will. By love, I can defeat all the attacks and temptations of hell. By love, I can endure all hardships and pains. By love, I can constantly love God more and more. Therefore, I will now begin, in all earnestness and fervor, to love God in a very holy manner, so that I may attain the end for which I was created, and that by me He may be praised, loved, and honored through all eternity."

[1] Kolb, p. 27.

These words concerning love already prove the fervor of the love within her. Other expressions and prayers give us a deeper insight into this seraphic heart, and excite our admiration at the greatness and purity of her love.

"I could not live if there were anything in my heart not striving after God and His love. Nay, if I had a thousand hearts, with all of them I would love God and Him alone ; for He alone is worthy of love. My life is to love, and my love is to suffer ; for then only is love worthy of the name of love, when it is crucified. If, then, all men and devils were to persecute and torment me in all manner of ways, it would only be pouring on oil to cause the fire of love within me to blaze with a loftier flame."

At another time she said : "If I knew that there was a drop of blood within me that did not love God, I would immediately let it out. If I could become an angel by speaking one word that did not come from the love of God, I would not speak that word."

In the year 1722 she wrote :[1] "O Lord, give me only love for Thee, and I shall be rich enough! I desire nothing more, save that Thou shouldst leave me in my nothingness, and, if I may so express myself, from the very vehemence of love, that Thou shouldst continue to be *All*, Thou, who in Thy infinite perfection art always like unto Thyself, and art *All in All.* In what I do, I will love Thee as Thou lovest Thyself ; I will love Thee in Thyself, as in the Supreme Good which Thou art to me ; I will love Thee in Thy divine gifts and graces ; I will love Thee, because to me Thou art all in all ; I will rejoice in nothing save in Thee alone, and on account of Thy love."

The height and purity of her love were more clearly and distinctly marked by some other expressions. With a glowing countenance, overflowing eyes, and indescribable fervor, she often said : "*To love God because He is what He is,*" and not seldom was she thereby rapt in

---

[1] Kolb, 1722.

ecstasy. In her unguarded moments, she was at times heard sighing thus: "My God, I love Thee above all, because in Thyself Thou art the Supreme and Infinite Good: this is my only joy, that Thou art all and that I am nothing."

The love of complacency in the infinite beauty and perfection of God, which constitutes that sea of bliss in Heaven, in which all the members of the triumphant Church are, as it were, submerged, was, in this seraphic heart, so powerful, so continuous, that all other feelings were thereby silenced. In the purest love she wished nothing for herself, but all for her Beloved, and because she reserved nothing for herself, she received, instead of joy in herself, which she had renounced, the joy in God and from God, which she had abandoned to Him and ascribed to Him alone.

The following prayer preserved by Father Ott[1] bears a beautiful testimony to the sublime purity of her love: "I rejoice with Thee from the bottom of my heart, on account of Thy Divinity, and on account of the endless happiness that Thou art in Thyself and that Thou enjoyest from all eternity. Oh, that I could, alone, render Thee as many services and love Thee as ardently as the whole number of Thy elect love Thee! Oh, that I could love God as His Saints love Him in Heaven, and that there were many millions of heavens and worlds, so that in many millions of ways glory and honor might be bestowed on my Beloved! Ah! wound my heart with such a wound of love, that I may love Thee infinitely more than I love myself or aught else. But wound it also with suffering, that for love of Thee I may, throughout all time, suffer more and more and be by all men contemned and despised."

Wishes, such as those so often uttered by Saints in an excess of the pressure of love, were very familiar to her.[2] "Did I know for certain," she said, "that I had but a

---

single moment more to spend on earth, and that, immediately after death, I was to be condemned by God, I would still love this all-loving God alone, for that moment, and hell would be hell to me because there we cannot love God." But since love consists more in actions than in ardent affections or grandiloquent words, we must apply the rule of the inner and outer life, in order to acquire a correct knowledge of the greatness of her love.

St. Bonaventure [1] defines the highest degree of love possible here on earth as follows : "The highest degree of love which is possible on earth, is reached when the soul is so far united to God that with all its powers and faculties it is recollected in Him in such a manner as to become one spirit with Him, so that it remembers nothing outside of Him, and that all the affections united in joyous love are at rest in a delightful communing with the Creator."

Her confessor, Father Pamer, once asked her what she was doing day and night. She answered : "I cannot say otherwise than that I am thinking of God, I am loving God." She said the same thing, when in a half-ecstatic state, to her beloved Sister in religion, M. Joachim. In her resolutions of the year 1741, we read : [2] "I will constantly raise up my mind to Thee, and in the most profound repose and quietude of my heart, by a peculiar light and perception, I will meditate upon, marvel at, and delight in Thy divine perfections."

Outward occupations did not disturb this interior uninterrupted intercourse of love with the beloved One ; because it was sustained by an entirely extraordinary light and was exercised with amazing facility in the most profound depths of her soul, which soul was, with her higher countenance, as mystics express it, turned wholly to God. Nay, whatever happened to her outwardly seemed to fan still more this interior flame. A single word about God and divine things was a breeze which at once struck the

---

[1] De Process. Relig.   [2] Kolb, p. 50.

strings of her heart, causing them to resound with the melodies of love.   And since everything .was to her spiritual eye a mirror of God and the Godlike, so everything gave forth to her ear an invitation to love, which excited her heart to a renewal of that sentiment.   Thus she rejoiced in all the works of God's hands.   In the beautiful she beheld the Most Beautiful, in every melodious sound she heard the echoes of the Highest Love, and in this way she followed every trace which God has left of Himself among His creatures.   Panting with desire, she was ever pursuing her Beloved.   And thus, even as creatures became a ladder to her soul to enable her to ascend to the first Truth and Beauty, so they also became a magnet to her heart, drawing it beyond all gifts to the Giver, whose original goodness, love, and beauty she was seeking, and of which she obtained a taste from the little brook of creatures which flowed from this great ocean.   "My Beloved," she said, "reveals Himself to me in all that I see or hear.   Everywhere He meets me, everywhere He follows me ; in short, He is mine, and I am His."   In the year 1727 she writes thus :[1] "Because God created all things for His own love and honor, therefore must God be honored in and by all His creatures, with the same love and honor with which He honors Himself.   I will leave off loving myself ; Thee alone will I love, O my God, and indeed so thoroughly will I love Thee alone, that I may become one with Thee."   In the year 1722 she writes thus :[2] "O God, as far as I can, I separate myself from all creatures, to give to Thee, my Creator, my entire love !   I will love the Creator in all creatures, because I find in every one of them signs, nay, as it were, footprints of my God."

These traces of divine omnipotence, beauty, and love, met her in every grain of sand, and in every leaf of a tree, with an exhortation to love.   Flowers and stars filled her mouth with thanksgiving and praise sent to the *Triune*, and her heart was lighted up by a flame that transfigured

---

[1] Kolb, p. 34.   [2] Ibid. p. 23.

her, as she stood rapt in ecstasy, with her eyes fixed on Heaven. She named the stars chandeliers burning before the throne of God, or sometimes she called them a brilliant diadem of her Beloved. "You are indeed beautiful," she would add, "but how much more beautiful is the great God who created you out of nothing! Ah! crown His head, and tell Him that I love Him."

The singing of birds made a similar impression on her. Like her Seraphic Father, Francis of Assisi, and the holy virgin, St. Rose of Lima, who were animated with a like fervor, Crescentia vied with the birds in praising the Lord. "Beloved birds," she would say, [1] "strike up the hymn of love and praise to my Beloved." Then, oft-times she would find fault with herself: [1] "O God, what a difference between these Thy creatures and myself! Thou givest to the bird only food and water, and for this little provision he sings with all his might in thanksgiving to his Creator. But I, who have received such great graces from God, love and thank Him so little, nay, even offend Him!"

Blest eyes of a loving heart! They penetrate the dark veil of creatures, and behind the shadow of finite things perceive the Eternal Light which, unmixed and infinite in its sublimity, supports all things, sustains, vivifies, and gives motion to all below, and which, without being in any degree finite itself, is nevertheless in all and above all. From this interior light, which beholds the Supreme One in the least of finite things, and in the meanest creature loves the Most High God, the following sayings, to which she frequently gave utterance, proceeded: "My God, I do not see Thee face to face; nevertheless, I am already happy, for I love Thee. Every creature invites us to love; for the Creator manifests Himself in His creatures. The creature is a ladder, an incentive leading to God. It seems to me as if there were nothing existing save God and Crescentia. My home is in the heart of Jesus: there I dwell as in

---

[1] Summm. N. 9, § 63.

a sweet and lovely solitude, intimately united to God, even in the tumult of human affairs."

Such a love endures no word, no work, not even a wish or a thought, as far as these are voluntary, which does not come from or exist on account of love. This she expressed in the beautiful words : "No heart but to love, for love, on account of love," which in fact she practised day and night. As Sister Gabriel says, in spite of her many affairs she never did go forth from herself or from God. By the most sublime intentions she connected every temporal work with Heaven, or rather with Christ. Hear what she says herself : "In my little occupations nothing human shall intermingle ; love alone shall rule ; the *beginning*, the *centre*, and the *end* shall be love, namely : at the beginning of the work I will do the will of God from love ; at the middle I will obey for love ; at the end I will love as Christ has loved. Not I, but God and Christ live in me through love and suffering. Grant, then, O God, that love and suffering may increase within me, that with the cheerful mind that proceeds from love I may love Thee ever more and more !"

All kinds of love, the acts of complacency, of well-wishing, of resignation, of contrition, succeeded each other and made of every day an uninterrupted, marvellously varying golden chain of love. The simplest, together with the sublimest exercises and expressions are found therein. Let us hear more of them : " This alone gives me heartfelt joy, that God is what He is in Himself, O my God, my only Good, my all !' O God, I give Thee Thyself ; everything that Thou art in Thyself ! I salute Thee, Most Holy Trinity, through Thy sweetly-sonorous and incomprehensible heart, and I praise Thee with the honor Thou hast been unto Thyself from all eternity, which Thou hast given Thyself from eternity to the present time, which Thou wilt render to Thyself for all eternity, and which will be given unto Thee by all angels and men throughout eternity.' I

____

... tion of sayings.

desire to love Thee, as all the holy angels love Thee, and as Mary, the Mother of God, and the humanity of Jesus Christ love Thee eternally. But above all, I wish that I had Thy own Sacred Heart, that with it I might sufficiently love Thee, O most beautiful God! But what rejoices me most, is that Thou, O Supreme Good, canst love Thyself sufficiently and in a manner worthy of Thyself!"

That the love of Crescentia was no mere fanatical ebullition of feeling, but a power of God, is proved by three effects, which were manifested in her in a very high degree, namely, her angelic purity of conscience, her ardent thirst for greater love, as well as for greater suffering. Conscience is pure, in the measure in which God's will rules the human being. Ven. Crescentia's mottoes were:[1] "God's will is my will."—"My food is to do the will of my Father."—"Nothing of my own will is reserved." Indefatigably she repeated: "Thy most holy will be done, O God!" She used also to say often: "I would rather lift a straw from the ground by the will of God, than raise a hundred dead men to life by my own will."

She knew how true was the saying of an old master: "In order that God may enter a heart, the creature must first depart from it." For this reason she endeavored, with astonishing zeal and perseverance, to divest herself of even the faintest particle of love of the world, together with that of her own free-will, and to sacrifice her liberty, without reserve, to the divine will, that thus she might attain to the full liberty of the children of God. According to the word of the Lord: "He that hath My commandments and keepeth them, he it is that loveth Me,"[2] she observed, with unswerving fidelity, all the commandments of God, of the Church, and of her Rule, from the very first day of her entering into religion, with such exactitude, that even envious and malevolent observers never could discover the slightest transgression of even the least rule; this

---

[1] Gabriel, p. 87.   [2] John xiv. 21.

was publicly affirmed by Sisters who had lived with her for forty years. In this matter she did not trust to herself, but several times, with the general and particular printed examinations in hand, she examined with painful exactness every step she had taken, every thought, and every word, so that no fault might be overlooked. These she noted in a little book she kept for that purpose.

Her heart was pierced when she saw or heard any Sisters not caring about keeping the Rule in minor details, and when they excused themselves by saying : "This Rule does not bind under pain of sin." With sighs and tears she would then say that such talk as that is the language and Rule of a luke-warm religious, that it leads to indifference in regard to perfection, and is by all means to be avoided, because, even in minor matters, we either please or displease God.

The purity of her conscience astonished all her confessors. We have from them all, beginning with her first confessor, Rev. Charles Heiland, to whom she confessed while living in the world, express testimony, not only that she had ever retained her baptismal innocence, but that in her whole life they could scarcely discover anything which was for certain even a venial sin of her youth, so that they could base an absolution upon it. So say Father Lachner, S. J., who was her confessor for six years; Father Bartholomäus Binner, who tried her almost too severely ; Father Michael Bauer ; and Father Pamer. Father Bonifacius Schmidt, the Provincial, her extraordinary confessor, assures us that if an angel were to confess, his confession would scarcely be different from hers.

The greatness of her love caused such an abhorrence of sin in her soul, that she would turn pale at the mere mention of it, and would exclaim with incredible emotion :   "O my God ! only no sin ! send me whatever Thou pleasest : sickness, sorrow, contempt, sufferings of the soul, only no sin ! no sin for all eternity ! I had rather endure all the pains of purgatory from now to the last day, than commit one venial sin." At times she expressed herself more forcibly yet, saying: "O Lord, were it possible, I would rather suffer the pains of hell without sin, than be in Heaven with a venial sin!" This abhorrence of sin reached such a height that she besought the Lord rather to let her die, than to offend Him by a mere imperfection. The least neglect in spiritual life was more abhorrent to her than a serious crime is to many an ordinary Christian. "O Divine Sower," she writes,[1] "do not permit me to suppress by my carelessness, or suffocate by my sins, the divine seed which Thou, from pure grace, hast sowed in my barren heart. I will diligently look after the field of my heart by general and particular examinations, and when I find weeds therein, I will root them up, as far as I can, by contrition and sorrow, by confession and penance." This she did also, after the example of all the Saints, and experienced an incredible sorrow of contrition at every little speck of sin, which she, illumined by the sunlight of the Holy Ghost, noticed or thought she noticed within herself.

She confessed every week, at least two or three times, and during the last years, nearly every day. She prepared herself very carefully for confession, sometimes for hours, and for the most part experienced such profound contrition, that she shed many tears and could not suppress loud sobs. She then appeared as cast down and as contrite as if she had been a criminal led forth to execution. Her Sisters could not look at her without compassion, nor indeed without a feeling of shame and a salutary emotion conducing to contrition. In the confessional she shed so many tears, that the Sisters who came after her often found the place wet with these precious tears of penitential love, and the confessors themselves were confused and touched by such a sorrow for faults in which they could not find sufficient matter for absolution.[2] The acts of contrition which she made in the confessional were, as Father Pamer expresses himself, so intense, that it seemed as if her heart was about

---

[1] Kolb, p. 17.   [2] Summ. N. 9, § 300, 302.

to burst from her bosom. As soon as she left the confessional, however, she appeared entirely changed, as if she was endowed with new life, and beaming with joy and consolation ; she then poured forth from her heart long and fervent acts of thanksgiving. This great contrition, proceeding from love, was a grace which she had repeatedly and continuously implored of the Sacred Heart. She writes in the year 1740:[1] " Oh, my merciful, beloved Jesus ! Give me tears, that I may bewail and repent of my sins ! I am not—Thou knowest it well—a Moses to call forth a spring, by knocking at the hard rock of my heart. Thou knowest that I do not possess the love of the much-loving Magdalen; Thou knowest that I can do nothing without Thee."

Such a perfectly penitential life produced the effect that in the last twenty years of her life she became, as it were, dead to the world and to herself, and without difficulty controlled all the impulses of nature. Like the blessed angels, she was scarcely conscious any longer of the first movements of resistance of repugnant nature, and could therefore concentrate her strength on the uninterrupted exercise of love, instead of having to use it in overcoming inordinate self-love.[2] Such a pure heart is the most glorious and pleasing temple of the Saviour ; He comes and takes His abode therein, because " to be divested of every creature means to be full of God," as an old teacher of spiritual life expresses it. Hence the Saviour said, in a vision to His beloved child, Crescentia:[2] " My child, I like to dwell in a pure heart ; therein is My joy and My pleasure. Blessed are the pure of heart, for they shall see God."

When a soul has obtained a high degree, not of imperfect contrition, but of a contrition springing from pure love, she then feels nearly the same sorrow for the sins of others as for her own ; and this pure virgin, loving God as she did, had no greater cross on earth than that of beholding that Love, Love made flesh, is not loved upon earth, but is so often atrociously offended. When

---

[1] Kolb. p. 42.   [2] Ott. B. II. C. 4.

she heard of great sins committed by others, she turned as pale as death, terror was depicted in her countenance, she could not suppress the emotion of grief; she exclaimed: "Oh, what a frightful thing is sin! Woe! woe! how it torments me that Love is not loved!" With a bleeding heart and with tears in her eyes, she would then call on Heaven for grace and mercy for these unfortunate sinners and for removing such a dishonor from the Divine Majesty. "Defend Thyself, O Lord," she sighed, "defend Thyself from such monstrosities committed against Thee by men! Either prevent them by Thy Omnipotence, or at least annihilate these injustices by an immediate interposition of Thy mercy."

She then felt an almost invincible pressure urging her to make some atonement to the Divine Majesty by performing severe penances in union with the sufferings of Christ. Then, in no way relying on her own actions, she besought her Sisters in religion with burning words, to love God more and to implore Him that no more sins be committed. "Because," she said, "if by our prayers and penances we prevent but one sin, it will be of more worth than if we were doing heroic acts before men and even raising the dead to life. What a horrible thing it is to offend God! Oh, beloved Sisters, only no sin!" How she sought to atone for the sins of others and how to prevent them we shall relate further on.

The word of the Lord: "Blessed are they that hunger and thirst after justice, for they shall have their fill,"[1] is said of love. It is peculiar to love always to hunger and thirst after greater love, for although it already fills the heart in some way or other on earth, yet this satiating and appeasing only gives rise to an increase of hunger, in complete contrast to what takes place with regard to our physical needs, in which desire, when succeeded by its fulfilment, is naturally superseded: so that one excludes the other.

---

[1] Matth. v. 6.

St. Laurence Justinian says:[1] "When a soul is altogether burning with love, even the constant exterior increase seems to it too little, from the intense desire it cherishes for a still greater love." Love of God knows no word like: "It is enough." With the seraphic Crescentia this hunger grew greater and greater, till it became a true, though sweet, martyrdom. We will add a few beautiful expressions of hers to the testimonies we have already adduced. In the year 1727[2] she wrote: "My joy shall be to grow and increase in the Lord in suffering, in love! I will frequently contemplate, with deep interior attention, the infinite perfections of God, and especially dwell with marvellous admiration on His love, that I may come to know God rightly, to enjoy Him, and aspire to Him, and always do that which is most perfect in His sight. I will love Thee, O Divine Majesty, O my most beloved Jesus, as the angels and as the Seraphim love Thee. My Divine Spouse says to me: 'Be perfect as your heavenly Father is perfect.' I will immerse my humanity in the divine essence and love Thee as Thy Divine Father loves Thee. Would I could love Thee like God, could suffer like Jesus, rejoice like God, and yet remain, the while, buried in my own nothingness." This lofty flight of love shows how nearly she had attained what St. Paul expresses in the words: "But he who is joined to the Lord, is one spirit,"[3] and this not in the Pantheistic sense, but in that of the most wonderful and comprehensive union. And since her own heart did not suffice to the love for which she longed, she desired to inflame all hearts, that by them God might be loved in a higher degree. She writes in the year 1729:[4] "I offer Thee, therefore, my heart and all the hearts of the whole human race, and place them in Thy Divine Heart, O Lord, for an eternal love. I pray Thee make of all these hearts but one heart, but one fire, but one love!"

Sister Rafael Miller says: "To excite me to love and

---

[1] De Disciplin. Monast., C. 6.   [2] Kolb, p. 35.   [3] I. Cor. vi. 17.   [4] Kolb, p. 39.

chase away my lukewarmness, Crescentia said to me, that
every day she made a compact of love with God, with the
purpose and intention that every beat of her pulse, every
breath she drew, and every movement of her body, by day
and night, should be so many acts of love and sighs of burning fervor, in order to attain that love that is completely
merged in Jesus Christ. Wounded by the arrow of heavenly love, she even dreamed about it and made acts of love
in her sleep. She sighed and conjured all the Saints and
angels with the words of the bride in the Canticles : " If
you find my Beloved, tell Him that I languish with love."
About this she once said :[1] " The quiet night is the best
time to love, which fact must be well considered by a
spouse of Jesus Christ. Every person consecrated to God
must not only be engaged in love for Him during the day,
but must continue this exercise during the night, even in
sleep, by making an intention to that effect, beforehand;
for love must never rest."

This thirst for love had encouraged her to make that
sublime vow, to do in all things what she considered to
be the most perfect ; which vow, from the testimony of
her confessors,[2] Fathers Januarius Mayr and John Baptist
Pamer, she certainly made. This vow, by which she bound
herself to avoid, not only the least sin, but every known imperfection, she took, with the permission of her father confessor, in the year 1725—shortly after Christmas—and kept it
faithfully for nineteen years, until her death. But all this by
no means satisfied her hunger for love; she always believed
she was trespassing against the Highest Love by her own
want of love. With tears she would exclaim : " O my God,
how canst Thou suffer on earth so miserable and sinful a
creature as I am, who am not worthy that the sun should
shine upon me ? Let me know myself, let me know Thee,
hope in Thee, love Thee. Until now, although I am old,
I have not yet properly begun to love. To-day I will begin to love Thee in very truth."

---

[1] Gabriel, p. 75.   [2] Summ. N. 9, § 590, and Act. B. Inform. N. 111.

She was not satisfied with the love attained until this time; she still stretched forward to what was before her, to the possession of the Supreme Good through love. " O my dear Sisters," she said, [1] " let us ascend up to Heaven ; up to Heaven, to God, let us fly! Who will give me wings like a dove, that I may fly and rest in the clefts of the rock, in the sacred hollow places of my Beloved ? If, in order to find my Beloved, I had to climb the highest mountain, with great labor and in danger of death, or that it were needful to dive into the depths of the ocean, I would not hesitate a moment, but would undertake to do so with joy."

Another time she exclaims: [2] " O my God, I succumb to Thy sweet power ! I cannot do more, my poor heart is too little. O great God, instead of my loving Thee, love Thou Thyself, as Thou art infinitely worthy of it ! " This desire finally made her a true martyr of love. " O God," she said, " this pain surpasses all other pain ! To suffer for God is the highest joy and delight ; but not to be able to love Him enough is a great martyrdom. I love God so much that I almost die of it. But if this love were taken from me, I should absolutely die, because I was not loving my Love."

These expressions cannot be understood by such as love not God, but they are very familiar to the great Saints. It is not a play on words but a great truth, the fullest truth, that is contained in the following verses of St. Theresa, which we add here as a parallel to the sentiments expressed above :—

VERSES BY ST. THERESA.

I live! yet not in self I live!
My wooing doth such living give
That 'tis in dying *not*, I die,
For what is life with Thee not nigh ?
With Thee remote what doth remain,
In very truth, but death's sharp pain,

---

[1] Gabriel, p. 74.   [2] Ott, p. 60.

More bitter than the world can see?
I woo the wail of sympathy ;
For the sharp pain 'neath which I sigh,
Is—that in dying *not*—I die.

This interior fire of the soul produced its effects on the Ven. Crescentia's body ; feeble and emaciated as that body was, a remarkable heat was diffused through it, even in the cold of winter. The Sisters noticed it when she was so weak that they had to support or sometimes to carry her into the choir. Her hands were so warm, even during the severest cold that it was noticed their warmth communicated itself through the three-fold garments of others. She frequently could not endure the exceeding heat burning in her veins, but had to obtain relief by the application of cold poultices.[1] Her frequent attacks of violent bleeding of the nose are probably to be attributed to this cause ; it seems, even, that most of her sicknesses were occasioned by it. This was the opinion of the physicians who attended her, even of the Protestant doctor and apothecary, Mr. Schmid, who visited her in a serious attack of sickness she had two years previous to her happy death. He spoke of it publicly, and thought that no medicine could cool the inward heat consuming her, because it was supernatural and came from God, from which he believed that this nun had an extraordinary love for God.[2] The ecstasies, returning nearly every day, are, in fact, but manifestations and effects of love, of a love so great that the weak vessel of frail nature could not absorb these effects of the Holy Spirit. This Holy Spirit worked so powerfully within her, that she was even in her normal state more passive than active at prayer when she made her acts of love. God was near to her as an immeasurable light, casting its rays into her interior, inflaming it and so moving it that she believed herself to be living and acting within this very light. In the course of years her interior life was transfigured into an incredible state of repose, peace, and firm-

---

[1] Ott, B. II. C. 3, and Gabriel.   [2] Summ. N. 9, § 513.

ness, as if her soul were immovably attached to Him who is immovability itself.

But the pure gold of her love was more surely tested by the crosses and sufferings which are the touch-stone of love, than by all her mystic states. Great love cannot exist without love for suffering. We will relate in a subsequent chapter in what a high degree this seraphic soul possessed and practised a true love of the cross. As a conclusion to this one, it will be sufficient to note some resolutions and affections referring both to suffering and to love.[1]

"Oh, what a consolation it is, what a pleasure, what sweet delight, to love Thee alone, O Highest Good, to serve Thee, to cling to Thee ! If, instead of heavenly wine, Thou givest me to drink of genuine wine mixed with myrrh, the love that suffers for Thee is still sweet and lovely. Yes, indeed, the more Thou visitest me with bitterness, the more consoling to me, the more endearing is Thy love, O God ! Lord, give me a love that suffers firmly, constantly, and immovably ; such as no waters of affliction can quench. Since true love consists in suffering, I beseech Thee, O God, that I may suffer ! suffer and not die ; and when it is Thy will that I should die, let me not die merely to pay the debt of nature, but out of pure love for Thee. O Lord, I say with the prophet Isaias : Shoot at me ! I am prepared like a target at which they shoot with arrows. What could make one happier, than to be wounded by an arrow of the love of God, discharged by God Himself? Behold, O Lord, my heart is open and ready for Thee : shoot and hit me with the sweet arrow of divine love ! I love Thy arrows, O God, even when they occasion only pain and smarting. They come from the bow of love and aim only at love. O God, Thou knowest that I love Thee, and should there be anything in my heart that does not love Thee, tear it out ! My heart shall be Thine forever ! O my God ! keep it, and never return it unto me."

True progress, when viewed from the stand-point of

<hr>

[1] Kolb, pp. 16, 37, 53.

eternity, consists solely in an increase of love ; and this being the case, it would certainly be desirable that the bawlers after progress, in these our days, should go to the poor, despised nun, to learn of her the only right road to progress, namely, a holy love thirsting after God. And since the true happiness of the human heart is only to be found in a well-regulated and everlasting love, how pitiable must be the numerous spoiled men and women, true children of this world, educated according to the exterior training of the age, but whose hearts know nothing of the source and proper object of all love. Would that such as these maturely reflected on the undeniably beautiful words of Crescentia : "People deceive themselves very much if they imagine that the real pleasure of a soul consists in exterior things, or in fleshly joys, or in the absence of every cross. No, no ! it consists in the spirit alone, and only in this, that we do and suffer everything, according to the will of our heavenly Father."[1] O faithful reader, look into your own heart : it will never come to true rest, until it rests in God by love. Look up to the cross ; thus it speaks to you : "Christ died for all, that they also who live, may not now live to themselves, but unto Him who died for them and rose again."[2]

CHAPTER IV.

The Blessed Sacrament, her Heaven on Earth.

 HE divine will and the Blessed Sacrament are my Heaven on earth." It was thus that the Ven. Crescentia once expressed herself, and this was the perfect truth. Her faithful and loving heart had discovered the gate which alone, in this valley of tears and

---

[1] Gabriel, p. 63. [2] II. Cor. v. 15.

sins, forms the entrance to that better Paradise which we have lost in Adam. Her devotion to the Blessed Sacrament, the miracle of miracles, was in itself to be considered miraculous, and is consequently well fitted to explain the really prodigious occurrences to be related in this chapter, and which would otherwise be scarcely credible. Rev. Januarius Mayr, S. J., her confessor, in the report dictated by him on his death-bed, makes the same remark concerning the virtues of this godly virgin, and adds to this, that even a very superficial observation must convince those around her that she must possess a very extraordinary devotion to the great mystery of divine love. To prove it, he adduces two exterior signs, as reasons : First, that whenever the weakness of her sick body permitted her to do so, she dragged herself to the oratory, in order to adore the Saviour in the Blessed Eucharist, and that in all her leisure time, she would spend, not hours alone, but half-days before the Tabernacle.

We may here add from other witnesses, that when she could not walk, she had herself led, or sometimes even carried thither by other Sisters, and that there she knelt for hours like an angel, never raising her eyes ; that no noise, however sudden and startling it might be, could for an instant divert her attention from the object of her veneration and love ; that, moreover, the change of her color, the sighs of ardent love she uttered unconsciously, the seraphic expression of her countenance betrayed the interior fervor which consumed her heart. There, before the Tabernacle, she became, as it were, transfigured ; there all sufferings, even the sorrow of exile from the vision of the Supreme Good, were forgotten ; there she drank in full draughts of the living water promised by our Saviour, and from this Jacob's well of the Blessed Sacrament she drew light and hope, consolation and joy, nay, even bodily strength. On the other hand, the sense of exile stole over her as soon as absent in body from this, her "Heaven on earth."

Her Sisters in religion sometimes endeavored, from a compassionate feeling, to induce her to spare her sickly body, and not remain so long in the Church during the severe cold weather. But she would not let this hinder her, and answered:[1] "What do you mean? where will you find more strength and heat than in the Church?"

When the Blessed Sacrament was exposed for adoration, she remained kneeling before it all the time; obedience alone could then withdraw her from the Church. The Octave of Corpus Christi was a real jubilee for her. For the whole eight days she scarcely stirred from the oratory. Her devotion burst forth in higher flames at the thought, that throughout the Universal Church so many prayers went up, and so much honor was paid to our Lord in the Blessed Sacrament. During these days, her soul seemed to be in an ecstasy of delight and rapture. In a similar manner, she every Thursday celebrated the great mystery of love, and took pleasure on that day in thus expressing the feelings of her heart: "O Thursday, O wonderful day, O sweet day, on which God gave Himself to us as food!"

When she passed the Church, she always knelt down and devoutly adored the Blessed Sacrament. Whenever she heard of an accident, or when she was asked for advice in any difficulty, she went before the Blessed Sacrament, there to ask for light and help. When she was compelled to leave the Church, it was easily seen what force she had to use to compel herself to quit this "gate of Heaven." Although, in point of fact, it was only her body that left the holy place, her heart still remained before the eyes of the Lord. Besides this, on such occasions she constantly invoked one of her holy patrons, praying him to take her place and to praise and love the Saviour for her. When outside the Church, her eyes, when it was possible, turned towards the direction in which the Church was situated.

Father Mayr, S. J., adduces as the second exterior sign of her love to the Blessed Sacrament, the great care she

[1] Ott, B. II. C. 5.

took of everything that had reference to the Blessed Sacrament in the Church, the reverence with which she handled everything about it.   She decorated the Tabernacle and the altars as magnificently as it was possible, and wanted to have the chalice, ciborium, or whatever else was used, as beautiful and costly as they could be made.   She said that no expense ought to be spared in order that the Divine Majesty might not be altogether unbecomingly served.   The presents which, at a later date, were often made to her, she handed over immediately to the Superioress, with the request that they should be used in ornamenting the Church.   Nearly all the precious articles which the convent Church (which had been very poor in the beginning) afterwards possessed in abundance, came from her.   There was no work she liked better than to clean and decorate the Church, and to make or repair articles used at the Holy Sacrifice of the Mass.   She spared no pains to make it thoroughly clean and neat.

Often and willingly she spoke of the Blessed Sacrament, and did this with so much light and warmth that, as Sister M. Raphael Miller testifies,[1] her conversations on that subject far surpassed in intensity anything we hear in the common run of sermons, or read about in books.   Not seldom, however, she was suddenly struck dumb ; then she remained standing motionless, and the ecstatic expression of her face spoke more forcibly than the most eloquent words could do.

Above all, she endeavored to impress devotion to the Blessed Sacrament on her pupils, teaching them to visit it as often as possible, frequently to make a spiritual communion, and in every need to seek counsel, consolation, and help from the Redeemer.   Even when they were at work, she taught them to direct their heart and soul to the Blessed Tabernacle, and frequently to salute our Lord with the well-known greeting :   "Praise and honored be the Holy Sacrament of the altar !"   When she was Mother

---

[1] N. 12. § 73.

Superior, she introduced the pious custom among the Sisters of repeating, as they passed the Church, the angelic song of praise : " *Sanctus, sanctus, sanctus, Dominus Deus Sabaoth,*" "Holy, holy, holy, Lord God of Hosts." As she observed the greatest reverence in the Church, she required her subjects to do the like. It can hardly astonish us that the Redeemer should reward so extraordinary a devotion in a striking manner ; we relate two instances out of many, given by Father Ott :[1]

Crescentia had been the whole day hard at work, which she had carried on, however, while maintaining an uninterrupted union with her Saviour by prayer. She was tired out, but in spite of this, she, according to her habit, paid a visit to the Blessed Sacrament before she retired to rest, offering up her day's work and sinking her bodily weakness within the Sacred Heart; she then heard the following words proceed distinctly from the Tabernacle : "How beautiful are thy steps..... O prince's daughter !"[2] At another time she was obliged, in attending to her work, frequently to pass by the Blessed Sacrament, without being able to tarry. She could only, as she passed, frequently direct this ejaculation to her Redeemer : "My God, for love of Thee, and in obedience!" When she passed the altar for the last time, she noticed several flames hovering above it; she was confounded, and asked the Lord what it meant. The Lord answered: "These are the aspirations of love you sent up to Me when passing."

As the love of the Redeemer, in the Blessed Sacrament, manifests itself in the highest degree, not alone by gifts, but by giving Himself as food to the soul, that the soul "may abide in Him, and He in her,"[3] Holy Communion was for this angelical soul peculiarly "Heaven on earth." "O miracle of miracles!" she exclaimed, "Love—God is Love—has given Himself to me, poor creature as I am, for food, and left Himself to me in His last will and testament ! O banquet sweet to the soul, how I hunger and thirst after

---

[1] Ott, B. III. C. 2.   [2] Canticle vii. 1.   [3] John vi. 57.

Thee ! But because it is not permitted me to receive Thee as often as I desire in Holy Communion, I will bear the deprivation in patient silence and with the resignation I ought to feel, but I will prepare myself every day, that my Lord may find me always ready." On another occasion she said : "It seems to me that it would not be possible for me to refrain from Holy Communion, from the motive of humility, although I justly consider myself as the greatest of sinners, and truly unworthy of this grace. From obedience I do thus refrain, because the desire to do the will of God outweighs all other desires; I therefore do it without fail, when I am required to do so by obedience to my superiors and confessors."

Every one who saw her approach Holy Communion was not only edified, but altogether amazed ; among many others who bear witness to this, Alderman John Peter Kollman says :[1] " I have seen her at Holy Communion hundreds of times, and always with new amazement ; it was like seeing an angel, and not a mortal being, communicate." "Her face," Sister Gabriel says, "then became as beautiful as that of an angel, and she frequently diffused around her a fragrance of heavenly sweetness, that I have myself often perceived." Sister Raphael Miller gives a still closer description : "Her desire for Holy Communion was so intense, that as the appointed time drew near for her to receive, every delay appeared to her intolerable. Her hunger for this divine food reached such a height that she frequently appeared nearly dying. Before Holy Communion she was frequently so weak and frail looking, that she could scarcely walk or speak ; it was necessary to support her on both sides in order to lead her into the Church and to Holy Communion. After receiving, she acquired new strength, and I frequently perceived on these occasions an exquisite fragrance emanating from her. Her thanksgiving lasted as long as the duties of her office or obedience permitted, generally several hours. During

____

[1] Summ. N. 9, § 462.

that time she seemed beyond herself, and remained, immovable as a statue, on her knees. Her countenance appeared sometimes pale and white as wax, sometimes inflamed with a glowing redness like a rose, but so lovely, so marvellously beautiful, that whoever witnessed it was moved to devotion and love. All this I have myself seen, heard, and experienced."

As she not seldom fainted on the morning of Holy Communion, her confessors, especially Father Pamer, were of opinion that her unspeakable desire for this heavenly food was the cause of it. Perhaps her own words confirm this ; she said : "For one communion I would gladly suffer all the sicknesses of all mankind ; and, with the exception of possession and vision of God, I would rather forego the enjoyment of the pleasures of Heaven, than miss one Holy Communion."

We have already indicated with what care she prepared herself for Holy Communion ; we meet particulars of this in the communications of Sister Gabriel :[1] "Her whole life was spent in constant preparation for Holy Communion, and in thanksgiving for it. Everything she did was directed to that end by holy intentions. She commenced her preparation at midnight, or, at latest, at two o'clock, by multifarious acts of virtue. After this, she occupied herself with the mysteries of the passion of Christ, from the institution of the Blessed Sacrament till the Sacrifice upon the Cross, the commemoration of which is celebrated in the Holy Eucharist. She presented the bitter sufferings of the Redeemer with great interior recollection to the heavenly Father, clothing herself, as it were, in the merits of Christ, in order to be worthy to receive Him. After Holy Communion she first greeted her heavenly Bridegroom with ejaculations of ardent affection, such as : ' My heart and my body rejoice in the living God;' or, ' Whence proceeds this happiness, that the Son of my beloved Mother comes to me ?' After which she would say the Magnificat, add-

---

[1] Gabriel, p. 147.

ing appropriate explanations ; but she seldom got farther than the words : *'because He hath done great things to me.'*[1] The reason for this she did not give, but it lies in the fact that her soul was by that time carried away by the plenitude of light and love, that it entered into God and rested in Him without any further voluntary act."

A remarkable occurrence related by many witnesses shows to what a degree her eagerness for Holy Communion had attained. Sister M. Helena Kurz tells it as follows:[2] "When we approached Holy Communion on the day after Christmas in the year 1742, in the usual order, Crescentia's longing for Holy Communion revealed itself by a singular incident. Although, as Mother Superior, it was, according to our custom, her place to come last to the table of the Lord, this time she came as if flying after the two youngest Sisters who came there the first ; of these I was one, the other was Sister M. Raphael Miller—and she hastened to the communion-railing. By the construction of the place she could not avoid meeting us, yet we neither of us noticed her, nor did the other Sisters, until they saw her suddenly at the communion-railing. The space is so limited that only two Sisters can kneel there side by side, yet no disturbance took place among the communicants, which surprised every one, when it was seen that Crescentia was kneeling at the railing. At the dinner-table some of the Sisters asked her why she had broken through the custom and preceded the Sisters at Communion ? She blushed and answered humbly : 'Did I go too soon ? I do not know myself what I did. How stupid of me to make a disturbance everywhere. Dear Sisters, if I was in any one's way, or disturbed the usual order, I pray you, pardon me.'" With these humble words she sought to explain the occurrence, as if it had been occasioned by her awkwardness, but any one who examines the space in which it happened, which remains to-day as it was then, and considers well the circumstances, will scarcely doubt that in this

---

we have an example of ecstatic flight, of which Görres enumerates many cases.[1]

But we have to relate a still more marvellous incident which was successfully maintained by the defenders of her beatification, in spite of the sharp opposition made by the *Promoter fidei*.[2] It is said that on those days when the Sisters did not communicate in common, Crescentia for two years received the Blessed Sacrament from the hands of an angel. Such a wonderful mode of Holy Communion is also related in some few cases of Saints, as of St. Bonaventure, of the Blessed Clare of Montefalco, of St. Catherine of Sienna, of St. Mary Magdalene of Pazzi, and some others. But such a frequent repetition of the favor as was the case here, is perhaps unknown. Naturally these facts rest on her own testimony alone, but it is certain that she told them to her confessor, Rev. Ignatius Lieb, S. J., to her Superioress, Mother M. Johanna, as also to Sister M. Justina. Some exterior circumstances have also concurred in corroborating her own testimony. According to various reports of this most extraordinary event, it happened as follows:

Her desire to communicate every day had reached an incredible height, yet it was hardly to be expected that the Superiors would make an exception in her favor in regard to the usual number of communion-days permitted to the Sisters. In the year 1721, on the feast of her patron Saint Crescentia, July 15, the desire for the Blessed Sacrament increased during Mass to an intolerable height. Whilst the priest was saying the "*Domine non sum dignus*," "Lord, I am not worthy," the spouse of Christ saw a procession of angels coming from the altar to her. One of them, a seraph, carried the Blessed Sacrament and gave it to her according to the rites of the Church. This was repeated for two years, on every day when the usual Com-

---

[1] Görres: Mystik: B. II. p. 511—553.

[2] Summ. N. 9, § 25.—Act. B. Summ. Object. N. 12, and Resp. N. 144-150. Also Ott, B. II. p. 95, seq.

munion did not take place in common, until October 27, 1723.

When she told this remarkable case to her confessor, Father Ignatius Lieb, he became troubled and doubtful. But he expressed himself to the effect, that she ought to receive such a grace with great humility and gratitude, resolving in his heart, the while, to scrutinize this most extraordinary case severely. At once he had recourse to God in holy prayer, in order to acquire light from above in such a difficult matter. Without speaking of it to any one, he besought God not to permit her Holy Communion through angelic ministration for the next three days, while interiorly he forbade it to his penitent. He used to say Mass in the Sisters' Chapel and it had been at this holy Mass of her confessor that the miraculous communion had taken place, according to the information given by Crescentia.

At the third day he asked the servant of God how she was. She replied: "I cannot be easy; for three days I have not received Holy Communion and I fear that I have committed some sin." He dismissed her with some commonplace words. Then he prayed God to grant her this grace again, if indeed it proceeded from Him. On the day after, the virgin told him that the holy angels had again communicated to her the Bread of Heaven. Her confessor said nothing in reply, but afterwards he spoke to the Mother Superior of the affair, and said that he no longer doubted its truth. He was soon to be yet more strengthened in this opinion, as we shall relate immediately. The true spirit of the Ven. Crescentia was shown also in this : that these rare graces were not pleasing to her soul, on the contrary, she mistrusted anything out of the usual course of things. Holy Communion from the hand of the priest seemed to her to convey more certainty and merit, inasmuch as faith and humility were more exercised thereby. She ceased not to pray earnestly to God that He would permit her daily to receive the Blessed

Sacrament in the usual manner. This favor seemed the more difficult to obtain, as, in her great humility, she esteemed herself unworthy of consideration and could not venture to ask for so striking an exception to the usual order. Divine Providence, however, so ordered it that her desires were granted without a petition being presented by herself on the subject. She became seriously ill from excess of love ; an inexplicable heat parched the very blood in her veins ; no remedy had any effect ; she was nearly dying. At this emergency a thought struck her father confessor, who had already directed her for four years, and at the same time the same thought came to Mother Johanna, that the best remedy would be for the priest to give her Holy Communion every day. When they had communicated this thought to each other, they resolved to consult the Father Provincial on the subject. Father Sebastian Höss, who then filled that office, had himself, as we have already related, received indubitable proofs that God was conducting Crescentia by extraordinary ways ; and God having thus disposed it, he gave his consent at once. The joy and gratitude of the servant of God was beyond all conception. The 27th of October, 1723, she made use of this privilege for the first time. To this permission the condition was at first annexed that she should not receive publicly, but only in the presence of her fellow-Sisters. Later on this restriction was removed. The expected effect of this grace was justified in the event. She recovered her health immediately, without other remedy.

This same father confessor, a short time afterwards, thought it right to test once more the spirit and obedience of his penitent. One day he forbade her Holy Communion. Silently, in all humility, she submitted to a command so hard to her. God rewarded her obedience, while He, at the same time, forcibly bore witness to the truth of the extraordinary manner in which she had previously received the Bread of Heaven by the hands of angels.

When her confessor, on the same morning on which he

had denied her Holy Communion, was at Mass, and about to receive the Body of the Lord, he perceived, to his great alarm, that only one-half of the host previously broken was on the paten. He searched most carefully for the other part, but in vain; finally, he had to continue and conclude the holy Mass. When the doors of the Church had been locked, he recommenced his search; he examined the whole altar carefully, but could find no trace of the missing particle. Altogether confounded and dejected, he mentioned the occurrence, which was most inexplicable to him, to the Superioress, and both together concluded to ask Crescentia about it. She replied in confusion: "My angel guardian communicated me with the other half of the Sacred Host." From that time no confessor ever again withheld Holy Communion from her, although she presented herself, time and again, for the acceptance of this *to her* most difficult act of obedience. Thus, she received daily, for more than twenty years, until her happy death.

Even before the year 1721 she had received the Blessed Sacrament in a manner equally wonderful.[1] Father Ott[2] calls this case a forerunner of the grace so often subsequently repeated. In order to carry out the directions given by the Father Provincial to test the servant of God most strictly, Mother Johanna, the Superioress, commanded her to go into the kitchen instead of into the Church, on a day of general communion. Humbly obeying, she still remained interiorly absorbed in devotion, while she performed her work. God rewarded her by having the food of angels served up to her by angels' hands, in the very spot where obedience had placed her.

The ways of grace enumerated above belong, in fact, to the rarest of which we have any knowledge; but since God never lets Himself be surpassed in generosity by any creature, and since Crescentia possessed the grace to give herself to God without reserve, and with the greatest fidelity

---

[1] Act. B. Summ. Obj. N. 12.   [2] Ott, B. II. p. 268.

and perseverance, it becomes in some slight degree intelligible why the most generous King extended more and more the miracles of His power and love, as contained in this Holy Sacrament, to so holy a soul. In regard to the effects produced by Holy Communion in her soul, we can only point to them, not describe them. All the brilliant promises which the Saviour has attached to this Holy Sacrament [1] were fulfilled in her, particularly the promise: "He that eateth My flesh . . . . . abideth in Me, and I in him." This heavenly food tested in her person its transforming power of changing the receiver into the living Bread, into Christ, inasmuch as she could say: "I live now, not I, but Christ liveth in me." [2] Her thoughts and wishes, her words and actions, her life, love, and suffering, all moved round one central point, Christ, who, as Lord and King, alone occupied the throne of her heart. She herself could find no words in which to explain to her confessor the effect produced in her by Holy Communion. She could only say that she beheld the humanity of Christ in an ineffable light, and that in the highest of all mysteries, that of the Blessed Trinity, she understood how the Son from all eternity is begotten of the Father, and how the Holy Ghost proceeds from both. [3]

The ecstasies already mentioned, and which nearly always came to her after Holy Communion, as well as the remarkable bodily strength which she always received therefrom, bear evident witness to the richest streams of grace which flowed from the Blessed Sacrament into her soul. Even the extraordinary effect, that Holy Communion often for a long time took the place of all bodily food, is undeniable. During the last six weeks of her life it was her only nourishment, as we shall see hereafter. During her severe illness in the year 1742, which lasted six months, she took scarcely anything else than this celestial food, so that every one thought it could not be by a natural way that her life was sustained; the quantity of bodily nourish-

---

[1] Compare John vi.   [2] Gal. ii. 20.   [3] Ott, B. I.

ment she took was too small for that.' Instances of this
kind, concerning the effects of the Holy Eucharist on the
bodily frame, are numerous in the lives of the Saints ; not
a little of it is to be found in the Mystic of Görres.'

In union with devotion to the Holy Sacrament of the
altar, she, from infancy upwards, practised with great pre-
dilection and affection the devotion to the Sacred Heart
of Jesus, so closely allied to the other, and which in these
later centuries has been spread in such an extraordinary
manner over the whole Church. She could not tire of
meditating on the love and mercy of the Heart of the Man-
God, of praising it, of loving it ; she lived, as she herself
expressed it, more in this Heart than in her own. The
words which she, when a child, had heard from the mouth
of the Lord Jesus in the vision we related before : "Thy
heart and My Heart shall be but one Heart," were most
deeply impressed upon her. Other visions and other words
addressed to her, which had reference to the same object,
came at a later date, and enkindled in her a still greater
love for the Most Sacred Heart of the Redeemer. We give
some of these, culled from Father Ott : '

Once, when she was kneeling before the Blessed Sacrament, immersing her own heart with great fervor in the
Sacred Heart of her Divine Redeemer, as she often used to
do, it appeared to her as if many brilliantly shining rays
came from the Tabernacle and penetrated her heart ; at the
same time she seemed to hear these words : "These are
the marks of My love towards you, with which I will inflame
your heart and unite it to Mine." This grace gave her
courage to ask for a still greater favor, namely, that God
would give her His own Heart, so that she might thus be
enabled to love Him worthily. This petition was granted
her, later, on the Feast of the Sacred Heart of Jesus. In a
sublime vision the Saviour appeared to her, and gave her
His Most Sacred Heart, not, indeed, in the ordinary way,
as He gives it to all pious Christians at Holy Communion,

---

¹ Act. B. Summ. Add. p. 14.   ² B. III. p. 370.   ³ Ott, B. III. C. 2.

but in a peculiar mystic union, so that she possessed a special title and grant of donation to this exalted treasure. Carried away by surprise and love, she, on her part, gave her own heart to her heavenly Spouse without the least restriction, praying that He would make it wholly His own, subject it entirely to His royal sway, make it ready to do His holy will, equally in pain as in pleasure, in life as in death. The effect of this vision was inexpressible ; it appeared as if from this happy exchange of hearts a fresh start had been made for a new life, a more perfect one, one more carefully modelled after the virtues of the Divine Heart.

Once, in an unusually great interior abandonment for many days and nights, she sighed with the desire, and in the words of the Spouse in the Canticle of Canticles, after the presence of her only Love. The Saviour then appeared to her, brilliant in the glory of inaccessible light ; His Heart was open and pierced with many arrows. When the spouse of the Crucified compassionately asked : " My Lord, who has wounded Thee thus ? " He answered with a benign countenance : " My child, it is thou who hast wounded My heart with the sighs of love thou art continually sending up to Me ; they are so many arrows of love. I am well pleased with it. Thy joy shall increase by suffering and love." These words proved their divine origin by producing in her soul the effect they described ; that is, an insatiable desire for greater sufferings, and for illimitable love.

Dear Christians, Jesus Christ has taken His abode among men in the Blessed Sacrament for your benefit also, and for you also was the word spoken : " He that eateth this Bread shall live forever." [1] For you, too, the sanctuary lamp is lit, to show you the Tabernacle where there is Heaven on earth. Then turn no longer a deaf ear to the sweet invitation of the Lord : " Come to Me, all you that labor, and are burdened, and I will refresh you." [2]

---

[1] John vi. 59.   [2] Matth. xi. 28.

CHAPTER V.

The Life and Passion of Christ, the Subject of Crescentia's Constant Meditation. [1]

O wish to know nothing save Jesus Christ and Him crucified, with Him to live in the most intimate spiritual union, with Him to suffer, die, and rise again, is, according to the doctrine of the Apostle St. Paul, the interior, the true life of a Christian ; it forms the quintessence of the lives of all the Saints, and is also the spirit of Ven. M. Crescentia. We must say that she lived wholly in Christ and that Christ lived in her. From the very first years of her life, her thoughts and feelings, her hopes and affections, attracted by extraordinary grace, turned to the Man-God, and this germ of interior life grew up to such an extent and in such strength, that all the faculties of her soul took fast hold in this direction alone—she knew but Christ, and Him crucified. Lovingly to meditate on Him, her Spouse, in all His mysteries and to love so to meditate, was the only business she had at heart ; it was her life, her Heaven on earth. Led by the guiding hand of Holy Church, which every year, so to speak, sets before the eyes and hearts of her children the great work of the world's redemption, by the feasts of the ecclesiastical year, her soul followed, with undivided sympathy, the development of this truly divine drama, accompanied every scene with pious meditations and spiritual exercises, or rather by sublime contemplation and mystical participation. She renewed in herself and lived again the life of her Celestial Head, of whom she was a living member. Jesus as a Child in the manger ; as the only Teacher of truth ; as the Sacrifice on the cross ; as her Reward in Heaven, as her Spouse in the Blessed Sacrament ; these were the principal headings under which she

---

[1] Summ. passim.

meditated upon the unfathomable riches of His grace and love; they were the sources whence she derived, not only an infinite fervor of devotion, but also a plenitude of sublime acts of virtue, which, like to ring within ring, linked her life together till it became a glorious imitation of the life of Christ.

The holy season of Christmas, with its feasts before and after, was to her a time of heavenly joy and love. Her heart was indefatigable in calling down from Heaven the Divine Child, reverently to adore Him, and to receive Him with inexpressible delight and thanksgiving. During the whole of Advent, and for three weeks beforehand, she was intent on duly preparing herself for the birth of our Lord. Every moment of time and every action of the day was pressed into this service and directed to the realization of the great mystery of the Incarnation. With interior and exterior virtues she, incessantly occupied in its erection, built a crib for the Divine Infant in her heart. The longing sighs of the fathers of the Old Testament for the coming of the Redeemer of the world continually rose with like fervor from her heart towards Heaven, increasing in intensity as the anniversary of the day of salvation drew near. She had constantly before her sight the Virgin Mother and the blessed Fruit of her womb, and vied with the angels in adoring and loving the only-begotten Son of the Father, who, by the instrumentality of the Holy Ghost, became the Son of a mortal Mother. And as the praise and love of the angels themselves seemed to her all too little, she turned towards the Immaculate Mother with the petition that she would praise, love, and affectionately embrace the Infant in her (Crescentia's) name.

Fastings and many other works of penance were her daily offering for the glory of the Redeemer, and in honor of the "silent Word" she kept silence so rigidly, that she scarcely uttered a word, unless charity or obedience called it forth. On the holy Christmas eve she appeared to be more in Heaven than on earth. We cannot follow the flight of her spirit, rapt in joy and love, even at a distance. According to the accounts given by herself, the days from Christmas to the Epiphany of our Lord were the sweetest and loveliest days of the whole year. When the word "Bethlehem" alone, uttered at any time of the year, was sufficient to raise her to an ecstasy, we may form some idea of the effect the feast-days themselves must have produced.

Concerning the impression produced by that one word, Sister Raphael Miller, among many other witnesses, testifies: [1] "I noticed this impression in a special way, when I made my profession at her hands. From sickness, Crescentia was at that time as pale as death, but the 'Babe of Bethlehem' was scarcely mentioned when her face grew red as fire and she became as if 'out of herself.'" During this season she was favored with many visions, and with words addressed to her. We will give a few of them from the report of Father Ott: [2] As she in Advent once greeted the Virgin Mother and her Divine Infant with the words familiar to her: "Praised and blessed be thy noble treasure, O Mary, which thou didst receive from the Holy Ghost ! and praised be the blessed Fruit of thy womb," the Mother of God appeared to her with the Infant, surrounded by the splendor of Heaven ; she presented the Child to her, saying : "This is the blessed Fruit of my womb." The servant of God felt her heart penetrated by inexpressible feelings, as she held the Divine Child in her arms ; her spirit became transfigured from the light streaming into her and lost itself in God.

But the deepest impression made upon her mind was that caused by the passion of Christ. She was uninterruptedly occupied with it and it was more than a mere meditation with her. Her whole interior being seemed as if it were drawn in and had lost itself in the suffering Redeemer ; she could say with St. Paul, in a mystical

---

sense : "With Christ I am nailed to the cross."[1] On merely hearing the words " Passion of Christ," she would break forth into tears and say, at times, with a broken voice : "Oh! what is that ? God suffering and dying!"[2] When, on Thursday evening, the signal of the bell was given for the agony of our Lord, and on Friday for that of His death, her color would change, and tears flowed abundantly from her eyes.

There was nothing which she more earnestly recommended than a constant meditation on the sufferings of Christ ; in that, she would say, " lies an infinite treasure and the living fruit of Paradise : whoever eats of it, shall never die. For a religious, the holy cross should be the main book; in this book, written outside with blood, inside with love, every perfection is taught, as well how to act as how to suffer." She did this herself. As the bee, flying from flower to flower, sucks the sweet juice and prepares it for honey, so did her mind fly to all the wounds of the Lord, to gather from His sorrows the sweetness of love and the honey of grace ; for the more her mind dwelt on the passion of our Lord, the more abundantly did He pour on her the flood of His graces, which seemed to drown all the faults of nature, to fructify every virtue, and transform all suffering into love and delight.

In her spiritual intercourse with those subject to her, she instructed them how to enter into the particulars of the sufferings of Christ, both when at meditation and at work. She divided the whole history of the passion into many points for them, distributing these points to the days of the week, and the hours of the day, and instructing them how to unite their own work and occupation to the corresponding mysteries and merits of the suffering Redeemer. In order to get an external hold they were to consider the objects and tools of their occupation as a mirror in which some mystery was reflected. For instance,[3] when drinking they should think of the gall and vinegar

---

[1] Gal. ii. 19.　　[2] Summ. N. 12　　[3] Summ. N. 12. § 67-71.

presented to Christ on the cross : when drawing water, of the brook Cedron. The linen before them should remind them of the sheets in the sepulchre, or of Veronica's veil. Forks and knives, of the lance ; plates, of the crown of thorns ; when ascending a stair-case they should in spirit go up Mount Calvary ; when carrying wood, help the Saviour to carry His cross ; and so of the rest. By diligently practising exercises of this description, the servant of God maintained that they would soon acquire an aptitude to see, as from themselves, some remembrance of the suffering Saviour everywhere and be spontaneously impelled to perform every action in union with Christ. Yet this exercise, she prudently added, must be carried on without any violent exertion of the mind, and was not to be entertained as a mere play of thought, which would only bring forth leaves instead of fruit ; on the contrary, the aim should be rather to unite one's interior affections with the Redeemer and imitate His virtues, alike in our hidden as in our public life. This is the aim and end of every true devotion. If, for example, they wished to represent to themselves the mournful parting of Christ from His sorrowful Mother, they must excite the same affections in their own hearts: " Oh, with what sorrow do the holiest persons part ; then will I also separate myself willingly from parents, relatives, and from everything that is not God." And when they remembered the blow Christ received on His cheek, they should at once say within their hearts : "I, too, will silently and meekly suffer all humiliations for love of Him." In order more and more to foster veneration for the passion of Christ in her religious community, and thus open for them the most copious fountain of spiritual grace and consolation, she, as soon as she was appointed Mother Superior, had large pictures of the Stations made; these are still in the convent. Also, with all the influence she could command, and yet more by her example than by precept, she fostered the salutary custom of performing the Stations, a custom which, thanks be to the Lord, is now spreading more and more over the whole Church. As long as she could drag herself along, she never omitted, for a single day, performing the Stations with edifying devotion. At the beginning and end of this devotion she tarried a long while before the statue of the Mother of Dolors. At the beginning she chose her for her companion on the sorrowful road, and at the conclusion she offered everything, through those hands, rich in grace, to her beloved Saviour. At her last sickness she had the pictures of the Stations set up in her room, to have them always before her eyes while on her couch of suffering.

Among the mysteries of the passion she had a special reverence for the silence which Jesus observed when calumniated and scoffed at. The words, " Jesus held His peace," served her as a shield which enabled her easily to ward off the most fiery arrows of abuse. She also liked to tarry a long while in the Garden of Olives, which offered her, in Christ's agony unto death and in the mysterious sweating of blood, abundant matter for pious reflections. There her heart was filled with bitter sorrow and with ardent love. The heart-rending parting of the Mother of God from her Son, her station beneath the cross, the three hours' martyrdom of Christ, were to her an inexhaustible ocean of holy meditation and of ardent affection, nay, a means by which her interior being seemed to be transformed into a likeness of the suffering and loving Redeemer. In Lent, and more particularly in Holy Week, her mind scarcely left the cross at all ; she would kneel for hours, with arms extended, rigid, and immovable, before a picture of the Crucified, or of the Mother of Sorrows. No one could understand how one so sick and feeble as she was could continue so long in such a position.

On the Fridays of Lent, and particularly in Holy Week, she observed her usual fasts in a yet stricter degree : sunk in profound silence and recollection, she never turned her eyes away from the suffering Saviour. Her sympathy for Him tore her heart to pieces, and manifested itself by irre-

pressible tears, by copious bleeding of the heart, and by
her whole appearance, which was that of one so exhausted
and so intensely suffering, that she often appeared to be almost dying from sheer pain of the heart.

Such an uninterrupted and loving occupation with the
suffering of Christ could not fail to bring forth extraordinary effects. Her imagination was so filled with holy representations of the passion, that she had scarcely room for
anything else. Even in sleep she was in spirit on the
Mount of Olives, or in other places where the Redeemer
had suffered. Her mind read in these pictures nothing
but love, given and returned. It was a striking fact, that
she could give the slightest historical or geographical circumstance of the life and suffering of Christ with as much
exactitude as if she had seen it herself. It was impossible
that she could have acquired this knowledge from books.

A higher light must have at least co-operated here ; a
light such as we so often find in holy souls, and particularly must acknowledge and admire in the saintly Anne
Catherine Emmerich. A Father of the Franciscan Order
who had spent many years in the Holy Land, spoke to her
of the holy places. He could not suppress his astonishment
when she gave him a most accurate description of Jerusalem, Bethlehem, Nazareth, and the rest : he expressed
himself to the effect that she knew them all better than he
did himself. This assiduous meditation on the passion of
Christ produced the most precious effect in her soul, for
thereby she died totally to everything that is not God
Himself, her heart melted away entirely in her Crucified
Love, and she acquired an ardent desire for suffering of
every kind. She seems to have considered it the most enviable lot a mortal can attain to, that of being enabled to
share the martyrdom of Christ and of experiencing the
interior and exterior torments He underwent.

It would be surprising if Christ had satisfied this crav-
ing for His passion, infused by Himself, merely by sufferings of an ordinary and exterior character. We should

rather expect that she, like so many contemplative Saints, was to be made worthy to participate in the passion of the Crucified, in a mystical manner, even though she did not precisely receive the grace of stigmatization. The reality of such a suffering in her is placed beyond doubt. She sought, indeed, to conceal such a mystery from the eyes of men, but it could not always remain hidden from her Sisters in the convent. They noticed [1] that on Thursday evening, when the bell was rung for the devotion of the agony, her whole being was so painfully changed that she resembled a dying person. On Friday morning she could scarcely walk or speak, so crushed was she with pain and grief; she was then a real picture of misery. This misery reached its height from nine o'clock in the morning till three o'clock in the afternoon. For the most part she, on Friday, neither ate, drank, nor spoke at all, or, at most, scarcely at all. The Mother Superior very often commanded her then to go to bed, where she found her several times wholly stiff and apparently half dead. After three o'clock she revived; she was, however, so exhausted, that frequently she could not even eat anything. This manifestation recurring at regular intervals and no one being able to find a natural cause for it, the conclusion arrived at was, that on these days the servant of God was not so much meditating on the sufferings of Christ, as sympathizing with them, and by this sympathy reproducing them in her own person. For many years (one report says three years) this state of hers appeared prominently in the highest degree and in a striking manner ; [2] it then became less visible to the eyes of others. Father Ott [3] says that by continual prayer she had obtained the grace, that while the pains continued the same, they should not reveal themselves exteriorly in so great a degree before the eyes of others. But a closer observation could not fail to apprehend that on such days a most extraordinary suffering continued to be

---

[1] Summ. N. 12, § 23, 61, 66.—Gabriel, p. 224.—Ott. B. II. C. 5.

[2] Katzenberger, Life, etc. C. 13.   [3] Ott, B. II. C. 13.

felt. Sister Joachim Kögl confidently asserts that she had noticed it for eleven years, and Sister Bernardina Gast had observed it for nineteen years when they were living together.

More reliable details are not forthcoming, especially as the reports of Sister M. Anna Neth and the narrative founded upon them of Father Kilian Katzenberger, are not trustworthy. A remark of the latter may, however, find a place here; he said that Crescentia herself had acknowledged to him that she suffered pains in her head, as if it were pricked with thorns, and in her left side, as if it had been pierced by a double-edged sword. We add two more miraculous occurrences, which are undeniable, and are related at full length by Father Ott.[1]

In Crescentia's cell there was a large crucifix for which she had a special veneration; several marvellous things, which she considered it necessary to tell the Mother Superior, had occurred in reference to it. The prudent Superioress feared that there might have been some deception practised; therefore, one morning, when the servant of God was in the choir with the rest of the Sisters, she secretly took the crucifix away from the cell and concealed it in a place to which no one had access. All through the day she waited, in expectation that Crescentia would notify her of the loss of it. But, as no word came, she herself, on the second day, asked Crescentia if she still had the crucifix; she, however, had never missed it, and the Superioress convinced herself that it still hung in its usual place, though no human hand could have carried it back. Herein she found a just confirmation that the communications made to this favored soul contained no deception.

The second occurrence is still more remarkable, and every one who enters the cell formerly occupied by the servant of God can, with his own eyes, assure himself of it. Once, when meditating with great recollection on the bloody scourging of Christ,[2] she was rapt in ecstasy and the

---

[1] Ott, B. II. C. 13.   [2] Act. B. Resp. § 173.

instruments of scourging were shown to her, namely, a whip twisted of sharp thorns, and a scourge with fifteen pointed hooks. When Mother Johanna heard of this vision (in what way does not appear), she wished for a proof of its truth, and commanded Crescentia to make a drawing of both the instruments of torture, just as she had seen them, and to do this in the room in which they were, before the very eyes of the Superioress, so that every possibility of her receiving foreign help should be excluded.

She knew that Crescentia had never received any instruction in drawing or sketching, nor practised either in even the least degree. But the heroic obedience of the spouse of Christ shrank from no difficulty, was terrified by no obstacle ; it could accomplish what was naturally impossible, as we shall also see elsewhere. Speedily she went to work, and drew on a large piece of paper the rod of thorns and the scourge, using the simplest means, and producing the effect in but few touches, but these so artistic and perfect, that no one can comprehend how she could have rendered the work so complete without ever having received any instruction or practice in sketching. Many thousands of people who have seen these drawings, and among these some great masters in painting, have expressed their admiration of them. [1]

Yet in reality it is less marvellous, less important, that this holy soul should have represented the scourges on paper, than that, through the power of the Holy Ghost, a vivid image of the Crucified should have been imprinted on her heart, or rather that she herself became a living picture of the suffering Redeemer. But this latter is re-

---

[1] The photograph added here will certainly convince the reader of the masterly construction of these pictures : the writing on them is a certificate that M. Crescentia, though entirely ignorant of drawing and sketching, made them herself. Mother M. Joachim Kögl, July 1, 1744, a few months after the death of the servant of God, testifies to this officially. A supernatural assistance from God in the performance of this work seems to guarantee in an unmistakable manner the genuineness of the vision. Yet no absolute certainty is here arrived at (as the teachers of mystical life explain more particularly) that the actual instruments of scourging were such as are here described.

Compare Scaramelli, Mystic, B. II. i. Sect. c. 18.

quired of every Christian, namely, that in the sight of
God he "be made conformable to the image of His Son."[1]

Therefore, O Christian, if you are really in earnest concerning your salvation, learn in the living book of the
Cross, and direct your mind and soul to your suffering
Saviour: "Christ, therefore, having suffered in the flesh,
be you also armed with the same thought."[2]

CHAPTER VI.

The Holy Ghost the Sweet Guest of her Soul.

BY Baptism the Holy Ghost, with the Father and the
Son, takes in a mysterious way His abode in the
heart of a Christian; in the ordinary development
of the life of grace, His action is, however, so concealed
in the interior being, or so limited, by the free activity of
mankind, that but few traces of it penetrate to the outside.
With Crescentia, the peculiar child of grace, however, the
operation of the Holy Ghost, manifested itself so openly
from the very first years of her childhood (as we have already related) that every one was astonished at it. She
alone knew it not; but she honored the Holy Ghost, by
faith, with the most affectionate reverence. Her aim and
strenuous desire was to become a pure temple of the Holy
Ghost,[3] to cleanse her heart from every particle of the dust
of imperfection, which could in any way offend the eyes of
the heavenly Guest, and then to embellish it with every
virtue. In every difficulty, temptation, and suffering, she
at once invoked the Holy Ghost. As a preparation for
Pentecost, she made a novena with extraordinary fervor.
To severe penitential practices she added many reflections,
prayers, and continual aspirations of love. With special

---

[1] Rom. viii. 29.   [2] 1. Peter iv. 1.   [3] Summ. N. 12, § 128.

relish she repeated the beautiful Church hymns of the Holy Ghost, particularly the "*Veni Creator Spiritus.*" Thus it can scarcely excite surprise that on that solemn feast, and during its octave, she used to receive the gifts of the Holy Ghost with extraordinary graces in great abundance. This interior intercourse of her heart with the Holy Ghost was accompanied with many apparitions, as He often appeared visible to the eyes of her soul, in the form of a young man. This is stated in the Acts of her Beatification [1] and also by Father Ott, [2] from whom we will quote but one vision out of the many he relates:

The Holy Ghost appeared to her on Pentecost Sunday and filled her soul in an ineffable manner with His sevenfold gifts. At the same time she heard these words: "Whoever loves nothing but Me alone, I will confirm in Myself and in My grace." Connected with this vision, was an operation of enlightening grace, which she had hitherto never experienced, which, as she says herself, could not be explained by words, but which left in her soul a light altogether new to her. This unveiled to her the abyss of her nothingness, and disclosed every movement of nature in a manner clear as daylight; and more yet, it enabled her to notice and distinguish plainly, in her own soul, the slightest movement and effect of that grace. This light was doubtless a most singular and precious grace, enabling her to advance with giant strides on the road to perfection.

These visions of the Holy Ghost appearing to Crescentia under the form of a young man, gave occasion to great difficulties at the preliminaries of her beatification. In order to place the reader in a position to distinguish truth from falsehood, we find ourselves obliged to depart from the temporal order of the succession of events, and to pass to occurrences which happened after the death of the servant of God. We also venture to hope that this apparent digression will not be read without interest and instruction.

---

[1] Act. B. Summ. Obj. N. 11, § 2.   [2] Ott, B. III. C. 2.

During the latter years of Ven. Mother Crescentia's life, the renown of her sanctity spread far beyond the boundaries of Germany, and even reached the ears of Pope Benedict XIV., so renowned for his astonishing erudition, and who then ruled the Church. Perhaps the reports he had heard of her marvellous sanctity had, as it often happens, received additions, exaggerations, or erroneous constructions on the long road by which they travelled to him; be that as it may, the prudent Pope, who was specially experienced in this branch of theology, thought fit to address letters, dated May 17th, 1744, to Bishop Joseph of Augsburg, Landgrave of Hesse, concerning the servant of God, admonishing him to oppose in due season probable fallacies, and ordering a summary report to be sent to himself of her life and miraculous gifts. He acted upon the supposition that Crescentia was still alive, although, in fact, she had died six weeks before, on the 5th of April. The commission to examine her life thus fell through of itself, but the bishop believed that he was acting in accordance with the wishes of the Holy Father, by instituting the projected inquiry even after her death.

In order to carry this out he intrusted the design to two men of distinction, well versed in theology: these were the spiritual counsellor, John Baptist Bassi, canon of St. Mauritius, and the renowned writer, Eusebius Amort, regular canon of Pollingen, and episcopal theologian, who is known by his works on moral theology and canon law, which are widely circulated, as also by his acute criticisms of the book of the Ven. Maria D'Agreda, entitled, "The City of God." By said criticisms he had come into a learned controversy with several Friars of the Order of St. Francis, who defended the work. This matter, at that period, excited considerable attention and interest among the public. These two gentlemen engaged Father Celestine Agricola, O. S. B., Notary Apostolic, as their notary, and on September 16th, 1744, began the investigation intrusted to them, in the convent at Kaufbeuren. They by no means observed the customary canonical formalities ; they questioned the witnesses not individually, but collectively, without swearing them in ; then the questions asked were of such a general character that but meagre information could be obtained. This was the judgment pronounced by Benedict XIV. himself, as the Brief we will shortly bring forward shows. The Acts drawn up in consequence of this investigation were transmitted to Rome, and by the Pope they were in the first place intrusted to a special commission for examination, after which they were read by himself.[1]

The result was, that the Holy Father did not find the suspicion of deceit in any way confirmed, but neither did he discover any convincing proof of extraordinary sanctity.   On the contrary, he believed that he had found indications of something very objectionable in these Acts ; namely, that the servant of God had originated, published, and approved pictures of the Holy Ghost under the form of a young man ; moreover, that she had distributed beads, crosses, and other blessed articles of devotion, which the people believed had been blessed and indulgenced by God Himself ; and since the bishop had written, in a letter which accompanied the Acts, that representations of the Holy Ghost in said form had been promulgated in his diocese and had been prohibited by him, the Holy Father, on October 1st, A. D. 1745, issued a new brief to the Bishop of Augsburg, which occupies six folio pages in the Bullarium.[2] A short synopsis of this brief will explain the state of this affair to the reader :

The Holy Father first advises the bishop that in the investigation concerning the sanctity of the deceased servant of God, the rules should be faithfully observed which in such cases are applied at Rome and which he himself had

---

[1] The original manuscript of this report was not to be found at the process of beatification ; nor even an authenticated copy, notwithstanding every effort made to obtain one. A sketch of it without the conclusion was discovered and is printed thus : Act. B. Summ. Obj. N. 5. The author of this biography, however, found an authenticated copy in the parish archives of Kaufbeuren, which had been brought thither from a suppressed convent.

[2] Bullarium Bened. XIV., tom 1, edit. Rom. p. 500, edit Luxemb., p. 318.

compiled in his work on Canonization ; then he desired that the whole subject should be for the present postponed, as present circumstances seemed to require this, while meantime watch should be kept, as to how things would develop themselves. He then refers to the pictures of the Holy Ghost. The question as to whether Crescentia originated, distributed, and approved these pictures, he will at present leave undecided ; he descants, however, at large, on the question as to whether it is permitted to represent the Holy Ghost in the form of a young man, and to use and venerate such pictures.

He first approves of the measures taken by the bishop against such pictures, and exhorts him not to permit them to be made and promulgated, nay, even—prudently and without noise—to put those out of the way which already exist. He then gives his reasons for this prohibition with great clearness and astonishing erudition. In this he proceeds from the acknowledged principle of the Church, that the Godhead being in itself spiritual and invisible, cannot be represented by any imagery, and can only be pictured in that form in which it has deigned to appear to men, according to the testimony of Holy Writ. He establishes this sentence as the correct one, and applies it to the representation of the Holy Ghost ; according to this, and to the custom of Holy Church, the Holy Ghost is to be represented by the symbolic form of the Dove, or, when picturing His descent on the Apostles, etc., in the form of fiery tongues. Any other representation illustrative of the Holy Ghost is not in accordance with the principles and customs of the Church. He then solves several objections, and finally touches upon the second accusation, which falsely attributes to Crescentia the charge that she had promulgated false indulgences, superstitious blessings and practices. Of this, however, we will speak in another place.

This letter of the Holy Father had manifestly decided nothing respecting Crescentia and her beatification. Yet it gave occasion to postponing the opening of the canonical process of her beatification, and it surrounded the beatification itself with more difficulties than otherwise would have arisen. But, on the other hand, it caused the whole affair to be thoroughly investigated, and finally to terminate to the honor of the servant of God. It was because the *Promotor fidei*,' referring to this Brief, objected to the opening of the process, that a special investigation was instituted by a papal commission, concerning the points in question, in the place itself, and the depositions of many witnesses were taken under oath. The result of these lengthy proceedings we will here give in a few brief words.

First : Ven. M. Crescentia was, in no sense, the originator of this manner of representing the Holy Ghost: such pictures had been in vogue from time immemorial, in many churches of Germany, especially in the dioceses of Salzburg, Passau, Constance, and Munich-Freising ; for instance, at Munich at St. Peter's, on the main altar of the Church of the Carmelite nuns, and elsewhere. In the convent at Kaufbeuren, also, the Sisters had some old copper engravings, made before Crescentia was born, representing the Holy Ghost in the shape of a young man, with this inscription in Latin : " In this form the Holy Ghost revealed Himself to the holy virgin Theresa." Secondly, it was not Crescentia, but her Superior, Mother Johanna, who had the little copper engravings made, as well as the large and beautiful picture of the Holy Ghost. Under this Superioress, such pictures were frequently distributed by the convent; on several of them the name of Crescentia appears, but the writing on all those, at least, which the author has seen, betrays the hand of Sister M. Anna Neth. Thirdly, as soon as Crescentia herself became Superioress, she forbade those under her rule to distribute any more of these pictures, and to cut off the opportunity of transgressing this prohibition, she took away from them all

---

¹ The officer whose duty it is to establish the validity of all objections made to a beatification or canonization.

they had left. This is affirmed on oath by the Sisters who themselves had to give them up. In this way all the suppositions on which the *Promotor fidei* based his objections fell to the ground.

The truth of the matter seems to be, that not infrequently Crescentia had had a vision of the Holy Ghost in which He became visible to the eyes of her spirit as a young man of beautiful form, clothed in a garment as white as snow, bare-headed, with curling hair, His head being surrounded by seven tongues of fire. It is thus stated by Father Ott, and by several other witnesses, who are mentioned in the Acts, and who assert that they heard the matter from others, who in turn had heard it from herself. The genuineness and reality of this vision we may safely leave to the defender of Crescentia in the process of her beatification, and with him maintain, that no probable reason can be alleged against the possibility and divine source of such a vision.

If we rely on the report of Father Ott, which is confirmed by the tradition of the convent, Sister M. Crescentia had her own share in producing the large and beautiful picture of the Holy Ghost.[1] According to his statement, it happened thus : Mother Superior Johanna, who had already ordered many little pictures of the Holy Ghost to be printed, wished to get a large one made after the form Crescentia had seen in her vision. In the year 1727 or 1728, she commissioned a painter of Munich, named Rufin, to carry it out. This the painter found it difficult to do, from the testimony which Crescentia was compelled to give him. The servant of God was now commanded, under obedience, to furnish the painter with full particulars and do all in her power to cause this pictorial illustration to exactly resemble the vision she had beheld. Hard as this command was to her humility, she faithfully complied with it, and in a few days the picture was completed with perfect success. No one was more astonished at the

---

[1] Ott, B. III. C. 2, p. 262.

facility with which it had been achieved, and at the perfection of the work, than the painter himself. He wished to make a copy of it at once for the Countess Amalia, afterwards Empress, who was a great admirer of Crescentia. But, strange to say, no matter what pains he took, he had no success with the copy. He acknowledged afterwards, with tears in his eyes, that through the merits of Crescentia the Holy Ghost Himself must have helped with the first picture. All who saw the picture admired it beyond expression. A countess afterwards donated a splendid frame for it. It was not publicly exposed, but kept in a room. Father Ott adds the following literally : "I myself, while here, had the great honor of showing this picture thirty times, or thereabouts, to distinguished persons, noblemen, and men of princely rank. The most honored Empress (Amalia) was so pleased with it that, in 1735, she had a similar image made of drawn silver, (as far as the goldsmith could catch the shape), and most kindly presented it to the convent."

As it was from obedience that Crescentia assisted in the making of this picture, surely no one will venture to declare this obedience, under these circumstances, unlawful, when under the eyes of spiritual authorities and father confessors, this kind of picture had been in use from time immemorial. We are even justified in supposing that she herself held a different opinion ; for it by no means follows from her silence and the assistance she rendered to the painter that she inwardly approved of the act. In the report made to the Pope immediately after her death by Amort and Bassi, which report confirms Father Ott's statement, Sister M. Justina affirms:[1] "From the very time that the picture of the Holy Ghost was published, she took only water to drink, and continued the practice to the time of her death." If to this we add that as soon as she became Superioress she confiscated the pictures, it is not improbable that the whole proceeding displeased her,

---

[1] Act. B. N. 15, § 19.

although she humbly submitted her judgment to that of her Superiors, or at least preferred to keep silence. And suppose she had in previous years unconditionally consented to that custom, such an inculpable error, in a mere matter of discipline, not of faith, is no evidence whatever against her eminent sanctity. Great Saints, nay, Doctors of the Church, have erred unconsciously, in real matters of faith, when, in their time, the Church had not yet pronounced her decision on these points.[1]

Veneration for the Holy Ghost should be cherished by every Christian, inasmuch as he is called to be a pure temple of the Holy Ghost. "Therefore grieve not the holy Spirit of God : whereby you are sealed unto the day of redemption."[2]

CHAPTER VII.

Crescentia's Fervor in Honoring the Mother of God, the Angels, and Saints.

"HE who loves Jesus, will also love His Mother. He who loves the Mother will likewise love the Son." These were words frequently heard from the lips of the servant of God. They are well adapted, not only to vindicate the teaching of the Church against heresy, but also the practice of her Saints against the irresolute hesitation of tepid and superficial spirits, who rend asunder elements which in life naturally flow on together, and think they perceive an injury done to the honor due

---

[1] Said picture of the painter Rufin is still in the convent, but carefully kept behind lock and bolt. The author has seen it, but it was as an exception to the rule and he must acknowledge that few pictures ever made so touching an impression on him. The silver statue modelled from it was confiscated by the state in 1801. This present of the Empress, together with many silver and gold votive tablets, has probably passed into the hands of speculating money-grabbers.

[2] Eph. iv. 30.

to Christ in every fervent devotion to her who, as Virgin and Mother, received and brought forth for us the "Word full of grace and truth."

Crescentia, from her very infancy, entered into a very sweet and tender relationship with the Mother of God. This became more and more perfected as years rolled on, until it reached such a high degree that she finally appeared to live only in and by the hearts of Jesus and Mary. Whoever heard her speak of Mary, could not fail to be touched by the love-breathing words with which she extolled the Mother of mercy, and recommended devotion to her. She could neither hear the cherished name of Mary mentioned, nor utter it herself, without bowing her head and showing exteriorly the love and devotion which penetrated her heart. She generally called the Queen of Heaven her dearly loved Mother, and maintained that on numberless occasions she had experienced that Mary, as the best and truest Mother, had kept the promise she had made to her in the years of her childhood : namely, that as her Mother she would always be at her side, assisting her.

She took a special pleasure in speaking of the prerogatives of the Blessed Virgin Mother, and it was in words of glowing enthusiasm, full of light and love, that she extolled the exalted Daughter of the heavenly Father, the Mother, full of grace, of the Son, the Immaculate Spouse of the Holy Ghost, the Mistress and Queen of Heaven and earth, the joy and delight of the angels, the miracle of created beauty,. the Mother of mercy, and, after God, through Christ, the principal mediatrix of our salvation, by whom we receive all graces. [1] With regard to the two mysteries of the Immaculate Conception and the Perpetual Virginity of Mary, she, (to use Sister M. Gabriel's expression) stood like a wall. She often repeated : "It would be my greatest delight, if, as a slave of love, I might sacrifice my life for the sublime mystery of the Immaculate

---

[1] Gabriel, p. 155, etc.

Conception ; and with my own blood bear witness that Mary was a Virgin, before, in, and after the birth of her Divine Son."

She was often heard to say certain verses in honor and love of Mary, which doubtless she uttered still oftener in heart. As, " Deign to let me praise thee, my dear Mother," or, " My heart is glad in the Lord, and rejoices in Mary, my beloved Mother."—"O Mary, show thyself to be my merciful Mother!"—"O ye powers of Heaven, sing a new song to Mary, because she is full of grace!"—"O Mary, remember me, and say that thou art my Mother ! that suffices me." [1]   Every day she recited the usual Office of the Blessed Virgin Mary in honor of her beloved Mother, as also that of the Immaculate Conception, for which she had a special affection ; moreover, she said the beads, the litany of Loretto, and often during the day, the beautiful prayer, " We fly to thy patronage," as also the glorious "*Magnificat.*" When the bell rang the " *Angelus Domini,*" she said the prayers kneeling : not hurriedly or superficially, as is often done, but with edifying devotion.

Before the principal feasts of the Mother of God she made novenas with strict fasts and penitential exercises, with the practise of virtue, meditation, and prayer, which she increased on the vigils.   On the feast-days themselves, she was altogether occupied with the praise, love, and congratulations which she tendered the Blessed Virgin, and she poured forth her heart in gratitude to God for the great things He had done unto Mary ; she could with difficulty finish, and her feelings could scarcely remain concealed from her Sisters in religion.   It was her inviolable resolution to refuse no petition if made in the name of Mary, unless such petition was opposed to the will of God.

Her confidence in Mary knew no bounds ; all the graces she had received she attributed to her maternal intercession.   She affirmed that no petition had hitherto ever been

---

[1] Gabriel, p. 155, etc.

refused, that none would in future time be unheard by Mary, nay, that with maternal solicitude the good Mother even grants blessings before being asked. She exhorted all persons with whom she came in contact to have the same confidence in Mary and to call on her for help. When Father Dominicus Gleich, O. S. F. spoke to her of some disease he had in his feet, which hindered him from walking, she at once earnestly exhorted him to have recourse to Mary, the "Help of Christians." He did so, relying the while on the prayers and merits of the servant of God, and immediately obtained an answer to his prayer.[1]

Whenever there was a case of converting a sinner, she addressed herself in full confidence to "the Refuge of sinners," and in fact, with surprising success ; but she did this on all occasions, when any need was felt, or any trouble, doubt, or difficulty, and this with the intimacy and reliance which a child uses in approaching its own mother. In all simplicity she told Mary of her joys and sorrows, asked her, as a child would, for advice, and laid all she thought, said, did, and suffered, in her hands, that she might present it to her Divine Son.

It was one of her fondest occupations to accompany, in spirit, the Blessed Virgin in all her ways, to share her labors and difficulties, to sympathize from her heart in her joys and sorrows, and willingly, continually, to serve her and her Divine Son, as a maid-servant should. Before Christmas, she .travelled with Mary to Bethlehem, stayed with her in the stable, practising the various devotions and intentions which were poured into her with rich abundance by the Spirit of God. With Mary she fled to Egypt, waiting upon her with the most tender love ; she then went back with her to Nazareth, where she tarried in her service, endeavoring to perform the same offices for her, in the spirit, which she actually performed in the body for the Community. During Lent she stood, full of pain, with the sorrowful Mother beneath the cross,

---

[1] Summ. N. 12, § 227.

or watched with her at the sepulchre. And when she meditated on the sufferings of Christ, she never forgot those of His Mother; she, too, felt in her heart the thrust of the sword, which Simeon had prophesied should pierce the heart of the Mother of the Lord.

It is scarcely necessary to say that her devotion to Mary did not consist in mere prayers and meditations. She used to say: "To imitate Mary in her virtues is the true veneration." From these sublime virtues she rarely turned away her eyes; to gaze at them, admire them, thank God for them, ask for them, and earnestly strive to imitate them, was her daily occupation. She never went to Holy Communion without having first shown her poverty to the Mother of mercy, begging an alms, often and lovingly beseeching her to clothe her miserable child with the garment of her own virtues, admired by Heaven and earth.

Such veneration and love could not remain unrequited by the Mother of divine grace. Father Ott [1] says on this subject: "In the holy strife of love, as to whether the child showed the Mother the greater love and honor, or the Mother conferred on the child the greater favors, the victory was always decided in favor of the Mother." From Mary she always found more than the needful protection in dangers, strength in trials, consolation in suffering. The more hell and the world stormed against her, the greater was the security. and protection afforded her by the invincible "Tower of David." She had frequent visions of the Most Blessed Virgin, who with gracious speeches, salutary admonitions, and instructions, filled her with a plenitude of delight and of efficacious grace.

We have already related that while still a child she received from the Mother of God the promise that she would be a mother to her, and assist her in every way. According to her own assertion, the Mother of God had deigned to

---

[1] Ott, B. II. C. 5.

put the Blessed Infant in her arms.[1] This often happened when the Litany of Loretto was sung. On the Feast of the Assumption of the Blessed Virgin Mary she beheld, as in a vision, the glorious entry of the Queen of Heaven into the Holy City of God.[2]

When the persecutions against the servant of God, during the first years of her religious life, had reached their highest point, the "Help of Christians" once appeared to her, and said : "You must not fear them, because I will assist you."[3] Such words from such powerful lips may well have inspired her with that firmness as of a rock, which was inexplicable to all, and offensive to some. Another time, when the waves of persecution rolled mountains high, she cast herself on her knees before a picture of the Blessed Virgin in her cell, not, however, to ask to be relieved of suffering, but to beseech Mary to take these sorrows with her virginal hands to her Divine Redeemer and to lay them as a sacrifice of love in His Sacred Heart. The Queen of Heaven then appeared to her crowned with surpassing glory and said, with a lovely smile on her face : "I rejoice to bring such a pleasant offering to my Divine Son, and I assure you that it will win for you a copious stream of grace to flow into your heart. Prepare for new persecutions, bearing ever in mind what my Divine Son spoke to His disciples : 'If they have persecuted Me, they will also persecute you.' "[4]

She prayed most earnestly, like a poor beggar, to the "Mother of fair love," for the gift of constantly increasing love of God. When she was once asking most fervently for this glorious "gift of love," the Virgin Mother appeared to her with the Infant and said : "My daughter, if you humble and annihilate yourself like this Child, you will love Him truly and perfectly." The spouse of Christ replied : "O Mother of God ! I will do this with His divine grace ;" then, turning to the Child, "O my dear, darling

---

[1] Act. B. Summ. Obj. No. 11, § 27.—Gabriel, p. 157.   [2] Ott, B. II. C. 5.
[3] Act. B. Summ. Obj. N. 11, § 27, and Ott.   [4] John xv. 20.

Jesus, deign to accept me as Thy slave and to grant me Thy grace, that I may follow Thee with all my strength." The Divine Child looked at her most lovingly and said : "My beloved, I present you with My love : love Me as much as you desire to love Me." The vision then disappeared, but left in the heart of the consecrated virgin such an ocean of delight, such an overflow of fervent love, that she could hardly stand it.[1]

One Christmas she was seriously sick in bed, suffering severe pain in every limb. She felt a burning desire to suffer all these pains for love of the new-born Infant, to increase His honor and pleasure ; she therefore addressed the petition to the Mother of God, that she would be pleased to offer the sufferings she endured to the little Jesus, in the manner most pleasing to Him, inasmuch as an offering by the hands of the Mother would be incomparably dearer to the Infant than that coming from a despicable hand-maiden. After this beautiful act, the Virgin Mother, with the Infant, appeared to her, and smiling graciously, said : "My daughter, your sufferings will be assuaged." She then put the Divine Infant into her arms, who caressingly said these words : " My child ! your humility and suffering have drawn Me to you. Because as one seeks Me, so he finds Me ; and he who seeks Me shall have life, and have it abundantly. I do not allow Myself to be surpassed in love and generosity. Behold, then, how well pleased I am when you suffer much for love of Me. Persevere and be faithful to Me, My grace will be great." Then the Child returned to His Mother's arms, and the vision ended with the words : " I am the Mother of fair love, of fear, of knowledge, and of hope : I will always remain your Mother."[2]

Such visions as these, with demonstrations of tender love, joined to condescending words, may, to the luke-warm Christian, scarcely seem credible ; they are, however, found in the history of mystical Saints of every century, as ordi-

<hr>

[1] Ott, B. III. C. 4.   [2] Ott, B. III. p. 258,

nary occurrences, and are partly explained by the fact that on the part of the happy souls who receive this sublime privilege, intercourse with the inhabitants of Heaven is incomparably more intimate than that of ordinary Christians, and on this account it is almost natural that a condescension, incomprehensible to us, should take place from on high on the part of the inhabitants of Heaven. The love and the trust which Crescentia placed in her dearly loved Mother, far surpass the intensity of affection by which children are united to their own mothers in the flesh. How, then, could that Mother-heart, which is of all *The Best*, not overleap the bounds of the usual order of things and bend down from Heaven to her beloved child on earth ?

The sources of this biography state that Crescentia had very many other similar visions of the Blessed Virgin, the particulars of which remain unknown. To these reports we add but one remark, that the love of this favored soul to her heavenly Mother showed itself conspicuously, shortly before her death. She had ordered two silver crowns, studded with precious stones, to be made for the picture representing St. Ann and Mary ; she was almost dying from inexpressible pain when these two crowns, just finished, were brought to her couch of death ; then her love for Mary was so gratified by the honor thus shown to these Saints, that, to the astonishment of every one, she was, as it were, beside herself with joy. She was, however, in close communion, not with the Queen of Heaven alone, but with all of the household of God who dwelt in the triumphant city of Jerusalem. Her love, reverence, and devotion to all the angels and Saints were most extraordinary. She used to say : " Since I am so poor myself, and so devoid of every virtue, I go in spirit from one class of Saints to another, like a poor Lazarus, begging for their prayers, partly for myself, partly for others."

She was specially familiar with her guardian angel, whom she saw, as she assures us, by a peculiar spiritual light, always by her side, and of this she had a greater certainty than if she saw him with her bodily eyes. From this circumstance she had from childhood upwards ever had so sensible a feeling of reverence from being in his presence, that it would have been impossible even to think of anything unbecoming, much less to say or do such before him.

From this resulted, with her, as with many other Saints, that a spiritual intercourse was developed between her and her guardian angel which was as intimate and full of loving trust as only an exceptionally obedient child can establish between itself and its own father. Her heart overflowed in daily acts of gratitude, veneration, and love towards him; she consulted him in doubts and difficulties, and endeavored carefully to follow his advice in everything. As often as she went to Church, she asked her guardian angel, and all the angels present, to come to her side, to assist her in adoring Christ worthily; and when she went away, or retired to rest, she commissioned this same angel to take her place, and to praise and love her heavenly Spouse in her stead. And here again we find that her devotion and love were corresponded to in a striking manner, and that her angel assisted her in remarkable ways. He often appeared to her in a visible form, instructed her in the mysteries of faith and the ways of interior life, and told her how to mortify her senses and suppress the movements of passion. While she was yet a child, when her mother gave her a piece of bread, the angel would at times appear to her visibly and admonish her thus : "My child, for the love of your Spouse, do not eat that piece of bread; rather give it to a poor person whom I will immediately point out to you."[1] Whenever she called on him, in any distress, she obtained help at once, and after she had chosen him as her monitor, she could entirely rely upon him. He would remind her in due time of everything she had to do, and spur her on to the doing. Thousands of cases proved that he helped her in even the least things. She used, therefore, to counsel the other Sisters,

---

[1] Ott, B. III. C. 4.

when they complained of forgetfulness, to pray confidently to their guardian angels to notify them of their duty at the right time. As for herself, she looked on the help of her guardian angel as a perfectly natural occurrence.

That she was favored with frequent visions of the holy angels, appears from the report already noticed, that she for two years received Holy Communion from the hands of an angel. The angel manifested his care for her in very small, nay, as our notions would esteem them, in very unimportant matters. When employed in the kitchen, her feeble strength often gave out in lifting heavy burdens ; she called on her guardian angel—he helped her immediately. This help she is said to have received, especially when the evil spirits, whom God had at that time permitted to exercise great power over her, placed obstacles in her way and caused her many vexations. The extinguished fire was rekindled, the broken windows repaired, as soon as she called on her guardian angel. One of her novices declared:[1] "In order to urge us to adoration of the Blessed Sacrament and to make us comprehend the goodness of God, Crescentia told us, in a spiritual conference, that, once when she had to cook pease in the kitchen, she asked her angel to attend to the fire on the hearth, that she might go to Church to adore the Blessed Sacrament ; that after a time she had returned, and seeing the angel busy at the fireplace, she felt herself justified in returning to the choir, which she did."

She also honored with a special devotion the holy Archangels, Michael, Gabriel, and Raphael, and prepared herself for their feasts in the manner we have already mentioned. St. Michael, whom she acknowledged and loved as the most glorious defender of God's honor and the protector of the Church militant, often appeared to her, strengthening, consoling, and defending her against diabolical attacks. St. Gabriel was her special intercessor with the Blessed

---

[1] Act, B. Obj. N. 11, § 14.

Virgin. When there was question of the conversion of great sinners, she used to send up her sighs, prayers, and penitential works, through the hands of this heavenly messenger, to the Mother of mercy. Surprising conversions were the ordinary results.[1] The following narrative, told also by Father Ott, is lovely indeed :

Once, when the bell was rung for the Angelus, she begged of the Redeemer to let the sound of this bell vibrate in the ears of all men, that thus they might, with the angels and Saints, and especially with St. Gabriel, salute the Mother of God, as the great Archangel had once saluted her in the name of the Blessed Trinity. This prayer had scarcely ascended from her heart to Heaven, when the Archangel appeared to her and with an unspeakably sweet air intoned the *Ave Maria.* Then her soul became rapt in ecstasy, she saw the Celestial Court drawn up in admirable order and heard all the voices join in the glorious chorus, saluting their Queen with the *Ave Maria.* St. Raphael, too, sometimes appeared to her and accompanied her on some little journeys ; he had also, to her great consolation, promised to accompany her on her last journey into eternity. We shall see, later on, how he kept his promise.

We will relate another vision, given by Father Ott, which is worth mentioning, especially for religious : it took place on the Feast of the Holy Angels. When the choir began to recite the Divine Office in the morning, she saw the guardian angel of every Sister standing by the side of their respective seats. She also noticed one standing by a vacant seat, with an expression of great displeasure on his face. The Sister who was to occupy the vacant seat came too late, from laziness.

In the Saints she honored the living members of Jesus Christ. When the annual celebration of their feasts came round, she venerated and called on them with special confidence ; at these times she was fond of recalling their virtues and proposing them for imitation to herself and Sisters.

---

[1] Ott, B. III. C. 4.

She had a special veneration for St. Joseph, the foster-father of Jesus Christ. She had an exceedingly great confidence in him, and asserted that she had received the greatest favors from God, by means of his intercession,[1] particularly in temporal affairs.

The grandparents of the Redeemer, St. Joachim and St. Anna, were also her chosen patrons. From her infancy she had endeavored to obtain, through their intercession, a perfect love for Jesus and for Mary. The pictures of both, beautifully ornamented, she exposed for veneration, both in the Church and in the cloister. She greatly regretted that St. Joachim was so little honored in the Church, and did not rest until, by negotiations with noble and princely persons, she sent a petition to the Holy See that the feast of St. Joachim should be solemnly celebrated throughout the whole Church. Her joy was great when Clement XII. granted this request on October 3d, A. D. 1738, and directed that it should be celebrated on the Sunday within the octave of the Assumption of the Blessed Virgin, as a feast of *duplex majus*, in the universal Church.[2]

Besides this, she had an intimate reverence for St. John the Baptist and for all the Apostles, particularly for the relatives of Christ, St. John the Evangelist and St. Judas Thaddaeus ; the latter for the very tender reason that on account of his name Judas, he was less likely to be venerated.

Other personal patrons of hers were St. Mary Magdalen, St. Dismas, St. Crescentia, and St. Barbara ; while among the Saints of recent date, St. John Nepomucene figured as the patron of her beloved silence. Then she venerated St. Ignatius Loyola, St. Francis Xavier, St. Aloysius, and St. Stanislaus Kostka, for their innocence and their great love of God ; St. Theresa and all holy martyrs, as also all the Saints of the Order of St. Francis. But, above

---

[1] Gabriel, p. 157.

[2] Note by translator : It is now a feast of *Duplex Secundæ Classis*, by order of Leo XIII.

all, she honored the blessed Fathers, St. Francis and St. Anthony of Padua, who also conferred most surprising favors upon her.

She daily practised particular devotions to St. Francis, at which she held familiar converse with him, such as a beloved daughter might hold with her father. His feast, October 4th, she anticipated by at least a fervent novena and appropriate exercises of the virtues of poverty, humility, and charity. She had many visions of this Saint. Father Ott[1] relates that once, on the vigil of his feast, she had honored the "burning Seraph," as she called him, by many hundred acts of love, and thanked him for having adopted her as one of his children. On the feast-day the Saviour showed her, after Communion, the holy Father Francis, with many arrows, which were explained to her as symbols of the holy exercise performed by her on the previous day; at the same time the Saint took her anew, as his dear child, under his paternal care.

She was very fond of St. Anthony of Padua, and invoked his aid especially for the conversion of sinners. In such cases she reminded him that he is invoked by all Christendom as the patron to restore lost articles, and that where grace, the greatest of all things, is lost, his aid in this is the most requisite of all. How this Saint accompanied her to the holy shrine at Lechsfeld, and how he cured her of a mortal sickness, has already been related.

As Father Ott says, it would be impossible to give the full particulars of all her marvellous intercourse with the Saints of the triumphant Church. From this same Father Ott,[2] we will, however, add some characteristics, which show at one and the same time her great simplicity and confidence:

During several days she had at one time been oppressed by bodily and spiritual sufferings. St. Bernardine, whom she specially honored among the Saints, in the third place of her Order, then appeared to her; in child-like simplicity

---

[1] Ott, B. II. C. 5.   [2] Ott, B. III. C. 4.

she addressed this complaint to him: " My holy Bernardine, are you come at last? Where were all of you staying so long ?" Instead of replying, the Saint cured her at once and filled her soul with joy and consolation.

As the servant of God was so sorely oppressed and was forsaken by every one during the first years of her religious life, while she was at the same time tormented by scruples and anxieties, without being able to obtain help from her father confessor, she earnestly besought God for a spiritual director. St. Ignatius then appeared to her, instructed her in different matters, admonished her to walk heroically on the way of the cross, and also promised that God would help her, and that he himself would not forsake her in these interior afflictions. True to his promise, this Saint appeared to her at other times when she was grievously tormented by exterior causes, and restored to her interior serenity and security.

She invoked St. Francis Xavier more particularly for the conversion of the heathen and of heretics. Father Ott says that the Saint, at times, showed her in a vision the fruit that her prayers and penitential works had produced among the heathens in Asia and America. Sometimes she appeared unusually cheerful ; when the Superioress, Mother Johanna, inquired the reason, she replied modestly and abashed : " My dear St. Xavier was with me, and told me that many unbelievers had been converted to the Catholic Church. Therefore, I rejoice."

St. Aloysius, who was so dear to her, [1] is said to have helped her at her work at times, as her guardian angel had done. Once she had to start a fire in the large stove in the visitors' room, and her feeble strength was unable to lift some heavy blocks of wood to put them into the stove ; she called out : " My holy Aloysius, do help me !" At once he was there, visible, and pushed the wood into the stove with the fire-tongs. The tongs are still kept as a relic, in memory of this event.

---

[1] Act. B. Summ. Obj. N. 11, § 5.—Ott B. III. C. 4.

The wise of this world will shrug their shoulders and laugh at this naïve narrative; but it is written : "I will destroy the wisdom of the wise, and the prudence of the prudent I will reject,"[1] and "The foolish things of the world hath God chosen that he may confound the wise."[2]

It is scarcely necessary to remark that, according to the enlightened spirit of the Catholic Church, she held in reverence, and admonished her Sisters to a similar reverence. all that is held sacred or that appertains to the Saints : such as relics, holy pictures, consecrated articles, and also the ceremonies and usages of the Church. She went so far as to collect the drops of holy water spilled on the ground by the Sisters, to save them from profanation.[3]

Since God is not only sanctity itself, but also the Source of all sanctity ; since He as Law-giver demands sanctity of His rational creatures : "Be ye holy, because I am holy,"[4] and as Sanctifier, liberally imparts this sanctity by His Spirit ; and since He further commands that we should bestow the highest adoration on Himself as the original Source of all sanctity ; it follows, of itself, that the sanctity of the Saints, which flows like a little rivulet from the original Source of divine grace, demands from us a tribute of veneration which of itself flows back to God, even as created sanctity comes from God and returns to Him. And as he who praises the rays of the sun does not lessen the honor of the sun itself, but rather increases it, even as a child withdraws no love from its mother by contemplating her picture, in like manner the veneration of the Saints by the Catholic Church deprives God of no honor due to Him. On the contrary, He is doubly honored thereby, being honored as sanctity itself and as the Author of sanctity in His creatures.

Therefore, O Christian, practise both injunctions of the Apostle : "To the only God be honor and glory :"[5] because supreme adoration belongs to Him alone ; and on the

---

[1] I. Cor. i. 19.   [2] Ibid. 27.   [3] Summ. N. 12, ₵ 127.
[4] Levit. xi. 44.   [5] Tim. i. 17.

other hand, " Render, therefore, to all men their dues. .. .. honor to whom honor (is due)." [1] But next to God, among mere creatures, the highest honor is due to the Blessed Virgin Mary, and then to all the citizens of Heaven, because on them "resteth that which is of the honor, glory, and power of God and that which is His Spirit." [2]

CHAPTER VIII.

The Great Gift of Prayer and Contemplation which God bestowed on Ven. Mother Crescentia.

E ought always to pray, and not to faint." [3] This injunction of our Lord has, perhaps, been carried out by few, in this miserable earth-life, in the degree and with that perseverance with which Crescentia practised it. We know already, from what has been said, that her short sleep scarcely interrupted her prayer, and that she considered every moment in which she lost sight of God as an irreparable loss, nay, as a misfortune to be bitterly bewailed as a crime.

From this we may conclude that the Lord had granted her a sublimer mode of praying and meditating than is practised by ordinary Christians ; in fact, even as a child, she was already elevated to an extraordinary state of contemplative prayer, although we do not know the exact time at which it occurred. It is certain that at a later period she was not obliged to follow the usual rules for meditation and to make use in various ways of the different faculties of the soul in order to seek God : a higher light drew the powers of the soul towards the interior, into the presence of the Highest Good : the spirit, penetrated by the light of faith and elevated by the gifts of

---

the Holy Ghost, knew, without labor and toilsome inquiry, the things of Heaven in a manner far more profound than the mere human idea can comprehend ; the will, captured by astonishment and love, reposed quietly in God. Sister M. Gabriel says : [1] "As soon as she wished to be recollected, she was drawn quite out of herself, and by the infinite power and goodness of God, was carried upwards by the straight road, and either immersed in the infinite mystery of the ever-blessed Trinity, or in the rocky clefts of the most sacred wounds of Christ, and plunged therein so deeply that she believed herself, from very vehemence of love, to be transported out of herself and changed into another being. When she came to herself again, all creation seemed something foreign to her. At prayer there was no need of her making long preparation, no reflection was necessary ; she grasped the truth at once, gazing alternately at her own nothingness and at the fathomless abyss of the Godhead. She became constantly more and more humble."

In this way her prayer was, as a rule, not a hard seeking or a painful knocking, but a marvellous vision, a loving attention, a joyous surrender of herself to God, an enjoyment of His presence, a pouring forth and taking up of her heart which she then totally plunged into God, the Ocean of everything good. We have no report of the order she went through in climbing the various degrees of the higher stages of prayer; we only know that she attained the highest points of contemplation. She was silent about these ; only once, in obedience, she made the general remark, that at the beginning of prayer her will and her intellect were attracted by a sweet power and became as if lost in God. It was God who worked within her; she herself really did nothing. Whoever observed her could not fail to notice that this was true. She had scarcely knelt down, ere her face betrayed that her soul had left the sensible world and had interiorly turned itself towards Heav-

---

[1] Gabriel, p. 67.

on ; she then lived more in God, whom she loved, than in her mortal body, which remained motionless as a statue. She was so occupied with God that she neither saw nor heard anything, and no disturbance near or around her disquieted her in the least. This state of recollection often became a real ecstasy ; then no words addressed to her, no shaking had any effect on her ; obedience alone re-called her to herself. She was unable to prevent or to put an end to these states. They occurred almost regularly af-ter Holy Communion ; but also outside of the Church, when a word, a hymn, or a prayer affected her mind by reminding her of a mystery of faith. Nay, these states of mind happened so often that the Sisters ceased to pay at-tention to them, although every one witnessing her posi-tion and the expression of her countenance was filled with devotion and shuddered with holy awe. Eye-witnesses, who had often watched her, describe her outward appear-ance during these ecstasies as follows : [1]

"Her position was then very becoming : she was a strik-ing image of profound devotion ; her face wore an expres-sion of heavenly radiance ; her eyes were half closed and motionless ; her hands were hid under the scapular ; her body kneeling without movement, and at times shedding a sweet perfume around her."

The following narrative, taken from the Acts of her Beatification, confirms and illustrates the foregoing state-ments : [2]

Sister M. Joseph Anger, who had but just been received in the convent, and had not seen the servant of God in this state, relates : "One day, Mother M. Johanna Altweger sent me to the choir, where Crescentia was making her thanksgiving after Communion, to call her, as a certain gentleman wished to see her. When I got to her prie-dieu in the choir, I found her kneeling, stiff and immovable, so that I was quite frightened. Yet, I recovered myself and said : 'Sister Crescentia, please come down ; somebody

[1] Summ. 19, § 90.   [2] Summ. N. 9, § 560.

wants you.' I received no answer and could not perceive any sign of life in her. Then I became thoroughly alarmed, ran with all speed to the Mother and said: 'Crescentia is dead at her kneeling-desk.' Mother M. Johanna, however, bade me return and tell her that the Mother Superior commanded her to come. I had scarcely uttered the words 'Venerable Mother,' than she at once recovered consciousness, arose and went to her. In this manner, after Holy Communion, Crescentia was always spiritually elevated to God, as long as I lived with her in the convent."

According to the statements of other Sisters, these ecstasies often lasted for several hours, even until obedience recalled her to herself. Yet, it requires but little acquaintance with the interior life to feel assured that such sensible consolations and fulness of light did not always accompany her prayer. For if the interior life consists in our mystically assimilating the life of Christ in ourselves, and permitting it to develop itself within, then must we also partake of the death of Christ, as St. Paul emphatically assures us: "If we have been planted together in the likeness of His death, we shall be also in the likeness of His resurrection."[1] Yes, according to the teaching of the masters of spiritual life, participation in the sufferings and death of Christ, as also in His resurrection, repeats itself in the interior life ; or, in plainer words, a period of painful probation and purification of the spirit, precedes every or nearly every higher degree of enlightenment and union. Thus Crescentia also had her hours, days, and years of painful abandonment of the spirit, so absolute, that only the dim light of faith could point out to her the direct and certain path.

But she loved and sought God not less in the darkness than in the light, in poverty than in riches, on Mount Calvary equally as on Mount Thabor : it even seemed that in her bereavement her zeal and fidelity were doubled.

[1] Rom. vi. 5.

She herself describes this state after she had borne it for almost four years.[1] " Oh, for very torment have I been seeking among all creatures, and asking them, beseeching them dolefully, if they knew where He could be, whom my soul loveth ! How often have I wandered in spirit with St. Mary Magdalen in the streets and gardens, and cried out : Tell me where you have laid Him and I will get Him, else I must die of love and desire ! But the more I sought Him the further was He from me ; it seemed to me not otherwise than that I was in a dark wilderness. Oh ! no one can imagine what interior dereliction is. One would run through a thousand naked swords, and sacrifice one's life a thousand times, if only one could obtain what is so earnestly sought for. But I sought and found Him not."

She often used the words : " I thirst for the strong and living God ; " or, turning to creatures, she cried out : " O all of you, help me to bemoan the absence of my Beloved, or rather the cause of His absence—my sins ! " Yet, even then, her soul was already so disengaged from all self-love, that had she had the choice, she would have preferred this incomparably painful state of abandonment to the delights of Thabor. She frequently said so herself. She also gives expression to similar exalted sentiments in the resolutions written down in 1723 :[2] " O my glorious Redeemer ! Thou sayest : I am the Resurrection and the Life. In Thy resurrection Thou hast given me a new life. Before this, my heart was a true Limbo of dryness and dereliction. But since Thou hast come to me in the Holy Eucharist, Thou hast dispelled all darkness and made me rise again to Thee. Thus I have a joyous Easter, thus my soul can sing, Alleluia. But, my God, is this to love perfectly ? No ! That, therefore, I may love Thee in future, I beseech Thee to grant me the grace, not only to preserve an equal tranquillity of mind, in consolation as in dereliction, but to rejoice alike in both."

The following remarkable occurrence, which happened

---

[1] Ott, B. III. C. 13.   [2] Kolb, p. 26.

during that four years' abandonment, is well attested : [1]
Once, when with ardent desire she sought her Spouse in her
own cell, and with the most dolorous expressions adjured
all creatures to tell her if they had seen Him after whom
her soul languished, her guardian angel appeared to her
and bade her look through the window. She hastened to
the window and on the branches of a pear-tree standing
near the water-basin in the yard, she saw the dearly loved
Spouse of her soul, sitting quietly and motionless, although
the tree was very violently agitated by the wind, and the
branches which seemed to bear Him were tossed to and fro.
Full of joy at this sight, the servant of God exclaimed :
"My Saviour, what art Thou doing there ? Come to my
heart and rest." The Lord answered : "My daughter, as
I remain in peace on this tree, however violently it may be
agitated, even so I rest in thy heart : thou mayest think
there is a great storm there, but I am in the midst, all the
same." The vision then vanished, leaving great consolation
and delight in her soul ; this lasted, however, only a quarter
of an hour, and then the previous dereliction returned. [2]

When she was not in a state of dereliction she very often
had supernatural communications, revelations, words addressed to her, and visions ; indeed, according to the testimony of her confessors, she had visitations of every kind
that occurred to other mystical Saints. The state of dereliction took place very often, but except during the four
years mentioned before, it did not last long.

We here remind the reader that the masters of mystic
theology distinguish three kinds of visions, namely :
First, bodily, that is, seen, heard, or felt, as when our Saviour appeared to His Apostles after His resurrection, which
happened in reality. Secondly, imaginary, when the
force of imagination pictures divine things and represents

[1] Act. B. Summ. Obj. N. 11, § 14 and 31.

[2] This vision was made known to several Sisters, and also to outsiders, by the
Mother Superior (Sister Johanna). After the death of Crescentia, many visitors
wished to get a leaf of the tree as a remembrance of the vision. Several sick persons used these leaves when pulverized, addressing a prayer to Crescentia. Their
prayers were heard and many miracles were wrought.

them as real ; this is easily subject to deception. Thirdly, intellectual, whereby the soul is enabled to perceive by an extraordinary light the highest conceptions of divine objects, more after the manner of angels than of men. These last are by far the most exalted and the most efficacious ; and when they are purely intellectual they are not exposed to deception. These last the servant of God had frequently.

What were her governing principles with regard to such revelations and visions we shall learn best from her own words.[1] Following up the words "do not fear" spoken by the angel to the holy women on the day of the resurrection, she continues : "I, too, will lay aside that excessive fear at visions which is a hindrance to me, and keep myself between the love and fear of God ; I will confide in God, and while doing so, I will pay good attention as to whether these visions are conducive to or a hindrance to my last aim and end. Especially will I communicate them to my confessor, though it may be hard for me."

The objects which entered within the circle of her vision in a supernatural manner are of various descriptions. Sometimes souls from purgatory appeared to her, either to ask for help or to return thanks for help received. Sometimes angels and Saints, and then again the Mother of God with the Divine Infant ; now, it was Christ, either suffering or in glory ; and often she had visions of or communications from the Godhead, especially the Blessed Trinity, in a purely intellectual manner. To this mystery she had an incredible devotion ; every word concerning it, that she heard or spoke, was accompanied with strong emotions of mind and heart, frequently occasioning ecstasy. In later years this mystery was the usual subject of her contemplation ; her mind was herein lost in wonder and adoration, in praise and thanksgiving, with a loving offering up of herself, and human words cannot express what sublime illuminations, and what fulness of heavenly joys were then imparted to her.

---

[1] Kolb. p. 11.

Once, on the Feast of the Blessed Trinity,[1] she offered, in a vision, her intellect to the omnipotence of the Father, that it might be enabled more clearly to comprehend the immensity of the Divine Majesty and her own nothingness; to the wisdom of the Son she donated her own will, to be consecrated for the most perfect imitation of the divine perfections; to the goodness of the Holy Ghost she offered her memory for an uninterrupted remembrance, love, and praise of the Most High Godhead. She had scarcely laid this offering of her faculties on the divine altar, with great affection, than her soul heard these words distinctly: "We three are one." Then she exclaimed in an ecstasy of holy love: "O most Holy Trinity, I give Thee Thyself and all Thy perfections!" Thereupon she heard the angels sing: "Holy, holy, holy, is the Lord God of Hosts," and her soul was immersed in an ocean of bliss, so that she believed it must part from the body.

One day,[2] after Holy Communion, her ecstasy had lasted unusually long. Mother Johanna asked her afterwards what had been communicated to her. In obedience, she replied that the Redeemer had appeared to her, and had held a very interesting conference with her. "He said: 'I am the good Shepherd, and I give My life for My sheep.' I replied: 'Yes, my Beloved, Thou art the good Shepherd, and the Lamb of God; Thou whom I have just received under the appearance of bread.' Then I offered this, my good Shepherd and the Lamb of God, for myself and for all men, to the heavenly Father for His eternal praise and complacency, even as He had offered Himself to the same Father when He gave His blood and life for His lost sheep. The heavenly Father accepted this offering with the greatest satisfaction; the Redeemer turned to me with a gracious love, uttering these blessed words: 'You are My dear little sheep, and will be so throughout eternity.' He then pointed out to me a very rich and fertile pasture, which was, nevertheless, filled with thistles and thorns, and

---

[1] Ott. B. III. C. 1.   [2] Ott. B. III. C. 3.

said to me : ' Do you see this pasture ? It is indeed full of thorns, yet it is very good, nay, the very best ; for there My love feeds you, with many sufferings leads you to Myself, and renders you conformable to Me. During My own life, suffering was My daily portion ; I ordain the same for you, because you are My darling little sheep. I will always assist you with My grace, and after this life will feed you with inexpressible joys and quench your thirst from the fountain of delight. Increase in My love, walk in the way of the cross, until you come to Me in My kingdom.' "

Another vision is so instructive and consoling that we must not omit it : [1]

The Saviour appeared to her, surrounded by angels, with an expression of great joy. In humble confidence, she inquired the reason of this. The Lord replied : " I appear to you in this manner, because yesterday, again, you spoke so expressively to your Sisters about My divine perfections and the many gifts and graces I bestow upon mankind. By this discourse you have caused them to recognize and set a high value upon My mercy ; to admire and venerate My goodness, My love, and My generosity; it is a great joy to Me when people recognize what is good, and strive after it ; it provides the occasion for Me to confer on them more abundant mercy. I am always seeking their happiness alone. *Go, therefore, and tell the children of men how good I am.*' "

Then her soul poured itself forth in praise and thanksgiving and she besought the Lord that He would Himself fill the hearts of all men with the knowledge of His goodness, that the current of His grace might flow without any obstacle being in the way. Then the Lord gave her His blessing and concluded with the words : " My child, where two or three are gathered together in My name, there I am in the midst of them."

On New Year's day, Crescentia [2] had, according to her wont, made a New Year's gift of herself to the Lord, offer-

---

[1] Ott. B. III. C. 3.   [2] Ott. B. II. C. 3.

ing herself with extraordinary fervor as a holocaust, to be immolated according to the divine will. and consumed in the holy fire of suffering, of crosses, and of love. She fell into an ecstasy, and heard from the lips of Christ these words : "This thine offering pleases Me ; but thou must know that I do not allow Myself to be surpassed in love." Then showing her His opened heart, He said : "Behold My heart, laid open by love ; I give it thee as a habitation, a security, and an asylum against all thine enemies." This vision produced incredible and indescribable emotions in the heart of the virgin ; the flame of love increased to an almost intolerable degree the desire to suffer crosses and even to die for her Beloved.

As we have said so much of her ecstasies and visions, we cannot forbear mentioning here, that according to the doctrine of sound mystical theology, perfection by no means consists in such apparitions, nor is the highest and most precious degree of supernatural enlightenment to be sought therein.   Accordingly, the servant of Christ experienced the generosity of her Spouse when such extraordinary illuminations did not take place.   She had always, at her usual prayers and at work,. a bright light within her, which quietly and peacefully placed her spirit before the face of God, and, as it were, kept it there.

The veil of the body which hides from our eyes the world of light which surrounds us, was either half-raised or quite transparent to her.   A witness in the Acts thus expressed himself on this point:[1] "God was to her as infinite light, in which she lived, by which she was surrounded, wherever she was and whatever she was doing." By virtue of this light she could, without any exertion, direct the higher eye of her mind to God, dwelling in the interior depths of her soul, and continuing in an uninterrupted intercourse of love with Him, could enjoy Him and repose in Him.   That mysterious separation of the interior and exterior being, of which several masters of the spiritual life make mention,

---

[1] Summ. N. 9, § 380.

had taken place in her. The higher part of the soul, peacefully attracted by the sensible presence of her Highest Good, yielded itself absolutely to the sway of the Holy Ghost working within and powerfully exciting her will to the most sublime acts of love, to the sweet surrender of her whole being to God, and to repose in Him. This did not prevent her from holding converse with people of the outward world, or from attending to her duties. Whatever touched her soul exteriorly was but as a passing shadow, which could in no way darken the fulness of the light in the interior of her soul. This grace, which is as rare as it is precious, is a participation in the perfections of the holy angels, who, as St. Bonaventure says, [1] "hasten within God, whithersoever they are sent."

We can therefore say, that in consequence of this union with God, and this surrender of her being, which we have described, that she became, in word and act, more passive than active, that she was impelled by the spirit of God rather than self-acting and resolving. And by this fact, the child of God had reached its perfection, and in the fullest sense realized St. Paul's meaning when he says : "Whosoever are led by the Spirit of God, they are the sons of God." [2] This influence of divine grace went so far as actually, in important cases, to lay the words on her tongue. It had always been her practice to weigh her words before she spoke ; later on, it frequently happened that she said something different from what she had intended. This often happened when she was giving instruction to the novices, at which times she sometimes remained for a quarter of an hour in an ecstatic state, speaking then such marvellous words that they inflamed the hearts of all who heard them. To strangers also, especially when they were in mortal sin, she sometimes spoke words, which could only come from Him who proves the reins and the heart, and of hearts hard as stone makes children of God. A few

---

[1] Brevilog. P. II. C. 8. "Intra Deum currunt."   [2] Rom. viii. 14.

words from her penetrated the coldest hearts with a crushing repentance and contrition, and drew forth from their eyes floods of tears.

Nevertheless, exalted and interior as her prayer and her conduct undoubtedly were, she was far removed from the sham devotion of those who despise outward exercises, considering them beneath their dignity. The servant of God took pleasure in performing faithfully all the exterior exercises and vocal prayers of the community, and even added many of her own accord ; but the exterior exercises were by her rendered interior, so that she adored God in spirit and in truth. We have already noted many of these exercises of hers ; as a picture of her whole life of prayer, we will give a short description of the manner in which she spent the days preceding Lent (carnival).

During these days, in which, almost everywhere, people seem to claim the privilege of forgetting God and of offending Him by sin, as if by prescriptive right, she knelt constantly before the Blessed Sacrament, to honor the Divine Majesty the more for the many offences then committed against Him, and to crave for mercy to the many blinded souls who run after empty and gloomy shadows, forgetting the Eternal Light in its infinite loveliness. Even in the last years of her life, her great weakness and sickness could not keep her from making this exercise.

She also gave her fellow-religious earnest admonitions and comprehensive instructions to make a careful use of these days as a time of penance and of prayer for the sins of the world ; and since we must suppose that she herself carried out, in the most perfect manner, the exercises which she prescribed to others, we will copy one of the many methods arranged for the use of those days. They have been substantially written down by her pupils, and are preserved in a book already mentioned, styled : The Purposes of Ven. Crescentia : Die Meinungen der Ehrw. Crescentia. This one method is substantially as follows : " Since the goodness of God is so very much offended at this time, a soul that loves God should endeavor to replace these offences, committed by the children of the world, by pious exercises, and for these five days keep up a spiritual drama for our dear Saviour, consisting of meditations on five mysteries taken from the ignominious and doleful Passion of Christ. These they might represent to the heavenly Father and offer them up in behalf of sinners. On the Thursday before Quinquagesima Sunday, they should meditate on the contempt, ridicule, affronts, and fulness of sorrow which Christ suffered in the court of Caiphas, and should offer their meditation up to God. On Quinquagesima Sunday they should choose the contemptuous and painful treatment He underwent before the court of Herod; on Monday, the scourging, on Tuesday, the crowning with thorns, and on Ash-Wednesday, the drama of the '*Ecce Homo.*' Early in the morning of these days all the faculties of the soul should be directed to the consideration of these respective mysteries, making the intentions to perform all their works and exercises and to bear the inconveniences of the day in union with the infinitely meritorious mysteries of the suffering Redeemer and for His greater glory. All their prayers and meditations should be referred to the suffering Saviour ; especially at the Holy Sacrifice of the Mass is His Passion to be offered with all fervor, as a reparation for the contempt cast upon the Divine Majesty. At the same time, acts of thanksgiving, of petition, and of contrition should be made."

As an ejaculatory prayer, to be frequently repeated through the day, is given : "O my Jesus ! turn away Thine eyes and ears from everything displeasing to Thee and direct them to what pleases Thee !" The prudent remark is added, that these exercises should be performed in secret, without betraying any sadness ; but on the contrary, keeping the soul in peace and joy, while even during the cheerful conversation at recreation they were to keep the mystery before their minds by casually casting on it a spiritual glance.

From what has been said, we may apply to Crescentia the praise which the Church, in the Breviary, confers on St. Martin : "Turning her eyes and hands to Heaven, she with indefatigable soul never ceased from praying." Like the citizens of Heaven, she spent day and night in using the holy language of the eye and of the heart with her beloved Supreme Good. Her fidelity was priceless ; the Word of the Lord, "Ask, and you shall receive, that your joy may be full," [1] was already visibly fulfilled in her mortal life ; eternity, however, will fully reveal the fulness of her joys.

This exhortation and this promise were also given to you, dear Christian. Prayer, therefore, should be the constant breath of your interior life, that the words of the prophet may also be verified in your regard : "My eyes are ever towards the Lord ; for He shall pluck my feet out of the snare." [2]

CHAPTER IX.

How Crescentia Loved Christ in Every One. [3]

HE love coming from Christ produces two shoots from one root, and by a two-fold exercise fulfils two commandments : the first and greatest is the love of God, and the second, which is like unto the first, is the love of one's neighbor. And as this second exercise of love presupposes the first and makes that first visible, the whole law is summed up in the words: "Love thy neighbor as thyself." [4] Would to God that this truth were as commonly put into practice as it is commonly known!

From the fulness of that divine love, which inflamed the

---

[1] John xvi. 24.   [2] Ps. xxiv. 15.
[3] Summ. N. 10, § 1-443.—B. Inform. § 119-144.   [4] Gal. v. 14.

heart of Ven. Sister M. Crescentia, a stream of love for her neighbor poured forth powerfully and brilliantly, a love which all the waters of unkindness, injustice, ingratitude, and hatred could neither quench nor weaken ; they but served to make it more manifest. The Spirit of God incessantly urged her to practise this virtue in the most perfect manner possible ; she said herself, a voice continually resounded in her heart : " Thou shalt love thy neighbor as thyself." She herself neglected not to encourage it with new resolutions. In 1741 she writes: [1] " I dare not admit anything in my heart which is against the love of my neighbor. Thou, my Redeemer, art my neighbor, and next to Thee all rational creatures are my neighbors. I will, therefore, love Thee in my neighbor, and my neighbor I will love as myself." She looked on every day as lost in which she could not exercise love. But by this love she altogether understood the supernatural, the specific Christian love of which Christ is at once the source and the end, the measure and the rule. Natural love, on the other hand, comes from human affection, and whoever loves from this source, seeks more or less his own satisfaction, honor, or interest. And because this natural love takes its own will for its rule, it cannot yield to the first and supreme will of Him who is love itself.

Crescentia had, indeed, naturally, a heart rich in love and compassion, and tender in affection ; yet with this heart she had given herself up absolutely to the service of Christ, and had so intimately united it with the original source of the eternal and most holy love, that the natural power of love became penetrated through and through, was transfigured and regulated by the love that proceedeth from and leadeth to eternity.

Mere natural love was an abomination to her : she used to say that it became a consecrated person very ill and was for such a person a kind of idolatry ; consequently she spoke often and very severely against the pestilence of par-

---

[1] Kolb, p. 51.

ticular friendships, which sometimes cause so much mischief in religious communities : originating in the natural affections, albeit not exactly of the lowest order, they can only aim at natural ends, such as the responding to temporal and perishable inclinations. She warned her hearers that they who entertain such friendships can never attain to interior peace, and consequently never arrive at perfection ; they are even in a very critical condition with regard to their souls, and at the same time can easily become a stumbling-block to others. Such friendships gradually destroy the universal love and peace, nay, even obedience itself ; they smother devotion and are capable of effecting the ruin of a whole community.

She herself was so penetrated with the light of faith and the love of Jesus Christ that the exterior of persons and things to which the sensible affections attach themselves was for her altogether in the back-ground. Her enlightened eye acknowledged in every human being the image of God, and, as such, one entitled to great respect and love ; further, each one was the property of Jesus Christ, bought by the high price of His Blood, nay, was the living member of the Redeemer, or, at the least, destined to become a member of Christ and to remain so forever. Jesus Christ, the great King, met her in the person of every one, even were it the most miserable human object possible, to call forth the tribute of love, to which He alone has an inalienable title, to collect it through His representatives, to take possession of it and reward it by returning eternal love for it. And since Christ was the origin, object, and aim of her love, it explains itself how it was that her love became so disinterested, so forgetful of self, that ordinary people, who "all seek the things that are their own, and not the things that are Jesus Christ's,"[1] considered it as exaggerated and foolish. To sacrifice her own, to deprive herself of it, by giving it to others, was so peculiar to her, in a measure, that a wit-

____
[1] Phil. II. 21.

ness stated : "She seemed not to have been born for herself, but for her neighbors."

Therefore it was that she neither expected nor claimed any return for the love she showed, no thanks, no love in response, no service from men, for it was to Christ alone to whom her love and service were tendered. More yet, when for her good offices she was met by evil, when her love encountered ingratitude, rudeness, and offence, which often happened, she thought it a double gain, and it was remarked that she was unusually gay and cheerful. Her gain was double, because, in the first place, an opportunity had been given to exercise *active* love, and in the second, to practise *patient* love, which is still better. Whoever afforded her occasion to practise this virtue was her benefactor, who deserved her thanks. According to this, the giver of a gift should rather consider himself under obligation to the receiver than the receiver to him. This view is, indeed, the order of the world reversed, but blessed is he who can comprehend and practise it. It is but the application and natural sequence of the words of eternal truth : "It is more blessed to give than to receive."[1] She looked upon all rational beings from the same exalted stand-point of universal love. Grace had burst asunder the narrow limits with which *self-love surrounds its sphere of action,* and her heart extended its sympathy and love over the whole communion of Saints, over the entire human race. Her faith was catholic, that is, universal, and so was the love of her heart. As faith, in coming forth from God, overleaps the boundaries of time and space, and even in its visible and temporal extension can permit in the Church no barriers of nationality or of political restriction, so love must never say : "Thus far, and no farther, I have nothing to do with yonder man." No ; catholic love must be perfect, even as is the love of the "Father in Heaven, who maketh His sun to rise upon the good and bad : and raineth upon the just and the unjust."[2]

---

[1] Acts xx. 35. [2] Matth. v. 45.

Ven. M. Crescentia possessed this catholic heart; she felt that beating of the pulse of the love of God, that runs through all creation, and reveals itself in the highest degree in the children of God. It gladdened her heart to see others glad, she mourned with the mourners, suffered with the suffering, and fought with and for such as were in danger and in need. How her soul rejoiced with the members of the triumphant Church, and poured itself out in that endless praise and thanksgiving which she offered to God for the love He had bestowed upon the Saints! On the other hand, the compassion she felt for the poor souls in purgatory and for all the sufferings and needs of the Church militant, is beyond the power of expression. In contemplating these, she forgot her own personal griefs, and did not hesitate to make every imaginable sacrifice, in order to help and console any one whom she found suffering. From this same disinterested and universal love proceeded the pious habit she had of thanking God for any good she noticed in any one else, as she would for a benefit conferred upon herself.[1] "O God!" she would then say, "I thank Thee a thousand times for this grace which Thou hast bestowed on my fellow-man. Alas! I am not worthy of such a grace, as this my neighbor is; but Thou, O God! shalt be loved and praised for it forever. Increase Thy grace in my neighbor, that he may seek nothing and love nothing but Thee alone." One of her usual prayers was that God would let her die the most painful death for the salvation of those who were in the state of sin. Such sentiments can only be inspired by the Holy Spirit of love. This is true, practical Christianity, as expressed in the words of St. Paul: "If one member suffer anything, all the members suffer with it; or, if one member glory, all the members rejoice with it. Now you are the body of Christ, and members of member."[2]

Although she embraced all mankind in love and by her

<hr>

[1] Gabriel, p. 105.   [2] 1. Cor. xii. 26, 27.

will, nevertheless, in the exercise of her love, she observed the order appointed by the will of God. The salvation of men was the first object of her love, and therefore, in prayer, she gave the preference to those whose salvation was in danger. "A religious," she said, "must not be intent on her own salvation alone, but must labor for the salvation of sinners and the conversion of heretics and infidels, with all her strength, by holy desires, fervent prayers, and a life of penance." For that reason she had also a maternal compassion for those who were tempted and afflicted, and she endeavored, even when she was without consolation herself, to console them in all possible ways. She frequently prayed :[1] "O God ! console my neighbor, according to Thy divine will, when, according to that same will, I am left without consolation. If it fare well with my neighbor, then let what may happen to me : I am Thy slave, and the work of Thy hands."

She possessed a peculiar gift in consoling the afflicted, and it is said that no one who was grieving ever left her presence unconsoled. It was, however, principally the misery of sinners that excited her love to the most strenuous exertions. The bitter tears which she shed nearly every day will show how great the grief was which she experienced on their account, as also the fainting-fits into which she fell at times, which were occasioned by the pain she felt at hearing of great sins. This is shown also by her incessant prayers for them, especially at holy Mass, where she offered up her tears in union with the Blood of the Saviour; by her severe works of penance, her fastings, her scourgings, all offered up every day with the same intention. In regard to the latter, her love would have made her transgress the limits of prudence, had not obedience restrained her fervor. She found it hard that the will of her Superiors only permitted her to scourge herself three times a day.

God Himself sometimes enlightened her concerning extraordinary perils incurred by some souls, that she might

---

[1] Gabriel, p. 100.

pray for them. Sister Gabriel says,[1] that Crescentia sometimes heard voices in the air, of persons in great suffering, calling on her for aid, which request she fervently complied with. Father Ott relates,[2] that on one occasion she suddenly rose from prayer and called on her fellow-Sisters to help her to pray for one in the agony of death, whose name she mentioned ; afterwards they ascertained that that very person was at that time really dying, a fact she could not have become acquainted with by any natural means.

The thought that so many persons are actually in the state of mortal sin, caused her a painful oppression of the heart. She would willingly have died for each one of them, if by the death of her body, she could have acquired spiritual life for them. On the other hand, her joy was inexpressible when she heard of the conversion of a sinner. On the great festivals, when many Christians usually approach the Sacraments, her prayers were very fervent on behalf of the penitents, while her joy was great, because she presupposed that many a sinner became again a child of God.

For the same reason, she rejoiced excessively whenever the Holy See proclaimed a Jubilee or an extraordinary indulgence. She very appropriately called the Jubilee an "invention of love, by which many sinners were led back on the road of penance." She then admonished the Sisters in these words : "Pray, beloved Sisters, pray, because now is the time of grace for the earth, and of joy for Heaven ; innumerable souls will be converted from sin to penance." It is scarcely necessary to mention that she herself availed herself of such an occasion by increasing her prayers and penitential works.

Modest and retiring as she naturally was, she knew no fear of man when the conversion of a soul was in question. With frankness and irresistible power she would then exhort even persons in authority to do penance; and as the Spirit of God frequently revealed to her the secrets of

<hr>

[1] Gabriel, p. 117.   [2] Ott, B. II. C. 5.

strangers' consciences, she sometimes, by her earnest and
loving words, completely took by surprise persons already
hardened in sin and made them tremble. Once, when
urging a sinner to be converted, she knelt down before
him and exhorted him with such piercing and passion-
ate words, that he acknowledged that it would have
been impossible for him to withstand her. At times, an
expressive glance cast at a sinner sufficed to pierce his soul
and move it to contrition. In this way, as the Acts assert, she worked innumerable conversions by prayer and
exhortations.[1]

When she prayed for a sinner, she did so with such ardent fervor, scourged herself so cruelly, persevered therein
with such deep interior pains and heartfelt aspirations, that
she did not leave off until her prayer was heard. This soon
became known far and wide, and when all other means had
failed to convert a hardened sinner, people had recourse
to her. Thus the Acts make mention of a miserable
wretch who, on his death-bed, obstinately refused the Sacraments. They wrote about him to Crescentia, who at
once used all means to obtain grace for him, and with such
success, that all who knew him were not a little astonished,
especially at the edifying fervor of the penitent.

We have already related the glowing zeal that animated
her for the conversion of the heathen ; to this we may here
add, that she most earnestly besought all the priests and
preachers of the Word of God, to be indefatigable in casting the net to catch souls. No sacrifice could be too great
for that purpose. There was nothing more pleasing to God
than to labor for the salvation of souls, and he who would
not tend the souls for which Christ shed His blood, could
not be a friend of Christ. When Father Flotto of the Society of Jesus, a renowned missionary of that period, told
her, that from age and infirmity he had resolved to discon-
tinue his missions, she spoke to him with so much em-
phatic earnestness, that he yielded consent to consecrate

---

[1] Act. B. Inform. § 127.

his last strength to this fruitful but difficult work. The nearest circle in which her love was actively called forth was naturally the convent itself; and we must say that the love which she felt towards her Sisters was shown by her being so accommodating, so kind and painstaking, so active and patient, that no mother could do more to express her love to her best loved, darling child.

According to the unanimous testimony of all the Sisters who lived with her, the tender consideration with which she avoided doing anything that could give the least offence to others, and the readiness with which she sought to gratify any reasonable wish of another person, could not be carried further. In forty years, no impatient, contentious, or in any way offensive word was ever heard from her, neither did she speak of her Sisters' faults, even of such as were publicly known ; she praised everybody except herself, blamed no one except when duty required her to reprimand those subject to her, and she ever stood up in defence of the honor of others. Were the faults public, she would sometimes say : " Oh ! these are but little failings, while my own are very great and without number." When it was possible, she explained everything in a charitable manner, or would say : " Under similar circumstances I should have done a thousand times worse myself." She knew how to say something good of everybody and would enumerate their virtues without noticing their faults. If she saw a poor person, she would say that he was far more patient in his poverty than she could be. If she saw persons gaudily dressed, she would suppose that under their soft garments they were perhaps mortifying their bodies a thousand times more than she did herself. It was in this way that she guided the Sisters : " We must, " she said, " act like the bees, which suck out the honey alone, from every direction, while spiders seek poison. Like the bees we must seek the honey of virtue and of good example and teaching from our neighbors."

She always preferred the will of another to her own, be-

ing ever ready to serve every one with pleasure. She had
the beautiful saying, "I am the handmaid of the Lord in
the house of the Lord," not on her lips alone, but cheerfully she made herself the servant of all, becoming all things
to all men.[1] She considered it her duty to select the hardest and meanest work for herself, and without being
asked, to assist her Sisters in every necessity of body or of
soul ; she was therefore styled the "universal helper," because, notwithstanding her own feeble health, she was always ready to help when a Sister was taken sick or was in
any other way hindered in her work ; and this she did so
cordially and so cheerfully, that her loving heart could be
felt by every one.

The sick and the feeble experienced her love and had
most of her assistance. Her compassion for them was so
great that she could not keep back her tears ; she wished
to suffer with them and for them, nay, to be sick with the
sick. She tended them cheerfully day and night, performing with pleasure the most difficult and repugnant services in
their behalf, consoling, tending, praying ; she did everything that she imagined they would like. The sick Sisters
often said that she was a true mother to them, rather than
a nurse. In the service of the sick, she carried her self-
denial to the extreme, especially when she assumed the care of
Sister Dorothea Osterrieder, an aged religious.[2] The age and
the nature of the sickness made nursing this Sister so hard,
that the other Sisters could no longer conquer their loathing and disgust ; Crescentia then undertook the case, and
her zeal grew in fervor as the sickness increased ; nay,
perhaps to punish an involuntary feeling of disgust, she, in
the same heroic manner as we read of in the life of St.
Catherine of Sienna, once mortified herself by forcing herself to take into her mouth the stinking expectorations of
the sick woman.

She gained a similar victory over herself, when the Sisters M. Anna Neth and M. Angelina Aichel had very bad

---

[1] I. Cor. ix. 22.   [2] Summ. N. 10, § 203,

wounds on their feet : not content with cleansing and dressing these, she conquered herself so far as to suck them out. The former of these Sisters was thereby cured at once without the use of any other remedy.' It is self-evident that she had a greater care for the spiritual welfare of the sick than for their physical health. She consoled and admonished them by salutary instructions and proverbs, and was specially careful to provide for them a timely reception of the Sacraments. She even had the special grace of foreknowing the hour of their death. When it drew near, she did not stir from the bed of death, but rendered bodily and spiritual help up to the last moment. Other Sisters were once tending the sick Sister M. Clara Perl, and did not at all apprehend that death was near; suddenly Crescentia entered the infirmary, saying : "See there ! Clara is dying." And so it was ; had she not come, Clara would have expired without the other attendants remarking it.

The salvation of her Sisters was as dear to her heart as her own. She sometimes said, with inexpressible emphasis: "Oh, my beloved Sisters ! Could I but carry you in my arms up to Heaven, how gladly would I sacrifice my honor and my life to do it !" With eyes upturned to Heaven, she frequently repeated the loving words of the Saviour : "Holy Father, keep them in Thy name, whom Thou hast given me." [2] How as Mistress of Novices and as Superioress she continued to work in the same spirit, we shall hereafter give in detail.

The crown of all the practices of love for one's neighbor is patience with the failings of our fellow-men, and especially "love of one's enemies." The great precept of the Lord : "Love your enemies, do good to them that hate you, and pray for them that persecute and calumniate you," [3] Crescentia inculcated not only by word of mouth, but by such conspicuous and heroic example, that the universal conviction found expression in the words : "The more bar-

---

[1] Summ. N. 10, § 401.   [2] John xvii. 11.   [3] Matth. v. 44.

barously one behaves to Crescentia, the dearer one becomes to her." Deviating from the view generally taken, she declared that her persecutors and enemies were her greatest benefactors. "Consider it as undoubtedly true," she used to say, "that our enemies are our greatest benefactors. They pay such diligent attention to our faults and remind us of them, so that we can look after and amend them." To these words of the servant of God, we can safely apply the saying of the Lord : "Blessed art thou. . . . . . because flesh and blood hath not revealed it to thee, but My Father who is in Heaven." [1] In the same sense she expressed herself when she was told that such and such persons were her enemies ; with a smile on her face she gave her opinion in the following words : " I know nothing about enemies. For, indeed, my greatest enemies are my greatest friends, since they give me an occasion to go to my beloved God, and to suffer a little for love of Him." She once said to Sister Joachima, that if she were most cruelly put to death by any one, and then restored to life, she would confer every act of love she could think of on her murderer ; " for," she added, " it is God's command that we should love our enemies, and that must be sufficient for us." God granted her the most abundant graces to carry out in actions these exalted sentiments. Few men have encountered such reckless disregard of justice, such ingratitude, such spite and contempt, in return for the practice of sublime virtues, in the degree that befell Crescentia. Yet, as we have already stated, all these floods of mighty wrongs could not extinguish the fire of love within her, nay, they served but to increase it.

When she had favors to confer she gave the preference to her enemies, even when doing so laid her open to the imputation of stupidity, want of feeling, or hypocrisy. No one could finally withstand such kindness. She not only kept silent respecting the offences she received, but she took the offender's part. She often kissed the

---

[1] Matth. xvi. 17.

footprints of those who had just before grievously insulted her. It happened, at the time when she was calumniated as a witch, that some one, instigated by the devil, spat in her face ; she immediately knelt down and asked pardon of the offender. Sister M. Josepha relates other similar cases, where she at once asked pardon, thereby moving every one, even the offending party, to tears. Then she continues: "I saw that once, when singing, she received a push from an old Sister named M. Antonia. Though she had committed no fault, and had been greatly insulted, she asked forgiveness with such sincere humility, that I could not refrain from weeping aloud." In later years such great offences did not recur, but God so ordained (many think at her special prayer) that she was never without an occasion to exercise her patient love. Some mocked at her ecstasies and revelations, laughed at her works of penance and heroic virtues, or declared them to be hypocrisy. Others maintained that her sickness was mostly laziness, that she would rather sit in the Church than work, and they were the more regardless in what they said against her, from the fact that she said that they were right, and undertook to defend them. It certainly came to pass, at times, that the other Sisters and the Superioress wished such unkindness to be punished ; then the servant of God came forward as mediatrix, knelt down and with tears prayed for the pardon of the Sisters' faults, and that a penance should be put on herself as the real offender. It was at all times with a heavy heart that she saw the Mother Superior impose a punishment on any Sister for a fault ; she would then never omit to ask the Superioress to put the penance on her as the worse one of the two.

Even on her death-bed, she gave a brilliant example of her love for her enemies.[1] She declared, with a countenance glowing with love, a few hours before her death : " I forgive, from my whole heart, all who may not have been

---

[1] Summ. N. 10, § 335.

favorably inclined towards me during my life-time; I wish
them every good, temporal and eternal.   Besides this, I forgive, beforehand, from my whole heart, every one who,
after my death, may judge ill or speak unfavorably of
me."

We have already spoken of the love with which she cherished the poor.   The mere title " Mother of the Poor," which
was given her during the seventeen years in which she was
door-keeper, to express the gratitude of the poor people,
speaks more than would many words; this title she never
dishonored in after times.   As Mother Superior especially,
she increased the usual daily dole of alms, and provided,
with special kindness, for poor families, as well as for the
sick and feeble.   In what spirit she did this, the following
words will show: " I thus feed the *Divine Word*, who
Himself said: I was hungry and you gave Me to eat."   It
was for this reason that she was so willing to be with the
poor, without being in the least repelled by their failings,
or their frequently over-exacting demands.   She listened
to their complaints with a mother's love, wept with them
over their sufferings, and instructed them how to win from
their poverty the benefit God intended to confer by its
means.   The kind and cordial manner with which she bestowed her alms perhaps did the poor more good than the
gift itself.   The most friendly smile and most endearing
words were reserved for the poor and sick.   When the conversation turned on these unfortunates, her eyes immediately
filled with tears, and if she was at table, she could no
longer eat ; she then requested of the Superioress to be
permitted to give her share of the food to the persons in
question.   She restricted her own physical needs to the
lowest point possible, that she might be able to give more
bounteously to the poor, and had not obedience restrained her, would have given everything away to the poor
members of Jesus Christ.

In the exercise of love, her catholic heart recognized no
limitations of country or of creed.   She frequently sent to

sick Lutherans victuals which she had in secret prepared, appropriate to their particular sickness. " For," she said, " every one is my neighbor ; the command to love excepts no one." [1] Such heroic love for her neighbor renders credible the reports that Christ Himself and some Saints appeared to her several times in the form of the poor, and received at her hands the gift of charity. The like occurrence is related of many of the Saints.

The following instance is related by Father Ott [2] and Sister M. Gabriel : [3] On a cold, wintry day a miserable old beggar came to the convent door and asked Crescentia for a pair of shoes. Full of compassion, she ran through the whole convent to get a pair of old shoes from somebody. When she returned to the Superioress with empty hands, she knelt down before her and most earnestly begged to be permitted to pull off her own shoes, and to offer them to the poor man. Having at length obtained permission to do this, she joyfully gave the poor man her shoes. He immediately vanished, leaving, however, bloody foot-prints on the spot where He had stood. By this, it became known to whom Crescentia had had the happiness of giving alms. In a document signed on August 28th, 1752, by several Sisters, and kept in the archives of the convent at Kaufbeuren, several similar cases are stated : especially that Christ, at one time in the form of a poor priest, at another in that of a pilgrim, had asked Crescentia for the alms of a dinner. But as these facts have not been sufficiently proved, we give them but a casual mention.

We conclude this chapter with the beautiful eulogy pronounced on her by a witness in the canonical process : " Nobody ever came in contact with her, without receiving from her light, consolation, and assistance." It is infallibly true that, " he that loveth not his brother, whom he seeth, how can he love God, whom he seeth not ?" [4] It is certain, beyond a doubt, that every Christian must render

---

[1] Summ. N. 10, § 177.   [2] Ott, B. 11. C. 6.
[3] Gabriel, p. 122.   [4] I. John iv. 20.

a strict account at the tribunal of Christ, as to whether he has paid the tribute of love to his Redeemer through the hands of his fellow-men.

Therefore, O Christian, look up to Him who is at once your Redeemer and your Judge, and listen to the assurance He gives you that He will look upon everything done to or withheld from your neighbor, as done to or withheld from Himself; having done this, ponder over the words: "Judge not and you shall not be judged. Condemn not, and you shall not be condemned.   Forgive and you shall be forgiven. Give and it shall be given to you." [1]

CHAPTER X.

On the Love and Assistance Conferred by Crescentia on the Suffering Souls in Purgatory. [2]

HE thoroughly catholic heart of Ven. Sister Crescentia, which embraced the whole communion of Saints, felt so great a compassion for the helpless and suffering souls who are detained in purgatory to be purified for Heaven, that a mother's heart could scarcely sympathize more with the sufferings of her sickly babe, than she sympathized with them. Her heart, therefore, continually urged her to use all the means to help them which the communion of Saints offers to its militant members here on earth through the teaching of the Church. She was ready joyfully to accept all the pain and affliction possible for their welfare. She had, as she states herself, made as it were of herself a voluntary sacrifice of propitiation to the Lord on their behalf, beseeching Him to let her suffer all their sufferings by virtue of the passion of Christ, that she might in their state satisfy the divine justice.

---

[1] Luke vi. 37, 38.   [2] Summ. N. 10.

Consequently, every day she did what she could to help them; she said many fervent prayers, practised severe works of penance and offered up her sufferings for them; in a word, like the widow in the Gospel, she threw the whole of her property, her entire living, that is, all her works of satisfaction for temporal punishment due to sins, into the treasury of the Church, in favor of those who have to pay their debts to the last farthing in the other world. She also recommended the practice to others, especially to her Sisters in religion. Many were induced by her, not only to perform many good works with this intention, but to give to the poor souls whatever they had acquired as a satisfaction to offer to God, for the payment of their temporal penalties for sin. This heroic act of love, which, as is well known, has of late been recommended by the Holy See, and enriched with special indulgences, she practised in preference to all others. Even on her death-bed she, as her confessor, Father Painer, relates, appointed the suffering souls as her universal heirs, and willed to them not only her past good works, as far as they were competent to discharge temporal debts for sin, but also all the holy Masses, prayers, and indulgences which others might offer up for her after her death.[1] Such love naturally evoked reciprocal love and served to knit more closely the ties of love which the spirit of Christ has, in a mysterious manner, cast around His living members, thereby elevating their intercourse in an extraordinary manner to a full consciousness of their mutual bearing. We must first remark that Crescentia, on her side, believed that she had many times received help from the poor souls in purgatory when she prayed to them.

She acknowledged, that when she desired a peculiarly great favor from God for herself or others, she also invoked the " beloved poor souls," and that then her prayers were usually answered at once. She entertained the conviction, which is now almost universal among Catholic

---

[1] Summ. N. 10, § 181.

people, that the souls in purgatory, who can no longer merit anything for themselves, can show their love effec- ively by praying for the members of the Church militant. Moreover, by permission of God, such souls often appeared to her, detailing their sufferings and appealing to her for help. Her compassion was in this way increased beyond measure ; she could not allow herself to rest until she had obtained for them either relief or deliverance. Souls thus liberated often returned to her in great glory to thank her, and to let her who had had so much compassion on their sufferings participate in some degree in their present joy. It can scarcely be told what hard sacrifices were laid on the servant of God, by this frequent intercourse with the souls in purgatory. Her night's rest, already so short, was in this way often completely taken from her. Scarcely had she gone to sleep when she was awakened by the groans or speech of such a soul, after which sleep was no longer to be thought of ; she had to pray or to chastise her innocent body. It was the general conviction of those who knew of her interior life that she had brought effective assistance to a great many souls. We gather from our sources of information some instances which will cast a light on this intercourse, and are to a great extent deserving of attention.

In 1718, Mother Johanna Altweger [1] asked Crescentia, when she was very sick, whether she could sleep. She said she could not, and on being further ques- tioned, acknowledged that the poor souls appeared to her and that their moaning, and groaning, and urgent prayers rendered sleep impossible. The compassionate Superior- ess thought that she must now interfere, and said : "You must have rest, absolutely, else you cannot stand it in the long run; so if the poor souls return to-night, tell them to go to the Mother ; obedience now requires that you should sleep." The servant of God punctually obeyed ; but the poor Mother no sooner saw and heard these apparitions

---

[1] Act. B. Summ. Object. N. 11, § 10.—Ott, B. III. C. 5.

in her own cell than, struck with fear and terror, she could find no other escape than to send them again to the good sick Sister. She herself told this occurrence on the next day to several Sisters (some of them bore witness to it in the canonical process), and she added that she never again, during her life, would make a similar attempt.

We take the following from Father Ott : [1]

Father Ignatius Wagener of the Society of Jesus, a man of great piety, erudition, and experience, who from October, 1713, to the autumn of 1715, had been at the head of the house of the Society in Kaufbeuren, had, at the special wish of the Father Provincial, Sebastian Höss, O. S. F., undertaken a particular investigation of the spirit of the servant of God. Through this, he himself had been filled with a high degree of veneration and admiration for her, and had directed her with great circumspection and charity. This had, on her part, led her to feel the greatest gratitude and veneration for him. This Father died October 19, 1716, at Regensburg, to which place he had been removed the year before. The notice of his death arrived at Kaufbeuren on the 21st of the same month. At the Angelus bell on the evening of the 19th, Crescentia, when going to the choir, noticed a white shadow advancing before her ; as the poor souls frequently appeared to her under that form, she contented herself with offering up some fervently devout prayers for this unknown soul. On the 21st, however, the soul appeared to her in the form of the deceased Father, stating that he had not been permitted to make himself known to her the first time. He asked her help, with God, that he might soon get to see the desired face of the Lord ; he added that he suffered no pain in the senses, but that he was kept away from the vision of God, because, during his life-time, his desire for that vision of God had been so feeble, and now this desire has become his greatest torment and punishment. It need scarcely be

<hr>

[1] Ott, B. II. C. 6, and B. III. C. 3.

mentioned that she did all she could to help this, her spiritual father ; and on October 23d, when she had prayed for him with great fervor at the holy Mass said for him, she had the consolation of seeing this same soul, surrounded with celestial splendor ; he appeared to her, thanked her, and assured her, that with her assistance he was inexpressibly happy in the possession of the Sovereign Good.'

The soul of one of the Sisters of the convent who had been dead six years, appeared to her and begged for help with the piteous words : " Oh, how I thirst for the strong and living God ! Oh, help me, who am unable to help myself ! " Bitterly weeping, Crescentia promised to do all that lay in her power, and shortly afterwards she received the assurance that this soul was redeemed.

While Crescentia was yet in the novitiate, and was one evening on a fast-day partaking of a meagre collation with the other Sisters, the door of the refectory was suddenly thrown open, and as suddenly closed. The Sisters were so much frightened that no one ventured to go out to see what might be the cause of so strange an occurrence. Crescentia alone was not alarmed, and immediately offered herself to Mother Theresa Schmid, to go and see if any one was outside. The Mother Superior bade her go, and she went and saw a nun, who said in a pitiful tone that she had formerly been in that convent, and had already for nine years been suffering in purgatory. She begged for assistance that she might be soon freed, and specified certain prayers and good works to be offered for that purpose. This was done, and by Crescentia especially with the greatest fervor ; she soon had the consolation of being assured of that soul's redemption.

 ' The opinion that some souls in purgatory suffer only the punishment of loss and not that of the senses, and that this is on account of the want of desire to see God, is defended by many theologians, among others by Cardinal Bellarmine. Many apparitions of souls, recognized as of known sanctity, favor this notion. The story of a particularly remarkable apparition and similar to the one related above, is related in the life of a great servant of God, Clara Gherzi, Abbess of the Poor Clares at Gubbio ; she died in 1801, and the process of her beatification is already far advanced. Her life is written by Father Capistranus, General of the Franciscans.

Even the souls of the faithful departed whom she had never seen, and who had died in distant lands, had recourse to her for assistance. Once, for three nights in succession, she heard a moaning in her cell, without any words. She then asked the soul who it was. A voice replied that it was the soul of a young deceased soldier of the Count's body guard at Munich : that he had lately been present at the convent of Kaufbeuren, to witness the profession of his own sister, M. Elizabeth ;[1] that he had shortened his own life by immoderate drinking, and must suffer the temporal punishment for this fault, by enduring inexpressible torments. If she did not come to his help, he would have to suffer as many years as he had cut off from his own life by intemperance. She did a great deal for this soul, and after a while saw it enter Heaven gloriously.

But the most remarkable history is the following, which we relate, following strictly the same authority : In the year 1718, on November 21st, Mr. Francis Joseph Scholl died. He had been counsellor to the court, and administrator of an important office at the Count's court in Kemnat. On the same day on which he died, Crescentia heard a peculiar fingering and rattling among the papers in her cell, which was repeated in the evening and early the next morning, although she had earnestly prayed for the soul who had probably caused it. On the morning of the 22d, she asked who was there. Then she distinctly heard : "I am the soul of Scholl, dear Crescentia, pray for me to your Beloved." She then asked what was the meaning of the noise among the papers. He answered, that he would return to her several times, and as soon as God permitted it, would tell her the reason of it. Thenceforward, she noticed the noise among the papers every day, thereby divining the presence of the soul. During the night of December 7th, the same voice spoke more particularly to her, stating that in his last sickness

---

[1] A Sister by the name of M. Elizabeth Krimer died in the Convent of Kaufbeuren Dec. 13, 1767,—born Aug. 11, 1696.

he had intended to settle all his affairs ; that somebody had come to him to complain of having been wronged in a certain matter ; that he had sent the man away with a few short and harsh words, giving him to understand that, according to the showing of his papers, no wrong had been done him. He (Scholl) had made a mistake in this and was not without fault in doing so : the complainant had really been defrauded of four florins. He then asked the servant of God to speak to the parish priest at Kemnat and get him to persuade his wife to make good the damage. On the Feast of the Immaculate Conception, December 8th, Crescentia told all this to the parish priest of Kemnat, Dr. Philip James Meichelbeck, who was at that time the father confessor of the convent. He at once remembered that a man, whose name he mentioned, had, on November 2d, complained to him of the wrong suffered, and of the harsh words of the deceased councilman, and strangely enough, the man had repeated the same words that Crescentia had heard from the apparition. The wrong was repaired at once : the rattling in the papers ceased ; not so, however, the moaning and entreaties of the deceased, for these were especially urgent on Christmas eve. Immediately after New Year the apparition told her that God had announced to him, by his guardian angel, a speedy delivery. On January 6th, 1710, Crescentia had offered up, for that soul, four holy Masses, which four priests had promised her to say on that day. The last of these Masses was said between ten and eleven o'clock, and at the same time the deceased appeared to her in wondrous splendor, and thanked her for her help ; she then saw in spirit how that soul was conducted by the angels into Heaven, and received with infinite joy before the throne of God. At the end of this report Father Ott says : " Dr. Meichelbeck, parish priest of Kemnat and confessor of the convent, to whom Crescentia had to tell every particular of this occurrence, wrote out the whole history in all its details, giving all the circumstances in such a manner that we cannot doubt the truth of it."

And now, having related so many apparitions of these poor souls, we can scarcely suppress the remark that on this field, fallacies or even deceptions may very easily creep in, and that unless such reports are attested by persons of extraordinary sanctity and of supernatural knowledge, as was the case with Ven. M. Crescentia, prudence requires caution in giving credit to them. To deny the principle on which they are founded is scarcely reconcilable with the doctrine of the Communion of Saints, or with the respect due to the thousands of Saints who maintain that they had similar apparitions. The Catholic Faith does not by any means rest on the private revelations of individuals, but on the Word of God deposited in the Church in verbal and written form, laid by her before the faithful and explained with infallible certainty. This Holy Church teaches us :[1] "'That there is a purgatory, and that souls detained there may be helped by the prayers of the faithful, but especially by the sacrifice of the altar, so pleasing to God."

This faith must be the rule of our actions. The apparitions and revelations mentioned above may, however, help us to practise more and more catholic love towards these holy, but helpless suffering souls. Therefore, O Christian! do for them what you would have done to yourself when you yourself suffer in this purifying fire: "It is, therefore, a holy and wholesome thought to pray for the dead, that they may be loosed from sins."[2]

---

[1] Trid. Sess. 25.   [2] II. Mach. xii. 46.

CHAPTER XI.

Her Fortitude and Love of the Cross.[1]

"HO shall find a valiant woman ? the price of her is from afar off and from the uttermost coasts."[2] This high praise of the Holy Ghost the servant of God deserved in a rare degree. She trod from her infancy the rough paths of the most difficult exercises of virtue and of fearful suffering without, so far as the eye could detect, swerving one moment from the difficult task, or wavering under the heavy pressure of the cross which God had laid upon her. We do not know which to admire the more in her, the spirit of fortitude in her actions, or the patience, joy, and love she showed in suffering. In both respects we encounter a superhuman strength in the weakness of her sex. She herself points out the source of her strength in the beautiful expression : "The true means of being immovable is, O Lord, no other than to adhere to Thee."

A retrospective view of what we have already related shows us with what admirable fortitude she trod the most sublime paths of mortification and of self-denial, overcoming all obstacles ; and not that alone, but constantly advancing in the steps of a higher progress, subduing all natural feelings, even the most justifiable, in order to attain her one end and aim, that of the Supreme Good. How courageously did she not keep her heart from the world, even when in the midst of the world, to keep it filled with God Himself! How she stept over the love she bore to her family, to seek the Crucified in the convent ! and when in the years of her novitiate, mountains of difficulties and temptations towered up to assail her, the tender virgin never looked back, but removed all the mountains by faith. She never withdrew her foot from the path of self-denial

and suffering. The repugnance of nature, the contradictions of men, the most violent persecutions of the world
and of hell could neither turn her away from the straight
and narrow path, nor retard her progress thereon. Faithful unto death, forever fighting and gloriously conquering,
she followed the sorrowful road of the imitation of Christ,
and because, here below, she sowed in tears, we have reason
to believe that the seed thus sown has ripened to a wonderful harvest in Heaven.

To conquer one's self is, even according to the heathen of
antiquity, an indication of a higher degree of courage
than to fight with one's enemies. According to this measure, Crescentia is a heroine of the first rank. The naturally powerful feelings of hope and fear, joy and sorrow,
were so completely subjected to her will, that no worldly
consideration could influence her, even in the smallest
things. She was as if dead to the enticements and threat-
enings of the world. In every lawful matter she preferred
the will of others to her own, with the greatest readiness ;
but firm and unyielding, full of calm and peace, she was
not to be persuaded by any mockery and persecution to deviate from the road pointed out by obedience and the Holy
Ghost. Peace was always present with her ; she smiled
amidst the greatest storms and sufferings ; there was no
trace of cowardice in her, but also no bragging of heroism.
She did not shrink from telling the bitter truth, even to
persons of high-standing, when the spirit of God moved her
so to do ; nor, when Superioress, did she hesitate to curb
faults and put an end to abuses, but she did it with such
prudence, love, and firmness, that no one resisted her.
The boldest mocker was silenced by her glance, and hardened sinners bowed their stubborn heads before her admonitions. Yet, she ever preserved a modest, disciplined deportment, without showing coldness or repugnance. She
was full of love without particular attachments, pious
and meek, thoughtful, amiable, and regularity itself, without pedantry. There was no affectation or coquetry in her

behavior, all was nature and grace ; a noble soul and God were mirrored in every word, in every movement.

Fortitude of soul manifests itself yet more in suffering than in action ; and on this stage of suffering, where we can least hide ourselves behind a deceitful mask, God revealed, in the highest degree, the spirit of courage He had laid in this tender heart. What St. Paul writes of the Philippians was accomplished in her in the highest degree: "For unto you it is given for Christ, not only to believe in Him, but also to suffer for Him."[1] In love to suffer with Christ, means also to suffer for Him, and this was granted to her abundantly. She considered all her sufferings as graces. She once said: "One of the greatest signs that God cares for me is this, that He always gives me opportunities to suffer something for Him." She said, "to suffer something," yet at times she expressed herself like this: "I suffer nothing at all, and have never suffered anything, although I am the greatest sinner !" But it was her insatiable desire for suffering which applied this depreciating view to torments, which to ordinary human nature appeared terrible, nay, insupportable. Father Ott[2] says with justice: "Under the special inspiration of the Holy Ghost, and an extraordinary gift of fortitude, she, during the forty years of her convent life, had borne and stood firm under such great and terrible trials that even a man's heart shudders at the mere recital of them." The reader already knows that envy, calumny, and persecution, which, like lightning, like best to strike the heights and summits of Virtue, poured forth their whole rage on Crescentia, that the devils tormented her in their most cruel fashion, that she suffered continually from physical pain, and frequently even more severely by interior spiritual distress. In regard to her bodily condition, this, at its best, would have been a state of severe suffering for other people. Within she was consumed by a constant fever, and a tormenting thirst, which she neither could nor would quench,

---

[1] Philip. 1. 29.   [2] Ott, B. III. C. 13.

as the luke-warm water which she drank rather increased than lessened it. To this were added extremely painful head-aches, and frequently still more painful tooth-aches, while from time to time came severe and painful sicknesses of a serious character.

In all her sufferings she showed not only an admirable patience and resignation, but—and this is at once the test and the summit of Christian patience—a veritable joy in and with suffering, and a *great desire to suffer more.* She sought no alleviation, and only from obedience took the medicine prescribed, which for the most part rather increased than lessened her malady. When told to ask God to diminish her suffering, she replied: "What! am I to ask my Jesus not to permit me to follow Him in His sufferings? If I could turn away from me all crosses and pains by saying a single Hail Mary, I would not say it for that purpose."

Not one of her Sisters in religion ever heard her utter a word of complaint, either about her suffering or concerning the neglect to which she was exposed by the indiscretion of others. Not even the ordinary complaint of heat, cold, or other inconveniences, which so easily escapes one's lips, ever came from her, and what is still more, no one ever remarked in her any sign of sadness, dejection, or despondency, on account of personal suffering, and yet such sometimes occurs in the hour of weakness to the strongest hearts. "Indeed," she once said, "I do not know what despondency is." This fortitude in suffering is more than human, its source can be in God alone, as a remark of hers clearly indicates: once when suffering acutely, she was asked if she did not wish for a stimulant; she answered: "The will of God is strength, and it is stimulant enough for me."

She had given herself up so completely to God, that the most painful sufferings could not compel her to desire an alleviation of them. Her will rested so completely in the divine will, that she did not in the least wish to know what

the future might have in store for her.   Once she said: ''A
religious person must not busy herself with troublesome
thoughts concerning the future; her sole solicitude should
be *now* to love God above all things, and serve Him with
all her strength.   The anxiety as to what will become of the
soul and body at some future time, we must leave to God
alone, as the all-providing and merciful Father."   This
calmness and resignation in suffering increased to such a
degree that she knew how to draw from it, not alone no
sadness, but *peace* and joy in the Holy Ghost.   Her motto
was: '' On earth nothing is great and sweet till it is crushed
and roasted," and of herself she said: ''To love God
and to suffer for Him are the two props of my life."

That these were not mere empty forms of speech is
proved by her whole life, especially by her behavior in
severe sicknesses.   Father Ott[1] relates a special instance of
this :   In a severe sickness, she was once cramped in her
hands and feet, or rather, by a contraction of the nerves,
her feet were bent backward in such a way that she had to
lie in bed rolled up like a ball, in inexpressible pain.   The
pains were worst in the back and between the shoulders.
Yet her courage and peace of mind never wavered.   She returned a thousand thanks to her Redeemer, asserting, with
a cheerful countenance, that these pains were specially dear
to her, because they continually reminded her of Christ's
carrying His cross.   Nay, the force of love so controlled
the feeling of pain, that she often broke forth with the
words: '' O ye my bones ! praise the Lord, for having given
you the capability of suffering."   Many days and nights
she lay upon this rack.   At length her guardian angel appeared to her, and promised that on the next day, after Holy
Communion, she should get well.   In the natural course
of things, this was impossible.   Yet after Holy Communion she arose from her sick-bed in good health, to the wonder and admiration of everybody.

Her joy in suffering was bound up with a genuine hun-

---

[1] Ott, B. II. C. 13.

ger for still greater sufferings. She had recognized the treasure that lies hid in suffering, and maintained that it surpassed all understanding, that all the honors, dignities, and riches of the world, taken together, could not compare with the slightest degree of contempt borne for the love of God. In this spirit she prayed for suffering as for an undeserved grace, and loved to repeat these words of a Saint : "Lord, not to die, but to suffer." She expresses this sentiment very beautifully in a little prayer which she wrote in 1727, and which she often repeated ; it is : "O Lord, love for love, suffering for suffering, pain for pain, mockery for mockery, contempt for contempt, life for life, wounds for wounds, death for death—and all this for no other reward than love."[1] In like manner, she expressed herself in the following words : "Lord, let the reward of my love be pain and sorrow ! And as a recompense for the calumnies I have undergone, heap upon me new contempt, inflict on me new and deeper wounds ; for that love which has no desire to accomplish great things and to bear heavy crosses, is no love at all ; it is not fire, it is an icicle. If you were to put in one scale all the mockeries and sicknesses, fire and sword, and every imaginable evil, and in the other, all the pleasures, riches, and amusements of the world, I would turn my back on the pleasures and treasures of the world, and with outstretched arms hasten to the torments and contempt ; nay, my greatest desire would be to rush forward to meet the most agonizing death."

Even in the last years of her life she once, on her knees, besought the Father Provincial, Boniface Schmidt, O. S. F., to pray to God for that singular grace that she might not be at any time without suffering, and that he, the Provincial, would also grant her the merit of obedience in all her sufferings. When he consented, she was extraordinarily glad, because she now believed herself to be more like Christ, who suffered so much, out of obedience to His Heavenly Father. This glowing thirst for suffering remained in un-

---

[1] Kolb, p. 33.

diminished vigor until death ; it stood firm under every
trial, and under the pressure of suffering burst forth more
powerfully than before, increasing in flame like a furious
fire under a jet of water. She then prayed in a cheerful
tone and with a sweet voice : "O my God, I thank Thee
a thousand times ! Increase my torments, but increase my
patience also. My heart is ready, O God, my heart is ready
to suffer all, as it pleases Thee!" If she were asked, when
suffering thus, how she was, she would answer : "Quite
well, since I am fulfilling God's will." To love and to suffer were the same thing to her ; and since her life was entirely consecrated to love, we may well understand how she
could assert the principle : "*There is no cross like that of
living without a cross.*" This is, indeed, a complete conversion of nature, it is the triumph of grace. The great
God who, as the Rev. Alban Stoltz asserts, has decreed for
His elect, "a sword through the heart on earth, and in
Heaven a crown on the head," breathes into His Saints
the sentiments which correspond to so noble a destiny.
This love of the cross showed itself prominently in Crescentia. Whoever beheld her sufferings and heard her
words scarcely dared to trust his own senses, so marvellous
in the frail vessel of flesh appeared the power of grace
which could change pain into joy, contempt into honor,
the pressure of tribulation into consolation, darkness into
light, and even death into life.

For the edification of the reader, we subjoin some sayings of the servant of God concerning the value and object
of suffering ; they are taken from the Acts and from the
writings of both Father Ott [1] and Sister Gabriel: [2] "To
love God without limit, and to suffer for Him are two in-
separable things. Afflictions are the nutriment of love ;
they keep alive and nurse the flame of love. Love which
does not long for great things, and is not willing to suffer
much, is not a golden love, but a brazen one. There is

---

[1] Ott, B. I.   [2] Gabriel, p. 86.

no other road to Heaven but the way of the cross ; it is the surest and the noblest ; God Himself trod that path. Who would not constantly endeavor to advance on that road with giant strides ?   Nothing excites in us the love of God more than many crosses and sufferings. Sufferings are the touchstone by which God tries whether the virtue of a spiritual person is genuine or not. We must not love this life for any other reason than because we can here suffer for God's love. Crosses are generally the greatest favors of God, and nothing can properly be called a cross, except to be without a cross; that is, indeed, the greatest cross. Whosoever aims at a union of love with Christ, must never desire to be freed from crosses ; rather must he seek his consolation therein, and look on them as the surest road to God."

We will close this chapter with the grand hymn which, far and wide, is known by her name and which has already afforded consolation to many a drooping heart.

Hymn of the Blessed Mary Crescentia Höss, of Kaufbeuren.

Sweet hand of my God, how my heart dost Thou cheer!
  I can joke with my suffering, while feeling Thee by ;
God strikes as with balls, yet His blows become dear,
  For the harder He strikes me, the higher I fly.

Yet I must acknowledge God planes very thin ;
  He cuts me, He chips me, I think it not rough.
Would you wish to know wherefore?   Thus does He begin
  To make me an angel by carving enough.

Oft am I abandoned, on cross or in woe,
  Then I think God rejoices, He wills it be so ;
He is hiding as hunter, the wild prey to snare ;
  We see not, we hear not, we feel not His care

Like a tree springing up in a garden am I,
  God Himself is the gardener, He prunes me in time,

He cleanses, He trims, and supports by each tie,
   That my fruit may be larger, that higher I climb.

'Tis therefore in sorrow I joy can maintain,
   Tho' Satan entice, tho' the world may complain,
I hear not, I heed not, to neither consent;
   My one, my sole aim, is on Heaven intent.

Oft I say to myself, thou flow'ret in bloom,
   Wilt wither already? Thus soon to forget
That pains me so sharply! Then I think of the doom,
   The leaves they must fall, that the seed may be set.

I fear then no suffering, great though it may be,
Which the hand of my God is conveying to me: `
More quickly is iron unto steel made alike,
When fiercely the smith with the hammer doth strike.

What can injure the eye, when you're melting away,
If the vine-stock of life is then shooting the spray?
Though one tear bring many: they fall to the earth,
And sorrow at length unto joy shall give birth.

Should torment continue, anxiety plague,
Like wave beating wave, in a wandering vague,
When it's God's hand that's fishing, then no one denies
The darker the water, the richer the prize.

God's pressure, tho' painful, yet patience bestows,
For then I think humbly, with heart full of throes,
I've deserved what I suffer: no organ alone,
When the keys were not pressed, ever gave forth a tone.

Come, blow, then, or trouble, since thus it must be,
All vain else the hope that we Heaven may see;
When the full sheaves are stacked, what of use doth appear,
Till the thresher has beaten the grain from the ear?

For a time, and a short one, God's hand with us plays,
Then to rain follows sunshine, joy sorrow allays;
   Endure, then, and bear what on thee God may lay:
   When discontent rises, be silent and pray.

To suffer in this life be ever content,
Till the threads of thy sorrow by God's hand are rent:
Then thy flesh to the worms: to the earth, then, thy bones:
Heaven's bliss to thy soul for thy sorrow atones.

Thus be it established: this proof of God's love:
Here cut and *here* burn, but be gracious above!
Then grateful inscribe I these words on my grave:
" Heaven's bliss, after sorrow, my God to me gave."

CHAPTER XII.

Crescentia Crucified with Christ by Severe Penances and Mortification.[1]

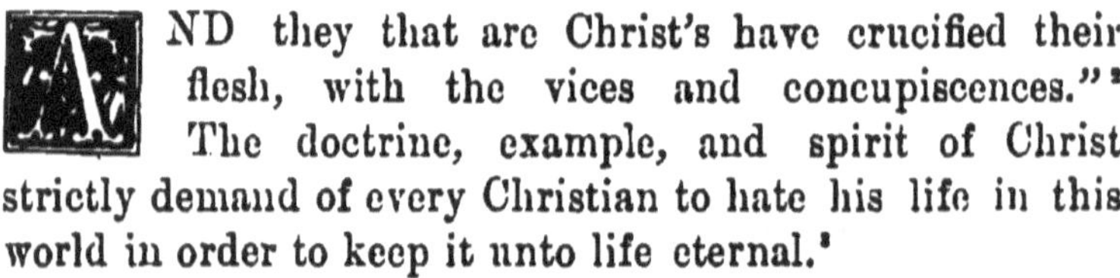

ND they that are Christ's have crucified their flesh, with the vices and concupiscences."[2] The doctrine, example, and spirit of Christ strictly demand of every Christian to hate his life in this world in order to keep it unto life eternal.[3]

These principles of the Gospel were deeply imprinted on the mind of Crescentia. She taught that "whosoever desires to love God must be entirely and forever dead to himself, so that he can say in very truth, I live, but now not I, but Christ liveth in me." And "the road to perfection does not consist in consolation and sweetness, but in continual self-denial, in frequent humiliations and in despising one's self." She often spoke thus and always acted accordingly.

As an inordinate self-love at first attaches itself to an inordinate enjoyment of the senses, and as "the flesh lusteth against the spirit,"[4] thus also doth the spirit of Jesus Christ rise up against the flesh and is an inveterate enemy of the pleasures of the senses. And hence Crescentia felt,

---

[1] Summ. N. 17, § 1-93 and N. 18, § 1-12.—Act. B. Inform. § 219-229.
[2] Galat. v. 24.   [3] John xii. 25.   [4] Galat. v. 17.

from her very infancy, that the interior spirit which she had received from above continually urged her not only to renounce the pleasure which she could have received from the outer world, but also permanently and voluntarily to bear pains and penances. The first enemy from the sensual camp is "love of eating." She called this inclination the "domestic enemy," and admonished her pupils to be well on the look-out against it, "because," she said, "no one knows how cunning this enemy can be. We must be very heroic if we would not yield to it, and we must at once suppress inordinate desires for eating and drinking, else the devil will capture us. We ought to take food for necessity's sake, not for enjoyment. There is nothing more odious than for a religious person to be enslaved by such things, feeding the heart with sensual pleasures. We should also, in taking what is necessary, call on the Holy Ghost, that the soul too may be fed, whilst the body is nourished."

On account of the great severity against herself in this very point, the Sisters often advised her to eat ; she used then to reply, in the words of the Lord: "Not in bread alone doth man live, but in every word that proceedeth from the mouth of God."[1] Her life was a continuous fast of such severity that no one could understand how life could be sustained on so little and such meagre food. But as sensual pleasure may arise and claim its share even in taking poor food, she imposed on herself the strict law, neither to seek the pleasure of taste, nor to attend to it, nay, not even purposely to admit it. The greater part of her life she took but one repast a day and that at noon. For many years she had permission to absent herself from the common table in the evening ; even when she was present she usually took nothing. Sometimes she ate nothing the whole day, at times not even in two or three days.[2] In her last sickness she ate nothing for six weeks, and in the illness before the last, which lasted a longer time, she took but little: daily Communion was then her nourishment. At dinner in the refectory she took only a little barley broth, which for many years was specially prepared for her; to this she added a few herbs, and in summer some lettuce sprinkled with warm water or tasteless broth. To conceal her mortifications, she said that she liked to eat it, and they could see by this how weak and luxurious she was. If she were busy in the kitchen, so as not to be at table, she would eat from the remnants brought back on the dishes; nay, if she were not noticed, she drank of the nauseous dish-water.

Water was for many years her usual and only beverage, and this not fresh, but lukewarm or warm water; this was a more severe mortification, from the fact that she suffered continually from thirst, being troubled with inward heats. Her mouth was frequently parched, so that she could hardly speak. Besides this, she mortified her sense of taste in the manner she had learned as a child from her own father: by mixing, when not observed, bitter things, as worm-wood, ashes, fish-galls, etc., with her eatables and beverages. If she had to take medicine, she made the mortification of her taste atone for the alleviation of the sickness: she would keep the most nauseous medicines a long time in her mouth; chewed her pills slowly, and sipped the most disgusting fluids drop by drop.[1] By this severity to herself she had reached the point that she could no longer distinguish food by the taste, and had no preference for one kind more than for another, yet she frequently complained, with tears, that she treated her body, which, like our holy Father St. Francis, she called her donkey, too effeminately and too delicately.

As for the rest, she never spoke of eating and drinking and did not like the subject. She herself says she did not think of it, except when the signal bell called her to the refectory, and then it was a real torture to her to be obliged to comply with this low and physical necessity. She then obeyed the call of obedience, but her mind was occupied with God and her will followed the divine will, which had imposed on her the yoke of the necessity of eating, rather than the impulse of the senses demanding nutriment. She said the grace before and after meals with angelic devotion, and at every mouthful she took practised the exercise of sublime intentions and reflections. At the beginning of the meal she cut a piece of bread in the shape of a triangle and in it contemplated the Blessed Trinity during the time of the repast.[1] Her intention in taking food was directed to that perfection of motive which Jesus and Mary might have entertained at such a time. Her thoughts, while she was eating, were not for a moment averted from the spiritual reading, or from the subject of her meditation, and thus it often came to pass that she was rapt in ecstasy at table. Who does not feel a wondrous admiration for this holy soul, who was more recollected in God when attending to the wants of her body than we ourselves are at prayer or at Holy Communion.

As with the sense of taste, so with the other senses ; she withdrew from them the pleasant sensations which nature craves : she permitted not that her ears should hear or her eyes see even the most innocent things, except in so far as they might serve the soul. She not only did not allow the organ of smelling to enjoy perfumes artificially prepared, but she denied it even the fragrance of flowers, while she compelled herself to accept all repugnant impressions, nay, even went in search of them. The infirmary was welcome to her on this account. When other Sisters turned away from the bad odors occurring there, or held their noses, she would say cheerfully : " This shows me very clearly what I shall be one day," or she used the words of Job : " I have said to rottenness, thou art my father: to worms, you are my mother and my sister." [2]

She denied herself all comfort in the carriage and position which she might so easily have indulged in. No matter how weak or sick she might be, she never leaned

---

[1] Gabriel, p. 167.   [2] Job xvii. 14.

against anything when at prayer or at work. That God wished that mortification on her part, appears from the following occurrence related by Father Ott :[1] Once she was so tired by long and hard work that she thought she could no longer keep on her feet. She then asked the Saviour to permit her to support her hands a little by the screen of the choir, but she at once heard the words : " My child," thus the Lord usually addressed her, " this is no time to rest."

All these mortifications, however, did not satisfy the spirit of penance animating Crescentia ; her motto was : " The more we nail the body to the cross, and the more patiently we bear offences from others, the more grace we may hope for in this life, and the greater glory in the next." She, therefore, was always inventing new ways of torturing her body, being, however, even more intent on mortifying her will by obedience. She attempted nothing without previously receiving permission from her father confessor. The more he permitted her, the greater became her desire, the more urgent her petition to obtain permission to carry out yet greater works of mortification.

Her sleep at longest lasted but two or three hours, and often not that, as her confessor, Father Pamer, relates. During her short night's rest she gave pain to her body by keeping it in an inconvenient position. During her youth she often slept on the hard floor ; later on, she slept on a bed, indeed, yet it was on a large wooden cross, which is yet preserved with great veneration in her cell. When she became old and feeble she was not permitted to do this any more ; yet leaving this off was no advantage to the comfort of the body, for God sent her such pains that as soon as she lay down, she was either tortured by heat as great as if she were lying in fire, or suffered such a degree of cold that it seemed to her as if she were frozen to an icicle.[2] This torture was scarcely endurable, nevertheless she persevered in it until permitted by obedience to rise.

---

[1] Ott. B II. C. 8.   [2] Ott. B. II. C. 8.

To these privations she added the chastisement of her body by the use of painful instruments of penance. She encircled her arms and body with sharp cilices or girdles, which she scarcely ever laid aside; these often penetrated into her flesh, so that it was with difficulty she drew them out. On her breast, in memory of the Passion of Christ, she wore a cross almost a foot long and set with sharp points. On her bare head she wore, in memory of the crown of thorns, a hoop set with iron prickles, causing her, like the cross, immense pain.

As often as she received permission, that is, at least once a day, but mostly three times, she scourged herself with disciplines, in which iron wires or spurs were interlaced. She used these so ruthlessly against herself that she shed much blood and the skin of her neck was flayed. Several times, on this account, her garments stuck to her body so firmly that she was unable to loosen them, and had to get others to help her. Sister M. Elizabeth Krimer, at the command of the Mother Superior, frequently rendered her this painful service of charity. She carefully concealed her instruments of penance; nevertheless, Sister M. Gabriel once caught sight of her discipline, and saw, with a shudder, that it was quite bloody and that pieces of skin were sticking to the little iron wheels of the spurs.[1]

Some of these instruments of penance are still in existence; but the Sisters say[2] that she herself destroyed the most painful of them shortly before her death. Thirty years after her death, they still plainly showed traces of blood and diffused a marvellously pleasant odor all around.[3] Numberless witnesses attest this from their own experience. She had also the habit of putting little stones in her shoes, in order to bear in mind and to venerate the bloody footsteps made by our Saviour in His last walk. This she did, for instance, when she made the customary little pilgrimage to St. Wendelin, at Germaringen; to the shrine of the Mother of Dolors at Ebenhofen, and to St.

---

[1] Ott, B. II. C. 8.   [2] Ibid. § 107.   [3] Summ. x. 8, § 107 et passim.

Michael's. We easily incline to think that such a pressure of hard works of penance, united with such a load of bodily sufferings, would surpass the measure of human strength and consequently the limits of discretion. But so strong was the sublime spirit living within her, that she, on the contrary, not only moved around easily and cheerfully in this heavy armor, but looked upon all this as trifling and insufficient. She thought that her life was altogether unmortified, effeminate, and useless, and therefore teased her confessors to grant her the great privilege of doing more.

If in her exterior mortifications she is more to be wondered at than imitated, she herself laid the greatest stress on interior self-denial, and as the account of her life everywhere shows, she attained to great perfection therein. All human passions seemed absolutely dead within her. No attachment or aversion, no desire or fear in reference to human affairs, no sadness or frivolous joy, no emotions of anger or dejection appeared exteriorly, or darkened the interior of this soul, so wholly weaned from the world, so utterly absorbed in God. Even the first spontaneous emotions of this description appeared but seldom in later years and were then easily and instantly suppressed. After the many heroic victories she had gained, the flesh so full of the pleasures of the world and of the senses, so full also of selfishness, scarcely dared to raise its head against reason, or to resist the direction of God in the loftier ways of the spirit. Hence came the visible, fascinating harmony and calm in her whole conduct ; hence the perfect display of the beautiful picture of all Christian virtues ; hence the steadfastness with which she ever remained equal to herself in all the situations and vicissitudes of life. Storms which usually overturn the heart of man, and lay bare abysses which reach down to hell itself, could not darken the mirror of her soul or even excite its waves to a gentle movement. The powers of her nature easily obeyed the movements of the Holy Ghost dwelling within her; the holy fire which blazed within her heart, burst forth outwardly and consumed every fault adhering to the flesh, making of her body and soul a true holocaust of love.

O most happy virgin, so similar in spirit as in body to the Lamb of God crucified, sacrificed ! Happy virgin, who united the lily of virginity to the most fragrant rose of voluntary martyrdom ! If the sword of persecution did not take away her physical life, yet did love adorn her life with the sufferings and merits of the holy martyrs.

O Christian ! do you desire one day to partake of the resurrection and glory of Christ ? Then do not now refuse to feel the death of Christ in your own flesh, by dying to the world, by denying your natural affections and by practically accepting the sufferings of this life ; to you, too, the words of the Apostle apply : "You are dead and your life is hid with Christ in God."[1]

CHAPTER XIII.

How the Humble Servant of God Takes the Last Place.[2]

THE words of Isaias the prophet apply to the faithful child of God : "It shall take root downward and bear fruit upward."[3] That is to say, it takes a lowly position from humility and is on that account elevated in grace and merits, and adorned with the "fruits of light;" with more than human virtue.

In order to avoid the downfall of Lucifer, who wanted to rise higher, when he ought to have humbled himself, there is but one means left to a privileged soul and that is, to become as much less in his own estimate of self, as he becomes proportionally greater by grace in God. Nay,

---

[1] Col. iii. 3.   [2] Summ. N. 19, § 1, 224.—Act. B. Inform. § 230–238.
[3] IV. Kings xix. 30.

these two conditions are so inseparably united by the power of divine ordinance, that we can affirm that this lowering of one's self and rising to God are one and the same thing, as in a balance, where one scale goes down as the other goes up. St. Gregory says : " The greater the light of virtue poured by the Holy Ghost into the hearts of the elect, the greater will be the gift of humility with which He enriches them." [1] According to these principles the reader can scarcely expect anything else, than that the humility of Ven. M. Crescentia should manifest itself in a manner barely comprehensible to the ordinary class of people. She knew it would be folly to erect an edifice for eternity on any other foundation than that of humility, which Christ, the only wise builder, taught alike by word and example. She therefore had these words of the Lord often on her lips : "Learn of Me, for I am meek and humble of heart," [2] and added : " On this rock, which is Christ, must all our virtues be based." She wished, by this, to say that this rock, Christ, can only be reached and a solid foundation laid upon it, by descending into the depths of one's own nothingness and sinfulness.

The nature of this mysterious virtue she well understood. "Humility," she said, "does not consist in hanging down one's head and giving free utterance to humble words and expressions, but in the light of a true knowledge of one's self and one's sins, as also of the greatness of God, and from these to conceive an aversion for the esteem and love of men." She constantly prayed for this light, that she might obtain this knowledge of God and of self ; using for this purpose the well-known words of St. Augustine : " Lord, may I know myself ! may I know Thee ! " How far God granted her this light is shown in the little prayer with which she concluded her resolutions : [3] " O my God !   Thou alone knowest my weakness ; I sink into my nothingness, and pray to Thee to work in me, and

---

[1] Lib. iv. 1 Reg. c. 5.   [2] Matth. xi. 29.   [3] Kolb, p. 68.

show Thyself great in this empty straw of mine. Accomplish in deeds what Thou hast given me by Thy grace. Amen."

She believed that with her hands she could take hold of the great truth thus expressed by St. Hugo of Grenoble: "The good which I do is never entirely good, and is not mine ; but the evil which I do is entirely evil, and is all mine." Sometimes she said : "What reason can a reasonable man find to exalt himself ? Do not all evils and sins come from man, and all good, whatsoever it be, come wholly from God, and from Him alone ? He who really knows God, must prize Him alone highly, and love Him above all things ; the knowledge of God is followed by a complete contempt of one's self and of one's nothingness."

. In recognizing clearly her nothingness and her sins as the capital properly belonging to herself, she obtained the stand-point that we must consider everything good as a pure alms from God and aim to refer it to its true source, the goodness of God. She used to say that, as all waters spring from the ocean and return thither, so must everything good go back to its source and nothing be kept as our own. This she practised herself ; she never sought her own gain or advantage in anything. No self-aggrandizement, no honor before men were in her thoughts ; on the contrary, the more liberally God manifested His goodness in her behalf, the deeper she dived into her own nothingness and unworthiness. She was fully conscious of these gifts, and of their magnitude, and indeed incessantly returned thanks for them to the Father of light, but her glance at the splendor and glory of this gift was accompanied by a glance at her own unworthiness and responsibility. The more she received, the greater the debt she believed herself to have incurred ; and the more God exalted her, the lower she kept herself down. "For," said she, "of him who receives much, much will also be demanded." And as every new gift of God increased in her the knowledge of her own unworthiness, ingratitude, and responsibility, so of every best and perfect gift, coming to her from the Father of light, she kept nothing for her own individual self but a conviction of being an unworthy hand-maid of the Lord ; and hence she succeeded in returning to God the current of grace, whole and in all its purity, she herself remaining in her sheer nothingness.

She descended deeper yet, even below her nothingness. Sin is far below the line of nothingness ; and this holy soul had in spirit gone down so deep into this abyss, that she considered herself to be the greatest sinner on earth, above whom every other sinner ranked immeasurably high. This opinion of hers may appear, to those who are but little acquainted with the interior life, barely credible, and in any case pass for an altogether untrue exaggeration. But two things are here to be considered : on the one side, that the comparison is not here instituted between the grievousness of sinful acts in themselves, as if she had meant that she herself had committed more sins, and these more grievous mortal sins, than those of other persons, but it refers to the contrast of graces received, she believing herself to have offered a greater resistance to the infinite fulness of grace conferred upon her, than others had done to the lesser degree bestowed on them. On the other side, it is peculiar to the God-given light, that it should point out to the interior eye the very smallest speck of its own faults, while it turns away that same eye from the faults of others, and only lets them see the good that is in them. Consequently, when the light of grace casts its illumination on one's own faults, it throws the faults of others into the shade, in such a way that the Saints can entertain a firm conviction that they are the greatest among sinners.

This holy virgin lived and worked, then, amid a light so great, that it made the smallest defect seem to be a crime ; therefore it was that she could not comprehend how any one could set any value on himself, after he had committed a single sin and thereby deserves to be held in contempt by others ; she felt a real disgust at herself ; she seemed to herself, " an abomination of desolation in a holy place," and would have liked to flee from herself. She was, therefore, greatly surprised that others, instead of heaping contempt on her, conferred favors upon her, and suffered her in " their holy company."

She maintained that no one on the face of the earth, who was in the enjoyment of such fulness of grace as she was, was so miserable and wretched as she. If God were to withdraw His assistance but for a moment, she was ready for every crime ; if God were but to take His own from her, nothing but sin and pure nothingness would be left to her; and even if she had committed no mortal sin, she was but the more indebted to the mercy of God, which had preserved her from it. If she heard that any one had committed a grievous sin, she used to say : "I should have fallen much lower than this unfortunate man, if Almighty God had not so powerfully upheld me ; had the man, on the other hand, had the grace I possess, he would live a thousand times more piously than I do. 'He that thinketh himself to stand, let him take heed lest he fall.'"[1]

It was a puzzle to her how people could ask advice from her, or beg for her prayers ; then she would often exclaim : " And I, what am I, then ? a sinful, ignorant woman, a despicable nothing, a feeble reed, a straw, a sinful worm ! what good can be expected from such a worm ? my whole skill consists in sinning." "Useless straw" was the usual title she applied to herself. She was of opinion that it was one of the greatest miracles of divine mercy that God tolerated her, the most contemptible of creatures, on the earth. "O God !" she once said, "the earth on which I tread is Thy creature, and I step on it with my feet, whilst I deserve for my sins to be trodden under foot by every creature." To the Sisters she sometimes exclaimed : "Dear Sisters, you can hardly believe how bad and miserable I am ; I am

---

[1] I. Cor. x. 12.

unworthy of the bread I eat, unworthy that the sun should shine on me, that the earth should bear me ; I deserve to be cast out from human society." This great self-contempt was appropriately expressed in the wonder she felt that the devil should tempt her so severely ; she could not understand how a spirit so noble as he is by nature, was not ashamed to trouble himself so much with such a miserable and sinful woman. From the same sentiment came the petition she uttered on her death-bed, that no crown of roses should adorn her corpse, but a crown of straw.

This low opinion of herself being once entertained by her with full and constant conviction, urged her on all occasions, interiorly and exteriorly, to take the last place as the one properly belonging to her. She considered it a settled fact that in every point she was the least and the worst among the Sisters. " I see," she said,[1] "in the face of every Sister a living virtue shine, but in me there is nothing to see but a dark shadow of sin. I cannot sufficiently wonder how people and all creatures can stand such a wretched creature as I am." When she witnessed public and undeniable faults committed by her Sisters, she first laid them to her own account and maintained that by her bad example she had given occasion to them; for the same reason she wished the Superioress to lay the penance on her for the failings of the others. Even the general calamities befalling the city and country she attributed to her sins, and thought it was only her duty to ask of God not to punish others on her account. In her outward behavior she always sought to occupy the lowest place. It had become to her a second nature to yield to all, to help, to anticipate their wishes and to obey them. When it was not against the prescribed order of the community, she always took the last seat, as being, in her own way of thinking, the most unworthy. She acted in this way also with the poor and with beggars, as if she felt herself unworthy to be in their company.

---

[1] Summ. C. I § 193.

Even when she had become old she still obeyed the youngest Sisters, like a child; she assumed their hard work, opened the door to them, let them precede her, served them in everything and had a special pleasure and consolation in being the least and the last.[1] She carefully avoided making any pretensions, and every appearance of vainglory; she never interrupted any one who was speaking; she willingly asked advice, even of the youngest and most inexperienced of the Sisters, and at once gave in, if contradicted. Even when Mistress of Novices, she frequently questioned her pupils, with the view of being instructed by them in many things. She had the simple eye, that is, the eye everywhere directed to good, edified by everything, and therefore she was enabled to say with truth, that every one in the convent gave her good example and edification. We will afterwards narrate more in detail how she practised humility as Mistress of Novices and as Mother Superior; we will here only remark that it was very painful to her when the Sisters, according to religious usage, knelt down before her on certain occasions: she could not then forbear telling them, that, at the washing of the feet, Christ Himself had knelt before the impious Judas. This beautiful virtue was brought into striking prominence in her conduct with persons of the outer world; to these she always appeared very modest and humble, plain and simple, without affectation or dissimulation. A priest says of her that she was considered a perfect model of humility by all who conversed with her. Persons of high distinction who visited her declared they knew not which to admire the more, her humility or her prudence.

She concealed with great care and prudence everything that could tend to her honor, especially everything extraordinary that she did or had received from God, and if by any chance anything of this kind became publicly known, she blushed and was as much ashamed as a child caught in

----

[1] Summ. C. I § 203.

some mischief would be. According to the assurances given by Father Ott,[1] she was so successful in hiding her virtues and graces, that during her lifetime not even those nearest to her knew one-thousandth part of them. When obedience required her to reveal them, it was easy to see what torture and confusion she underwent. At the same time she avoided all singularity and conformed so entirely to the usual demeanor of the others in the choir, at table, and at recreation, that a superficial observer would have seen nothing remarkable in her. She was full of jokes at recreation time, and when with children she was like a child ; her exuberant interior life broke forth at times, only when the power of the soul carried her away.

The poison of praise, so sweet to fallen humanity, she, from her childhood upwards, had loathed and abhorred more than death itself ; even at that time she would shed bitter tears when she was praised for her loveliness, modesty, and prudence, and would complain of the great wrong done in telling such falsehoods of her. In later years, when the success of anything was attributed to her advice or prayer, she would say, with blushes and with eyes cast down : "God has done it ; to Him alone be all honor and glory ; but to me shame and confusion of face, as is due to mere vanity and misery." If she was praised on other accounts, she would say :[2] "Ah, these good people do not know me, else they would think differently of me ; I am the greatest sinner, and weakness and wretchedness itself ; I am a straw, a broken reed, a most contemptible worm, a nothing, fit only to be cast away. I deserve that every one should tread me under foot and clean his shoes on me." On the other hand, the more severely she was blamed, the more she appeared to rejoice and said : "The useless and wretched Crescentia deserves no other praise than this."

When, in later years, visits from persons of high rank became constantly more frequent, it gave her great pain and she wept bitter tears because so many noble gentlemen

---

[1] Ott. p. 201.   [2] Gabriel. p. 201.

and ladies were deceived in her regard. Obedience alone
could prevail on her to converse with them, because, as she
expressed it, she only understood how to wash dishes in the
kitchen, and not how to converse with distinguished persons. This recognition of her sanctity and consequent veneration paid to her, might have been very dangerous to souls
not well grounded in truth, but this danger lay so far from
her, that, as her confessor, Father Pamer, asserts,[1] she never
even had the temptation to indulge a thought of vanity;
on the contrary, the honor paid to her but humbled her
the more. She could not sufficiently express her astonishment that such wise and virtuous gentlemen should condescend to "speak to a poor, silly, ignorant weaver's
daughter." She sometimes exclaimed:[2] "Oh, wretched
being that I am! how ashamed I feel before such noble
persons, who are so pious and humble as to condescend to
come to see a poor weaver's daughter, or to write to her.
Although I am a religious, I have no such humility. I
cannot wonder enough that even one single person in the
whole world should remember me, who am but a miserable
sinner, and a mere nothing. Others, from the secular
state, too, are so rich in virtues, and I, great sinner as I am,
have not even the shadow of one virtue, and in spite of
my religious vocation, am not worthy to touch them with
my finger. Oh, they will one day confound me before the
whole world!" At such visits as these, she behaved with
extreme modesty and propriety, but without affectation;
her eyes were cast down, and her hands hidden under the
scapular. It was especially before noble and princely
persons that she took pleasure in mentioning that she was
a poor weaver's daughter, received into the convent from
pure charity, since she had brought nothing with her.

It has been cast at her, as a sign of pride, that she had
allowed her picture to be taken, and this even in the stations
of the cross that were put up in the convent. But she is altogether blameless in this matter. Father Erasmus Osen-

---

[1] Gabriel, p. 53.   [2] Ibid. p. 266.

reuter, in whose house the pictures were made, had induced the artist, Joseph Schwartz, of Buchloe, to put the picture of the servant of God repeatedly in these pictures. The artist himself relates it in a document still extant, dated May 10th, 1752, and at the same time describes, in a most amusing manner, the embarrassment in which he had himself been placed. When Mother Crescentia's attention had been called to the fact that she herself had been painted on the pictures, she became much troubled, nay, exasperated. With an unwonted animation she demanded that the pictures should be altered, or, as she expressed it, that "those monkey-faces be removed at once." But the parish-priest was just as resolute that they should remain. The poor artist was sorely perplexed, and did not know which way to turn. At length he had recourse to diplomacy, and promised to alter the pictures when he returned from a journey he had to make. At the same time, "I thought to myself," says he, "that I would do it if the parish-priest so settled it;" she was now tranquillized. During the artist's travels Crescentia took sick and after a while died, and the pictures remained as they were.

To flee from honors is difficult; to accept with pleasure contempt and disgrace, and seek such with avidity, is still more difficult. Nevertheless, we can truly assert that in no lady of fashion is the desire to please so great as was in Crescentia the desire to possess the treasure of contempt and disgrace. When this celestial pearl was presented to her, she received it with joy and gratitude. It is not known that she ever avoided an occasion of disgrace, or ever said a word to excuse herself; yet she was many times falsely accused and was often grievously insulted. The revered words, "But Jesus held His peace," hovered before her eyes, and she kept silent with a cheerful countenance, or rather, she thanked those who upbraided her for their kind admonition and promised to do better. Even when the harsh accusations which we have mentioned were brought against her, she still remained the same silent, patient lamb, asked pardon from her accusers, and would then say : "These know me better than I know myself, and if everybody were to act in this way with me, I should come to know my faults much better, but miserable wretch that I am, I do not amend and do not deserve the good bread and the place I have in the convent." A stranger, who knew her by name only, once told her and several Sisters that he had heard that Crescentia was a witch and was now really in prison. She smiled at this and said cheerfully : "Praise be to God, I know nothing about that, but for my sins I have deserved that and even greater punishments."

It was her real conviction, which she once said with the most touching humility, when they imprisoned her in a dark room and treated her with glaring injustice : "They treat me much too kindly; I deserve the insults heaped upon me, and more still. This place where I am imprisoned is too beautiful and too comfortable for such a great sinner as I." Such heroism can only result from profound humility and the most powerful love for the Crucified. When a Sister once asked her how she could stand such injurious treatment, and what she thought of it, she replied : "Jesus, my Spouse, although innocent, suffered much more for me, and I am not without guilt ; but even if I suffer as guilty, I still rejoice that I can suffer for love of Him."

She knew what a sweet kernel of grace lies hidden in the bitter husk of contempt and humiliation, therefore she considered it as a priceless gain to exchange a passing, temporal disgrace for eternal glory, and besides this, to become likened to the crucified Redeemer. For this reason she let no opportunity pass of incurring shame before others, without availing herself of it ; and with insatiable hunger she longed for still greater humiliation and contempt. As often as obedience and love permitted it, she would intentionally, now and then, make blunders in singing, at work, and in her conversation, or make some silly remark, in order to be laughed at ; she then joined in the laugh, saying :   "I am a silly woman ; but God is so good as to show me that I really know nothing, can do nothing, that I am nothing."   Somebody says truly of her :   "Humility and love are the characteristic features which strike the eye most forcibly in her regard."

We conclude this chapter by bringing forward the testimony of her confessor, Father Adolphus Lachner, S. J., who knew her well.   He said that he was convinced that he could not by any praise stir up the least temptation to a thought of vanity, that she would rather be driven by such praise to humble herself the more profoundly ; that never in her whole life had a proud thought risen within her heart.   This is something so great and rare that we should hardly believe it possible, did we not know that what seems impossible to men is possible with God. "Where pride is, there also shall be reproach ; but where humility is, there also is wisdom." [1]   The whole of history bears witness to this sentence ; and yet we use so little and so negligently the opportunities to humble ourselves, opportunities daily sent by God Himself, that we even count as a misfortune that which, according to the ordinance of God, should lead us to happiness.   Attend, O Christian soul, to what St. James teaches :   "Be humbled in the sight of the Lord, and He will exalt you." [2]

---

[1] Prov. xi. 2.   [2] James iv. 10.

CHAPTER XIV.

How Perfectly Crescentia Practised the Obedience of Faith.[1]

LL who refuse to obey are far from the spirit of God."
This infallibly true principle the servant of God
often asserted, and was so convinced of it, that she
would rather have given her life a thousand times than
deviate a hair's breadth from obedience. She styled obedience her "pilgrim's staff, with which the soul walks securely on the road of virtue, nay, if need be, flies, until on
the narrow path of perfection it has happily completed
the journey from this temporal life to the eternal."

By this obedience, however, she understood Christian
obedience springing forth from the root of faith. For,
there is also a purely human obedience, proceeding from a
pliable disposition, which when it is supported by a corresponding education, and assisted by natural motives, at
times achieves great things and exteriorly resembles true
virtue very much. Such acquiescence is, however, rather
slavery than human virtue, or at best man-service and not
service of God. Only the one who by faith acknowledges
the will of God in the ordinance of the Superior, and who
in the mortal obeys Christ Himself, exercises the virtue of
the obedience of faith. To this may be applied "to serve
God is to rule;" and he who practises it rises spiritually in
the same degree in which he humbles himself exteriorly.

The servant of God carefully drew the line of distinction
between the obedience of nature and that of faith, and
frequently inculcated on her pupils the necessity of their
adopting the latter; and, as the first and most important principle, she taught them to acknowledge in the person of the Superior or father confessor, God Himself, and

[1] Summ. N. 15, § 1-206.

to accept their commands as respectfully and as cheerfully as they would receive the orders of God Himself.

Such an obedience she could not sufficiently praise and recommend ;[1] it contained the greatest liberty attainable on earth ; a liberty not to sin, for inasmuch as we act by obedience, we become sinless ; it is also the surest and shortest road to perfection ; but this refers to blind obedience alone ; an obedience which does not investigate the command, but immediately carries out what is ordered ; an obedience to which a glance of the eye suffices, which does not listen to the objections of the senses, but sees nothing but the person of Jesus Christ, whose person the Superior represents, which relies on nothing save the words of Eternal Truth : "He who hears you, hears Me." The effects of this virtue are really marvellous, even in the most insignificant exercises; it brings forth the greatest fruits ; it gilds everything which other virtues would but silver over. It renders sweet what is bitter ; and what is meanest and lowest it makes precious before God. It is better to pick up a straw from the floor in obedience, than, of your own will, to accomplish deeds of heroism. She herself continually practised this virtue and expressed her sentiments by the following prayer :[1] "O God, my Creator and Sovereign Good ! I accept this Thy command with pleasure and from the purest love for Thee ; graciously accept the good-will and obedience of poor Crescentia, Thy slave, which I now offer to Thy honor."

The first effect of this exercise of faith was to abstract her view completely from the qualifications and motives of those who brought to her the will of God. In this she resembled her holy Father St. Francis, who, as he himself assures us, would, with the grace of God, as readily obey the novice who had just entered the Order, as the oldest and worthiest Brother. She considered it a matter of indifference, whether the person whom she obeyed were young or old, clever or a blockhead, attached to her or averse.

---

[1] Gabriel, p. 174.   [1] Ibid. p. 175.

Without minding who the person was, she directed her attention to God, and followed the direction of her Superiors with the simplicity of a child. She therefore called her Superiors "her shining stars," by which she had to be guided. She used to say:[1] "By the grace of God I would obey a sulphur match, if God set it up as my Superior. The Superior is only the tool by which God rules us. God commands the Superior, the Superior commands us; it is therefore absolutely necessary that we should obey, not men, but God Himself."

From the same reasoning it became easy to her to sacrifice everything to this acknowledged divine will; and to give up wholly to the will of her Superiors her body and soul, her judgment and will, her entire exterior and interior life. Like her Spouse she was obedient unto death, as she gave herself up to the disposal of her Divine Master unto life and death. Many witnesses give evidence of the exactness of perfection which she acquired in the exercise of this virtue, in little as in great matters, in easy as well as difficult things. Father Ott expresses his opinion that hardly any religious had ever been more thoroughly and universally, or more constantly and severely tried, than she was, and this even in good and holy things, and certainly no one had ever stood these trials with greater constancy, cheerfulness, and subjection of the will and judgment.

We have already heard the testimony given by her parents respecting her obedience in their house; they said that she had never committed the least fault in this respect. Concerning her religious life, Sister Josephine Anger speaks as follows:[2] "Self-will was completely dead in her; she never examined the orders of her Superiors, and it made no difference to her, whether the command were easy or difficult. She beheld in her Superiors the command of God Himself, and desired nothing else than to live, to suffer, and to die in obedience and by obedience. This I always saw in her, and heard it of her

---

[1] Gabriel, p. 175.   [2] Summ. N. 15 & 180.

from others. Her obedience was entirely submissive and universal. It was united to a great facility and dexterity, cheerfulness and perseverance unto death. She obeyed, not commands alone, but also every hint of the Superioress, at every hour, day and night, without any exception whatever."

At the first signal of the bell, summoning the community to an exercise, or at the first hint of the Superioress, she left everything she had in hand, just where it happened to be; she did not complete the letter begun; nay, as the Sisters noticed with surprise, if at table she had already brought the spoon to her mouth, and heard the signal of obedience, she returned the food to the plate and first did what she was ordered. Nay, she even anticipated the wish or hint of the Mother Superior, so that the latter frequently said she must be careful in Crescentia's presence not to utter any wish, for she would immediately hasten to carry it out, even if it surpassed her strength. Moreover, she not only did everything which obedience ordered, but what is far more, she did nothing but by obedience. She was often heard to utter the beautiful maxim, " Nothing by self-will: everything by obedience." Indeed, she used every effort not to leave the slightest room for her own selection, or decision, not even in the least things, so that the divine will might exercise full sway in the dominion of her interior and exterior action, through the obedience she rendered to her Superiors. Every exercise of virtue, every work, every decision respecting the most indifferent and insignificant things, as, for example, care for the needs of the body, she subjected to the sceptre of obedience. On her knees, she entreated Father Provincial Boniface Schmidt to extend the merit of obedience to all things, even to such as were not commanded, that she might with certainty in all things fulfil the will of God.

An obedience springing wholly from the light of faith, and animated by the power of love, can stand the hardest probation. We see this in this soul consecrated to God

and to the "obedience of charity."[1] By the dispensation
of God, she had many occasions of becoming rich in merits,
and an edifying model for others by heroic acts of this
virtue. We will not repeat how she carried out her obedience under the unconscionably hard Mother M. Theresa,
when she had to expose herself to the mockery and laughter of seculars, but simply quote the memorable words she
then spoke: "If my Superior and an angel were to issue
commands to me at one and the same time, I would first
obey my Superior; because in this obedience there is no deception, since our Lord says: 'He that heareth you heareth Me.'"

We have also related, in general terms, the manner in
which Mother Johanna was induced, from high motives, to
impose hard trials of obedience upon her. We will here
subjoin some particular instances: Once, in the winter-
time, she told her to make snow-balls and dry them at the
hot stove. Without hesitation she obeyed, and when the
melted snow flowed over the floor of the refectory, many
Sisters became angry at such a "silly trick" and told her to
her face that such a stupid creature never came into a convent before. Then they complained of the spouse of Christ
to the Superioress, who imposed a severe penance on her,
which Crescentia joyfully and silently fulfilled, thereby
doubling the merit of her obedience. Sometimes, in
obedience, she would sweep with the bare handle of a
broom, would make snow-balls in winter and throw them
into the brook running through the premises, and
set plants with the roots upwards and the leaves in the
ground. The readiness, simplicity, and cheerfulness with
which she carried out such commands were admirable; she
performed them as if she were doing the holiest work. In
doing so she did not experience a natural repugnance, and
had, for instance, when setting the plants in the wrong way,
the profound thought, although it sounds oddly, that it
might be better so, since Heaven could certainly give more

---

[1] I. Pet. l. 22.

power to the roots than earth could yield. When the Sisters once asked her why she did such silly things, she concealed her virtue under the humble words:[1] "I am such a blockhead, such a simpleton. I thought the snow would dry up, and that it was better to sweep with the stick than with the broom. I am such a fool that my dear Superioress and my beloved Sisters must certainly have a great deal of trouble with me."

Mother Johanna once told her to remain at a certain spot in the garden; she obeyed at once. God permitted that the Superioress should forget to call her from it. She remained on this same spot for many hours, though Sister Bernardine Gast gave her a good scolding for such unaccountable idleness. She held her peace and remained there until finally the Mother called her away. Such a wonderful obedience deserved to be accompanied by visible miracles. This is proved by the following occurrence, which is attested by many witnesses and was published all over the town :[2] Mother Johanna commanded Crescentia to bring water from the well near the sacristy, in a sieve which had holes in it as large as one's fist. The daughter of obedience hastened with the sieve to the well, let the water run into it from the pipe, and carried it filled through the yard and the refectory up to the room of the Superioress. Three Sisters, M. Elizabeth Krimer, M. Benedicta Pez, and M. Felicitas Kempter followed her, wondering at such a sight. The Superioress was not a little perplexed and affrighted ; she praised the Lord, but she acted as if nothing out of the way had taken place. She bade Crescentia carry the water back again, pour it into the brook, and hang up the sieve in its proper place. Another time, in holy obedience, she filled a wash-tub with water from the same sieve, in the presence of many eye-witnesses, and then emptied it again in the same manner.[3]

---

[1] Gabriel, p. 188.   [2] Summ. N. 15, § 24 et passim.—Ott, B. II. C. 9.—Gabriel, p. 187.
[3] Summ. C. I. § 196 and 202.--Act. B. Resp. 151.   The sieve is still kept in the convent, as a remembrance of this wonderful occurrence.

These miracles of obedience, made so plain to the exterior senses, may excite the greatest admiration in those who look more to the exterior of things, than to their interior essence ; in reality, however, the rare and almost unheard-of grace that, amid all these trials, she was preserved from vexatious, or otherwise evil thoughts against her Superiors, is infinitely more precious and more wonderful.[1] " Rather to die than not to obey ; " this maxim of hers she obeyed literally, not hesitating to expose herself to manifest danger of death, when obedience required it. In the last years of her life, she was once so sick that she had eaten nothing for quite a time, and seemed to be near death. The Father Provincial was of opinion that she ought to eat something ; she replied that food was now injurious to her, yet if obedience required it she would be ready at once to take something. When the Superior ordered a little nourishment to be given to her, believing it necessary for her, she forced herself to carry out his orders. The food thus untimely taken, however, caused her most excruciating pains, and her state became so much worse that every one thought she was going to die at once. As the by-standers were beside themselves with anxiety and grief, she very calmly said : " It is not necessary to live, but it is indeed necessary to obey."[2] She showed the same readiness to obey during her last sickness ; when her confessor advised her to eat something her reply was : " If your reverence wishes it, I will take something at once, because it is not necessary that I should live, but indeed it is that I should obey." This time, however, he did not venture to insist on carrying his command out.

Concerning all her spiritual exercises she followed the direction of obedience, which obedience, indeed, took the first place among these exercises. Unluckily all religious persons do not possess this power of separating themselves from their own will, as is proved by the complaints they

---

[1] Gabriel, p. 190.   [2] Summ. C. I. § 14.—Ott. B. II. C. 9.

make when they are disturbed by their Superiors in exercises which have become dear to them.

Crescentia applied the maxim, "Nothing without obedience," not only to her works of mortification, prayers, and
occupations, but also to the receiving of Holy Communion,
although, without it, her physical·life seemed to pine away
in weakness and sorrow. She said one exercise of obedience was dearer to her than a thousand Holy Communions
without obedience. This sentiment was proved often
enough by her actions, when her confessors and Superiors,
in the early years of her convent life, unexpectedly
forbade her Holy Communion, on some feast-day dear to
her, and just when she was prepared to go with the rest to
the table of the Lord, sent her into the kitchen instead :
she obeyed without a wry face, and without any inward
irritability. Once she was ordered, immediately after Communion, to go to the door and tend it. Calmly she left
God, for God's sake, but only to profit by it. In the same
way, when the Infant Jesus had appeared, she left Him
and His sweet consolations in order to obey the signal when
the door-bell sounded. The virtue of obedience was more
precious to her than visions or miracles. Even in her
ecstasies, when she had no control over herself, and was inaccessible to exterior influences, the voice of obedience
brought her to herself ; even if it came but from the mouth
of a Sister bringing her a message, she at once rose and
punctually performed the duty. A sign without a word
would even be sufficient, as the following will show: [1]
One day after Mass her confessor passed through the choir,
and noticed that the servant of God was kneeling at her
prie-dieu in profound ecstasy, with her eyes closed. She
was in very poor health at the time and he thought it would
be better for her to be seated than to kneel. With this intention he raised his forefinger to indicate his will ; at the
same instant she seated herself. That by a special inspiration of God she often knew and fulfilled the commands

---

[1] Ott. B. I.

and wishes which her Superiors merely felt interiorly and did not express, Mother Johanna says she had herself many times experienced.[1]

Every trace of self-will was gradually extinguished within her by the grace of God ; hence it was her delight to submit her will, not only to the will of her Superiors for God's sake, but to that of all men and of every creature. The words of Thomas à Kempis,[2] "Endeavor rather to do the will of another than thine own," seemed to have passed into her flesh and blood. She showed this in a special manner, both when she had become Superioress, and at the time when she accepted the office; as also that she knew how to unite this office with the exercise and merit of an inferior. She could not imagine a cross greater than that of being the Superioress, and it was with tears that she begged of them not to impose it on her. Nevertheless, as soon as she heard the word "Obedience," she bowed her head in quiet resignation.

She then asked the Father Provincial to appoint a Sister whom she could obey with the merit of obedience, in everything relating to her person ; he appointed Sister M. Neth her assistant. It then became very edifying to observe how far she extended her obedience to this Sister and how punctually she fulfilled it : acting thus in the spirit of a true daughter and imitatrix of the holy Father Francis, who likewise used to obey his companion in all simplicity. Without humbly asking permission from her, she spoke to no stranger, did not go into the parlor, or make use of many rights of a Superior ; for instance, she would not grant permission to speak at table or at recreation without having first asked the assistant. To this humble submission to Sister M. Anna, we may perhaps attribute the many liberties which she took as secretary, and which Crescentia bore with such patience.

It deserves yet to be mentiond how perfectly in her sicknesses she obeyed the doctors and nurses. She was most

---

[1] Sumn. and Ott, loc. cit.—Gabriel, p. 190. [2] Imitation B. III. C. 23.

punctual in observing all the regulations of the doctor, although she knew very well that the medicines given her were rather an injury to her than a benefit. To the Sister in attendance she, as she expressed it herself, delivered up her whole body, and was indeed so much without a will of her own, that she let her determine the position of her body and would not change it without permission. With the simplicity of a child she would ask : "Do I lie right now, or must I change to some other position ?" How she practised obedience on her death-bed, even to the very departure itself, we shall have occasion to admire hereafter.

In conclusion, we would recommend all religious to ponder well the petition which she, as Superioress, presented to her confessor, Father Pamer, namely, that he would please to pay special attention to the preservation and increase of the spirit of obedience in the community, as in that case " everything would be well." Also, the beautiful passage of Holy Writ, which she often used to put before her novices, can never be sufficiently meditated on by all men : " Obey in all things your masters . . . not serving to the eye as pleasing men, but in simplicity of heart, fearing God. Whatsoever you do, do it from the heart as to the Lord, and not to men." [1]

---

[1] Coloss. iii. 22, 23.

CHAPTER XV.

Crescentia an Angel in the Flesh.[1]

IN the religious state, chastity is as the pupil of the eye; it must be carefully guarded from the smallest speck of the dust of impurity." With these words Crescentia used to exhort her Sisters in religion to the observance of the vow of chastity; but her whole appearance was so brilliant a picture of virginal chastity and modesty, that a glance at her inflamed the heart with a greater love of this virtue than the most beautiful words could effect.

The words spoken by our Lord of the glorified children of God, "They shall be as the angels of God in Heaven,"[2] were so suitable to her that nearly all who knew her applied them to her. Father Bartholomew Binner, S. J., often styled her an "angel made flesh," and Father Pamer assures us that, "in this virtue, she seemed to be not so much a human being as a Saint of Heaven, or an angel without flesh." In respect to this virtue she had three rare prerogatives:

First, her reputation was so spotless that not even the least suspicion was ever expressed against her virginal innocence. This is the more astonishing, from her having had during the greater part of her life to bear with wicked adversaries and cunning calumniators. But virginal modesty was so stamped on her whole being, and propriety and reserve were such marked features in her conduct, that the most mistrustful eye could not detect in her the slightest ground on which to base suspicion. Secondly, she was really free from even venial sin against this virtue, as far as men could judge; so said her confessors. She herself declared: "I would rather die a thousand times than suffer the shadow of a fault against this virtue." Thirdly, she was one of those rare souls who never had a tempta-

---

[1] Summ. N. 14 § 1-115.   [2] Matth. xxii. 30.

tion, even in thought, against purity. Like an innocent child she knew nothing of the opposite vice up to her old age, and did not wish to know anything of it. This extraordinary grace of God she, in all humility and gratitude to the Lord, several times revealed to her confessors and to her Sisters in religion. This very grace the devil made use of, at a time when she was in a state of extreme dereliction, to torture her with, by exciting her to entirely groundless anxiety, whether she herself had not brought this state upon herself by sins against holy purity, without being conscious of them. Her complete ignorance of the hateful vice of impurity, joined to her great humility, made her accessible to such anxieties. This truly angelic perfection of chastity presupposes an extraordinary grace of God, with, on her side, an extraordinary fidelity and care in guarding and fostering this beautiful lily.

In her sixth year she had already taken the vow of perpetual chastity ; she then selected St. Aloysius as her model and patron of holy chastity. The love of this heavenly virtue was ever on the increase within her heart and urged her onward to strive with the utmost care for its greatest perfection. Although no sting of temptation excited her to fervor, but love alone animated her, she took more pains to preserve purity than the generality of people can resolve to do when beset with the fiercest temptations and when they find themselves in proximate danger of falling into sin.

Since the fall of Adam this lily blooms only beneath the thorns of mortification. It was for this reason that she applied the bridle of severe discipline to all the senses of the body and to every feeling of the heart. She allowed her eyes no inquisitive looks, not even on harmless objects; she permitted her hand and other members neither movement nor convenient positions, without adequate, reasonable cause. The covenant she had made with her eyes, that they should not look on vanity, she kept so strictly, that for the most part she kept her eyes cast down to the ground, so that she knew very few persons by sight, or by their form or stature. Even Sisters who had been with her for many years had never seen her eyes so as to distinguish their color. Father Pamer asserts that he visited her often in her last sickness and for a length of time ; yet she never looked at him but once and that was half an hour before her death. The sight of one eye was already gone; she directed the other towards him to bid him "Good-bye." "At this look," he says, "there arose in my heart a sweet consolation, an unspeakable joy such as I have never felt during my whole life. She then closed her chaste eyes forever." [1] In religious pictures, also, she required the strictest modesty in the drapery of the figures. On this head she once earnestly remonstrated with an artist who was working for the convent and had permitted himself some liberties in the construction of a picture, which freedom she required him to correct.

As she would not even listen to the current news, we may imagine with what disgust she rejected any language that was too free. She became pale as death and trembled in every limb when a word was uttered which she considered immodest. She even blushed and turned away when the conversation touched upon personal beauty, vain dress, or delicious food, as she deemed such topics unfit for a spouse of Jesus Christ. She would then say : "God alone is beautiful, and the source of all beauty ; Christ is the most beautiful among the children of men. A spouse of Christ must look on no other beauty, think of no other, much less speak of any other. Her heart belongs to the heavenly Spouse alone ; her mouth must utter only holy things, and she must only speak on the subjects that lead to holy thoughts." Though she liked music, sang well, and loved to sing, she would only listen to religious hymns and to such music as excited holy feelings.

In her deportment and behavior she observed the greatest modesty. Before strangers, and, when feasible, even be-

---

[1] Ott. B. II. C. 10.

fore the Sisters, she kept her hands under the scapular. She would not even permit the Sisters to kiss her hands or even touch them. A report says [1] that she immediately and often washed her hands when they had been unexpectedly kissed by ladies from the outside world. She avoided every near approach of the body towards others, and cautioned her Sisters against the practice, especially with persons of the opposite sex.

If we now recall to mind that she crucified her flesh with the severest exercises of mortification, we shall be able to understand well, that all who knew her could say that no one could behold this angelical virgin without perceiving the sweetest fragrance of charity around her, together with a breath of heavenly purity which inflamed the heart with love for this beautiful virtue. Even the perfume that exhaled from her body after death and was often perceptible during her life, thus giving evidence of having a supernatural character, affords full proof of her appearing before God as a true lily among thorns, brilliantly shining in its snow-white innocence, and diffusing far and wide the sweet odor of Jesus Christ.

It would seem as if God had imparted to her the special grace of weakening the opposite vice in others, and of fostering the love and practice of chastity. Many confessed openly that when tormented by severe temptations to impurity, they were relieved from them by a mere look at this angel in the flesh ; or by a mere remembrance of her that they have been not only delivered from temptation, but filled with a sensible love for virtue. After her death she came to the assistance of such as invoked the help of her prayers for this purpose in a much more forcible manner. Father Pamer and Father Ott [2] alike testify to having met with remarkable proofs of this in their experience as priests. The latter of these mentions one case in particular of a young man who had long been habitually fettered by the commission of one of the worst forms of this kind of

---

[1] Act. B. Summ. Obj. N. 15 § 34.   [2] Ott, B. I.

sin; by his advice he had recourse to the intercession of the deceased virgin, and had been immediately and permanently preserved from any relapse into sin.

She wept bitter tears over the terrible lot of so many Christians who seek their happiness in the flesh, and find for time and for eternity nothing but pain of heart. She would have shed her blood a thousand times to procure for them the grace of enlightenment. She never wearied of exhorting her Sisters to come to the aid of these unhappy slaves of impurity by prayer and penance, as also in their own persons to strive to achieve the highest degree of this virtue. The doctrine which she inculcated for this purpose has lost nothing of its value for our own needs; we will then give a summary of it for our personal edification. She said: "We cannot be too much on our guard with respect to this dangerous point; we ought to be on the watch to catch the 'little foxes,'[1] lest they destroy the vineyard of the Beloved: these foxes are, inquisitiveness of the eyes, talkativeness of the tongue, immoderate laughter, effeminacy of life, idleness, and intercourse that might become dangerous. Religious (that is, persons belonging to a religious Order) have a very jealous Bridegroom, who wants the whole heart and suffers no one to divide it with Him. We ought to avoid even the remotest occasions as far as possible, and it is a veritable poison to be with persons for whose society we feel a sensible inclination. Towards such, whether they be secular, religious, or ecclesiastics, we should, when conversation is unavoidable, be cold and serious in our behavior; particular friendships, even if at first they appear to be altogether spiritual and holy, become at length dangerous and prejudicial; finally, humility is the only guardian of chastity."

O Christian, observe these admonitions! If God has given you a vocation to virginal chastity, be grateful to Him, be humble and devout; also consider well the words of St. Paul the Apostle: "The virgin thinketh on the things of the Lord, that she may be holy, both in body and in spirit."[2]

---

[1] Compare Canticle ii. 15.   [2] I. Cor. vii. 34.

CHAPTER XVI.

How Truly Crescentia Loved Poverty.

HE riches of Christ are only communicated to the poor in spirit. If the heart is not void of love for temporal goods, if the spirit is not humbled by self-contempt, and as it were annihilated in itself, there will be no room free in the interior for the Holy Ghost to enter; and reversing this, as a master of spiritual life says: "To be emptied of every creature, is to be full of God."

We have already seen how mortified and humble Crescentia was in self-love; from this it follow sof itself that she must have been so much the more free from the love for external goods, and must have possessed evangelical poverty in a high degree, for love for ourselves is the iron chain that binds us to what is beneath—to the shadows of creatures. In regard to poverty of spirit, she revealed the plenitude of this poverty in the following words, which came from the depths of her heart: "I would not lift a foot for all the treasures of the world." In the use of temporal things she always preferred poverty to abundance.

This love of poverty had grown up with her from infancy. There had always been great poverty and privation in her parents' home, and already as a child she had cheerfully borne the consequences of it; while, even then, her enlightened mind discovered the high supernatural privileges hidden beneath temporal want, namely, the gaining of grace, together with the glorious resemblance it bore to the holy family who lived in poverty, Jesus, Mary, and Joseph. In latter years she expressed herself on this subject as follows: She acknowledged it as a special grace of God that He had given her "poverty as a heritage." She loved to boast of it, thanking God and men, even on her death-bed, that it was only out of compassion that she had been received into the community.

Property and money were to this genuine daughter of the seraphic poor man of Assisi the most indifferent things in the world. "What have I to do with this straw and this stone?" This was the manner in which she spoke of money. When, by her profession, she had become "wedded to holy poverty," her love for it increased to that degree that she trod perfectly in the footsteps of the holy Father, and as he, in sublime words, had extolled poverty as his spouse and consort, so did she pour forth the enthusiasm of her love in most beautiful eulogies of the glorious "mother," poverty, which she loved more than the rich love their riches, or the vain their vanities. The source of this love, which exteriorly appeared almost fantastic, was faith in and love for Christ, who, "being rich, became poor for your sakes."[1] She willingly tarried in spirit in the poor little house at Nazareth and in the stable at Bethlehem, that in the marvellous mirror of the holy family of God she might comprehend the picture of perfect poverty. She used to call the little house of Nazareth, "her lovely cell." There the Redeemer could ever be found, poor, bereft of everything earthly; there we could learn of Him true poverty. And then the glance upon the cross, upon the Lord of the world, hanging there between Heaven and earth, may teach men to love that poverty which left Him no place on earth whereon to lay His head.

But beautiful words were not enough for her; she practised this virtue, and kept her vow in the most perfect manner. Since the vow of poverty excludes the right of private property, she avoided the least appearance of laying claim to anything, and found an inexpressible consolation in having nothing save God alone. "I have nothing of my own," was her expression; "God's treasures are mine; that is my joy." She avoided in every case the use of the word *mine* in reference to the temporal things appointed to her use; and it made her sad whenever she heard any of the Sisters use any such form of speech

____

[1] II. Cor. viii. 9.

as, *my beads, my cell.* She never failed to correct them with such words as : "Far be from us the cold words, mine and thine; for we are poor in Christ, and own nothing. It is my greatest joy that I have nothing but my dear God, and in Him infinite good." The most enviable lot seemed to her to be to resemble the Lord in not having whereon to lay His head; while to possess more and to be better taken care of than the Lord of Heaven and earth seemed to her something very unbecoming a religious, particularly for one like her, who had been taken into the convent for "compassion's sake," and could not make the smallest pretension to anything. For this reason she scarcely ate anything, and when the very worst was given her, such food as a beggar would have refused, she returned thanks with a heartiness rarely seen in others, when they have received great and undeserved favors.

As the vow of poverty permits the members of a religious order the use of things only as depending on the permission of the Superiors, she acted in this regard with rigid exactness. She would not accept, use, borrow, or lend the least thing without the permission of the Superioress ; not a needle, not a piece of paper, not a pen. She would never be satisfied with (which in trivial things is really permitted) a silent or a general permission. She accustomed her novices to a like strictness ; they could not go to bed without first having obtained permission for any pin they might have borrowed. The same strictness she exacted in regard to articles of devotion, such as religious pictures, beads, scapulars, which in latter years she distributed somewhat numerously ; even in things purely spiritual and which therefore do not come under the vow of poverty. Priests, both secular and religious, often promised to say Masses for her intention ; this gave her much pleasure, but she never accepted them, without first having obtained permission to do so. Many there were who found fault with this, calling it over-nicety or scrupulosity. She, however, considered these things from the stand-point of the greatest perfection and said : " I know of no difference between great things and small ; everything, however small it may be, is great if performed for God's sake and for the more perfect observance of a vow."

The perfection of poverty is very strikingly shown in another exercise of it, which St. Vincent Ferrer expresses in the following words:[1] "I know that merely to be poor is not praiseworthy, but rather in poverty to love to be poor, and cheerfully and joyfully to bear the needs entailed by poverty, for Christ's sake. Unfortunately, many plume themselves on the title of poverty, on condition that they want nothing : they style themselves friends of poverty, but flee from its companions, hunger, want, contempt." Not thus the servant of God ; she willingly restricted her necessities to the smallest measure ; selected for herself the worst, the hardest, the most severe lot, and welcomed with a pleasant face and cheerful heart all the privations and painful effects of poverty.

The great mortifications to which she subjected herself in regard to the quantity and quality of food which we have already mentioned, she also undertook in the spirit and under the impulse of poverty. What was left of the food of others, and what was set apart for the poor, she preferred from love of poverty, and when she had her choice, was satisfied with it. With regard to clothes, she begged for such as had been laid aside by the other Sisters as worn-out ; she then patched them up, kept them extremely clean, wore them as precious garments, and used them with such care and precaution, that a worn-out habit would last her longer than an entirely new one would the other Sisters. She had learned this practice of poverty at her very entrance into the community. The evil-minded Superioress had given the poor maiden only ragged garments, which had become unavailable to others. She accepted them in humility and joy, and knew very well how to make them suitable to herself.[2]

---

[1] De Vita Spirit.   [2] Gabriel, p. 207.

In after times she was compelled by obedience to wear new garments; she then considered these as the sacred property of Christ and was so careful of them that she generally made them last twice or three times as long as those of the other Sisters; and yet no one could ever see that they were stained or torn. "For," said she, "torn clothing in a religious is rather a sign of sloth or of negligence, than of holy poverty."

In her dwelling and in the furniture of her cell, she wished to feel the extremest privation and positive want, believing that this alone constitutes real riches, high profit, true pleasure. We have already noted the opportunity she had of putting these sentiments into practice and the heroic poverty which she exercised, when for two years she had no cell of her own, and also when she was shut up in a dark room; we will now add that even in her old age it gave her pleasure to think of this, and she asserted that she had never been so happy as then.[1] Out of love for poverty she would not have a light in her cell, even in winter, but availed herself of the light that glimmered from the opposite cell when she opened her door. She endured cold patiently and cheerfully in union with the holy family. During her many attacks of sickness, she never expressed a wish or desire to have anything special procured for herself; she thought even the worst too good, "because," she said, "we have not entered the convent to live according to our ease, but to follow Christ in poverty and contempt."

But severe as she was in regard to herself, she practised great love and consideration in favor of others, especially if they were old, feeble, or even sick. She looked on the poor with a kind of holy envy if their poverty seemed greater, exteriorly, than her own. Like her holy Father, blessed Francis, she then felt great confusion, and said: "Oh, how poor is this person in comparison with myself, and yet he loves and serves God better than

---

[1] Summ. N. 13 § 52.

I do ! Yes, I am unworthy to stand under the feet of beggars, who embrace poverty from love of God and endure it with such great patience."

She used the articles of the convent with the greatest economy. In the kitchen she let nothing spoil, neither a morsel of pulse, of fruit, nor a bit of bread ; she was saving with the wood, that no piece might be uselessly burned, and was as sparing as possible even with the warm water. Whatsoever could be used, were it but a thread or a chip, she picked up carefully, that "it might not perish uselessly, but attain the end for which God created it." With all these practices of poverty, she was even yet not satisfied ; she would like to have gone begging from door to door and then divide the alms she received with the poor. Had obedience not conquered her love of poverty, she would not have retained the most necessary articles in her cell.

Perhaps the greatest, or at least the most painful trial of her obedience, was when at times the Superioress compelled her to take things into her room which seemed to her not to be in keeping with holy poverty. Some ladies of the higher classes, for instance, importuned the Superioress to force the servant of God to accept and retain certain presents, such as beautiful pictures or flowers, with which to decorate the little altar in her cell. The Superioress could not always resist such petitions, and then Crescentia fell into great distress of mind. She yielded, but soon found a way to obtain permission to give these things away to the poor or to churches. Yet she was oppressed, and often sighed for permission to clear out her cell entirely. That this expression came really from her heart, was proved by her conduct when the Superioress, at the direction of the Father Provincial, once took away everything, even the crucifix, from her cell. On leaving the Church and entering her cell, finding it entirely empty, she rejoiced, saying : " Praise and thanks be to God ! at length I find what I have sought so long ; now, indeed, I am rich.

All my life-time I never had it so nice ; at last I can say with St. Francis : 'My God and my all !' Besides Him, I want nothing in Heaven and on earth."

Many persons of the higher classes, who visited her, wished to present her with abundant alms, to be used at her pleasure for the community, for the Church, or for the poor. She would never take anything for herself, nor would she interfere with the distribution of these presents, or even ascertain what became of them; she left the whole concern in the hands of the Superioress, even the support given expressly by several benefactors for Regina, her own sick and afflicted sister. When money or other articles were sent to her she would not suffer them for a single moment in her cell, but at once carried them to the Super·ioress, with the request that she would dispose of them in some other way. This was done ; many poor persons were assisted, many churches were provided with vestments and other needed articles. "Our own chapel in the house," says Father Ott, "can bear witness to this fact." The Duchess of Savoy, who had also made rich presents to the children of Crescentia's sister, wished to endow her with an annual rental of two hundred florins,' that with the approbation of her Superiors she might dispose of it. But she could not, by any means whatever, be induced to accept of this, either for herself or the community. She advised the Duchess to accord this support to the very poor con·vent of Clares at Heilbron, which was situated in the midst of Protestants. This disinterestedness edified the noble lady so much that she annually donated five hundred florins to the convent at Heilbron, and after·wards even seven hundred. And because Crescentia did not at all rely on human means, but trusted entirely and solely to poverty and to God, He blessed the con·vent so abundantly that in regard to its temporalities also, she may be regarded as its second foundress. Although, while she remained a subject, she never

---

¹ Father Ott says three hundred.

troubled herself about these temporal interests, and even as Superioress left them to her assistant, M. Anna Neth, who, with the aid of her brother, John Baptist Neth, the so-called spiritual father of the convent, took good care of these matters.

Her confidence in the Father of the poor was boundless. She said: "I should fear to sin, if I had merely an anxious thought about temporal things, since, by the virtue of hope, I can rely with absolute certainty on the Divine Providence, omnipotence, and fidelity. She was penetrated through and through with the feeling that she lived on the alms of divine mercy as one of the poor. On her death-bed she returned thanks to God, exalting Him highly for having caused her to be born in poverty and to live and die therein ; then, with deep emotion, she thanked the Sisters for having taken her in as a poor girl, for "mercy's sake," and supported her for so many years. She prayed that God might abundantly reward them for their goodness. She had still another favor to ask of them : it was, that after her death, they would receive another poor maiden for God's sake, in her stead, and without a dowry ; Christ had promised her that He would richly reward the convent for such an act of charity. All the Sisters promised, with tears, to fulfil this wish. There is even now preserved in the convent a paper, which was found after her death, written by her own hands, in which she repeats this petition, with the promise Christ had given. This is perhaps the only case in which she herself wrote down a revelation. A copy of it is as follows :

To the Honor of God.

Once I prayed my Beloved that He would deign to reward and repay the great love shown by my beloved Sisters, in having taken me, a poor unworthy creature, into the holy Order and admitted me to profession ; also that He would favor the convent with His holy blessing, that the Sisters might suffer no want of temporal goods, and be preserved and guarded from every evil of body and soul. Thy holy will be done. Then my Beloved said to me, the unworthy: "My child, I have heard thy prayer, and in this wise: after thy death, I will withdraw My blessing and grace from them a little, that they may know and see what My grace is. After that their eyes will be opened." Again I prayed: "Ah, my beloved and divine Father! I pray Thee, for Thy love's sake, do not keep Thy divine grace long away from them; hasten soon to their assistance." My beloved Spouse spoke further to me: "My child, if, after thy death, they take in again a poor person for love of Me, I will again give them My grace and blessing; but they must take in one who is virtuous and has a good will, and when this one dies, they must take in another and continue to do so. In this wise, My child, have I heard thy prayer, and these words which I have spoken to thee do thou write down, that they may be found after thy death and carried out." This, by His order and in obedience I have done. This petition has always, up to these last years, been faithfully fulfilled by the Sisters.

In conclusion, we append some few maxims of the servant of God, concerning religious poverty:

"The foundation of religious life is poverty; if that is gradually underminded by transgression, all other virtues will be overturned, and the convent approaches its ruin."—"A religious is never more happy than when she suffers the want of things really necessary."—"Gold and straw have an equal value."—"The effects of poverty are true riches, and I never possess so much as when I have nothing." With this we conclude the description of her virtues. The grand picture which we admire in her is but a copy of the original, of the Crucified.

You too, O Christian soul, must, as St. Paul says, be "transformed into the same image. . . . . . as by the Spirit of the Lord."[1] For that reason do not desist from "looking on Jesus, the author and finisher of faith, who having joy set before Him, endured the cross, despising the shame."[2]

---

[1] II. Cor. III 18.   [2] Hebr. xii. 2.

Third Book.

Crescentia's Work for Others.—Her Death and the Veneration paid Her

CHAPTER I.

Crescentia as Mistress of Novices.

GOD, who is rich in mercy, grants the treasures of extraordinary graces to chosen souls, in order to make use of them as instruments to conduct the current of mercy to others and, as it were, to diffuse it. The holier and humbler a soul is, the more she lives a hidden life with Christ in God, the more will she become a fruitful source of grace to the circle around her.

The subject of our narrative, little in her own eyes, as she was also little before the world, resembled the grain of wheat in the Gospel, which, when it had died, yielded much fruit. Her blessed influence extended at first from her poor cell to her own convent, then went out to continually widening circles. It cannot be counted how many souls God has led to conversion, or to a higher perfection, through her mediation.

First, we will describe her work as Mistress of Novices. This office, so important in a religious community, she held for many years [1] with the greatest blessing. The

---

[1] There is some discrepancy in the accounts about the time she held that office. Sister Gabriel says in her MS., p. 133, that she held it twenty-eight years; the document written immediately after her death by Amort and Bassi agrees with this account.—Act. B. Summ. Obj. But Summ. N. 10 § 69, sets it at nearly twenty-four years, and Father Ott, B. IV. C. 11, says: She was Portress seventeen years and Mistress of Novices twenty-four. But it may be that for a term of years she filled both offices at the same time.

light of a higher wisdom which guided her, the efficacy of
an example so perfect in every virtue, together with the
power of her prayer, had so great an effect that she brought
forth abundant fruits even in hearts but ill prepared.   Nobody could long resist the force of her humility and love.
It must have made a powerful impression on the youthful
minds of the novices, when they heard their mistress,
whom they knew to be a mirror of every virtue, say with
obvious simplicity and sincerity: " Beloved Sisters, do
not look at my evil deeds, and do not turn your eyes towards me, for I am a mere nothing ; but remember that
God speaks to you by me, the most insignificant of creatures,
and know that your merits will be greater, the worse I am."

Though she herself had the most exalted ideas concerning the religious state and the perfection suitable to persons consecrated to God, and well knew how to describe
the ideal to be aimed at, in plain and penetrating words,
she yet knew the weakness of human nature too well to
ask too much at once.   With a motherly love and patience
she condescended to the imperfections of her pupils, conquering even great faults by patience and forbearance.
One of the greatest difficulties in leading others is to pierce
through the veil cast by exterior faults, and find out the
depths of a soul already drawn by God's grace to good
works, and then to perceive where to take up the work
which grace has already begun, without being bewildered
by the action of natural weakness and corruption.

How well Crescentia understood this, and how, by her
patience, forbearance, and love, she would charm the
new-comers in the Order, we are told by the testimony
of her novices.   Sister Gabriel says, with great can-
dor :[1] " When by disobedience I had saddened her, or
by stubbornness offended her, she has humbly asked my pardon, which filled me with disgrace and shame before God
and man, for it was my place to have humbled myself and
to have asked forgiveness of her, since I had offended

---

[1] Gabriel, p. 200.

her ; besides, I was still a novice ; but the great humility of Crescentia conquered my pride also."

Sister M. Michelina Weiss speaks on this subject as follows : "When, as a novice, I showed myself stubborn against her, and listened to her motherly admonitions and loving rebukes with a wry face and irritable temper, she, indeed, as was her duty, remonstrated with me, in earnest words, but with her own hand she showed me most kindly how to perform the most menial work and explained how I should always have a good intention in doing it ; nay, with the same kindness and love she taught me the same thing over again, often as many as three or four times. I can truly say that the mere sight of Crescentia has been to me a constant instruction in humility, meekness, and charity." Sister M. Joseph Anger says[1] the same, to her great humiliation, adding[2] that Crescentia had also borne with inexhaustible patience the complaints and unjust reproaches uttered by some of the elder Sisters against the Novice-Mistress whenever the novices had made a mistake or committed a fault. "Frequently," says she, "I had to hear this, and my heart was like to burst, for I knew well enough that all the fault was ours; that is, it came from our youthful indiscretion and forgetfulness, and in no way from Crescentia, who, on the contrary, did all that could be done, and more than I can tell."

She was ready, day and night, to console and to instruct her spiritual daughters, and to lighten their difficulties by her maternal love. They might come to her at any hour. She helped them at their work, especially when it was hard and menial ; she told them how to perform it from the right motive, with the right intention, and thereby make it easier ; and she did all this with so much cheerfulness, meekness, and immovable patience that the greatest obstinacy had to yield to her influence.

All the novices had great confidence in their mistress, as also a great veneration for her. They soon knew by ex-

---

[1] Gabriel, p. 212.　　[2] Ibid. p. 219.

perience, that they never left her without having received
consolation, instruction, and strength.   Her gift of cheer-
ing and elevating timid and drooping hearts was here particularly manifest.   Sister Raphael Miller confesses, in regard to herself:[1]   "During my novitiate, I was very much
harassed by despondency, so much so that I had nearly
resolved to quit the convent.   At length I made known my
wretched state of mind to dear Mother Crescentia ; she gave
me such great and powerful encouragement to hope in God,
that I have enjoyed the greatest peace from that very day."

It is self-evident that she prayed with particular fervor
for those souls for whom she had to give an account to
God ; nay, she seemed to take Heaven by storm in their
behalf, especially when particular reasons called for it.
Innumerable times she repeated, with burning zeal, the
sweet words of the Redeemer :   "Holy Father, keep them
in Thy name, whom Thou hast given me ; Thine they were
and to me Thou gavest them."[2]   Great as her love was,
the watchfulness, prudence, and wholesome severity with
which she directed her pupils were equally great.   Sister
M. Joseph Anger testifies:[3]   "As for the rest, Crescentia
watched us novices very carefully, looked diligently after
our work and after all that we did ; often, when we least
suspected it, she was there, as if she came out of the earth.
She loved us beyond measure, and we too felt a sincere
filial love for her, but at the same time we had an indescribable fear, for with the erring or wrong-doer she could be
as stern as she was kind at other times.   This I have experienced myself."   As she laid so great a stress on having
a good intention, and on remembering the presence of God,
on which she gave lengthy instructions, she took care that
these should be carried out, and when she met one of her
pupils, would ask whither her thought and desires were
directed.   The novice would thus often have to acknowledge that her head was full of quite other matters.   Cres-

---

[1] Summ. N. 8 § 54.   [2] John xvii. 11, 6.   [3] Summ. N. 11 § 217.

centia would then sigh and say with great warmth :[1] "Is that serving God, is that loving God? Oh, how precious is time, which gives us the possibility of working and suffering for the love of God !"

With a holy fervor she inculcated the necessity of mortification: "We must put the axe to the root and conquer perfectly the inclination to sensuality, ease, and external things ; the reason that so many religious do not acquire true virtue is to be traced to this, that in their novitiate they did not learn to subdue the affections they brought with them from the world. We ought to learn to conquer ourselves heroically, for one single act so performed would forward one's progress more than a hundred ordinary ones." With resolute earnestness she combated the sensitiveness so dear to a woman's heart. When a novice complained to her of an offence or neglect, she would say, with mild but penetrating words: "Is that humility and an imitation of Christ? Instead of complaining about such trifles, you ought to thank God and rejoice at them. Self-love and pride occasion these feelings of sensitiveness; conquer them by all means, mortify them most diligently, for they are mortal enemies to true virtue." She recommended little mortifications of the senses and of the will to be practised daily, as being much more important than scourgings of the body and sweet affections of devotion. She did not want a sensational piety, but a manly virtue, built on the denial of self-will. The predominant passion must be fought out unto life and death ; the heart must be emptied of created things and consecrated without reserve to God, otherwise a religious could not live contented and die in peace. She frequently uttered the maxim which is so worthy of consideration, that many religious persons would attain to the highest perfection if they would only deny themselves and correspond to divine inspiration; but this perfection they would never attain if they foolishly retained a small particle of their hearts for them-

---

selves.   The first principle which she inculcated on her novices was the old adage, *Vince teipsum*, "Conquer thyself."

The holy veneration which the novices entertained for
their mistress had a still deeper foundation.   They soon
remarked that they were face to face with a great spiritual
power, the depth of which they rather imagined than
comprehended, and that their most secret thoughts were
frequently discovered by that penetrating eye which was
enlightened from above.   The servant of God looked
through the deepest recesses of hearts, not only in virtue
of a natural knowledge of mankind, but by the power of
a higher light.   This is proved by many examples :   Sister M. Joseph Anger[1] says :   "I have myself experienced
that Crescentia understood the secrets of my heart by a penetrating glance.   Sometimes she told me of things which
nobody but God could know ; I have also heard from my
fellow-Sisters that Crescentia had seen through and through
the thoughts of their hearts."   The same Sister mentions,[2]
among other incidents, that at a retreat she had been
troubled by a doubt.   Crescentia came to her suddenly,
told her of the doubt concerning which she, in a natural
way, could have known nothing, and solved it for her.
The following Sisters, Gabriel Merz, Benedicta Gast, and
Barbara Kiening, say[3] that Crescentia had told them of
their secret sins, and exhorted them to confess them.

We have already related that this mysterious insight
into hearts revealed themselves more especially after her
ecstasies.   Sister M. Raphael proves this by the following
statement :[4]   "When as Mistress of Novices she gave
her spiritual instructions, she frequently fell into an ecstasy : her face became, now pale as death, now glowing
with red.   She would remain silent in this state about half
or quarter of an hour.   We novices were struck with awe,
and not without reason were we frightened, for after these
spiritual conferences she whispered first to one and then to
another something which was not known to any one ; or in

---

[1] Summ. N. 11 § 287.   [2] Ibid. N. 21 § 105.   [3] Ibid. N. 33.   [4] Ibid. § 52.

her discourse she expressed herself so plainly that those who were hit knew plainly that their mistress had been reading their faults and temptations in their very hearts."

We have already spoken much of her enlightened addresses and instructions ; we will now add the report of Sister M. Gabriel:[1] "In the spiritual instructions she gave us, she spoke for two hours, sometimes for three or even more, about God or things referring to Him ; about the practice of virtue and perfection, with such wisdom and unction of spirit that we all perceived it was the Holy Ghost who directed her tongue. She then displayed an astonishing ability, meekness, and patience ; she spared no pains to lead us to a strict observance of the Rule and regulations of the Order ; and although she was sometimes so weak that she could scarcely speak, she never omitted her instructions to us. . . . . . Full of astonishment, we often said : Crescentia does not speak as a mortal ; the Holy Ghost speaks by her mouth. Beforehand, on her knees, she fervently invoked the Holy Ghost in these words : 'Speak Thou, O Lord, for Thy servants hear, and let all the words which Thy poor creature Crescentia pronounces, become fiery coals to set the hearts of my dear Sisters on fire with Thy love, that they may know, seek, and love nothing but Thee, the Sovereign Good!' She then said: 'Our help is in the name of the Lord, who has made Heaven and earth.' After which she began her discourse, and in all truth I can bear witness, that after every lesson in this school, it seemed to me as if I had been endowed with new life."

She strenuously inculcated the necessity and the manner of meditating on the Passion of Christ, on the complete surrender of one's self to God, on the poverty of spirit, together with that of the religious state, and on the obedience of faith. This latter point she specially recommended and watched her pupils very closely in regard to it ; for instance, as to whether they rose in the morning at the first signal given for rising, that they might begin the

---

[1] Gabriel, p. 124.

day in holy obedience. In reference to this virtue, Sister M. Raphael Miller relates that during the novitiate she had been very much troubled at night with timidity; then Crescentia had said to her that whenever obedience was concerned she must lay fear aside, and think that even if the devil himself should appear to her to turn her away from the path of obedience, she would pass by him undismayed, since he neither could nor would injure her. From that time every fear had been taken from her.

For the edification of the reader, we will here adduce some of the maxims Crescentia strenuously laid before her novices : "To love is better than to talk."—"The works which are not seen by any one, are the ones which we must perform with particular fervor, diligence, and love."—"If any work in itself seems trivial and menial, it is not so before the all-seeing eye of God, provided such work is performed with a good intention ; it then becomes great."—"Walk in the presence of God, because God sees all, God hears all, God knows all, God punishes or rewards all."

The two rules which she acted upon in receiving and training novices, deserve every consideration ; they are : "In selecting and receiving novices, no regard must be had to the riches of the world, but to the riches of virtue."—"Every novice must be treated and trained according to her peculiar qualifications, passions, needs, and divine indications. It is ridiculous to endeavor to lead all by the same road." Principles so enlightened, so holy an example, and so many prayers could not fail to yield fruit a hundred-fold ; in fact, she trained good and holy Sisters, the odor of whose virtues spread far and wide.

Oh, that all those to whom the education of youth is intrusted resembled her a little ! it would then certainly stand better with the family, the state, and the Church ; then in their regard the beautiful promise of Holy Scripture would be fulfilled : "But they that are learned shall shine as the brightness of the firmament ; and they that instruct many to justice, as stars to all eternity." [1]

<hr>

[1] Dan. xii. 3.

CHAPTER II.

Crescentia as Mother Superior.

HE Mother Superior, Sister M. Johanna Altweger, who was universally revered, died June 20th, 1741. On the 23d of the following month, the Sisters unanimously elected Sister M. Crescentia as their Superioress, the Father Provincial, Boniface Schmidt, presiding. The humble servant of God was almost beside herself with fright, a flood of tears streamed from her eyes, she could not utter a word, and she came so near fainting that she had to be supported by two other Sisters and conducted to the place, where, according to custom, she had to kneel down. She now refused to accept the office in these words: " My dear Sisters, you have elected the most wretched of all in electing me; I know nothing and understand nothing. I am a poor weaver's daughter and quite ignorant; there is nothing good about me, and as I cannot govern myself, how much less can I govern others !" But the presiding Provincial here interfered and commanded her under obedience to accept the office. Now, as ever, the word "obedience" had a wonderful effect : her tears ceased, her face assumed its usual serenity, and, with entire submission, she accepted the office from the hands of God, as a cross, but as a good cross. But, in order not to lose the merit of obedience, she, on her knees, begged the Father Provincial to appoint one of the Sisters to be her personal Superior, who should direct her in everything concerning herself individually. For this purpose he appointed the then Sister-assistant, M. Anna Neth. Crescentia accepted this appointment with gratitude and pleasure, and as we have already related, practised obedience so fully and perfectly in all points until the day of her death, that none of her inferiors could equal her.

She governed the community for almost three years,

with such prudence, firmness, love, and humility, that she drew forth universal approbation, nay, even admiration, and this not only in the community, but from those outside. She who had been so often compelled to hear that she had been received for mercy's sake and was but a burden on the community, and who, considering this to be actually the case, had always taken the last place, now, as "second foundress," raised the convent to its greatest splendor, temporally and spiritually. She introduced a stricter discipline, a greater seclusion and recollection ; and fostered such love and unity among the Sisterhood that the convent really became what a convent ought to be—a peaceable little kingdom of love amid the noise and din of the world's selfishness. Her maxims, ordinances, and regulations proved so beneficial, that after her death her successors adopted them as a Rule, and retained them with the greatest advantage to the community.

A Superior in religion must possess, as St. Bonaventure teaches, in a renowned little work entitled "*De sex alis Seraphim*—six wings of Seraphim—to wit : zeal for justice; compassionate love for the sick and feeble ; immovable patience under cares, contradictions, and labors ; an exemplary life ; prudence, and the gift of discerning spirits : and lastly, affectionate piety and devotion." All these virtues Crescentia had practised long since, but now that she was as a light put on a candlestick, the fulness with which she possessed them was revealed to every eye and in a new manner. This we will elucidate with a special reference to justice, kindness, and discernment of spirit.

In regard to justice,[1] it is scarcely necessary to mention that she exercised the ordinary Rule, in temporal matters, of giving to every man his own with strict conscientiousness ; this principle being the fundamental basis of social life. She watched carefully and with some anxiety to see that the wages due to the workmen and servants were paid in full and at the proper time, and that they were rather plenti-

---

[1] Summ. N. 12, § 1-291.

fully than sparingly supplied with food and drink. She insisted that the Sister-procuratrix should pay at once for the things bought, she examined the account books closely herself, and laid them before the Sister assistant and the two Sisters of the council four times a year (at Ember times), and before the Father Provincial at the Visitation, requesting that they should be carefully examined. She never made a promise without keeping it, neither did she postpone its execution any longer than was necessary. Her heart and her tongue were always perfectly agreed ; she never permitted herself or any of her inferiors to use an ambiguous word, any outwitting or crooked ways, not the least untruth, were it only in joke. In dove-like simplicity she always looked up to the divine will, from which alone she accepted every good, and endeavored, by faith, to persevere in the order of Providence, to work and to suffer just as God might desire and demand it, hour by hour. Beyond this, she wanted nothing ; nothing to conceal, nothing to reveal, nothing to gain, nothing to lose ; she desired no means, she had no object in view, otherwise than as God appointed them.

She hated detraction above all things, and was horrified when a shadow of anything that seemed like it was spoken in her presence. She then reproved the evil speakers with great energy. Careless of her own reputation, she was ever on the watch for the honor of others, always taking the part of the accused. In the distribution of offices and of work she acted with great circumspection, impartiality, and justice. She took into consideration the ability, character, and merits of each Sister, and knew how so to appoint the task for each that no one should be overburdened to the detriment of soul and body; when circumstances increased the work, she provided assistance in due time. Hereby she rendered all of them not only contented, but extremely happy.

A just soul is also a thankful one. She was always in a high degree grateful to all who conferred favors on herself or on the community, and was always afraid that she had not offered up to God enough prayers and works of penance for them. For the slightest service, as, for instance, when the door was opened for her as Superioress, she returned thanks. She never demanded anything for herself as a right, but asked for it in humble words, as for an undeserved favor. In her love for justice she often exhorted the great personages of this world and those in office with whom she became acquainted, not merely to avoid the unjust oppression of the poor themselves, but to watch that in their administration no subaltern should commit any injustice, also that widows and orphans should be protected. Even retributive justice seemed to her so deserving of respect, that she praised the government which enforced it, although she felt a heartfelt compassion for the culprit. Sometimes she would say: " If any one of my dearest friends or relatives were put to death for wickedness, I would not intercede for him, even were I certain of obtaining his pardon. I would rather kiss the avenging hand of God."

It is scarcely necessary to mention that she worked zealously for the promotion of the kingdom of God, and for the extirpation of vice. Let us hear what Sister M. Michelina Weis says about this:[1] " Mild, meek, and yielding as Crescentia was, when Superioress, she never neglected to remind such Sisters as were remiss of their duty, and also in the spirit of meekness to inflict such punishment as had been deserved, particularly if they had failed in observing the commandments of God, or in the perfection required by their state of life. In such cases she labored with an overwhelming force for the honor of God and the salvation of souls, and soon effected a change for the better." Sister M. Raphael says: " A single glance from her, without a word, was of such efficacy that we at once recognized our faults and were sorry for them."

In correcting, however, she acted with great prudence and often after long deliberation. In doubtful cases or

____

[1] Summ. N. 12 § 133.

when opinions differed, she first had recourse to God in prayer, and never spoiled anything by precipitation. She was of opinion that in the first excitement we often say that for which we are afterwards sorry, and that when accusations are made, delay in postponing the sentence often brings the truth to light and then reconciliation follows as a matter of course; therefore, when a complaint against any one was brought to her, she would not believe the accusation at first without further evidence, but she prayed and inquired closely into the case; she then considered what might be the best mode of correcting the delinquent. She never corrected important faults immediately; if she had to reprimand she prayed to God so to direct her tongue that she should use the requisite moderation; she then reproved with so much humility, mildness, and firmness that success was insured. She never again mentioned the faults that had been amended.

The old rule of prudence, " do nothing without counsel," was sacred in her eyes. By consulting with the older and more experienced Sisters, she sought, on the one hand, to obtain greater security against blunders, on the other, to gain a higher authority for what was decided. She convened this council more particularly for the regulation of temporal affairs, for which she deemed herself utterly unfit. The execution of details she also left, as far as possible, to such Sisters as were adapted for it.

The manner in which she held the customary chapter of faults is admirable. Sister M. Gabriel says:[1] " When, as Mother Superior, she held the chapter, it should rather have been termed a school of virtue than a chapter (of faults). She encouraged and consoled the failing and neglectful with maternal tenderness and gave to each and all the most wholesome advice to serve God with zeal and fervor, to keep their holy rules and vows with great exactness, to practise virtue, and every day to strive after greater perfection. In the chapter itself she was the most humble of

---

[1] Gabriel, p. 269.

all, publicly confessed her shortcomings, on her knees before all the Sisters, and humbly asked us for pardon, for God's sake, for the many faults and omissions of which she had been guilty and the bad example she had given. This on her part was a sheer act of humility and of self-annihilation, for to us she had always been a model and mirror of every virtue. When she had held the chapter, she knelt down again and humbly asked pardon for having admonished and corrected us for our faults, adding: ' My dear Sisters ! I am ashamed from my very heart that I have to admonish you for your failings, knowing, as I do, that I myself have the most and the greatest, and that I do not in the least do as I say: but I beg of you, follow not my deeds but my words; 'God will assuredly not allow these words to err in her whom He has ordained to fill His place. The all-seeing God, who provides everything, knows why He selected me, the most unfit, to this obedience. I know nothing, understand nothing, and how can I govern you who cannot direct myself ? But I hope and trust in my dear God, that He may deign to direct me, a mere straw, according to His divine will, to His greater honor, and to your welfare and salvation ; for the meaner the creature is, the greater and the more conspicuous will be the power, wisdom, and goodness He displays through its instrumentality.' ''

Such humility and love could give rise to no dubious thoughts, as if her judgment was partial, and even the least humble were compelled to acknowledge their faults, when they saw their holy Superioress proclaiming herself a transgressor, nay, the greatest transgressor of them all. More than this, they were convinced that Crescentia really loved them all, so that she would have given her life for each one of them. They saw how, without being asked, she was careful to provide for their individual needs, bodily and spiritual, and that she thought of everything, and seemed forgetful of herself alone.

Sister M. Joseph Anger testifies :[1] '' When she was

Mother Superior, every Sister had at all times free access to her, to reveal to her any doubts, temptations, and needs with which she might be troubled. She listened to every one with more than a mother's love and condescension, and every one left her presence consoled by her, and feeling fervor and desire for religious perfection renewed. We frequently said amongst ourselves : Whenever Crescentia speaks to us we get a new life; all her words are spirit and life. She often said to us : ' Oh, how gladly would I sacrifice my honor, my life, and everything, if I could only carry you up in my hands to Heaven !' In fact, she spared herself no pains, neglected no effort to lead us, by word and example, to virtue and perfection."

She was exceedingly careful in receiving candidates for the religious state. She said : " Decision on this subject is very important ; God's honor and that of the community depend on it." Even on her death-bed she gave exhortations to proceed in this matter with great consideration and without over-haste. She herself only received two novices, namely, Sister Raphael Miller (who from 1769–1799 was Superioress of the convent) and Sister M. Helena Kürz, who died Nov. 6, 1800. Every consideration of riches and of influential recommendations she desired should be excluded at their reception. She said: " It is God's will that the community should be rich, not in worldly goods, but in virtues." She manifested these principles in a particular manner in a case where the Father Provincial had warmly recommended a very wealthy postulant of noble family and when the other Sisters had already been influenced to give their consent. For obvious reasons she did not make many objections, but simply said, on seeing the postulant : " This one is not for us." In reality, she soon returned home of her own accord, and the Sister who relates the incident adds : " We were all, the postulant included, very glad at the event."

She gave a special caution against receiving persons of a melancholy disposition or of weak intellect ; even if they had mountains of gold, she said, they should not be received, seeing that they were little capable of advancing towards perfection themselves and were only an obstacle to others. She kept the novices under strict discipline during their novitiate, and urged their mistress, Sister M. Anna Neth, to neglect nothing in watching and educating them. In regard to the other Sisters she was particularly watchful over their intercourse with the outer world. By her prudence she was successful in removing some inconveniences which had arisen from the frequent visits of ecclesiastics and seculars. She had strict maxims on these subjects and often said that Sisters of a religious community incur no greater dangers than those which arise from a too frequent and intimate intercourse with their relatives and other outsiders, even were such belonging to the ecclesiastical state. Though the beginning might be good, it would often lead to no good end ; at the least it disturbed recollection, distracted the mind, and easily turned the heart away from God and towards creatures. While, on the other hand, recollection and silence nourish good thoughts, holy intentions, and mutual love.

Neither would she permit the common gossip of the city to be brought into the convent. " Let the dead bury the dead," she would say on these occasions ; "but we must imitate Christ ; that alone is our vocation." When they were at work at times when silence was not to be observed, and the Sisters had strayed off in vain talk, she at once turned the conversation, and sometimes, too, would find fault, saying : " Seek and love God, who is present, and speak of Him ; for love is better than speech. Whoever would strive after God, as in duty bound to do, must begin with silence and interior recollection. Sin is never absent where there is much talk ; even if the conversation begins with God, it easily runs off into worldly gossip. It is then better to keep silence and to love, in order that Jesus may be in our midst when we are at work."

After the example of holy Father Francis, she hated idle-

ness very much and attacked it on all occasions. She said :
" It gives an easy entrance to the devil and brings him much
profit ; yet we ought not to work as eye-servants of men
for men, but as servants of Christ for God." She herself
was the very first at menial works, and often secretly performed such as there were to do, so that the Sisters who
had them in charge found them already completed. She
was never absent from any exercise of the community
unless confined to bed by sickness, and she exacted this
punctuality from the others. We have already related that
she did not fail to be present at the recreations, where she
cheered as well as edified the Sisters. She made, as an
eye-witness asserts, the recreation not merely physically
recuperative, but truly a spiritual one. She was very glad
to see the Sisters rejoice in the Lord. " Be glad," she
said; " to one who seeks and loves nothing but God, cheerfulness becomes a second nature. The Lord loveth a
cheerful giver and servant ; those who are melancholy
and sad in this service displease Him ; they fish in the
mud of their own perversity." All affectation of singularity
in conduct displeased her sorely ; it did not come from God,
she thought, and only tended to sow the seed of disunion.

It was no wonder that a Superioress who lived entirely
by truth and love should fascinate all hearts, and, becoming herself the central point, should be able to unite the
whole community in peace and harmony and raise it up to
God Himself. What is most to be admired in her is, perhaps, her interior recollection, which was so powerfully effective that no outward affairs, cares, or conversations could
interrupt or disturb her interior intercourse with God.
Neither did she ever omit her usual prayers and exercises ;
only very extraordinary causes could induce her to be absent from the common exercises. No occurrence, no
difficulty, no loss could disturb her peace for a moment;
she lived altogether by that truth spoken by the Redeemer:
" Seek ye therefore first the kingdom of God, and His justice, and all these things shall be added unto you."

We must speak of the serious sickness which befell her in the first year of her office.[1] She suffered for a quarter of a year with dropsy, and everybody, including the two doctors who attended her, thought she would soon die. The swelling increased to such a size that she could not lie down, and sitting up became also difficult. All at once a change took place in her sickness, and in a short time she became quite well, to every one's surprise. When the Sisters questioned her about it, she replied that St. Anthony, her patron, had appeared to her, and announced to her that she would not die of this disease. Then the sickness had disappeared.

Crescentia affords us a new example that God exalts the humble and makes them His instruments. It is peculiar to God to work great things in nothing, and by nothing; and " the base things of the world and the things that are contemptible hath God chosen, and things that are not, that He might bring to naught things that are; that no flesh should glory in His sight."[2] Whosoever is called by God to be His representative and tool in directing others, should never forget this sublime truth. But, alas! too easily does man interiorly exalt his person, when he is exteriorly elevated to dignities; whereby he sinks before God in the same degree that he rises before men. In this regard, the Wise Man says: " Have they made thee ruler? be not lifted up; be among them as one of them."[3]

---

[1] Act. B. Summ. Obj. N. 11 § 8.   [2] I. Cor. i. 28, 29.   [3] Eccl. xxxii. 1.

CHAPTER III.

How Much and how Successfully Crescentia Labored in and outside of the Community.

T pleased Almighty God to place the light, which He Himself had lit, and had kept for so many years under the bushel of contempt, in a candlestick, that it might henceforth give light to the House of God far and wide. "And the weak things of the world hath God chosen, that He may confound the strong." [1] For this reason "God had," as Sister M. Gabriel says, [2] "endowed His servant with marvellous wisdom and the gifts of the Holy Ghost. Persons of high rank have frequently acknowledged that they had received salutary counsel and assistance from her in most difficult cases, in which the ablest and most learned men scarcely ventured to give a definite decision. She possessed a wonderful ability for any business and could accommodate herself to all circumstances and all characters."

The fame of her sanctity and wisdom spread, not only over the whole diocese of Augsburg, but over all Germany, and even beyond it. Attracted by this renown and led to her by God, persons from the highest classes of society, or such as were prominent for knowledge and sanctity, came to the poor convent, to seek comfort in affliction, counsel in intricate matters of business or in spiritual affairs, or edification and the assistance of her prayers. Others corresponded with her by letter for the same purposes. Among those who visited her personally, we must name, in the first place, Amalia, wife of the Prince-elector of Bavaria, who, later, was by one section of Germany acknowledged as emperor, under the name of Charles VII. This noble lady came three times to Kaufbeuren, and, to her great edification and consolation, remained alone with Crescentia

---

for many hours.   Then we must prominently mention the two brothers of Charles VII., Cardinal Theodore, and Clement Augustus, Elector of Cologne.

Concerning the visit of the latter, the following notice is found :[1] Some years before his death, Clement Augustus, when on a tour through Suabia, visited Mary Crescentia, of the Franciscan Order, who was living in the reputation of sanctity and was said to be favored with the gift of prophecy ; being in a cheerful mood, he requested her to tell him somewhat of his life to come. The good religious hesitated at first to comply with his wishes, but finally acceded to his oft-repeated, earnest request. She foretold to the prince that though he had indeed built many castles, he would die in none of them. And so it happened. Clement Augustus fell sick when on a journey to Munich, in the Chur-Treves castle at Ehrenbreitstein, and died there the day after his arrival, February 6th, A. D. 1761, at 5 P. M. The remark is added that the prince kept a picture of Ven. Crescentia in his sleeping apartments at Bonn.

Moreover, Leopold of Firmian, Archbishop of Salzburg, visited her, also the Cardinal and Prince-bishop of Constance, Von Roth, who had an extraordinary veneration for her, and had already visited her when Dean of the Cathedral of Augsburg, as well as afterwards ; he often remained in holy conversation with her for hours. The bishop of Constance and Augsburg, John Francis of Schauffenberg, and his successor, Joseph of Hesse-Darmstadt, visited her twice. Anselm, the Prince-abbot of Kempten ; the Prince of Sigmaringen, the Grand-master of Waldburg-Scheer, and the Duchess of Savoy, *née* Princess Lichtenstein, who was more devoted to her than any one, also visited her. The Imperial General, Count Collovrath, came all the way from Moravia to speak to her, and when he left could not find words sufficient to express his admiration of her. Not to mention the many other counts, barons, abbots, provincials, doctors of theology and others, persons re-

---

[1] Geschichte der Burgen, etc. History of Castles, etc.

nowned for sanctity, knowledge, and influence, who came, often from afar off, to seek from the poor religious, inexperienced in secular knowledge, but wonderfully enlightened in the school of Christ, a wisdom that human enlightenment and power cannot give. Their expectations were generally raised very high, and yet no one, as far as is known,[1] ever left her without being satisfied; on the contrary, they usually acknowledged that their expectations had been far surpassed, and that they found themselves wonderfully consoled and enlightened, and knew not which to admire most, her modesty and humility, or her wisdom and enlightenment.

As may be supposed, some visitors came from mere curiosity, or even with an evil purpose ; some to get material for making fun, or to gather facts for piquant remarks. Such as these were not a little disappointed. She then assumed so reserved and serious an attitude, spoke but little, and on such general topics, that the visit soon came to an end, and the visitors found no other material for their criticisms than to say that the servant of God was an ignorant and stupid woman. Not infrequently, however, these visits had quite another ending : several parties, after a brief interview, went away ashamed and confused ; some were even honest enough to confess that Crescentia had laid open to them the sad state of their conscience. An ecclesiastic once came with the sinister intention of trapping her with a few critical questions.[2] Out of respect for the priesthood she at first replied only with a few kind and reserved words. When, disappointed in his object, he was about to leave, she told him that he would do better, instead of squandering his precious time, to use it in doing penance for and amending certain sins, which she distinctly named to him. The words struck him like lightning ; he went away contrite, amended his life, and told several persons that Crescentia had told him of sins which God alone could have known.

---

[1] Summ. N. 23 § 68.   [2] Summ. N. 21 § 27 and 83.

Another priest came to hear a yet more earnest truth. At the process the witnesses relate only in a summary way[1] what Father Ott tells as follows : "This gentleman, more given to playing tricks for fun than is exactly becoming to a priest, when he heard that the Archbishop of Cologne was about to visit the servant of Christ, would not lose a convenient opportunity for playing a joke on Crescentia. Accompanied by several persons, he announced himself as the expected prelate. The Superioress and the Sisters received him in all honor, as became a person in so exalted a position. The pious virgin was at once summoned, but to the annoyance and alarm of the other Sisters she comported herself in a very reserved and chilling manner towards the gentleman. When left alone with him, she told him something that had hitherto remained a secret, and then bade him prepare for death, for within three months he would die. Thoroughly staggered, he followed her good advice; a short time after he died.

The great concourse of people and the daily disturbance it involved was a great sacrifice to this pious virgin, who cherished so extraordinary a love for a hidden and secluded life; so great indeed was the sacrifice that only her love for Christ and for the souls redeemed by Him could render it in any degree bearable. But she never received a visit or spoke to a stranger except at the command of Mother Johanna, or, when she herself was Superior, at the bidding of the Sister-assistant. She never spoke a word or gave a hint of what passed in these interviews on either side ; we should have known nothing of the details had not the visitors themselves praised her language as full of kindness, wisdom, and strength, and communicated many things from which we may conclude that God had granted her the discernment of spirits, and a frequent insight into the secrets of conscience. For this reason her words often struck like lightning, and many were incited to do penance, either for a state of grievous sin covering many years, or for a state of

---

[1] Summ. N. 21 § 153.

dangerous lukewarmness. She told a priest who visited her, and who had a pack of cards secreted in his pocket, "It would be better if your Reverence had the Breviary with you instead of the cards." To another she gave the salutary admonition not to be an ecclesiastic in the morning only, but in the evening also, and to refrain from useless conversation and company. In both cases the reprimands had the desired effect. Many came to her for help and advice in their temporal needs and sufferings. Then it became manifest, indeed, that she had an extraordinary gift of consoling the sorrowing and afflicted, of exciting them to trust in God and to resign themselves to the divine will. In fact, those seeking her help were very often really delivered from their troubles, as shall be related in the next chapter. Nearly every one who visited her desired to have a souvenir of her. With the permission of the Superioress she therefore distributed articles of devotion : rosaries, scapulars, crosses, certain instruments of the passion, and to the sick, blessed oil and similar articles.

Innumerable examples show that God connected many graces and even wonderful effects with a believing and devout use of these articles ; on which account, and as it seems not without some fault of the very credulous Sister M. Anna Neth, a false report had got abroad that these articles had been blessed and indulgenced by Christ Himself. We have already related that it was proved by a strict, special examination, how innocent Crescentia was in this respect, and how careful she always was to have these articles of devotion blessed by a priest.

The correspondence by letter which she had to carry on with many persons who had visited her, or who were prevented from doing so, assumed in the latter years of her life such large dimensions that Sister M. Anna was kept busy, the whole day through, in answering the letters received, and another Sister often had to help her. Many thousands of such letters containing matters of conscience she burnt at once ; yet after her death many such were found, as is shown by a document issued July 13, 1747,[1] by Father Benjamin Elbel, whom we have already mentioned ; he was Commissary General of the Franciscan Order on the north side of the Alps.   According to this document, there were eight hundred and seventy-seven letters in hand, which he ordered to be burnt for conscience' sake, as they contained many secret things.   Among them from seventy to eighty were from persons of the highest position in Church and State ; for example, four letters from the Empress Amalia, wife of the Emperor Joseph I.; three from the Princess-elector Amalia of the Electorate of Bavaria ; several from the widowed Empress Elizabeth, wife of Charles VI.; one from Queen Josepha of Poland, and one from King Augustus III.; six from the Prince-elector of Cologne ; others from the Princes-electors of Saxony, from the Archbishop of Salzburg, and from the Bishop of Brixen, with the humble signature, "Casper Ignatius" the sinner ; some others from the Princess-elector Emanuela Teresa, Sister of Charles VII.; more than thirty from the Duchess of Savoy *née* Princess of Lichtenstein ; from the Prince of Lowenstein, from a Margrave of Baden and a prince of Hohenlohe.   The other seven hundred letters were for the most part from high personages, fourteen of them from princely persons, several of them ministers, generals, and men distinguished for learning.   These names show how great already was her reputation for sanctity, and how astonishing was the extent of her influence.

Nearly all the answers to these letters were written, not by herself, but mostly by Sister M. Neth, as is shown by the hand-writing of the many still in existence.   Crescentia doubtless gave the substance of the reply, and her secretary then couched it in the ceremonious forms at that time in vogue ; but as has already been said, the secretary is supposed to have acted rather independently, and whether from forgetfulness or from her own imagination, to have inserted many things which were not told her.

---

[1] Act. B. Summ. Obj. N. 20.

Among those who kept up a letter correspondence with her we may also mention Maurus Xaverius, Abbot of Plankstetten, who died in the odor of sanctity, of whom a somewhat lengthy biography was reprinted in the "*Eichstadter Pastoral-Blatt,*" A. D. 1857. From that paper we borrow the following :[1] "In the letters (of the abbot), we come quite often upon the name of blessed Crescentia of Kaufbeuren, with whom he carried on a correspondence by letter, and of whom he afterwards distributed some relics. Once he received from her a sapling of a pear tree which he gave to the gardener (John Trindorfer), with directions to plant it. The gardener replied, with a laugh, that it would probably be labor in vain, as the sapling was dry and withered. Father Maurus, however, insisted on his orders being obeyed, and the sapling really grew into a lovely tree, which bore still lovelier fruit. Father Erhard Richter, who told us of this, knew the gardener well, heard the story from his own mouth, and picked some of the pears growing on that tree."[2]

She was also in close communication with two priests of the Order of St. Benedict, of the monastery of Mury-Gries, as is manifested by several letters.[3] To Father Placidus Vigier († 1745), Dean of the monastery, who had asked her advice as to whether it would not be better to resign his office, as it was so much mixed up with secular matters, she replied, on March 11th, 1741, advising him to remain in the office imposed on him by obedience. When the Superiors had left to this same Father the decision whether on account of sickness he should resign or not, she again advised him to leave it to the Superiors, and to invoke the Holy Ghost to enlighten them, for which pur-

---

[1] No. 11. Jahrg. iv. p. 54.

[2] This history of the withered branch is confirmed by a manuscript found in the possession of the late Dr. Antony Sporer, which contains the life of the servant of God, by Kilian Katzenberger, together with one hundred and thirty-five reports of miracles, from the years 1753 to 1778. We are indebted for this notice, and also for some others, to the kindness of Father Constantine, of the Friars Minor of the Capuchins.

[3] Communicated to us by Father Martinus Klein, O. S. B., of Sarnen.

pose she also promised to pray. In a letter to him, dated March 1, 1741, the subsequent passage is found: "My God! I am a mere nothing, and from me nothing is to be expected, but from our great, merciful, and loving God, who is so kind and does not despise a mere nothing like myself, and of His goodness comes to the help of all men; to Him be given all honor, praise, thanksgiving and benediction!" To Father Anselmus Frei, of the same Order († 1762), who had offered to say Mass for her intention once every month so long as he lived, she writes to express her gratitude, and since he left it to her to fix the day on which Mass should be said, she selects Thursday: "Because on this day the greatest benefit was bestowed on us poor mortals, as our dear Saviour gave Himself to us as food, and also as a holy, daily, and unbloody sacrifice. This is a grace which can never be sufficiently valued."

Several letters, which are still in existence, written partly in the name of Crescentia, partly in that of her Superioress, Mother M. Johanna, bear witness to the veneration in which she was held by the pious Baron of Bodman and his family. From two letters of March, 1725, it is evident that this nobleman desired to enter into a closer union of spirit with her, and wished that "she might receive him as her spiritual brother." This was too much for her humility. The Superioress, however, writes to him that she had given her the command to comply with his request, and as his sister to remember him and always to pray for him. In all her own letters to him, Crescentia exhorts the baron to lay aside his over-anxiety, and put his whole trust in God, that He would not let him be lost, for His will is that every one should be blest. On April 2d, 1729, she communicates to him, concerning her own person, "that her Divine Beloved also took her to task a little, and that she was glad that she had yet longer to suffer, before she could enjoy something of His love." It will not be uninteresting to read what the Superioress wrote in Crescentia's name, March 15, 1732: "I am not at all opposed to the vow not to dance or masquerade any more, as these vanities are not pleasing to God; I wish a stop could be put to them over the whole world, for certainly no honor accrues to God by their means; on the contrary, they are injurious to God's honor and the salvation of souls." The petition of the same nobleman to be allowed to have a scapular made from the mantle of the servant of God, the Superioress very properly refuses, with the remark that "the like of that is not permitted during one's lifetime."

The day of judgment alone will reveal how many sinners she converted by salutary encouragement and prayer. We subjoin a few cases that have been made public by the Acts. The following conversion is very remarkable:[1] A certain military officer, holding a high position, who was recklessly living a life of excess, one day found on his writing-desk a closed note. He read it, and became as if thunder-struck. In it were enumerated all his enormous sins, and underneath was the signature, M. Crescentia Höss. A powerful feeling of contrition seized him; he made a good confession and from that time forward led a Christian life. He wrote to Crescentia with his own hand, told her of the course of his conversion, and in burning words expressed his gratitude towards the saviour of his soul. Sister M. Barbara, the witness, had read the letter herself.

Another gentleman of distinction had led a very scandalous life.[2] All the entreaties and prayers of his good and pious wife had been without effect. He went once to Kaufbeuren and had a long conversation with Crescentia. She spoke so thrillingly to his heart, that on his return home he prepared himself for a good confession, and ever after led an exemplary life. When on his death-bed he said publicly: "I esteem those happy who have recourse to the prayers of M. Crescentia; it is by her intercession that God has granted me this great grace, without which I should have perished eternally." Father Ott reports that

---

[1] Summ. N. 10 § 258.   [2] Summ. N. 21 § 76.—Ott, B. III. C. 7.

the soul of this gentleman appeared after his death to the servant of God, beseeching her by her prayers to deliver him from purgatory, as she had already delivered him from hell. Then, after a short interval, she received a revelation that he had entered the glory of Heaven.

A young merchant of Augsburg,[1] a brother of Sister M. Antonia Duboin, was so addicted to vice, particularly to drinking and gambling, that he lost many thousand florins and in a short time had dissipated his whole fortune. He would not listen to anything about religion or about reforming himself, and in spite of the entreaties of his mother, wife, brothers, and sisters, lived on in this infatuated manner. His sister Antonia at length recommended him to the prayers of Crescentia, who exhorted her to trust in God and promised to pray for him, holding out hopes of his conversion. Suddenly the profligate man was taken sick, and became converted in the most edifying way. When he was about to receive the Viaticum, notwithstanding his great pains, he insisted on being taken out of bed, knelt down, and received . the Blessed Sacrament with the greatest devotion ; he then assisted at Mass, which was said in his room, up to the end. They then put him back in his bed, where he received Extreme Unction ; the agony of death soon came on, and he died in the sentiments of penance and with the greatest resignation. According to Father Ott's report, he, too, after death, appeared to Crescentia, to thank her for her powerful assistance, without which he would have been lost.

If we resembled the servant of God in humility and in love, God would also make use of us to direct the currents of His grace and mercy to many souls now going astray. Grace well used begets new grace, not only in ourselves, but in others also, even if in another way. Therefore, O Christian soul, remember what St. Paul says : " Wherefore receive one another, as Christ also hath received you unto the honor of God."[2]

---

[1] Summ. N. 10 § 60, 182, 222. - Ott, B. I.   [2] Rom. xv. 7.

CHAPTER IV.

How Crescentia was Endowed with the Spirit of Prophecy and the Gift of Curing the Sick.[1]

OULS endowed by the Spirit of God with extraordinary graces for their own sanctification generally receive marvellous gifts for the temporal and spiritual welfare of others, and for building up the Church of Christ, which is His spiritual body. That this godly virgin was specially privileged in this respect follows from the traits of her life as already told. Nevertheless, we have here many things to subjoin. We have, in the first place, to remark that even in these gifts, which are not in themselves real virtues, and are consequently not meritorious, her sublime virtue nevertheless shone forth conspicuously from the fact that she had no attachment to these effects of the Holy Ghost, laid no stress upon them, was even distrustful of everything extraordinary, subjecting all such entirely to the judgment of her confessors.

Concerning the gift of prophecy, many cases have been attested in which she foretold the future and laid open hidden things. The testimony of Cardinal Von Roth, Prince-bishop of Constance, is very important. When this pious prince of the Church, in 1770, visited the sepulchre of the servant of God, he declared before the Sisters and many ecclesiastical gentlemen that during her life-time the deceased had told him many things of the future, all of which had come to pass.

Sister M. Constantia Leder,[2] in the year 1742, suffered from pectoral dropsy, yet so that she could take part in the religious exercises of the community, and no immediate danger seemed at hand. On the 31st of March the servant of God, who was then Superioress, said to her, very early in the morning. that she should prepare for death, and after di-

---

[1] Summ. N. 21 § 1-167.   [2] Summ. N. 21 § 88, 86, 94.

vine service receive Extreme Unction. The sick Sister, not having noticed any change for the worse, was much surprised at this bidding, but she believed in her Superioress, and was present at the holy sacrifice of the Mass, went to confession in her turn with the other Sisters to Rev. P. Januarius Maier, S. J., and then requested him to administer the Sacraments of the dying, which he did. The next morning she was again present at Mass and went to bed only at the command of the Mother Superior. The Sister-infirmarian was directed not to leave her for a moment. At one o'clock in the afternoon the sick Sister suddenly had a relapse of her complaint and died forthwith.

In the year 1737, Sister M. Barbara Neth[1] seemed to be in her last agony; the infirmarian Sisters therefore, at three o'clock in the afternoon, gave the usual signal on the bell for the Sisters to meet, to assist the departing Sister with their prayers. M. Barbara Kiening and Gabriel Merz, who were then postulants, hastened with the other Sisters to the infirmary. Passing through the oratory they beheld M. Crescentia there, undisturbed in prayer. They then asked her, their mistress, for permission to go with the other Sisters to the dying nun. But she answered : "Mary Barbara is not going to die now, but at five o'clock; so go quietly back again." And in reality that Sister did die when the clock struck five. Once Crescentia told Sister M. Benedicta Pez that she would get a sickness which would render it necessary for her to be separated from the other Sisters ; this really happened in the year 1749.

On February 23d, 1731, Crescentia[2] met Sister M. Coletta Gröbl at the stair-case and told her to prepare for death; it was high time. The one spoken to felt quite well, and did not believe these words. On the same day, at supper, she felt unwell, left the refectory, and at the door was struck with paralysis which deprived her of all consciousness ; remedies were applied, she recovered sufficiently to be absolved and anointed ; ten hours after the attack she was a corpse.

---

[1] Summ. N. 21 § 17, 90.   [2] Ott. B. III. C. 6.

The same Father Ott relates the following circumstance:[1] Father Ferdinand Troper, S. J., preacher at the parochial Church of Kaufbeuren, became a little unwell, without any indications, however, that his sickness was dangerous. But when Father Bartholomew Binner came to Crescentia, she begged him to go home at once, and administer the last sacraments to his sick brother in religion, for it was high time. He remonstrated ; but she insisted more and more earnestly in her petition. He resolved to go and tell the sick Father what had happened ; this Father, knowing the prophetic spirit of Crescentia, immediately received the rites of the Church at six o'clock, March 13, 1736. He lost consciousness immediately after and died before midnight. She told her own sister Regina that their beloved father would die on the following day, before noon.[2] She also told her the very hour in which her husband, Joseph Heinritz, would die. Both events happened exactly as predicted. Not infrequently she told the Sisters of persons dying, who lived far off, at the very hour when the death occurred ; this is especially mentioned, relative to the death of Father Ignatius Lieb, S. J., who had been confessor to the community.

Sister M. Bernardine Gast[3] was tormented with an exceedingly great fear of death. Crescentia told her she would have to suffer these spiritual torments until shortly before her death ; that then this temptation would make room for the sweetest peace. In the beginning of August, 1713, all this fear of death passed suddenly into an ardent desire to die. She died on the 11th of the same month, smiling and with incredible joy, being assisted by Father Ott.

John Baptist von Benedict,[4] having finished his studies, was firmly resolved to try his fortune in the military service. When on a journey, he paid a visit to the servant of God and told her of the state of life he had chosen. She smiled and said he would by no means enter the secular

---

[1] Ott, B. I. [2] Summ. N. 21 § 67, 68.

[3] Ibid. § 90 and Father Ott, B. I. [4] Ibid. § 151,

but the spiritual militia. He shrugged his shoulders incredulously. Not long afterwards, however, he suddenly
resolved to enter the Society of Jesus. He became a
priest and professor, and frequently told Dr. Joseph Meichelbeck, who was a pupil of his, of this remarkable
prophecy.

To John Baptist Neth,[1] a citizen of Kaufbeuren without
any literary education, she announced the most improbable events long before they happened. He was to become
the steward of a noble family, and after that a senator, and
then a member of the privy council of his native city.
When this man's two sons studied Latin, he too began to
study that language. He followed up this study with that
of others with such zeal that, being well-talented, he made
great progress. On account of his knowledge and honorable character he became, in the first place, steward of the
noble family of Imhoff, and then senator of his native
city. This office he kept up to the time of his universally
lamented death in 1762. We believe we ought also to
mention what Father Kilianus Katzenberger relates:[2]
Crescentia went, in the year 1729, on a visit to another
convent. There she told the door-keeper, a young and robust Sister, to prepare herself for death. The Sister, however, thought she was still so young and strong, why should
she have to die ? Yet she died in a few weeks.

While Crescentia was yet Mistress of Novices, she several times said to her pupils:[3] "You do not pay much
attention now to what I say, but the time will come when
you will gather up all my words." No one then understood
what this meant : but the words were fulfilled after her
death, when in the examination for her Beatification, the
Sisters carefully collected all her teachings and called to
mind every reminiscence concerning the servant of God.

We have already[4] spoken of the prophecy she uttered in
regard to the suppression and re-establishment of her own

---

[1] Summ. N. 21 ¶ 153.   [2] Life of Crescentia, C. 18.   [3] Summ. N. 21 ¶ 4, 16.
[4] B. I. C, 4.

convent. A similar one she is said to have made respecting the future suppression and restoration of the Saxon province of the Holy Cross of the Franciscan Order, to which the author of this book belongs. We can adduce no written document in attestation of this, but only give the tradition which was known throughout the province even before the French Revolution. According to this tradition, she, probably between 1741 and 1744, very distinctly told the Superior of said province, who visited her when on his way to Rome, that this province, which was then very extensive and flourishing, would at a later period be entirely suppressed, though practically some convents would continue to exist; that from this germ the province of the Holy Cross would revive at two different periods, at the first one imperfectly, but at the second it would attain to a greater extent and prosperity than ever before, and even carry its branches beyond the ocean. The first two parts of this prophecy were accomplished in the beginning of this century (1800). During the long pressure of the suppression of religious houses, the Fathers who survived the acts of violence often built their hopes for better times on the abovementioned words of Crescentia. The beginning of the fulfilment of the last part took place in the years 1829 to 1831, and especially since 1844, when the noble-hearted King Frederic William IV. granted sufficient liberty to the Order. And since the year 1858 the province of this Order has founded several monasteries in North America. God grant that the complete accomplishment of this consoling prophecy may come to pass!

The light given to her by God very often revealed to her secret things of the present time. It frequently happened that she anticipated the words of the persons coming to consult her, telling them before they spoke what they wished, what had been done already, and what was still to be done in the matter concerned. That she often, with love and discretion, disclosed the secrets of their hearts to the Sisters, we have before noticed, and we could add their testimonics.[1]   We will speak here only of the cases in which she knew the thoughts of outsiders.

When Father Adam Flotto, S. J.,[2] at that time a renowned missionary, was rector of the college at Mindelheim, a most difficult and important case of conscience was laid before him in the confessional to decide.   He could not come to a clear opinion upon the matter, whether to decide in the affirmative or negative, although he had looked through many books on the subject.   The seal of confession prevented his consulting other theologians, and thus he was not a little embarrassed.   After some time, Mother Johanna, accompanied by Sister Crescentia, came to Mindelheim on business and called on the said Father to obtain his advice.   As he was speaking to the Mother Superior, the servant of God said to him all at once: " Your reverence must in this affair (she mentioned it distinctly) give an affirmative answer, for that is the will of God."   The surprise of the priest was very great, and he afterwards asserted that he had kept his doubts to himself, without manifesting his thoughts to any one, and that no one could have known them.

When priests said Mass for her or for her intention, it was often made known to her by divine manifestation.   Father Placidus, O. S. F., had notified her that he had said one holy Mass for her; she thanked him in writing for having also offered another for her, which he had really done, but without any one's knowing it.   She also thanked Rev. Conrad Pföttlin, the parish priest, for a holy Mass he had said for her in the parish church.   This case had been so concealed that nobody knew of it.

Rev. Father Beda,[3] Abbot of the Benedictine monastery at Zwiefalten, had heard of the many revelations and ecstasies of the servant of God.   Fearing a secret deception of the devil, he said a holy Mass with the intention that God might either humble the deluded soul and thereby save

---

[1] Compare Summ. N. 21 § 33.   [2] Ibid. § 83, and Father Ott, B. I.
[3] Ott, B. I.

her, or, if her revelations were genuine, to carry them further still with His grace. This intention was known only to him and to God. Yet on the same day on which he had said the holy Mass, Crescentia revealed the thoughts of this pious priest to her Superioress, asking permission of her to write her thanks to him, which was done. The abbot himself mentioned this occurrence, which so well exemplifies the spirit of Crescentia, to several persons, of whom Father Ott gives the names.

The same author relates, with its minutest details, the following curious history, which so thoroughly attests the prophetic spirit of the virgin, and which we give here, omitting some non-essential circumstances. Anthony Aendras, a poor farmer of Thalhofen, near Oberdorf, had two children by his wife Agnes; one of them was five years, the other six weeks old. On October 28th, 1742, both the parents went to Church, and carelessly left the children at home alone. A wicked woman from Unterthingau, named Anna Körpf, who a few weeks before had enjoyed their hospitality, and had withdrawn from the place, apparently to lie in wait for an opportunity to kidnap the baby, entered the house while they were away. She hoped and intended, with the help of an accomplice in guilt, to sell the child at a high price to certain Jews who had then come to Augsburg on account of the war. In order not to be discovered, she strangled the oldest child, concealed the body under a heap of straw, set fire to the bedstead, and then with the youngest child secretly betook herself to Augsburg. When the mother came home and opened the door, the house was full of smoke and fire, the cradle was empty, and neither of the two children was to be found. At her loud shrieks the whole village ran together, among them the parish priest, Father John Leonard Lochbronner. The fire was extinguished, but no trace of the children could be found. The people searched for them for three days but without success; then a rumor arose that the parents themselves had caused this inexplicable disappearance of their children. This new trouble drove the unfortunate couple nearly to desperation.

More than once they were summoned before a court of justice, and as no one took their part, they did not know how to clear themselves of the charge made against them. In her extreme distress the mother had recourse to St. Anthony of Padua, that by his intercession they might find out where their children were and be freed from this frightful suspicion. She had scarcely sent up this cry of her heart to Heaven than it seemed to her she saw a religious standing before her, and she immediately thought that it must be the "pious Crescentia," who would help her. She wished to go at once to Kaufbeuren, but could not find anybody to accompany her, until at length Barbara Huber, who was but seventeen years old, went with her out of compassion. On the 30th of October both came to the convent and desired to speak with Crescentia, but she was very sick and could not be seen by strangers; then the unhappy mother, amid much weeping and sobbing, told the door-keeper what she wanted, that she might tell the whole story of her misfortunes to the servant of God.

But Crescentia did not listen to the story ; she told the Sister to say to the woman that she must bear her heavy cross with patience, prayer, and trust ; that God would bring it all to a happy issue ; meantime, she was to blame nobody, and forgive her enemies. It would be some time yet before her innocence was made known, but meantime she should suffer herself to " be walked over and trodden upon." Concerning the holy Mass—which the woman had not mentioned, but which she had intended to have said—Crescentia herself would take charge of that and have it said instead of her, and also promised that the Sisters should pray for her, that she might not lose her reason. She was, however, to make the pilgrimage she had promised at once, if not previously prevented. This last case did occur ; the innocent woman was arrested on the road by the police and taken before the court.

The poor mother, meantime, was in no way satisfied with the message received; she wanted absolutely to know whether her children were alive, and where they were ; she therefore sent the door-keeper again to Crescentia, who sent back word that she would find out where the eldest was as soon as she returned home; and that the youngest was still living, but very weak. And, in fact, the unhappy woman, on returning home from the court, heard, even before entering the village, that the body of the eldest child had been discovered under the heap of straw. The investigations by the magistracy and the insults and affronts of the frantic people continued for some weeks longer to harass the oppressed parents. Then a report was circulated that the baby had been found at Augsburg. The parents at once set out for that place; on their way they called at the convent of Kaufbeuren and heard from Crescentia that as soon as they came to the gates of the city they would ascertain where the child was ; and indeed, they found people there who, supposing the child to be in the foundling house, conducted them thither.

The murderers had, in fact, lost courage while entering the city by the "Red Gate," and in order to enter the town unobserved, had set down on one side the basket containing the child. A Protestant woman had discovered the half-frozen child and taken it to the foundling house. When the mother entered the room, in which were upwards of thirty little children reposing in their beds, she, as if guided by an invisible hand, went straight up to the cradle of her little daughter, exclaiming in her native dialect : "O my Annie Barbele, how did you get here ?" Strange to say, the child laughed aloud ! The mother fainted away for joy. Several gentlemen present were moved to tears, and provided effective assistance for these troubled parents.

Suspicion soon fell on the real culprit; she was arrested, found guilty, and with her accomplice, was executed. During the trial, the much suffering parents remained at

Augsburg at the cost of the city, and returned home at the end of July, 1743, with their child. On their way back, they desired to return thanks to the servant of God, and as they rang the bell at the convent-door, the prophetic virgin told the door-keeper, who happened to be with her, to "open the door, for the people of Thalhofen are there with their child." The good people begged of Crescentia to obtain for them the grace that they might carry home the child alive to the village; it was very sick, and its death might expose them to new detractions. On this account, although night was approaching, they proposed to go home that very day. The servant of God quieted them, desiring them to remain all night in the city, because the child would not die before their return home. In fact, it died four days afterwards.

That by her prayers she had procured the recovery of many sick persons, and relief to many in trouble, was the firm belief among all classes of persons, and numberless instances were related of her doing this. During her life very little of this was written down, and the remembrance of these cases has in great measure been lost. We subjoin a few miraculous cures from the Acts of her Beatification:[1]

Francis Joseph Krautmann, or Kreitman, of Kaufbeuren, the only son of a widow, lay hopelessly sick of a dangerous fever. The afflicted mother went to the Mother Superior Johanna, to obtain, through her, prayers from Crescentia. In the very hour in which the latter began her fervent prayers in the sick man's behalf, an unexpected change took place, followed by a rapid recovery.

The child of a teacher at Stettin, nor far from Kaufbeuren, was at five years deformed and lame in both hands and feet, and had been so from its birth. Many medical appliances had been used and had helped nothing. The mother, Maria Sattel, had recourse to Crescentia, who promised to pray for the child, and gave her some blessed oil and a large Latin T printed on paper as a sign of the Cross. Three

---

[1] Summ. N. 22 § 1-28.

days afterwards the child could walk, and his limbs were straight and sound.

Lady Anna Antonia Dorothea (*née* von Hörbens), of Pappus, had for a length of time had a cancer on the breast which was continually increasing. When all medical appliances had proved useless, and the pain was becoming unbearable, she, in the year 1733, had recourse to Crescentia, who only gave her a little blessed oil. The evil disappeared almost instantly. The healed lady with her own hands wrote out a testimony of this miraculous cure.

Besides the case, [1] already mentioned, when by an heroic act of love she cured the wounds on the feet of Sister M. Anna Neth, it is said that she also obtained by her prayers, to the admiration and astonishment of all, a sudden restoration to health of the Superioress M. Johanna, at a time when her death seemed near and inevitable. At a furious fire which originated in a brewery in Kaufbeuren, circumstances rendered the fire so dangerous that the worst was apprehended for the city, and it seemed certain that the nearest houses would assuredly be lost. People came to ask the servant of God to pray; she did so with great fervor. In the most striking way the fire seemed to go out, as if of itself. Lutherans, as well as Catholics, looked on the event as something supernatural, and it was unanimously attributed to the powerful prayer of Crescentia. [2]

Father Ott relates the cure of Joseph Filser, of Füssen, in the year 1739, which made a great sensation, as after a severe sickness which had lasted three months the several doctors who had been in attendance had given up all hopes. As soon as the sick man received some blessed articles sent to him by Crescentia, he became suddenly and perfectly well.

The miracles which the Lord promised should accompany those who believe in Him [3] have never died out in the Catholic Church; every century, up to the present moment, has witnessed them in immeasurable fulness, if not in the

---

[1] B. II. C. 9.　　[2] Summ. N. 22 § 27.　　[3] Mark xvi. 17, 18.

same degree. Many millions of reports of such signs of the divine power and goodness have been written down, but have often been forgotten and sometimes partly lost. And yet the infidel deigns not even to cast a glance on these works of God in order to verify their truth. In this consists his sin and his condemnation!

O Christian, beware of pride, which, more than any other vice, wraps up the soul in a dark cloud, which so veils his sight, that though he has eyes, he seeth not! Our Lord assigns this as the cause of infidelity in these words: "How can you believe who receive glory one from another: and the glory which is from God alone, you do not seek?"[1]

CHAPTER V.

Last Sickness and Happy Death of Ven. Crescentia.[2]

THE desire to be dissolved and to be with Christ increased from her sixteenth year, and gained so greatly the upper hand, that it became a painful martyrdom, so that only the will of her celestial Spouse and the love for suffering could form a counter-balance, and keep her heart in peace and rest. During the last two years of her life she was never weary of talking about death; sometimes she would style it "the prison-keeper," sometimes the "marriage-bidder," or "bride-man," sometimes also the "wise man." Love had banished fear; she considered it the zenith of happiness to die for love. Sister M. Gabriel writes:[3] "Nothing was sweeter to her than Jesus and because she considered death the door or the road to Jesus, she used to say, during her life, as also on her death-bed, 'Nothing is sweeter than Jesus, Mary and death.'"

---

[1] John v. 44. [2] Summ. N. 24 § 1–390.—Act B. Inform. 75–86. [3] Gabriel, p. 291.

Father Ott[1] reports that once during the life of Mother Johanna, she had such a long continuous ecstasy that the Superioress became alarmed and finally determined to recall her to herself by obedience. When she had not yet completely recovered her normal condition, she said: " Oh, Reverend Mother, how far I am from you !" She afterwards told the Mother Superior, who inquired about it, that her angel guardian had taken her in spirit to hell, to purgatory, and to Heaven, and while gazing on the last had said to her : "My foster-child, here, where God is venerated with His elect, shalt thou dwell forever; then I heard," she continued, "the sweetest harmony of divine praise, I saw the entire immersion in God. All the saints swim in an ocean of ineffable joy and happiness. More I cannot tell, but that no eye has seen, no ear has ever heard, nor has it ever entered into the human heart to conceive what God has prepared for those who love Him."[2]

Her last sickness, the peculiar nature of which was not known to the doctors, began in February, 1744, at the commencement of Lent. Her whole body was penetrated with a peculiar inward heat ; even the Protestant physician could only account for the sickness by ascribing it to the powerful ardor of love glowing in her soul. Marrow and bones seemed to be penetrated with flames of fire, head and sides were pierced with constant pains, all moisture had disappeared, an intolerable thirst excruciated her, the roof of her mouth and the mouth itself were parched ; the tongue which was much swollen and hard, like the bark of a tree, was wounded with deep cuts, from which matter issued, the lips were brown and split. The whole body was shrunk up to mere skin and bone, her back, on which she lay immovable, soon became without skin and was one entire wound ; the left cheek and shoulder were fearfully swollen, and the whole body was so racked with pains that she could say with truth, what she told with joy to her confessor, Father Pamer, when he asked her what pains

---

[1] Ott. B. IV. C. 1.   [2] I. Cor. II. 9,

she suffered : that she seemed as if she were broiled on a red-hot gridiron. It would have been but natural that such a disease should fill the room with bad odors ; this was not the case; on the contrary, a pleasant odor was discernible, although no perfumery was used.

The sickness began with insignificant indications, betokening no danger whatever ; yet she said at once, to her confessor and infirmarian, that she should surely die of it. A few days afterwards such dangerous symptoms appeared that the frightened Sisters feared a near and sudden end. She, however, assured them that they need not fear ; the sickness would be a long one, and she would die a slow and painful death, after long and severe sufferings. The prospect of such sufferings seemed to impart a special pleasure to her.

In this she was always true to herself, and her desire for suffering manifested itself throughout the six weeks, in which she had to endure torments utterly beyond mere human strength, and she did this in so sublime a manner, that none could witness without admiration and astonishment this spectacle of a soul wholly transfigured by love and suffering. Following the Redeemer's example, she would not use anything to relieve her suffering. She never asked for any help, or for ease ; she took no strengthening remedies, and passed the whole six weeks without food or drink, except a little luke-warm spring-water, and even this not without much persuasion, and in so small a quantity that it rather aggravated than quenched her burning thirst. Neither of her two doctors could explain how anybody already so subdued by weakness, could sustain for so long a time such intense fever heat, without any nourishment at all. The physician of the Prince-abbot of Kempten, then counsellor to the court, declared, in a written document still extant, that this surpassed all the powers of nature. They often urgently insisted on her taking something, though no one ventured to command her; she would then say : " My food is to do the will of my Father

who is in Heaven : He is my strength and my food." If
the Sisters spoke with sympathy about her taking nothing,
she would sometimes say : [1] "God, so full of love, is infinitely good to me, in giving me, a miserable worm of the earth,
what He Himself had on the cross. He was so grievously
tormented with thirst, and shall I, His poor slave, refresh
myself ? Oh, no, that must not, cannot be ! "

Her only nourishment for body and soul was the living
bread, which she daily received in Holy Communion, ex-
cepting on Good Friday. As the pains increased from day
to day, to an incredible height, so the vigor of her soul increased in like degree. No word of complaint ever issued
from her mouth, but, on the contrary, expressions of seraphic love were heard in the oft-repeated words : "All ye
limbs and bones of my body, praise ye the Lord, who has
given you the capability of suffering." If any one asked
her how she got along, she would answer : "Very well ; I
am tasting a drop of the bitter chalice of my Lord, and
fulfilling His will to whom I give myself for time and eternity."

Sister Gabriel says : [2] " When we, in great grief and compassion for her, once told her that we were constantly asking God to alleviate her great suffering a little, she, with
a cheerful countenance, gave this answer : ' That prayer
is very pleasing indeed to me ; but the divine will which
sends me these pains is still more pleasing. Jesus, who
cured my soul, first tasted the bitter chalice of His passion ; why then, should I shrink from drinking it ? My
dear Sisters, happy is he to whom this chalice of suffering is given. I would not move my foot with the view of
easing my pain.' This I heard from her own mouth,
and I have seen her marvellous patience with my own
eyes."

Yes, suffering increased the desire in her for greater
sufferings. Following the example of St. Mary Magdalen
de Pazzi, she said : "Not to die, but to suffer still more for

---

[1] Gabriel, p. 290.   [2] Ibid., p. 289.

Thy sake, and from love of Thee. May my joy be increased by suffering and love." And it really appeared as if, with exterior sufferings, her interior joy increased. With a smile she said : "Oh, these torments are nothing compared with those which my Beloved suffered for me ; much greater ones must befall me. Increase my pain, O God, but also increase my patience !" Another time she addressed the following words to her Sisters in religion : "We must constantly increase in perfection, and if it pleases God, spend our whole life in sighing and suffering, and through it all, love Him and serve Him with all our might. For this end God created us." When Sister Joachima, who was closely attached to her, and was her attendant, once wept with compassion, she spoke most affectionately and kindly to her in these words : "O dear Sister, shall not the will of God be done in my regard ? We should not weep for the pains which my most amiable and loving God sends me, but return Him thanks ; I am, indeed, most unworthy, but I am ready to suffer as much and as long as it pleases God ; it would be scant consolation to me were I to die without pain."

The flame of desire to possess God burst from her with a mighty force and made her exclaim, in the words of the Psalmist : "Show me, O Lord ! Thy countenance and I am content, for my soul fainteth within me, thirsting after the living fountain of all good. Oh, when shall I come and appear before the face of the Lord ?" This desire was, however, entirely controlled by God's will, for she said immediately after : "As God wills, what God wills, and so long as God wills ; if I can only accomplish His most holy will, I desire no other consolation in this life." A wondrous spectacle for Heaven and earth ! happy soul, in which the desire to possess Christ and the longing with Christ and for Christ to suffer, balance each other, so that she does not love life nor fear death, a soul which lived and died without care and without fear, without a wish, and without resistance, which of this temporal life loved only the pains, and of the life eternal sought only the will and the possession of God.

The impression which such sublime virtue made on all who saw her, is depicted in the following words of Sister Gabriel:[1] "In every sorrow her heart remained like an immovable rock in the deep ocean, which the waves may beat against but never stir; in this way were the heart and spirit of Crescentia engaged. The more her body was filled with pain, the more unimpeded were her heart and spirit in soaring upwards to their happy end, and in her crippled limbs we could behold an upright mind. Within her body crushed with pain we saw a calm soul, so that one might almost fancy two persons lived in Crescentia: the one loving, the other sickly; the one exciting admiration, the other moving us to sorrow and compassion. She looked cheerfully upon herself, and from her sufferings took occasion to descant upon the divine love, so that her room became a school of virtue, and her sick-bed a pulpit, from which she pointed out to us all the torments undergone by the crucified Jesus. For, though bound to the bed in body, her mind was unfettered and did not find itself in the presence of sorrows, but kept above with the Beloved One, in such a manner, that she drew from her sufferings the sweetest balsam for her soul, while she was at the same time on fire with the love of God. This I have partly seen with my own eyes, and partly gathered from her words and her admirable patience."

Whilst, even with good people, their faults and imperfections are usually shown during sickness, if severe, the sublime virtue of Crescentia appeared but the more prominent in its depth and fulness as she lay on her couch of suffering. Her humility, self-contempt, and the subjection whereby she subjected herself to every other creature displayed themselves in a most touching manner. The feeling that she was the poorest of beggars and the greatest of sinners shone through her whole conduct and con-

---

[1] Gabriel, p. 288.

versation. She accepted the slightest service of love with the greatest gratitude, and, indeed, considered it as a benefit squandered on one utterly unworthy of it. She frequently called the Sisters together, and in expressive, deeply-felt words, begged for pardon on account of the bad example she said she had given, and the faults she had committed, imploring them for the alms of prayer; all present wept bitterly. Nay, she begged with real earnestness that after death her head might not be adorned with a wreath of flowers, as was customary, but with one of straw, and that she might be buried in the manure pile, or in some spot unknown to men. She practised obedience up to her last moments, first towards the Sister-infirmarian, who had to decide even what position she should take in bed ; which, without doubt, must have frequently occasioned her severe pain and hardship, on account of her many wounds. Then, she wished not only to live in obedience, but also, after the example of Him who was obedient unto death, to die in and by obedience. She had therefore written to the Father Provincial, Rev. Boniface Schmidt, to issue the order of obedience to die; he replied, that as far as it lay in his power, he, in the name of God and according to His will and ordinance, imposed on her the desired obedience. The spouse of the Crucified then rejoiced in spirit and praised the Lord for allowing her to make an act of obedience even with the last breath. She also begged her confessor that when she should be in her last agony, he would repeat for her these words : " O God, I like to die, that I may not offend Thee any more ! O God, I will willingly die out of love to Thee ! O God, I will willingly die from the obedience which I owe to my Creator and my Father ! "

Hope in God, love of God, and union in prayer with Him were uninterrupted with her, for which reason she desired to be as much as possible alone; she accepted no visits, except from the Sister-infirmarian and from the father confessor, if such visits were made to afford her comfort or help, as, in the brief time left her, she wished to love God alone, without hindrance. It was the general opinion that it was the extraordinary fervor of her love which brought her blood into such violent commotion that during the last three days she lost what strength she had left by an irrepressible bleeding of the nose.

Difficult as it was to her to talk, she nevertheless received with great kindness and love the Sisters who wished to see her and to speak with her; she gave them most beautiful instructions, in words full of sweetness and meekness. At the very beginning of her sickness she had the younger Sisters summoned to her bedside, to give them one more instruction, which would be the last. The Sisters shrank from the expression and began to weep; she consoled them, and exhorted them with burning words to keep the Rule faithfully, and to sanctify themselves in religious retirement, in unity of spirit, and in the chaste love of God. Their hearts were moved to their depths and copious floods of tears streamed from their eyes. After the exhortation she told each one privately what she had to do, and omit, and amend; in this she penetrated each one's conscience so thoroughly and spoke with such force, that her words made an impression which lasted all their lives.

After some weeks the sickness reached such a point that frequent symptoms of the approach of death appeared. Those present, however, could not always decide whether the fainting-fit was not in part ecstasy. When she came to herself again she assured them that her time was not yet come. On the 27th of March, the Feast of the Seven Dolors of the Blessed Virgin Mary, the Sisters suffered great anxiety, for such a long state of unconsciousness occurred, that they feared she would never come out of it. The father confessor, whom they summoned in all haste, also thought that death was at hand. But after recovering herself, she assured them that the Saints, whom she had often asked to assist her at the hour of death, had been there, and had promised her that they would come again when she was really about to die.

On the thirteenth day before her death, she herself begged the father confessor to administer to her Extreme Unction and Holy Communion as the Viaticum. She made her confession under a flood of tears, and received the sacraments with indescribable devotion, the Sisters being present. Sister M. Gabriel[1] says : " One hour after receiving the sacraments, she penitently accused herself before the whole community of having led a careless life ; she humbly asked pardon of each Sister individually for her culpable life, and for the bad example she had given them, as also for the burden she had been to them, and the trouble she had occasioned them. Moreover, she returned them the greatest thanks that they had received her into the Order, in which she had never done anything good, but had always been an unprofitable creature. After this, her contrite self-accusation, she gave us salutary instructions for the strict observance of the Rule and constitution ; of religious seclusion and mutual charity ; begged of us most fervently to pray for her, and to recommend her soul to the merciful God. And all this she did with such zeal and earnestness, that we were all moved to frequent tears, and could not reply in words, but our silence spoke for us, and was answer enough."

From the time of this solemn act the double desire, apparently contradictory, to die, and to live longer that she might suffer more, became still greater. The Sisters often heard her sigh : " O Lord ! if it is Thy most holy will, give me to suffer yet more, that I may love Thee still more." The Lord seemed to have heard this petition. On Monday in Holy Week, a week which for many years had been for her one of real, yet wished-for martyrdom, the pains, which were already extraordinary, began to increase and seemed to grow in intensity every hour. No one could, without tears, look on this living picture of the Crucified, or rather on this pitiable creature, as it were " crucified with Christ."

---

[1] Gabriel, p. 283.

The pains were most violent in the head, hands and feet. But the power of God within her controlled this raging sea of suffering. She even consoled those who were with her, saying : " My dearest Sisters, return thanks to God for all my pains. My whole joy, my whole life, and all my strength consists. in suffering and in love. If I could see myself nailed to the cross with Christ, all my desires would be accomplished ; for this is a foretaste of eternal happiness and a paradise on earth."

During the last three days of Holy Week she was, for the most part, in an ecstatic state, namely, on Holy Thursday, after Holy Communion. [1] At the same time, it was distinctly noticed that a very fragrant odor proceeded from her, diffusing itself all through the convent. The Father Provincial, Boniface Schmidt, who had come to . visit her on the previous Sunday, found her in the evening still in a profound ecstasy. However, he had scarcely uttered the words, " Venerable Mother Crescentia," than this child of obedience at once recovered consciousness, and on being asked where she had been, and what she had seen, she replied : " My holy guardian angel took me to the Mount of Olives, where I saw my Beloved in prayer, and all dripping with blood. I approached Him, adored Him, and offered myself to suffer everything for Him. My Beloved said : ' My child, thou shalt suffer and rise again with Me.' "

On Good Friday she was the whole day beside herself, and looked like a dying person ; her soul, however, accompanied the Saviour through all the mysteries of the Passion till it came to the Crucifixion; then she recovered herself. Her confessor asked her if she had accompanied the Saviour to the Place of Skulls (Calvary). With a deep sigh, she replied : " Oh, what is that, to see a God become man, suffer, and die ! I should have died with Him from love and compassion, had not His Omnipotence upheld me." She added many other sublime expressions concerning the

---

[1] Ott. B. IV. C. 2.

passion and love of the Crucified and of His sorrowful Mother. She spent the whole of Holy Saturday, spiritually and ecstatically, at the sepulchre of the Redeemer. Easter Sunday—it was the fifth of April—was to be the last of her life on earth. It passed in love, suffering, and in visions of heavenly things; yet when the Father Provincial or the father confessor addressed her, she answered them. After dinner she had the Sisters once more gather around her; she repeated, in few but earnest words, her former admonitions to a holy, religious life, and emphatically bade them carefully avoid unnecessary intercourse with outsiders, whether of the ecclesiastical or secular state. She again said a few fitting words to each one of them. These last words of the loving and now dying Mother, made an inexpressibly deep, and at the same time a most painful impression.

She now directed her whole attention to God, and replied to the words addressed to her by her confessor or Superior only by signs. In the evening she seemed coming to herself out of an ecstasy and asked Sister Joachima Kögl what o'clock it was; when the Sister answered that it had just struck seven, she said distinctly, so that all could hear her: "At twelve o'clock I shall die." Then she again forgave all her enemies, even those who should speak ill of her after her death, and she prayed for them; she also appointed the suffering souls in purgatory her heirs to all the holy masses, prayers, and works of penance which should be offered up for her soul. At nine o'clock she lost much blood by nose bleeding, and entered into the death agony, without, however, losing her consciousness.

All the Sisters hastened to the room of the dying Mother, where Father Pamer was already; the Father Provincial and his secretary, Father Cesarius Grueber, came immediately. She lay there without motion, without making the least sound, her eyes directed to Heaven or to the crucifix, her parched mouth half open. Whenever the priests uttered pious maxims or acts of virtue, she made a sign of approval, especially when the usual words of humility were said, such as : "I am a mere nothing, a miserable worm of the earth." The Father Provincial told her, that as soon as she was in the Divine Presence, she should pray to the Holy Trinity for the welfare of the Catholic Church, of Christian princes, of religious Orders, especially of her own, the Seraphic Order, as well as of her convent, that it might shine forth as a light to other convents, by good example. She gave plain signs of her obedient consent to this. The hearts of the Sisters kneeling round her bed were almost breaking with grief and compassion ; it was only by great exertion that they could repress themselves from weeping aloud.

The father confessor now remembered that she had often said that the holy archangel Raphael would be her guide into Heaven. At half-past eleven he said : "Venerable Mother, the archangel Raphael will probably be here soon." She answered at once and very plainly : "He is here already." Those were her last words on earth. Shortly afterwards she opened her eyes, of which one already had lost the sight, and threw her first and last glance on her confessor, as if to take leave of him. At this glance, his soul, as we have said already, was so filled with heavenly sweetness that, as he says himself, he never, either before or after, had experienced the like. Then she closed her chaste eyes to the light of earth.

All present waited with strained nerves, in excited expectation of that hour of twelve which she had foretold was to be her last. She lay there without convulsions, without jerking, or any other sign betokening that the soul was about to leave the body. Finally, the clock in the steeple of the parochial Church, which was the city clock, struck the first stroke of the hour of twelve ; at that very moment she breathed her last, with a calm, placid countenance, without any movement or twitching of the features, or of the limbs.

Thus did this angelically pure soul, so rich in graces, virtues, and merits, leave the prison of the body, after it had sought nothing here on earth save to be like the Crucified in life and death ; and we have reason to believe that she entered as a pure and perfect spouse into the fulness of divine glory ; for at the very moment when the clock struck and the soul parted from her body, a double event took place, inexplicable in a natural way. The inordinately great sorrow experienced by her fellow-Sisters in religion gave place, in an instant, to a heavenly sweetness and joy in such abundance, that they scarcely knew how to contain it and all acknowledged that they had never felt the like before. In the canonical process, five of those who had been present bore witness, under oath, to this. A similar inexplicable joy filled the hearts of those present at the death of St. Rose of Lima. This occurrence is believed with reason to be a sign that the departed soul immediately entered into bliss, and that from the ocean of her own unspeakable happiness she was permitted to shed, as it were, some drops of it on those whom she had left behind. At the same time the corpse she had left exhaled a transcendently penetrating, sweetly fragrant perfume, which filled the whole convent. The godly virgin died thus, in the last minute of Easter Sunday, April 5, 1744, aged sixty-one years, five months, and fifteen days, of which she had spent forty-one in the convent.

Look back, O mortal man, on this noble life and this precious death, and pray to God : " Let my soul die the death of the just, and my last end be like to them." [1]

----

[1] Numbers xxiii. 10.

CHAPTER VI.

Remarkable Occurrences after the Death of Ven. Crescentia.—Her Funeral.[1]

HEN the Sisters had recited the prayers usually said for a departed Sister, they began to prepare the corpse of the servant of God and dress it for the burial in the customary way. They were all astonished at the great, the marvellous change that had suddenly taken place in it. The face, which had previously been emaciated, ashen-gray, more resembling a dead skeleton than a living being, was now superlatively beautiful, white and red ; the lips, formerly dried up, were lovely and red as roses ; she was like a blooming virgin asleep. When they raised the corpse in the bed, it stood perfectly upright without support, while in the last days of her life she had not been able to lift, for the breadth of a finger, her head, which had sunk on her breast from weakness. They then seated the corpse on a bench and there also it sat upright, without support, for upwards of a quarter of an hour, as if living ; no one could account for it. All the limbs were tender and pliable as those of a child. They then laid the corpse again on the bed.

The next morning early, the report of her death spread at once all over the city, and Catholics and Protestants, ecclesiastics and seculars, flocked in such numbers to the convent that it was soon overfilled. At first, by order of the Father Provincial, the doors of the church and convent were closed, but the impatient crowd made preparations to climb the walls and to force open the doors. It was then deemed necessary to permit entrance. The room in which Crescentia had died not being large enough to contain the number of visitors, many endeavored to satisfy their pious curiosity by climbing on the shoulders of their

---

[1] Summ. N. 24 § 25—Ott. B. IV. C. 3 and 4.—Gabriel, p. 295 et seq.

companions and looking through the windows. The
Catholics wanted, by all means, to have some relic of the
servant of God from the things she had used, or at least to
touch her body with their rosaries. The Father Provincial
would not permit it ; nevertheless, many by fraud or force
obtained their wish. The many Lutherans present also
showed every respect towards the departed ; and it was a
touching sight when James Metzger, a Protestant, a very
aged man, who for more than fifty years had lived in an
apartment of her father's house, and had known and valued her from childhood upwards, pressed through the
crowd and said with many tears : "I must once more
visit my dear, good old mistress. Oh, she always lived a
godly, pious life, and never offended any one."

Meantime people were saying on all sides: " What lovely
perfume is this ? it refreshes body and soul. I never felt
the like in all my life!" This wonderful odor of sweetness,
which according to history has been diffused by the mortal remains of many if not most of the Saints, was in this
case so exquisite, so obvious on the three days before her
interment, that the hearts of all present were filled and the
eyes of many were bedewed with tears; it came under such
general notice that half the city could have borne testimony
to it. No natural cause could be discovered for it, since
there were no perfumed essences of any kind in the room.
Among the testimonies of many witnesses we adduce only
that of the joiner, Pancratius Hütter, who often used to relate that when he brought the corpse to the coffin, a lovely
and strong odor was diffused around, such as he had never
experienced before, and such as he could not even describe,
and which had filled his soul with an unwonted pleasure.
While the body was exposed, three remarkable instances of
grace occurred, which were obviously to be ascribed to the
merits of her who lay asleep in the Lord.

The month old child of the tanner, Philip James
Meichelbeck, of Kaufbeuren, had come into the world with
a rupture, in respect to which the physicians could do

nothing, with all their medical means and appliances. The child, named Joseph Ignatius, screamed with pain day and night, and was withering away. The sorrow-stricken father, while kneeling by the corpse of Crescentia, recommended his child to her intercession, and at the very same moment the child became quiet at home; every trace of the rupture had disappeared, the boy became strong and robust, and as parish priest of Kaufbeuren, bore witness in the canonical process [1] that he had innumerable times heard from his parents the benefit which Crescentia had bestowed on him.

Mary Theresa Satzgar, of Kaufbeuren, a young lady twenty-four years of age, had for many years been troubled with many maladies and was so crippled that she could scarcely stand on her feet. The doctors could do nothing for her. With the help of a friend she succeeded in getting near the bier; she knelt down and prayed thus with great confidence: " My Mother Crescentia, now you can pray to the good God for me, that He may give me a sound body, if such is His holy will, and if it will contribute to my salvation. I firmly believe that Mother Crescentia is now in Heaven and can obtain anything she desires from God." Hardly were these words said before she was cured; she praised God with tears and ran joyfully back to that home from which she had come with so much difficulty, and, as Father Ott expressed it, "more crawling than walking." Every one could convince himself that she afterwards remained in good health.

Appollonia Metz had for ten years suffered, although otherwise a pious person, a terrible temptation, which almost reduced her to despair. In fact she had a constant feeling of hatred against her own parents, which she vainly endeavored to control. All the means and exercises recommended to her had not weakened the temptation in the least. When she heard of the death of the spouse of Christ, she hastened to the convent, and, full of confidence, invoked

---

[1] Summ. N. 24 § 375.

her intercession. At the same moment the temptation vanished forever, and instead of this deeply rooted bitter feeling, a very tender and enduring love for her parents entered her heart.

The funeral took place on Wednesday, April 8th. The condition of the corpse was in no way changed ; the same beauty of the countenance, the same flexibility and tenderness of the limbs and of the flesh, the same delicious perfume, only in a higher degree. Early in the morning, at six o'clock, eight Sisters carried the mortal remains of their much-loved Mother into the little chapel of the convent. All pomp was avoided, as the deceased had desired, and as the spirit of her Order requires. The crucifix alone was carried before and the one little bell of the convent was rung; the doors of the convent and the church were kept closed, and but few were present when the Father Provincial performed the customary ceremonies and said the prayers of the Church.

She was buried in the centre of the nave of the little church; the grave was closed the same day and covered with pavement-brick like the rest of the floor. Only a white stone slab bearing the initials of her name, with a cross and the date of the year was placed over it. It was not till the year 1771 that this pavement of brick gave place to another of hewn stone. On the pillar near it, which supported a small arch, an inscription was placed: " Here lies buried Venerable Mother Crescentia Höss, who died blessed in the Lord, April 5th, 1744, aged 62 years." Immediately after the interment the Requiem Mass was celebrated, and also on the following days the Requiem Masses, customary at the death of a Mother Superior, were performed in the convent as well as in the parish church.

The marvellous odor of sweetness, of which we have spoken before, continued until later times, nay, has not altogether ceased in these our days. Of this there are many testimonies, from which we extract some from the Acts, [1] some

---

[1] Summ. N. 24 § 380, 384.

from the more prolix history of Father Ott, and condense them here in one narrative. All the articles which had been used by the Ven. Crescentia, especially her books, instruments of penance, and many rosaries which she herself had distributed, diffused this marvellous fragrance. It was particularly discernible in three places: at the grave, in the room of the Mother Superioress, on the first floor, where she had died, and in that cell of the dormitory which she had occupied for many years, and which is even now kept as a sort of sanctuary and not used.

Besides the Sisters, thousands of pilgrims from outside the convent walls, have borne witness to this remarkable phenomenon. Among these are many Protestants and many persons renowned for their knowledge and erudition, both in the ecclesiastical and secular state. Strangely enough, some persons perceive this fragrant odor in all three of these places, others only in one of them, while their companions do not perceive it here, but in the other places. Often it has been noticed by a whole company, and then again, by only one of them. For instance, on the 9th and 10th of March, 1775, when the Princess Antonia, Electress of Saxony, with her numerous retinue, among whom were many Protestants, visited the Church and the Convent, all bore witness to having perceived this fragrant odor.

We mention among many others who were witnesses to this, the Cardinal Von Roth, Prince-bishop of Constance, the Bishop of Chur, the Abbot Maurus Xaverius of Plankstetten, O.S.B., of saintly memory, whom we have already mentioned, who testifies, by word of mouth and by writing, that although from his infancy and upwards he had been deprived of the sense of smell, he, too, had perceived the fragrant odor in those places ; moreover, the deacon of the Cathedral at Freisingen, Baron Von Egger, the Count and Countess Von Capris, the professor of canonical rights at ·Dillingen, Joseph George Wanner, the professor of mathematics at Innsbruck, Ignatius Weinhardt, the professor of philosophy at Salzburg, Fridolin Steiger, the professor, Francis Scherer, S. J., and Father Cesarius Grueber, O.S.F., the Secretary of the Provincial. All these, and many others who were experts in perfumery, assert that this scent is not like any other known as perfumery.

Father Ott relates the following, respecting his own person : "I acknowledge, of my own accord, that when, in 1760, I made a pilgrimage to the grave of Crescentia, in company with Mr. Andrew Calligari, a merchant of Augsburg, and with Rev. Ignatius Bonschat, preacher at the Church-institute of St. Maurice, I did not find a supernatural odor anywhere, although my two companions were in full enjoyment of it. But when I came there in 1770, as appointed confessor, I perceived, to my great consolation, an extremely pleasant, and to me unknown smell, in the cell and the room ; but this only once, or at most twice. From that day forward I perceived nothing, although I often entered the rooms with pilgrims from the nobility, until the year 1774, when I opened the cell to Herr Von Funkner, land-steward to Prince Lichtenstein. I then with much pleasure perceived the sweet odor of which I had heard so much for the past four years. I, however, enjoyed this unexpected pleasure but a few minutes, while Herr Von Funkner was delighted with it for almost half an hour, in the cell as well as in the room. The same thing occurred again at the votive tablets, when I was least expecting it."

The Sisters of the convent assure us that the fragrant odor, formerly so frequent, is even now, at times, perceived by visitors to these rooms. But frequently, even now, a peculiarly pleasant odor is perceptible from her relics, as, for example, from a piece of her linen. This exteriorly perceivable fragrance affords a proof that she bore Christ within her, during her life, and as St. Paul says, "manifested the odor of His knowledge"[1] by her words and deeds. This latter every Christian ought to

---

[1] II. Cor. ii. 11.

do. Endeavor, then, O Christian soul, to become more and more "the good odor of Christ unto God, in them that are saved, and in them that perish."[1]

CHAPTER VII.

Surprising Spread of the Veneration Paid to her.—Pilgrimages to her Grave.—Conversion of many Sinners.[3]

OME voices, indeed, were raised against the universal reputation of sanctity of this great servant of God; some persons, either from ignorance or from worse motives, promulgated calumniating rumors respecting her. This did not, however, retard in any degree the incessant progress of the veneration paid to her. The spread, continuance, and intensity of this veneration, can in reason only be ascribed to that Divine Providence which loves to exalt humble souls, and to render glorious the sepulchres of those who, during life, willingly bore the shame of the cross of Christ.

The Church, as such, had as yet done nothing in her honor ; nay, up to this very time[2] it is not permitted to honor her publicly, and yet the Catholic people were so impressed with love and devotion to the godly virgin, that her grave soon became a shrine, the most frequented by pilgrims ; indeed, there are but few of the Saints, even of those canonized by the Church in the last centuries, who have been equally venerated. Her plain and simple grave is, by the universal love and veneration of Christian people, an object far more glorious than the tombs of heroes embellished by the most splendid monuments.

---

[1] II. Cor. II. 15.   [2] Summ. N. 27.—Ott. B. IV. C. 5.   [3] May, 1885.—Transl.

On the very day of her interment, people already came in crowds, kissed her grave, and put their beads and pictures thereon, to keep them as souvenirs of her. Many extraordinary things were told of prayers at her grave being heard, in which her intercession was implored for the various needs of the petitioners. Already, in the first and second years after her death, pilgrims came from afar off; some to seek help at her grave, some to return thanks for favors received. Among these were persons of the highest distinction, and not from Bavaria alone, but from Bohemia, Hungary, Tyrol, and other Austrian countries. Many who could not come themselves sent votive tablets and other gifts to express their gratitude for help received. From the year of her death to that of 1779 more than eighty princely persons visited her grave. From 1770 to 1780, Father Ott alone, when confessor to the community, showed thirty-four gentleman and ladies of princely rank through the convent, as he himself assures us. Most of these persons had undertaken a long journey for the purpose of visiting her grave, where they received the sacraments and prayed devoutly.

In the first place we have here to mention the great Empress Maria Theresa, who several times sent precious gifts; the Princess-elector of Saxony, Maria Antonia; Maximilian Joseph, Elector of Bavaria, who, with his wife, Maria Anna, visited her grave and the convent at least seven times with great devotion. Moreover, the Princes of Sigmaringen-Hechingen, the Prince-elector of the Palatinate, Charles Theodore (1761), Prince Louis Eugene, of Wurtemburg, who, in 1773, examined everything minutely, received the Blessed Sacrament, and in 1779 made another pilgrimage thither in company of his wife. Besides this, he frequently wrote to the Sisters to have certain affairs recommended to the servant of God. The Margravine of Baden-Baden, Anna Augusta, sister of the Prince-elector of Bavaria, was at least three times there, and the wife of the Emperor Joseph II. twice.

Among the higher prelates must be named : Cardinal Von Roth, Bishop of Constance, who in 1770 knelt an entire hour at her grave, and next day said Mass in the little church; the Prince-elector of Treves (1774), the Bishop of Augsburg, Joseph of Hesse-Darmstadt (four times), the Bishops of Ratisbon, Chur (1774), and Freisingen; Louis Joseph of Walden,—of Chiemsee, Grand-master of Waldenburg (five times); the Prince-Abbot of Kempten, and Honorius, Baron of Schreckenstein, who visited her grave nearly every year. Also the Coadjutor-bishop of Paderborn, Joseph Francis Von Gondola; Bishop Von. Tempe was there from the 28th to the 30th of December, 1761, and in a document yet extant, dated December 30, 1761, he expresses his astonishment at all the wonderful things he had seen, heard, and read there, and affirms his conviction that after canonical investigation by the Holy See, Crescentia will be accounted worthy to be numbered among the holy virgins. Besides those named above, it is reported that from April, 1744, to 1749, over three hundred barons, counts, and prelates, and to the year 1779, even as many as three thousand five hundred and fifty visited the grave of this godly virgin and often with tears of devotion kissed the stone which covered her grave, and the floor of her cell.

The number of other pilgrims, not a few of whom were priests, scientists, and officers, cannot be given at all. They were supposed to average thirty thousand annually, but since the opening of the process for her Beatification the pilgrims have reached at least double that number, and in the year 1779 they amounted to more than seventy thousand. From the year 1772 to 1779, the number of pilgrims was put down as far as it could be done, and it was found that at least three hundred and fifty thousand persons had visited Crescentia's grave for the sake of devotion within that space of time.

The convent church, formerly so lonesome, was now filled with devout worshippers from early morning till late in

the evening.   Formerly it was seldom that any other Masses were celebrated besides the one said daily ; but from
1770 till 1780, during which time Father Ott was appointed
the confessor, there were at least three thousand said every
year, the most of which were at the request of some one or
other devout person and offered up for the intention of
such a one.

The votive tablets and commemorative gifts laid on her
grave can hardly be counted.   Up to July 1, 1751, there
were over six thousand, though for the most part made only of wax.   In obedience to the papal ordinance these were
carried out of the church and preserved in twenty-two cases
made for that purpose.   In the year 1779 the votive offerings made of silver and gold numbered nearly three thousand.   The images of wax, painted tablets, crutches, trusses, needles that had been swallowed, and the like, which
could not be counted, afford a plain proof that many persons had firmly believed that they had received miraculous
help through the intercession of Ven. Crescentia.   Several
of these offerings were sent from Saxony, Moravia, Bohemia, Hungary, Transylvania, Switzerland, and Holland ;
from Italy and even from Malta and Moscow.   Some devo-
tees offered valuable articles, such as wedding rings,
rare coins, pearls, precious stones, but especially articles for the church, among which were nine chalices,
twenty-three costly sets of vestments, several antipen-
diums, cruets for Mass and the like.   The Empress Maria
Theresa, in 1772, sent a vestment embroidered by her own
hand, and Maria Anna, Princess-elector of Bavaria, did the
same.

That she was also venerated in North Germany may be
inferred from a circular issued by the Prince-bishop of
Cologne, Clement Augustus, who was also Bishop of Paderborn, Munster, and Hildesheim.   On July 14, 1754, he
commissioned his Vicar-general of Paderborn to investigate
officially the cures which were reported to have been
wrought by invoking the intercession of Ven. Crescentia.

Pilgrimages to her shrine (which still continue), have been made for one hundred and thirty years. The circumstances of the age, especially that of closing the house of the Society of Jesus, have rendered it extremely difficult to find father confessors for the numbers of pilgrims; this has diminished the concourse somewhat; nevertheless, the annual number is still very large and has in late years again been on the increase. Instead of the votive offerings which had been carried away at the suppression of the convent, new ones have been brought in numbers scarcely credible in this very century. The cases set up in the court-yard are again filled with many thousands of thank-offerings for deliverance from temporal afflictions, mostly of sickness.

But what is most to be prized in the whole matter, is the conversion of so many sinners which occurred at her grave. If the conversion of a hardened sinner is, as many of the Fathers tell us, a greater work than raising the dead to life, then the little convent church, which Crescentia hallowed by forty years' prayer and by her mortal remains, is a place of special grace in which God works many miracles. Of course, individual cases of conversion can scarcely be brought under public discussion ; and therefore the general expressions of Father Ott, which we give in a condensed form, must suffice us. He says : " Father John Baptist Pamer, who was for twenty-five years confessor to the convent of Mayrhoff, after the death of Crescentia, and who heard many thousands of pilgrims' confessions and received many communications from them outside the confessional, assures us that the benefits which God bestowed on souls, through the intercession of Crescentia, are much greater and more numerous than those which affected bodily health. I, too, holding that same office now for ten years, perfectly agree with him in this. At her grave many and astounding conversions of the greatest sinners have occurred, even of such as had long ago given themselves up to despair, who had signed deeds with their own blood, making themselves over to the devil, who had in unheard-of ways heaped sin upon sin. I could, without violating the seal of confession, bring forward many examples of this : many persons have by word of mouth and in writing attested that they came from a distance in order at length to make a good confession with compunction, which they succeeded in doing. Others, who were hardened sinners, felt at her grave an irresistible impulse to penance, so that, after making a good confession, they left quite consoled. Several who even here had not made a good confession, had, while returning home, such remorse of conscience, that they came back again, when already far on their way, and made a sincere confession with great compunction of heart. One person who had a strong impulse to confess some long-concealed sins, at length, after a long struggle with herself, yielded to the devil and was about to leave the church without confession, when she was held back by an invisible power at the threshold of the church-door. She attempted with all her might to get away, but in vain. Terrified and contrite, she finally humbled herself, made a good confession, and then went home without further hindrance and full of consolation. Sinners who for many years had been fettered by evil habits, and had despaired of being able to amend, here cast off their chains and became good Christians. Such as were severely tempted, especially against purity, here received peace and strength ; those tormented by scruples and melancholy, even to the extent of incipient insanity, here found a calmness and peace of mind ; among these was one person who had suffered unutterable things for seven years and could find no help anywhere."

A widow of good family had, through great misfortunes, fallen into extreme want, and was even driven from her home. Urged thereto by a sensation of black despair, she sought a place by the river-side, where the banks were high, that she might find death in the water. She attempted the fatal plunge, and was already hanging with the greatest part of her body above the water, when an invisible hand drew her back. Startled, she looked back and beheld a Sister, who immediately after vanished. She thought it might be Crescentia, whom in her misery she had invoked. She now felt penitent, and obtained the grace of making a good confession in a neighboring convent. She also promised to make a prilgrimage to the grave of her redemptress. After that, her affairs took a better turn, so that she obtained a home and means of support. To give thanks, she often went to Kaufbeuren and sounded the praises of her who had saved her from temporal and eternal death.

We think we cannot here omit the conversion of a criminal who, it would seem, belonged to the higher classes ; his name was Stephen Weinrauch, and he was executed at Oberndorf, September 14, 1754. We select only the principal details taken from the more copious reports of contemporary writers—one by Rev. John Kögl, parish priest of Oberndorf, dated October 16, 1754, the other by Mother Joachim Kögl, already mentioned, dated October 27, of the same year, and signed by eight Sisters. Both documents are still in the convent of Mayrhoff. This criminal had a little daughter, called Frederica, who was little more than three years old when her father was arrested, but yet she entertained a love and devotion to Crescentia, which were quite inexplicable at her age. At the very moment that her father was summoned from the house to be conveyed to the prison, the child fell down stairs and lay as if dead on the floor. The frightened mother invoked Ven. Crescentia and the child came to her senses. The first words she said were : " O mother, I fell down-stairs, but Crescentia helped me, she was here already." The child, . who was seriously hurt, lived three weeks longer, during which time she always wanted to have a rosary and a picture of Crescentia by her, and prayed diligently for her imprisoned father ; then she would frequently say : " Father is not coming home again ; he will die and go to Crescentia, and I shall die to, and go to her." Three hours before her death, the little one begged her mother to remove the curtains from her bed, that Crescentia might come to her ; she pointed with her finger up to where Crescentia was, and died joyful, pressing her beads and the picture of the servant of God to her heart.

There were many reasons for doubting whether the father would be converted; but immediately after sentence had been passed on him, he requested Father Pamer to come to his spiritual assistance, and that simply because he had been Crescentia's last confessor. On September 12th he made a very contrite general confession. Afterwards, in the presence of many persons, he repeatedly asserted that, next to God, he was indebted to Ven. Crescentia for the grace of his conversion. On the day of his execution he held in his hands a crucifix and a picture of the Saviour carrying His cross, both of which had belonged to Crescentia, and he manifested extraordinary compunction and firmness. With touching words which brought tears to the eyes of the thousands of spectators present, he begged forgiveness of every one ; he then ascended the scaffold and died so edifying a death, that, as the assisting priest expresses himself, " Every one acknowledged that they had never witnessed such nobleness at an execution, or one which brought with it such good results."

That the influence of the servant of God must have been very great is confirmed by a miraculous event which happened at the very time of the execution, in the convent of Kaufbeuren, and is reported in the above-named document. When the Sisters at the appointed hour were praying most fervently for the poor criminal, by making the stations of the cross, the portrait of Crescentia, which, as we have said, the artist had painted against her will, among the weeping women of the eighth station, suddenly underwent a change. " The countenance," so runs the report, "became very beautiful, rosy-red, and so lovely and gracious, as we had but seldom seen this dear Superioress and Mother, when in life in the convent, and then only in extraordinary cases.

This stayed so nearly an hour, till by degrees the bloom faded away and the picture resumed its ordinary appearance. We wept in joy and wonder, and conjectured from the marvellously beautiful redness and loveliness of the countenance that all was well with Mr. Weinrauch. Respecting the eyes of that picture, the following happened at that time : Both eyes became very red and swollen, as is the case when a person has been crying very hard. In the left eye were two tears, one entire and full, the other was flowing down. The full and entire one hung on the cheek pretty low down towards the nose, and one could clearly see the wet streak from the right corner of the eye connecting it with the tear-drop. The other opposite tear was diffused over the cheek, yet we saw the wet streak from the left corner of the left eye, far down the cheek. These wet streaks and tears remained on the face of the picture from eight o'clock till eleven in the forenoon.

" To this we bear witness by putting thereto our own hands and the seal of our convent, Kaufbeuren, in the convent of St. Francis, Mayrhoff, of the Third. Order of the holy Father Francis, the 27th of October, 1754." (Here follow the signatures of the Superioress and of eight Sisters).

The Venerable spouse of Christ had, during her life, not sought for honor before men, but for humiliation and contempt. But now, we may safely assume, she has found not only eternal glory, but what she did not seek at all, the greatest honor before men. " They that sow in tears, shall reap in joy. Going, they went and wept, casting their seeds, but coming they shall come with joyfulness, carrying their sheaves." [1]

---

[1] Ps. cxxv. 5-7.

CHAPTER VIII.

Selection of Miracles.[1]

THE number of prayers granted more or less miraculously to those who venerated the servant of God, and the granting of which is ascribed to her intercessory merits, is astonishingly great. When the Ordinariate of Augsburg, between the years 1770 and 1780, issued a mandate that reports of such favors and graces as were considered miraculous should be sent to them, they were sent in by thousands. But as these, for the most part, either from defective form, or on account of the subject-matter, were of no value in regard to the Beatification, the Coadjutor-bishop of Augsburg petitioned the Sacred Congregation of Rites[2] to be permitted to burn this pile of papers and it was probably done. Father Ott, too, speaks of these reports as sent in by thousands, but is of opinion that scarcely the half of the prayers that had been really granted were written down. Several hundred were kept in the convent. In the one year of 1779 there had been two hundred and thirty such cases of prayer reported as granted there ; these occurred either simply at the invocation of Crescentia, or by using her relics, beads, or other blessed articles. He also relates that Herr von Hautzenstein, Privy-counsellor of Franken, had received one hundred and eighty testimonials in two years and a half, within a district of but few miles in diameter, many of which seemed to record true miracles. A whole volume would be filled were we to print all the cases which are of importance. We restrict ourselves, therefore, to some few of the most weighty of those related in the Acts, and out of the many hundred related elsewhere, we select only a few.

Over thirty miracles are enumerated in those Acts, eight of which were carefully investigated, by examining many

---

[1] Acta super fama sanctitatis, Romae, 1787.　　[2] Summ. N. 27 § 1–38.

witnesses, in order to make use of them at the process of
the Beatification.   In a condensed form they are contained
in the *Summarium*,[1] to which we add some circumstances
from the more copious report of Father Ott.

Mary Francis Prix, the daughter of a doctor at Ottobeuren, suffered for thirteen years from a tear-running fis-
tula of a very malignant character, which had such a pun-
gent and bad-smelling odor, that no one could bear to come
near her.   The wound was accompanied by violent fever,
and took the form of cancer.   Her brother, who was a
physician at Eschingen, sent her to John Michael Endres,
a surgeon at Ottobeuren, for him to perform an operation
upon her.   Herr Endres agreed that the operation was
necessary, but stated at the same time that the loss of the
eye would be the almost inevitable result.   The sick girl,
in her great distress, made a vow in January, 1773, to send
a silver eye to the grave of Crescentia ; she then invoked her
aid in all confidence, and then, without the use of any
other remedy, in a very short time the wound and the fis-
tula healed, to the great astonishment of the physicians.

Mrs. Magdalen Kollman, formerly proprietress of the
Hunter House at Augsburg, later on residing as a widow in
Pengen, had for ten years suffered from an abscess in the
breast, which, though it constantly increased, she concealed
from everybody, until, in 1764, the unbearable pain
compelled her to consult the celebrated Doctor Jacob
Appin, of Kaufbeuren.   He explained to her immediately
that the malady was a cancer far advanced, and that the
only hope of a cure was in having an operation performed.
The frightened woman betook herself at once to the grave
of Crescentia, invoked her intercession, and immediately
the sharp and harrowing pain ceased.   On the day following the surgeon found no trace remaining of the appalling
disease ; he himself bore witness on oath to this wonderful
cure.

Mary Josephine, a year and a half old, daughter of James

---

[1] N. 27, § 1-8.

Herterich, of Heimenogg, had, in the year 1770, a severe fall, by which she injured or rather broke her spine, so that her back was raised the width of two hands. The child screamed day and night and could neither sit up nor lie down. The parents commended their little daughter to Crescentia's care, promised to make a pilgrimage to her grave, laid her picture on the injured back, and gave the child some water which had been poured over a rosary of Crescentia's. All at once the pains ceased, the swelling subsided, the spine resumed its normal state, and the child could come and go at its pleasure. When grown up, Mary Josephine visited the grave of her benefactress every year. Seventeen witnesses swore to this fact.

Maria Anna Oegg, of Nassenbeuren, county of Mindelheim, sixty-five years old, had for thirteen years suffered from a dangerous rupture which caused her great pain and twice endangered her life, which both times was saved by the skill of the surgeon, Charles Andrew Hauser. On the 21st of February, 1772, the malady returned in a worse form, so that the bowels protruded (*hernia incarcerata*). The surgeon found her almost in a dying state and ordered the last sacraments to be administered to her. All his endeavors were baffled for five days; a fearful fever, terrible vomiting, and inflammation of the bowels indicated the approach of death; the surgeon lost all hope and left her. On February 29th, the sick woman sent her son again for Mr. Hauser, the surgeon, as she could not stand the pains; he refused to go, as he could not help her any more. His wife, however, said to the son: "Boy, has your mother no confidence in dear Crescentia? she has helped so many who have called on her. I will give you something from her." She gave him some "Crescentia powder," made from the leaves of the tree mentioned already. The dying woman took this powder, and immediately the vomiting and fever ceased, the bowels went back to their place of themselves; she slept quietly through the whole night; the next day the swelling had disappeared and the woman was in perfect health. Fourteen witnesses, among whom were the surgeon, the sick woman, and her husband, swore to the whole transaction.

Ursula Schmid, of Langenfeld, had both feet frozen and so covered with wounds that the doctor thought it would be necessary to amputate them. Full of confidence in Crescentia, she tied a rosary of the servant of God around the right foot : the next morning it was entirely well. With still greater confidence and with the same success she repeated the act on the left foot. Five witnesses swore to the event.

Elizabeth Russ, a young girl aged nineteen, of Wasserlos, in the arch-diocese of Mayence, in 1774 suffered so severely from diseased limbs that her ·whole body became swollen : she had already received the last Sacraments, and three hours afterwards appeared to be in the agony of death. The mother of the dying girl, in her extreme distress, sent to the kind and friendly Prince Louis Eugene, of Würtemburg, who was then staying at Wasserlos and who had lately been to Kaufbeuren, whence he had brought some relics of the Ven. Crescentia. The prince felt impelled to make use of them in this case, and went personally to visit the sick girl, whom he found even in a worse condition than had been represented to him. He saw clearly enough that it was a case in which God alone could help, and he exhorted the dying girl to trust in the Almighty power of God and in the intercession of Crescentia. He waited awhile till she seemed really to be passing away, when he gave her a little of the so-called "Crescentia water" and a small piece of her habit. Immediately the pains diminished and the swelling subsided : as the prince touched the greatly swollen arms and feet with the piece of cloth, to the great astonishment of the beholders, the swelling visibly went down and the pains vanished ; the distorted face resumed its wonted aspect, "quicker than thought," to use the prince's own expression of the occurrence. The whole sickness was from that time forth thoroughly cured. The noble prince himself, and eight other witnesses, among whom was Margaret Glaser, a Protestant lady, have sworn to the truth of this miracle.

Sister Mary Sophia, of Bodonan, [1] in the convent of the Third Order of St. Francis at Meckingen, in the diocese of Constance, had been ailing for four years with a kind of dropsy called tympanites. The help of the ablest doctors had brought periodical relief ; but in December, 1770, the disease broke out with renewed vigor, no remedy had any effect, and Dr. Flacho, then a renowned practitioner and physician to the prince, gave her up. In the night of the 11th of January, 1771, alarming indications of death made their appearance. When her confessor, Joachim Mayer, visited her the next morning, she asked permission to put away all medicines, since the physician had lost hope, and instead of them to invoke the intercession of the Ven. Crescentia, and take some of her powder. The father confessor assented, on the express condition that she should pray for her recovery only if it were conducive to God's honor and her own salvation. After ten o'clock he left the sick Sister in the same hopeless condition ; she then took the powder, amid prayers, and soon experienced the desire to eat something, although for several years she had had a loathing for food. After she had eaten and drunk something, she attempted, with the help of her two attendants, to rise from her chair. Suddenly she felt within her such a return of vigor, that she threw aside her staff, and when the Sisters came to visit her after dinner, she went all alone to meet them, to their joy and surprise. They sent in all haste to the father confessor, who came at once, to assist her, as he thought, in her death-struggle. Speechless with fear, he stood rooted to the ground, when he beheld her whom two hours before he had left lying motionless in her chair advance joyfully to greet him. Tears of joy streamed from his eyes; it was with great difficulty that he regained his composure, and then he wished immediately to return

---

[1] L. cit. § 7, and Ott.

thanks to God by chanting the Te Deum. The cured Sister first put on other clothing and then hastened down stairs, ahead of them all, to the Church. She sang the Te Deum along with them, and so energetically that her voice overpowered those of the other Sisters. It was afterwards noticed that the large swelling, which had been as hard as a stone, had disappeared, and what was very remarkable, without any effusion. The cure was so complete that she could attend all the exercises of the convent without experiencing the least trace of her former malady. When Father Ott wrote down this report she was Superioress of the convent. Dr. Flacho and Dr. Joseph Conrad of Wogan, physician to the Prince-abbot Von Kempten, both bear witness that this sudden cure surpassed all the powers of nature.

John George Frei, a farmer of Schwäbishofen, about six miles from Kaufbeuren, suffered for six years from a severe rupture, with frequent protrusions of the bowels. His doctor, the renowned surgeon, John Dumas Velder, a specialist in this branch, declared that only an operation could cure him. The sick man had recourse to Crescentia, and promised a votive offering at her grave. As he was hearing Mass there, he felt himself all at once perfectly healed, neither could the surgeon discover that any trace of the malady was left ; and ten years later, when he had to bear testimony to his own cure during the apostolic investigation, he was still perfectly sound and healthy. The surgeon, and the wife and relatives of the cured farmer swore to the truth of this miracle.[1]

Other miracles mentioned in the Acts of her Beatification we pass over on account of their length. The following miracle is not contained in the Acts but it was officially investigated by a commission appointed by the Prince-bishop of Eichstadt, Raymond Anthony ; the protocol or register of this commission is still preserved

---

[1] The translator follows, for the rest of this chapter, the abbreviated second edition.

among the episcopal archives.[1] Father Ott, too, relates this case at full length ; we are content to give a condensed account of it:

Frances Magdalena Oberhofer, born at Straubing in 1711, and since 1730 a professed Sister in the convent of the east suburb of Eichstädt, was always sickly and often afflicted with mortal sickness. Twenty years ago she had had a stroke of paralysis and had become lame in the right side. Since October 20, 1763, she had suffered from a violent puncture in the breast and other maladies, and had been bled fourteen times, when they feared she would be suffocated. Many times she had been near to death, and had twice received the sacraments of the dying. When she had violent cramps and a severe fit of vomiting, she took four or five times some of the so-called Crescentia powder with instant relief. On December 22d, in the evening, she fainted away, after which she fell into a state in which all believed her to be dying, and the father confessor said the prayers of the dying beside her bed. Soon she lost consciousness again. In this state, it appeared to her as if the picture of Crescentia, which she had before her, became alive, and said to her that she would not die yet ; it was not God's will, and she (Crescentia) would not permit it ; she had to live longer, but in suffering. She felt a strong impulse to say these words aloud before all who were present, and after she had first asked her confessor in a low voice, she said in audible tones : "Your reverence will please leave off your supplications ; I am not going to die; I cannot die." Then she added the above-mentioned words and some others; she then raised herself in bed without help, wiped the death-sweat from her face, and begged the father confessor and the Mother Superior, who was also present, to allow her to get up, which permission was granted. She then took some nourishment, said the Te Deum in thanksgiving, and slept calmly all night. The next morning she arose without any help, though previously she had not been able to stand alone for nine weeks; she assisted at Mass, and at it sang in a firm voice the solemn hymn of St. Ambrose, the Te Deum. The cure was perfect. Besides ten other witnesses, who swore to the truth of all that has been said, the surgeon, John Michael Hafncr, the physician, John Starkman, doctor of philosophy and medicine, who had attended the Sister for twenty-one years in her many sicknesses, and his son, Andrew Joachim Starkman, also a physician, all attest that this sudden cure surpassed all the laws of nature.

From Father Ott's narrative we cull some miraculous events, which he himself examined. Michael Dollinger, a day-laborer at the castle of Hautzenstein, had had a rupture for forty-two years, which, in spite of good trusses, had brought him often to the brink of the grave, from which the assistance of good surgeons had barely saved him. In the year 1771, his bowels again protruded so frightfully, that all endeavors to help him proved fruitless. The lord of the castle, Privy-counsellor Von Franken, sent the dying man some of the so-called Crescentia oil, and bade those who tended him excite him to trust in her intercession. As soon as some drops of oil had been applied, the pains ceased, the bowels returned of themselves to their proper place, the rupture was healed so thoroughly that, incredible as it may seem, in a few days no trace of the old malady remained.

Euphosina Hag, the daughter of Protestant parents of Kaufbeuren, became, in the third or fourth year of her life, totally blind, and no help could be obtained from the doctors. Maria Acklsperger, a Catholic servant girl of the house, made a novena for the poor child to Crescentia, paid a daily visit to her grave, and once took the child thither, and moistened her eyes with some drops of the so-called Crescentia water. Early on the tenth day, at eight o'clock in the morning, the child opened her eyes, which were as bright and beautiful as could be desired. This happened in 1766. "The whole city," says Father Ott, "knows of the fact: no one disputes its truth, though some one will not acknowledge it to be a miracle." The child retained good eyes till its seventh year, when it died of small-pox.

Francis Anthony Pilgram, a merchant, and afterwards a citizen of Munich, from the electorate of Saxony, in 1764, after a severe sickness, lay at the point of death ; then his wife made a vow to go on a pilgrimage to the grave of the servant of God. At the very moment the sick man raised himself up, returned thanks to God, and with those present said the rosary. For many years afterwards he frequently went to the grave of his deliverer, as a living witness to this miracle.

Veronica Stark, of Kaufbeuren, in 1776 thrust a needle so deeply in the palm of her hand that it disappeared altogether, and the surgeon, Charles Braun, could not draw it out. A plaster had no other effect than to increase the pains. Veronica, being compelled to earn her living by manual labor, and chiefly by washing, gave up medical help and invoked the aid of Crescentia, promising to have the needle set in silver, and to carry it to her grave if she should be healed by her intercession. The pain then disappeared all at once, she could do her usual work without any difficulty, although by close inspection the needle could be noticed in her hand. Twenty-one weeks afterwards, she felt, when wiping her hand, that it stuck to the towel, and then, to her great surprise, noticed the head of the needle, which had penetrated crossways into the interior of the palm, stuck out on the upper side of the hand. She now pulled it out with great ease.

Anna Heiber, of Landsberg, in 1776 swallowed a needle, which lodged cross-ways in her throat. It was impossible to extract it ; she made a vow to Crescentia ; a moment afterwards the needle jerked itself out with great force from her mouth, in the presence of many people. We may here remark that there are hundreds of instances reported in which needles, pins, and other pointed objects, which had been swallowed or otherwise inserted in the body, have been drawn forth in a remarkable manner at the invocation of Crescentia. No one can look upon the articles brought to her grave within this present century, without a shudder, as well as astonishment.

Baron Von Rossi, an officer, Commandant of Constance, fell so sick with an inflammatory fever, in 1779, that he could not move for weakness and his physicians gave up all hope. Finally, he had recourse to the servant of God, and sent a priest of the Order of St. Dominic to Kaufbeuren, in order to say a holy Mass at her grave on a Thursday between nine and ten o'clock, at which time Mass was also said in the room of the sick officer, and at it he received Holy Communion. Immediately after that his appetite returned ; his weakness vanished so suddenly that in a few days he could entertain guests at his table, and soon after made in person a pilgrimage to Crescentia's grave. He, himself, as also his doctor, Dr. Braunegger, attributed his cure to a supernatural cause.

Father Ott relates in 1753 : " When I was visiting my good friend, Rev. Anthony Galler, parish priest in Rottenburg, Bavaria, he complained to me that for a year past he had had no rest. As soon as he prepared himself for sleep the frightful phantasm of a black dog would rush upon him and rob him of his rest, to the great detriment of his health. I gave him one of Crescentia's rosaries, and exhorted him to trust in her. He then wound the beads every evening around his hand, saying a short prayer, and never again experienced an attack of that kind of annoyance.

One of the rosaries distributed by Crescentia herself was for upwards of two hours in the midst of the flames of a fire which broke out, in 1744, at Köngetried, near Mindelheim. It was drawn by chance out of the fire by an iron fork, and found to be quite whole and uninjured, which filled many of the spectators with holy awe. These beads were at that time very often used in cases of difficult child-birth, and many hundreds of such cases occurred, in which visible help is said to have been given, even in very desperate circumstances ; as soon as the mother had swallowed a bead of the rosary, the birth immediately followed. In some cases, it was even reported that the child had the swallowed bead in its hand, which is naturally impossible. It was particularly at Lucerne that such instances occurred ; nay, at that time it was said there that for eighteen years, when women in child-birth recommended themselves to Crescentia, only one unhappy delivery had occurred, and that was to a person who had despised the invocation to Crescentia and made it the subject of mockery.

That the Ven. Crescentia also helps those who venerate her in temporal matters of less importance, is manifest from what Father Ott tells us of what we heard in the year 1770 from the mouth of Prince Hohenzollern-Hechingen. This prince had a noble horse of great price, which took sick when the emperor's troops besieged Schweidnitz. The farrier's treatment did him no good ; the horse was dying; they had already taken off his shoes and left him lying there on the ground. The prince was very much troubled at this loss, and seeing that human aid availed nothing, he invoked Crescentia, for whom he had a high veneration, vowing to send a silver horse to her grave. At the self-same moment the animal sprang to his feet, ran to the stable, as sound as he had ever been, and began to feed.

At the conclusion of this chapter we will recount as briefly as possible some of the numerous miracles reported of this century, as they are kept in the archives of the convent. They are not, however, of these latest years.

Francis Caspar Versching, of Kissingen, a boy of thirteen years of age, lost his senses in consequence of a fright, and remained crazy for seven years. As soon as his mother invoked Crescentia he recovered entirely.

A daughter of Michael Shirmayer, of Ginzelhofen, near Fürstenfeldbruck, was sixteen years old when she had been given up by the doctors; she had been struggling with death for two years; she was recommended to Crescentia and in a few days was perfectly well.

Anthony Heymer, of Niederstolzingen, was for a whole year totally blind, having cataract in both eyes. An operation which was performed was a failure, and for another quarter of a year he saw nothing. He vowed a pilgrimage to the grave of Crescentia and in the following night recovered his sight. He himself bore witness to this cure, at the very grave of Crescentia, July 14, 1809.

Mary Ostertag, of Mering, had thrust into her right hand a piece of a broken spindle, which, after trying every means for three years, she could not get out. The hand had been unfit for any use and was much swollen. She had scarcely made the vow to go on a pilgrimage, when, taking off the bandage, she found she could easily remove the fragment of the spindle without other help. July 23, 1809, she went herself to Kaufbeuren, and took the point of the spindle with her.

John Loder, of Buch, near Fürstenfeldbruck, on Good Friday got under a heavily-laden wagon. Several ribs were broken, the abdomen seriously injured. A physician and a surgeon declared he could not be saved; after nine hours, his death was expected at any moment. After he had recommended himself to the servant of God by a vow, it seemed to him, as he himself said, "as if the bowels had been pushed back to their former place." In five days he could work again as before.

On the 23d of March, 1816, James Schönl of Ipfldorf, brought a great splinter of a bone, set in a frame, to the grave of Crescentia. After he had suffered for five and a half years from a bad sore in his foot that impeded him in walking and could not be healed, he vowed he would make a pilgrimage, and the bone came out at once, the cure following instantly.

Maria Crescentia Buchenscheid, of Göppingen, near Ulm, had, in 1816, her tongue so frightfully swollen that it projected from her mouth, and for twenty-seven days the poor girl was speechless. No remedy was effective. Immediately after she had vowed to make the pilgrimage, the tongue went back, and the sick girl was completely cured.

Anna Kuhn, of Tarrenz, in Tyrol, had, in 1818, been so much reduced by a deadly gall and putrid fever, that the priest who stood by her bed-side expected her death every minute. A few drops of " Crescentia water," which her sister gave to her, vowing, at the same time, a pilgrimage to Kaufbeuren, effected a sudden convalescence and perfect cure.

Katherine Strohmiller, from Donaualtheim, seven years old, was blind of both eyes, and according to the opinion of the physicians, with the incurable black cataract. She was indebted to her devotion to Crescentia for her perfect cure, as she herself and her mother declared on the 13th of March, 1820.

Richard Koller, of Ottobeuren, was wounded in the battle-field on the 19th of March, 1813, in the left arm and side, by grape-shot. He lay there in his blood, without any bandage, from nine o'clock in the evening until seven in the morning. The next day the bullet was cut out of his side, but the arm remained quite crippled. Dismissed as an invalid, he was unable to work until he had recourse to Crescentia, when in three days he was perfectly healed, and rendered capable of doing any kind of work, as he himself testifies on the 24th of May, 1820.

John George Stadler, a carpenter from Markback, near Sulgau, was in the last stage of consumption, and being given up by the physicians, he had received the sacraments. Then his wife exhorted him to call upon Crescentia. The cure was sudden and perfect. It is dated June 14, 1823.

Similar miraculous cures in answer to prayer occur up to this very hour, and in these last years especially, are again becoming more frequent. According to the testimony of the Sisters, seldom a week passes without at least one such instance occurring. But as the persons who claim to have received these graces are still alive, and as no close, no exact investigation has been made by the spiritual authorities, concerning the truth of the facts asserted, we think we do better by not publishing them.

As long as the Church itself has not spoken any decision concerning these presumable miracles, we have only a human certainty in their regard, and consequently, one subject to deception. More than this we cannot and will not claim for the miracles mentioned above. Nevertheless, the number of these remarkable deeds is so great, and many of them are so striking, that delusion in all of these cases can scarcely be assumed.

Trust then, O Christian reader, in the Venerable Crescentia's powerful intercession. The Church Triumphant joins hands with the Church Militant, and to the Saints in Heaven the words of the Apostle St. James can be truly applied: "The continual prayer of a just man availeth much."[1]

CHAPTER IX.

Process of her Beatification.—Opening of the Grave.

E have already stated[2] that Benedict XIV. advised the Bishop of Augsburg, in a brief dated Oct. 1, 1745, not to hurry on in any way the examinations concerning the life of Crescentia, the servant of God, but rather, on account of the great veneration in which she was held, to postpone it longer than might otherwise seem advisable. This brief caused the widely disseminated opinion that the beatification of the consecrated Virgin had no prospect of success. This opinion was altogether unfounded. Yet the advice given by the Pope had

---

[1] James v. 16.   [2] B. II. C. VI.

the effect of inducing the Bishop of Augsburg to resist the general pressure on all sides, which was intended to accelerate the beginning of the process. Various opinions of distinguished persons had no effect for the moment; among these was one very favorable to the cause, that of Father Emmanuel Azevedo, an experienced counsellor of the Congregation of Rites, given on May 11th, 1754, which deserves special mention.

At length the Prince-bishop, Clement Wenceslaus, yielded to the general desire, and on July 3d, 1775, appointed a commission to hear witnesses and institute the so-called episcopal investigation. This commission consisted of the Baron Von Ungelten, Dean of the Cathedral, of Celestine Nipp, the spiritual adviser, of three parish priests from the neighborhood of Kaufbeuren, and of the Notary Apostolic, John Schwicker. These gentlemen concluded their investigations in two hundred and twenty-nine sessions, on the 12th of July, 1777. Five and thirty witnesses had been therein examined. The Acts were forwarded to Rome with a petition from the bishop that the matter of the Beatification might be taken up, and the apostolical process be entered upon. Father Philibert Obwexer, of the Upper German Franciscan Province, and procurator of the Germanic and Belgic Provinces at Rome, was the *Postulator Causæ;* Adrian Tisson was business manager for the convent of Kaufbeuren. They succeeded so far as to induce the Pope to appoint a commission in 1785 to begin the "Apostolic Process," which means to investigate the matter anew, and to examine the witnesses.

The Papal Commissaries were : Von Ungelten, the Coadjutor-bishop of Augsburg, the spiritual counsellor Nipp, with six abbots, namely: Joseph Maria, of St. Ulrich and Afra, in Augsburg, Honoratus, of Ottobeuren, Michael, of Thierhaupten, Æmilianus, of Füssen, Josephus, of Wessobrun, Honoratus, of Irsen.

The sessions began on July 30th, 1785, at Kaufbeuren; the last, which was the two hundred and fifty-ninth, was held on July 20th, 1790, in Ottobeuren ; the Acts contained the evidence of thirty-seven witnesses. On August 21st, 1793, both processes were declared valid by the Congregation of Rites. But before the Apostolic See had come to the resolution of taking up the *Causa*, and had appointed the papal commission to investigate the matter, lengthy proceedings had taken place in reference to various difficulties.

The *Promotor fidei* relied principally on the Brief of Benedict XIV., which had expressed a suspicion that the servant of God had designed and disseminated a picture of the Holy Ghost in the form of a young man, as also that she had distributed beads purporting to have been blessed and indulgenced by Christ Himself. This affair could not be decided in the May session of 1782 ; on the contrary, the Coadjutor-bishop of Augsburg was charged to institute a special investigation on these points and some others, which was done with extreme accuracy in May of the following year.

The question respecting her reputation for sanctity (*super fama sanctitatis in genere*) was favorably decided in 1787. Then began the important and difficult investigation respecting the heroic greatness of her virtues, that is, of the three theological and seven cardinal virtues. This took a rapid course. On the 2d of August, 1801, Pope Pius VII. announced the decision that it is ascertained for certain that the Ven. Servant of God, Sister Mary Crescentia Höss, possessed and exercised in a truly heroic degree the theological virtues, and the moral virtues which are bound up in them.

In consequence of the great resolutions of the following years and from other causes, the continuation of the Beatification has been interrupted for seventy years ; it has now, however, been again set in agitation. The next point will be to prove two miracles wrought after her death by her intercession. It would scarcely be believed, save by one who has followed up these investigations, with that scrup-

ulous strictness and prudence the Holy See conducts examinations. Two facts are necessary to substantiate the evidence; the sickly state of the patient before the cure, and
the cure that followed ; and these must be sworn to by
three witnesses. The fact that only this saint and no other was invoked, and that no other means were used, must
also be established, though on these points few witnesses
are necessary. In order to prove these three points, so
many questions must be solved, that even an obvious miracle could scarcely stand the fire of the cross-examination,
if the evidence concerning it has not been very carefully
made out.

On the 1st of October, 1788, the grave of Crescentia was
opened and examined in the presence of the members
of the Papal Commission, with the addition of the
Father Provincial, Meinrad Köning, and several Sisters
and physicians. But as all these had promised under oath
not to reveal anything that they had seen, we do not
know in what state they found the body of the servant of
God, nor what state it is in now.

In taking leave of the exalted figure of this angelic virgin, which has become endeared to us by this our work, as
also of our reader, we would address a petition to the latter to do all he possibly can to promote the happy completion of the Beatification of this spotless Spouse of Christ,
if it be only to recommend the matter to God.

But to thee, O favored virgin, in purity a lily, in humility a violet, in love a brilliant rose ! to thee I dedicate these
imperfect pages, with the prayer that amid the storms of
the age, thou wouldst protect by thine intercession the religious state, and enlighten it with the shining example
of thy virtues. And if this poor and trifling work of mine
does not displease thee, then keep thy protecting hand over
me in life, and in death lay it on my head, and teach me,
after thy example, to verify the word of Holy Writ: "You
are dead and your life is hidden with Christ in God."[1]

---

[1] Col. iii. 3.

APPENDIX.

Decretum Augustanae

In matters referring to the Beatification and Canonization of the Venerable Servant of God,

Sister Mary Crescentia Höss,

Professed Sister of the Third Order of St. Francis in the convent of Kaufbeuren.

On the Question :

Whether in the case before us, and for the specified purpose, the heroic degree of the theological virtues, as faith, hope, and love for God and one's neighbor, together with the moral ones, prudence, justice, fortitude, and temperance, and the virtues in connection with these, is firmly established.

The purity of the Catholic Faith, which in union with all other Christian virtues, shone so brilliantly throughout the life of Mary Crescentia Höss, from her tenderest age to the last breath of her life, excited the admiration not only of her Catholic fellow-citizens, but also that of Protestants, to that degree that many among them conferred on her the greatest encomiums, and did all they could to obtain for her, in spite of her poor circumstances, official admission into the convent of the Third Order of St. Francis, as the surest safe-guard for her innocence.

As in consequence of her great reputation for sanctity, which she already enjoyed during her life, but which since her death has constantly increased and been farther and more widely spread, two investigations were set on foot, concerning the manner of her whole life. The first one, after the lapse of considerable time, with a view to try the constancy of her renown, was instituted by the Bishop of Augsburg ; the second, much more searching, was made in obedience to the mandate of the Apostolic See itself.

Among other things we have the pleasure to announce, that among the judges selected were four abbots of the Order of St. Benedict, an event not of common occurrence, which sustained the joyful hope already cherished that the work begun by them would be completed by the Sovereign Hierärch, who was himself a member of that ancient and venerable Order.

So in fact it came to pass : The particulars of the investigation concerning her brilliant virtues had been handed in to the Sacred Congregation of Rites, when this Congregation had, May 9, 1797, held their first sessions in the palace of the late Cardinal Archinto, who was then the notary of the process. Their sessions were continued on March 3d of this current year in the apostolic palace of the Quirinal, and were finally concluded on July 28th, in the same Quirinal. In a general assembly, in which his Holiness Pope Pius VII. presided, it was the unanimous judgment of the Venerable Cardinals and of all the judges there assembled, that the Ven. Crescentia had practised these Christian virtues in an heroic degree.

But his Holiness, who at that time refrained from giving a decision, in order, in so important a matter to seek counsel in prayer, that he might know God's will, selected a day venerated by the whole Franciscan family, as one on which the dedication of their first Church is annually commemorated, on which to honor this prudent virgin and daughter of the holy Patriarch, St. Francis, with the glorious name of a Heroine of Christian virtue. Therefore, after having celebrated the divine mysteries with great devotion in his domestic chapel, he summoned the Rev. Cardinal-vicar of Somalia, Prefect of the Congregation of Rites and also, during the process, its notary, together with the *Promotor Fidei*, Father Jerome Napulioni, and the undersigned secretary, to appear before him, and then he solemnly pronounced the following judgment: "It is certain that the Venerable Servant of God, Sister Mary Crescentia Höss, possessed and practised in a truly heroic degree the theological and moral virtues and those connected with them."

At the same time he ordered the publication of this decision and its insertion in the Acts of the Congregation of Rites, on the second day of August, A. D. 1801.

J. M., CARDINAL OF SOMALIA,
Prefect of the Congregation of Rites.
J., OF CARPINGEN,
Secretary of the Congregation of Rites.